Shadow Island

SUEÑO BAY  ADVENTURES 1

MIKE DEAS AND NANCY DEAS

ORCA BOOK PUBLISHERS

For Annie and Faye
—M.D and N.D.

Many thanks to Jenn Playford, Liz Kemp, Ruth Linka,
Andrew Wooldridge and the whole team at Orca
for all the hard work and for believing in the project.
Also a big thank-you to Aidan Cassie and Kathya
Bustamante for all your input and support.
—M.D and N.D.

Text and illustrations copyright © 2019 Mike Deas and Nancy Deas

Library and Archives Canada Cataloguing in Publication

Title: Shadow Island / Mike Deas and Nancy Deas; illustrated by Mike Deas.
Names: Deas, Mike, 1982– author, illustrator. | Deas, Nancy, author.

Description: Series statement: Sueño Bay adventures; 1

Identifiers: Canadiana (print) 20190076585 | Canadiana (ebook) 20190076607 |
ISBN 9781459819610 (softcover) | ISBN 9781459819634 (PDF) | ISBN 9781459819627 (EPUB)

Subjects: LCGFT: Graphic novels.

Classification: LCC PN6733.D43 S53 2019 | DDC j741.5/971—dc23

Library of Congress Control Number: 2019934049
Simultaneously published in Canada and the United States in 2019

Summary: In this graphic novel for early middle readers, mysterious raccoon-like Moon Creatures are
discovered on an island in the Pacific Northwest.

*Orca Book Publishers is committed to reducing the consumption of nonrenewable resources in the making of our books.
We make every effort to use materials that support a sustainable future.*

Orca Book Publishers gratefully acknowledges the support for its publishing programs provided by
the following agencies: the Government of Canada, the Canada Council for the Arts and the Province
of British Columbia through the BC Arts Council and the Book Publishing Tax Credit.

Cover and interior illustrations by Mike Deas
Photos of Mike Deas and Nancy Deas by Billie Woods

Design by Jenn Playford

ORCA BOOK PUBLISHERS
orcabook.com

Printed and bound in China.

22 21 20 19 • 4 3 2 1

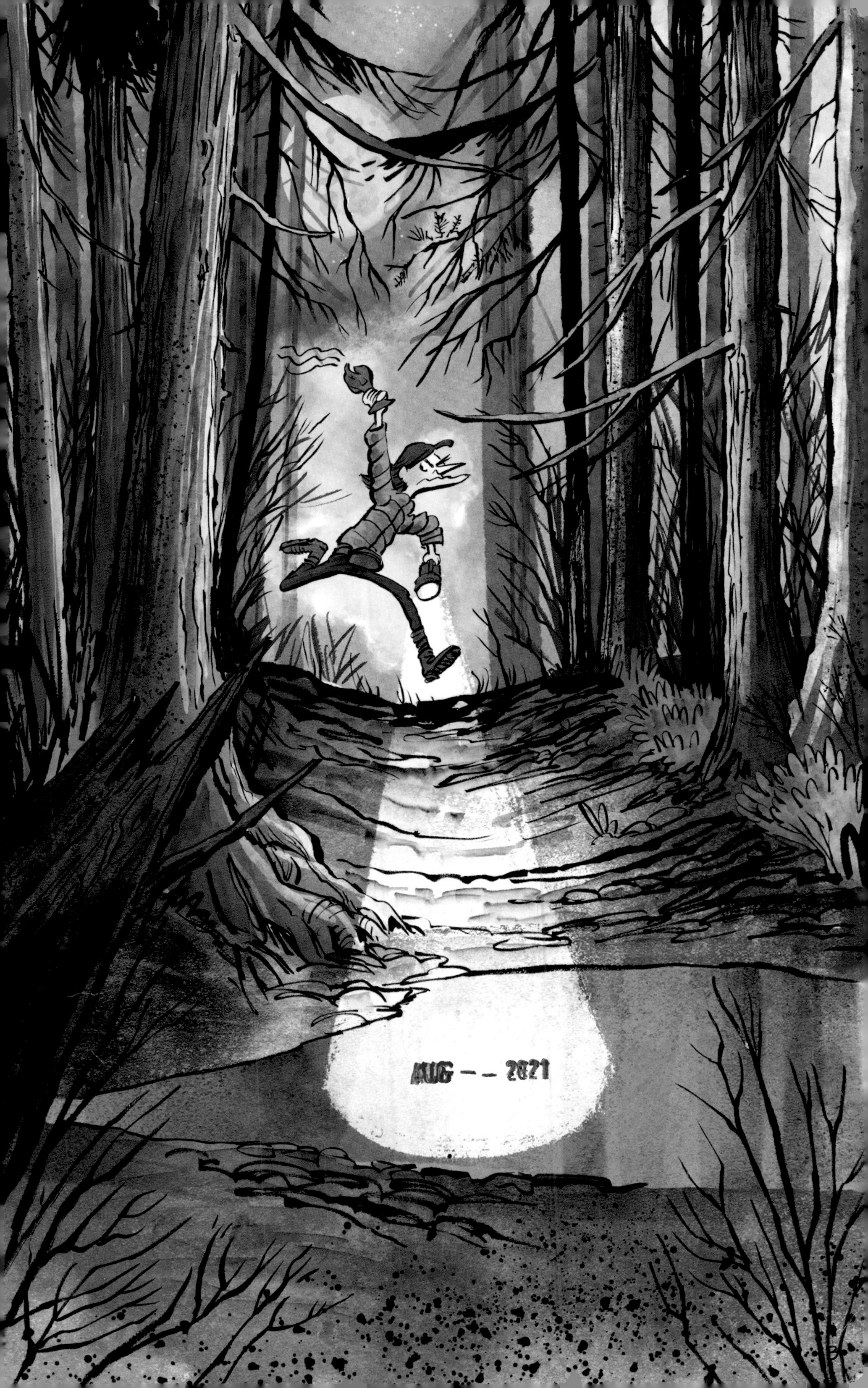

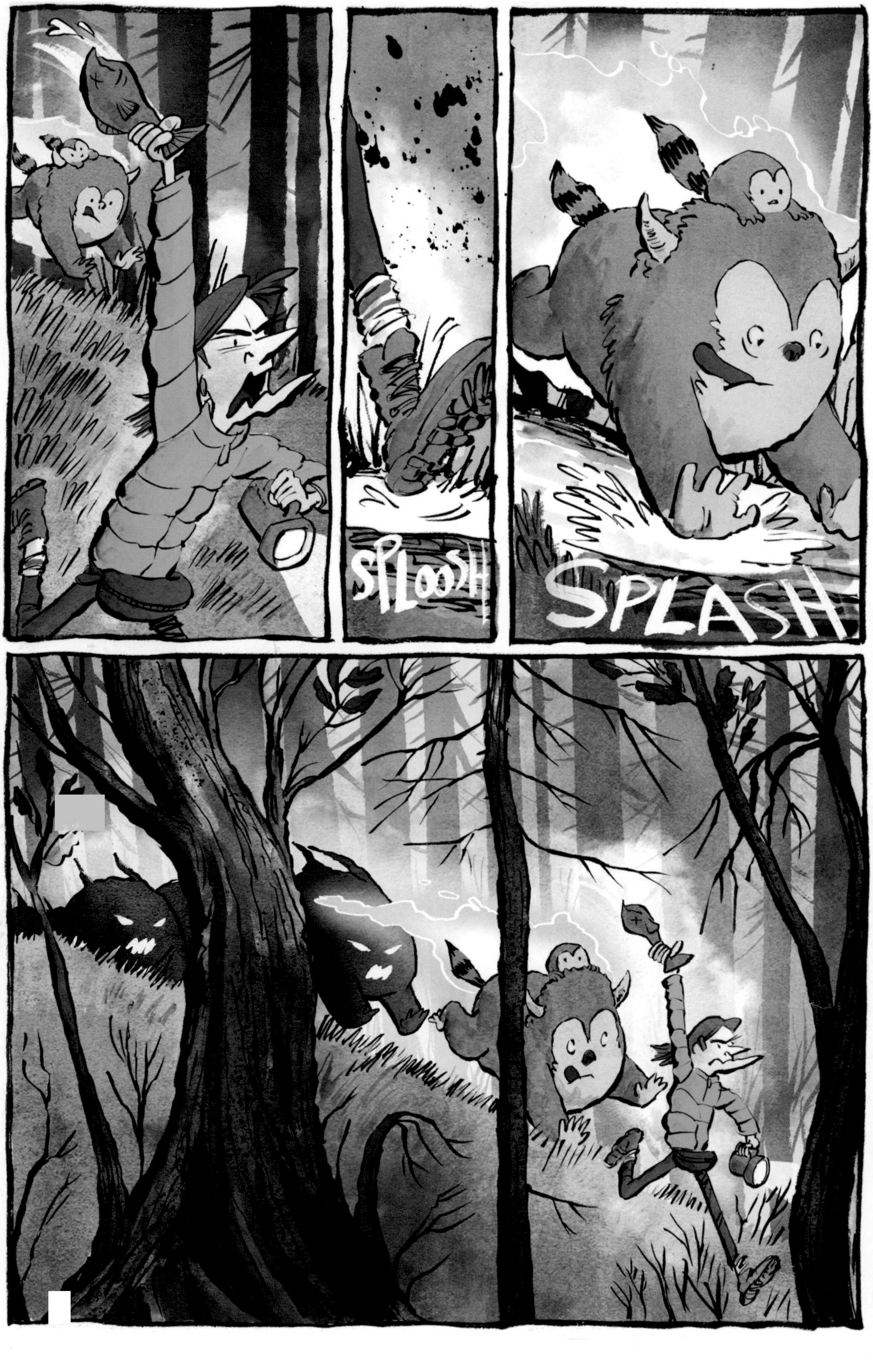
SPLOOSH
SPLASH

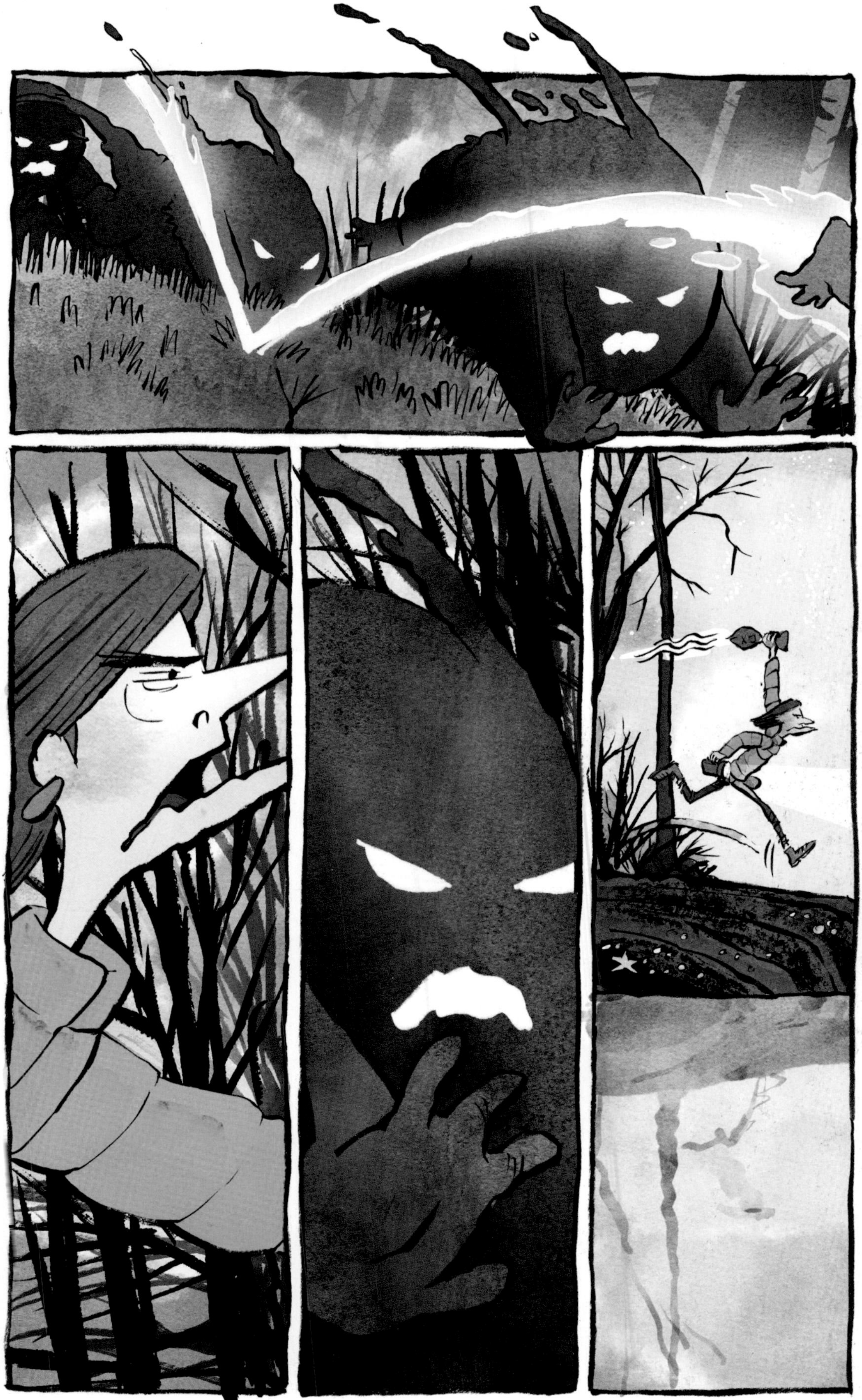

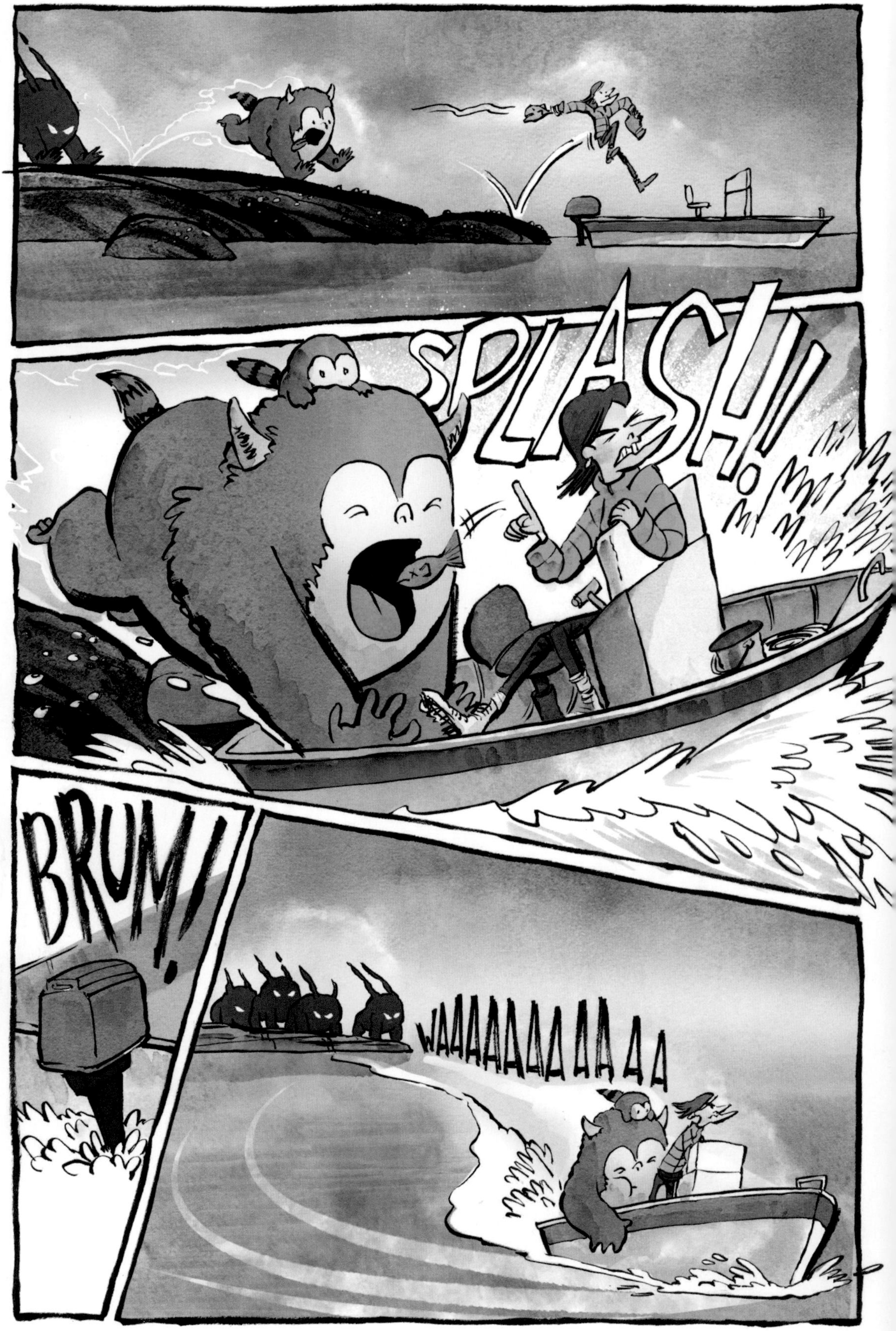
SPLASH!!
BRUM!!
WAAAAAAAAAA

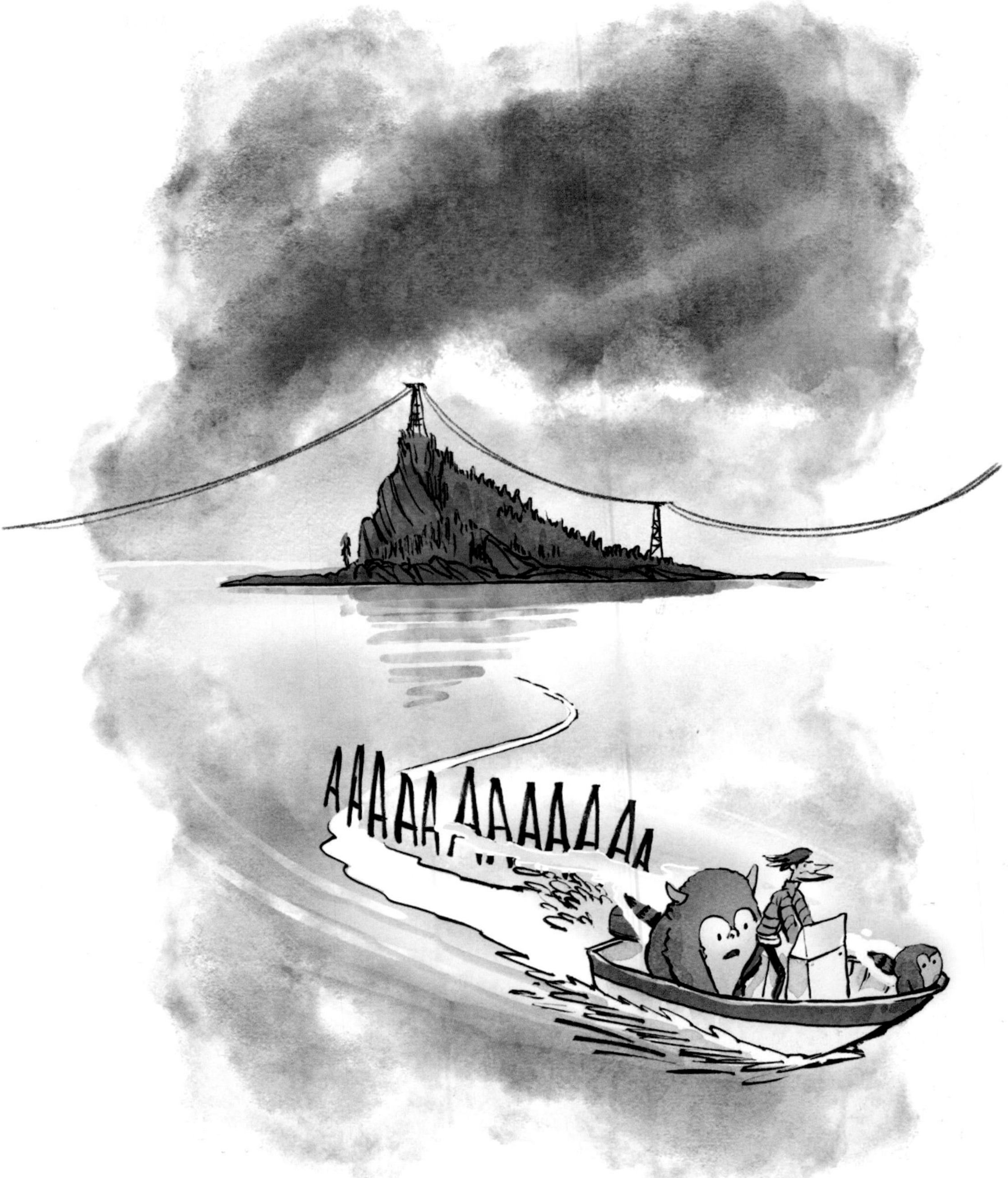
AAAAAAAAAAAAAA

CHAPTER ONE

Spring Break Begins

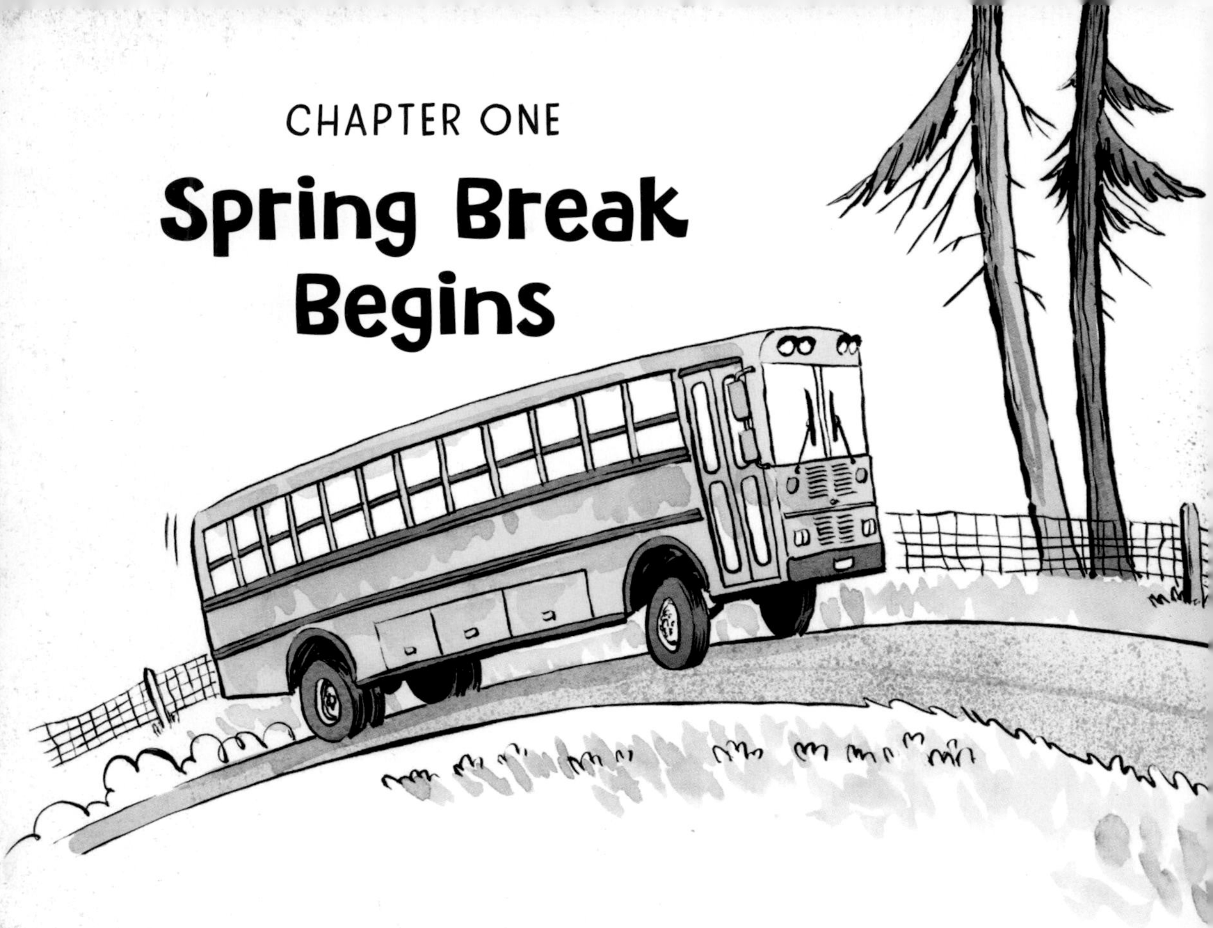

Here in Sueño Bay, Robertson Island, it rains over two hundred days a year. Central Shores back on the mainland gets less than forty-five days of rain. Oh, and there are earthquakes in Sueño Bay too.

Why would anyone live here? I've been here three weeks...

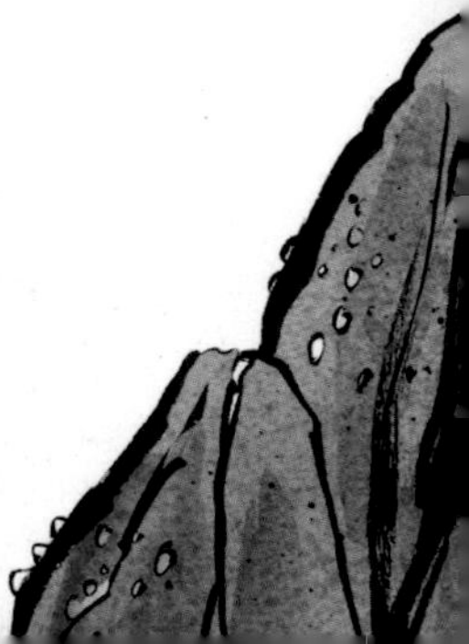

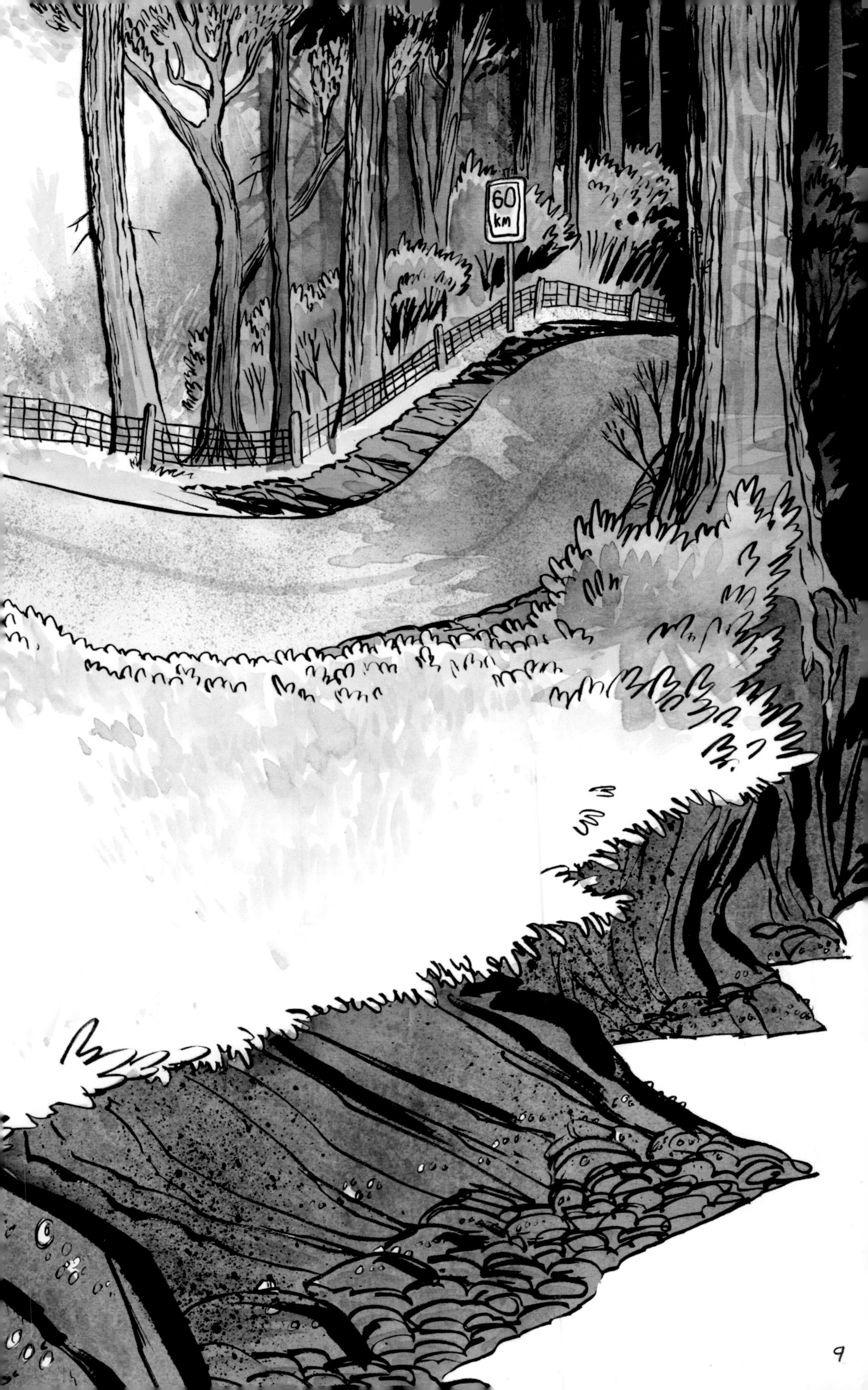
60
km

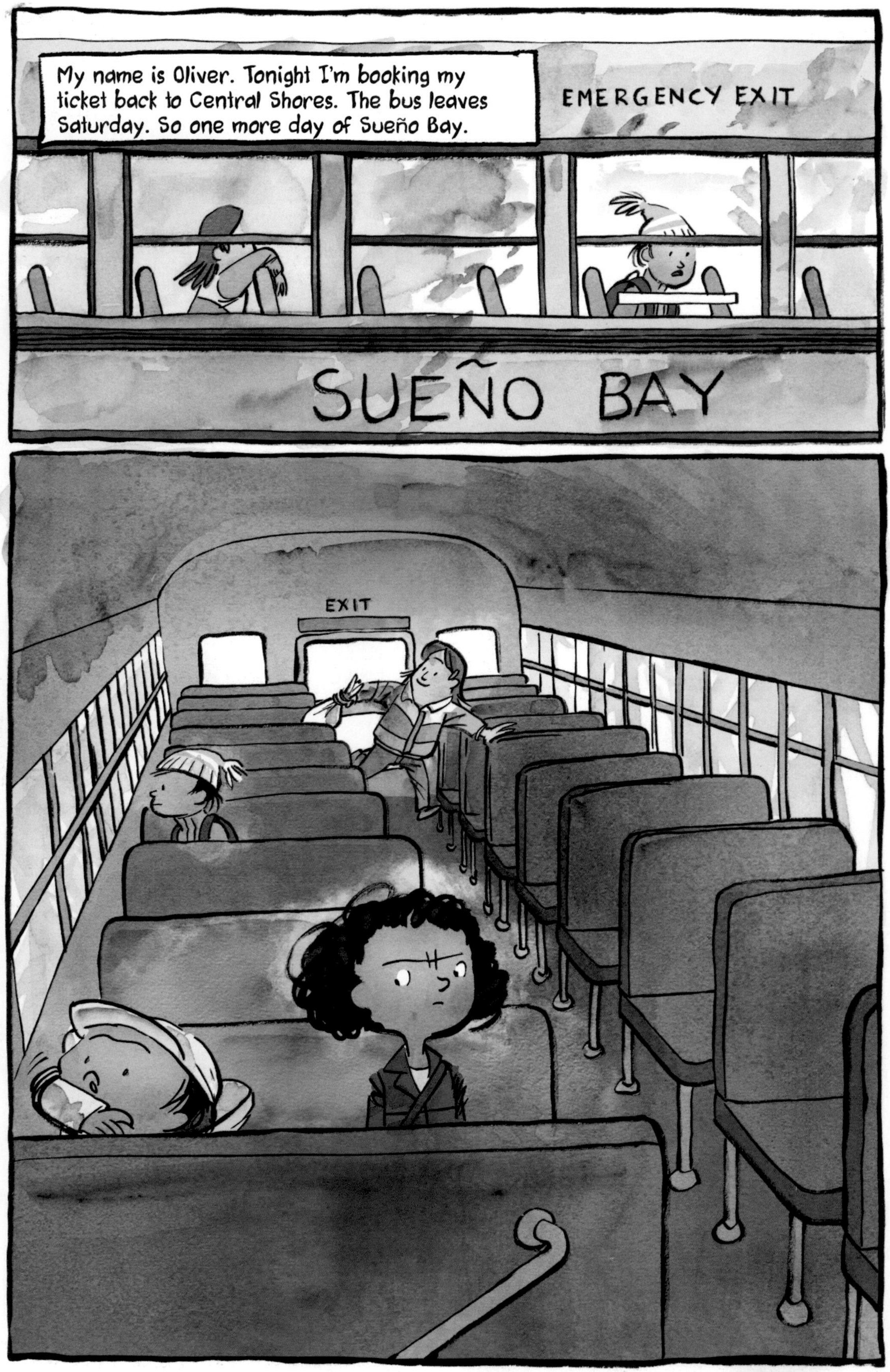
My name is Oliver. Tonight I'm booking my ticket back to Central Shores. The bus leaves Saturday. So one more day of Sueño Bay.
EMERGENCY EXIT
SUEÑO BAY
EXIT

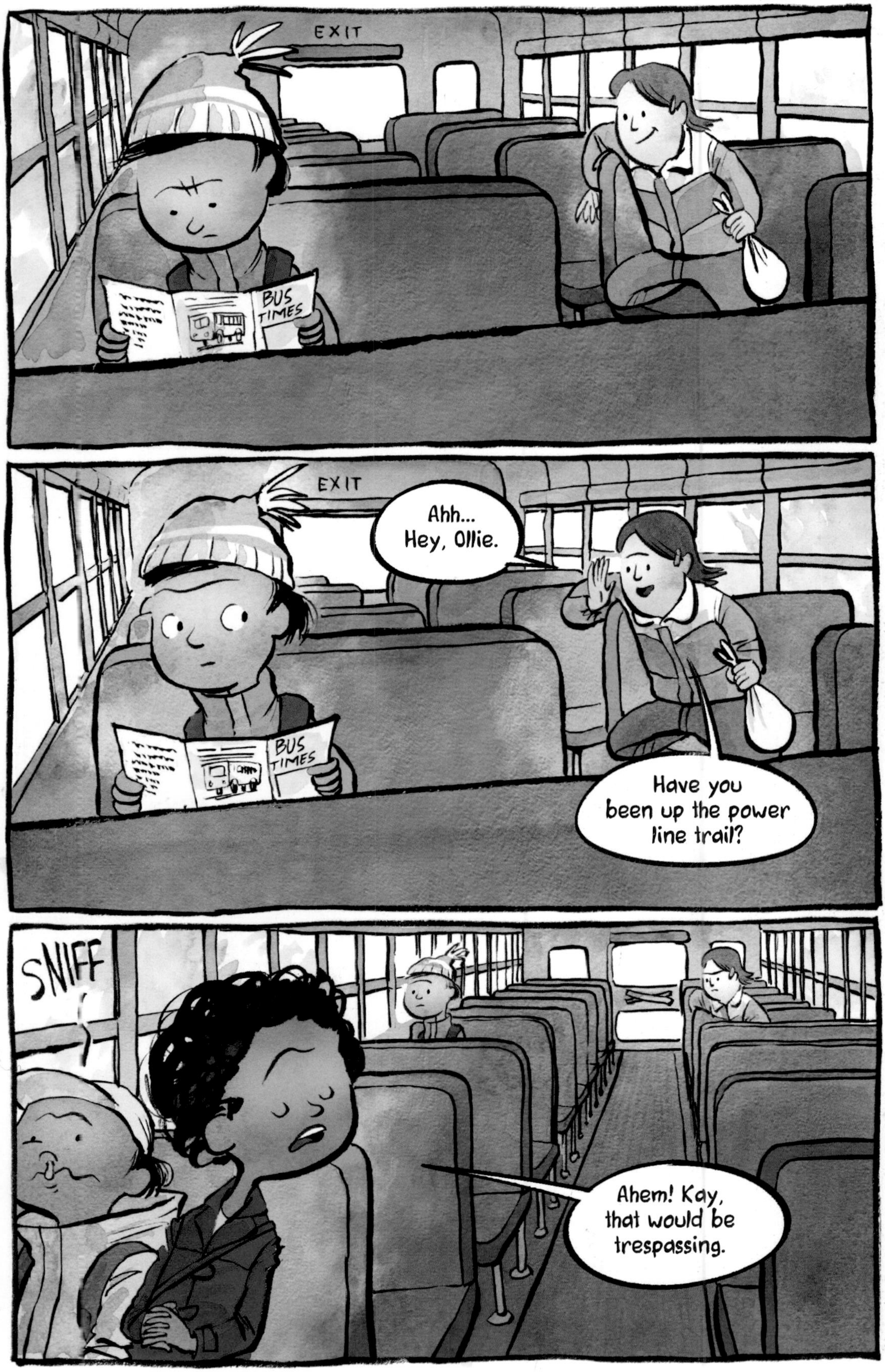
EXIT
BUS TIMES
EXIT
Ahh... Hey, Ollie.
BUS TIMES
Have you been up the power line trail?
SNIFF
Ahem! Kay, that would be trespassing.

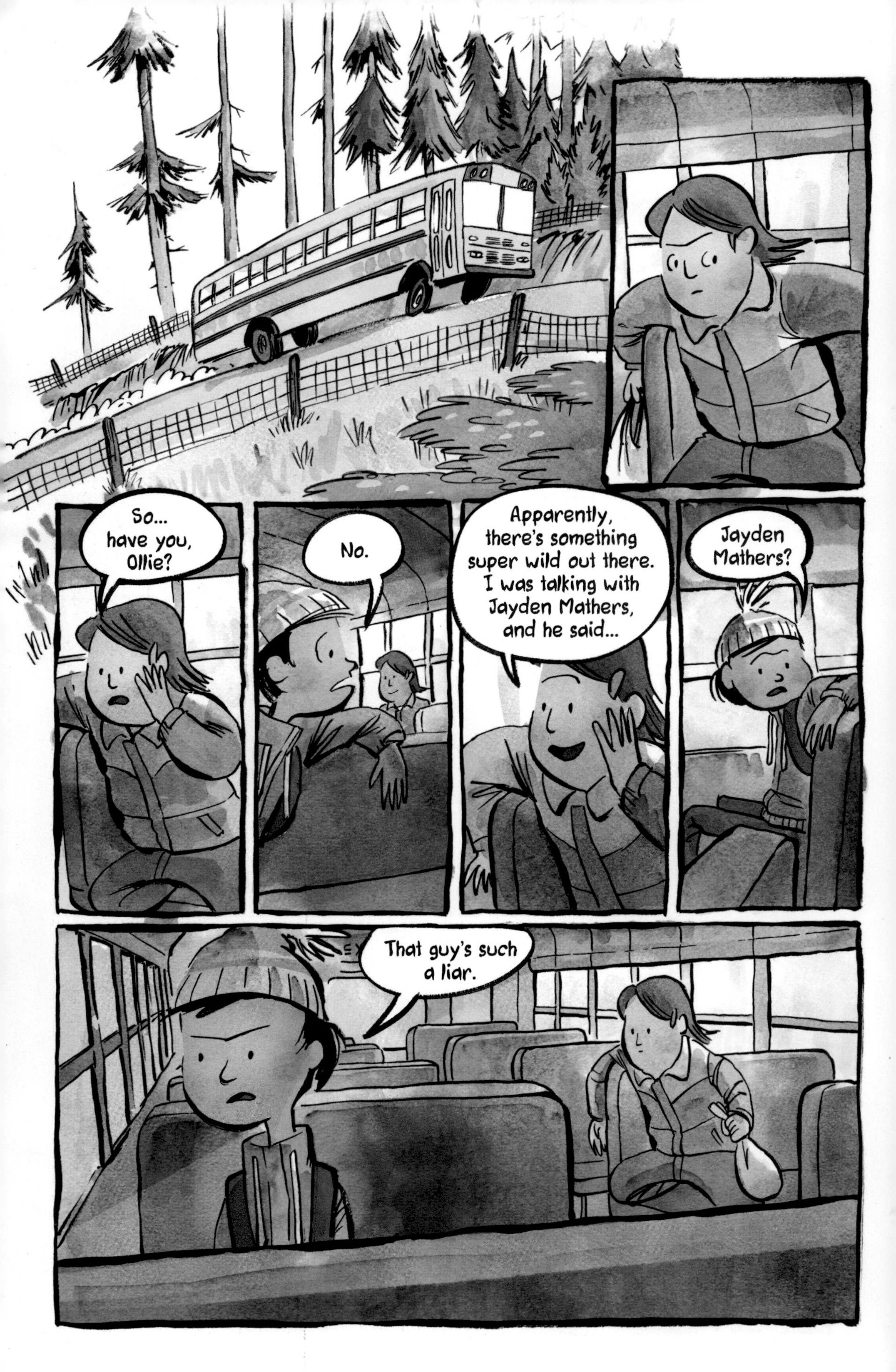

So... have you, Ollie?
No.
Apparently, there's something super wild out there. I was talking with Jayden Mathers, and he said...
Jayden Mathers?
That guy's such a liar.

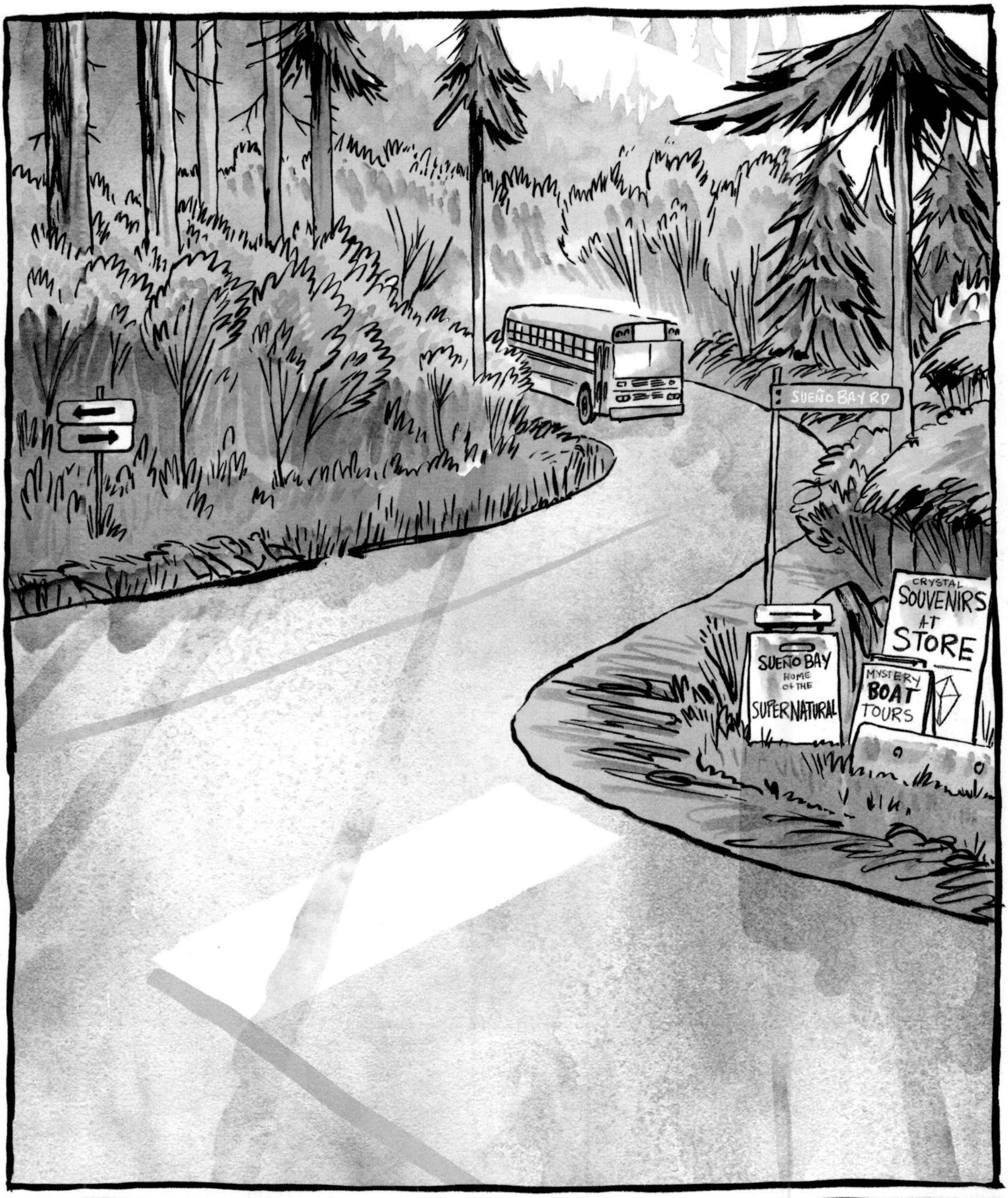
SUEÑO BAY RD
SUEÑO BAY HOME OF THE SUPERNATURAL
CRYSTAL SOUVENIRS AT STORE
MYSTERY BOAT TOURS

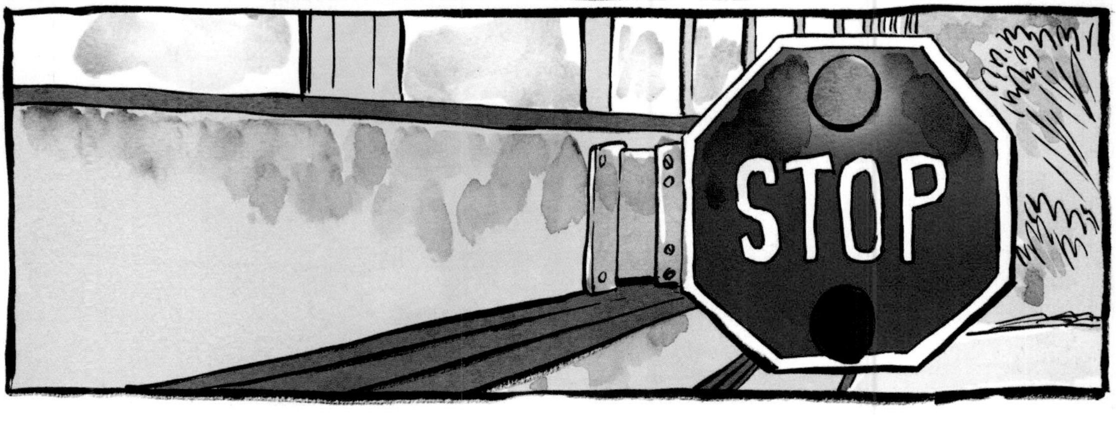
STOP

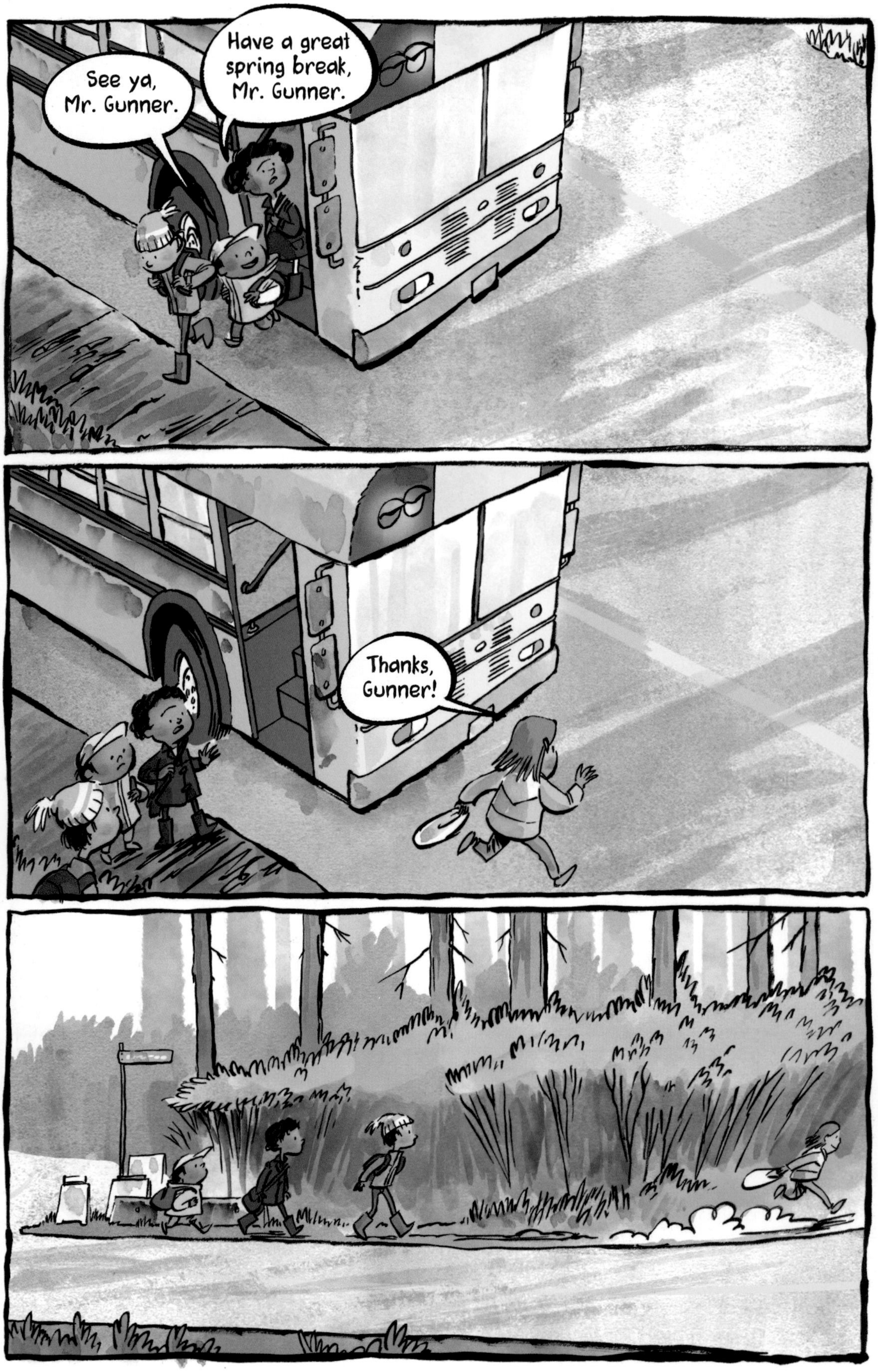
See ya, Mr. Gunner.
Have a great spring break, Mr. Gunner.
Thanks, Gunner!

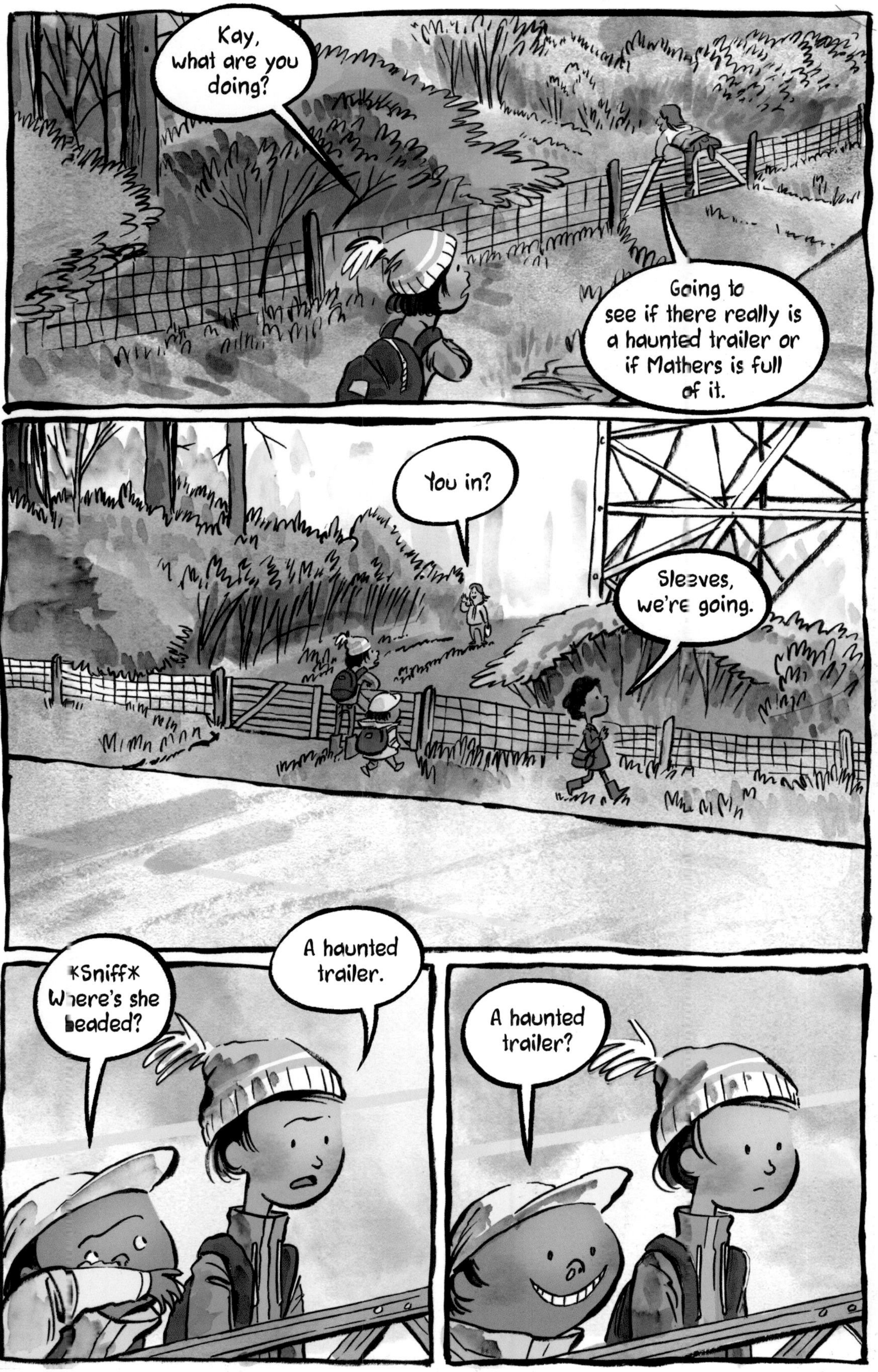
Kay, what are you doing?
Going to see if there really is a haunted trailer or if Mathers is full of it.
You in?
Sleeves, we're going.
Sniff Where's she headed?
A haunted trailer.
A haunted trailer?

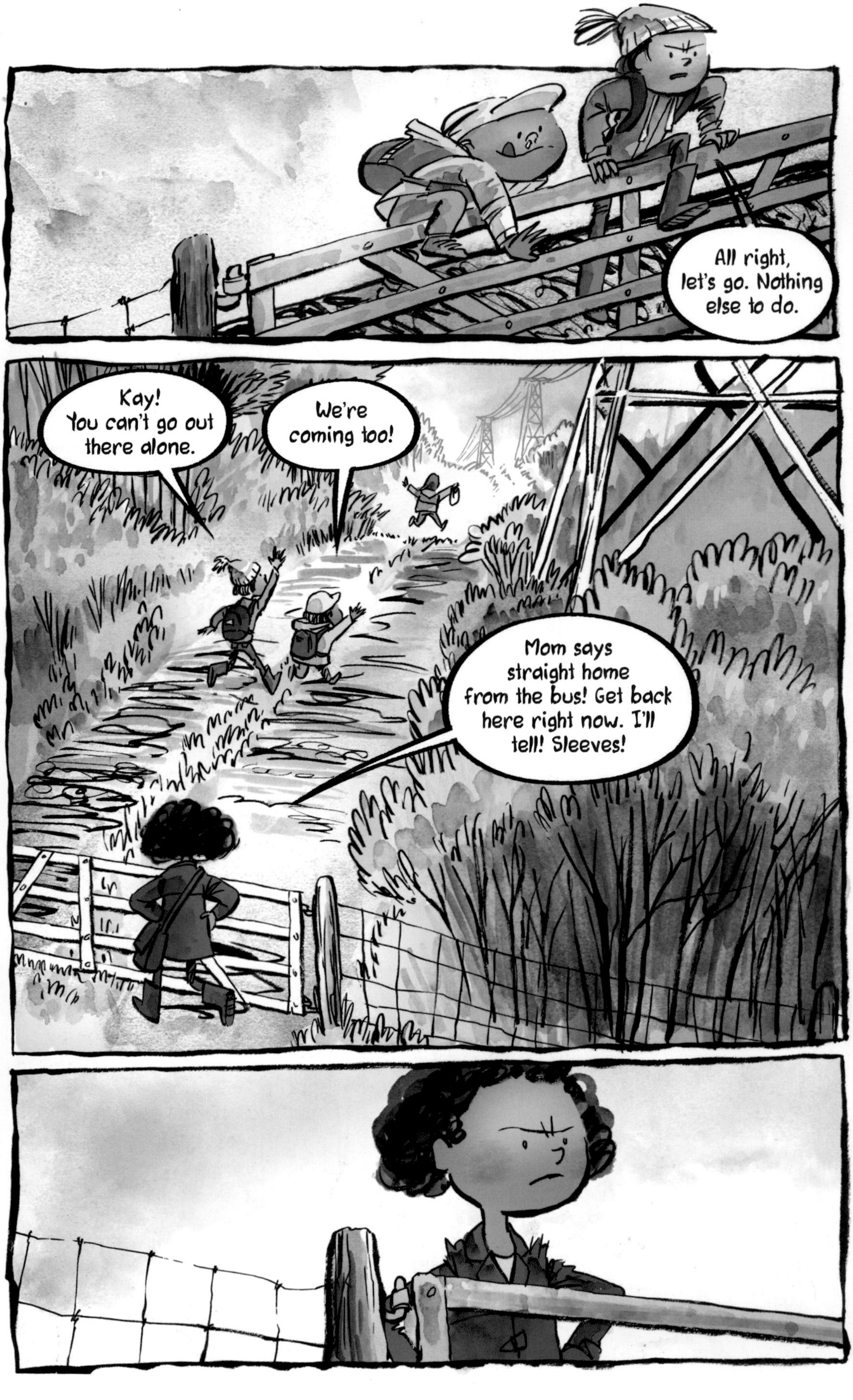
All right, let's go. Nothing else to do.
Kay! You can't go out there alone.
We're coming too!
Mom says straight home from the bus! Get back here right now. I'll tell! Sleeves!

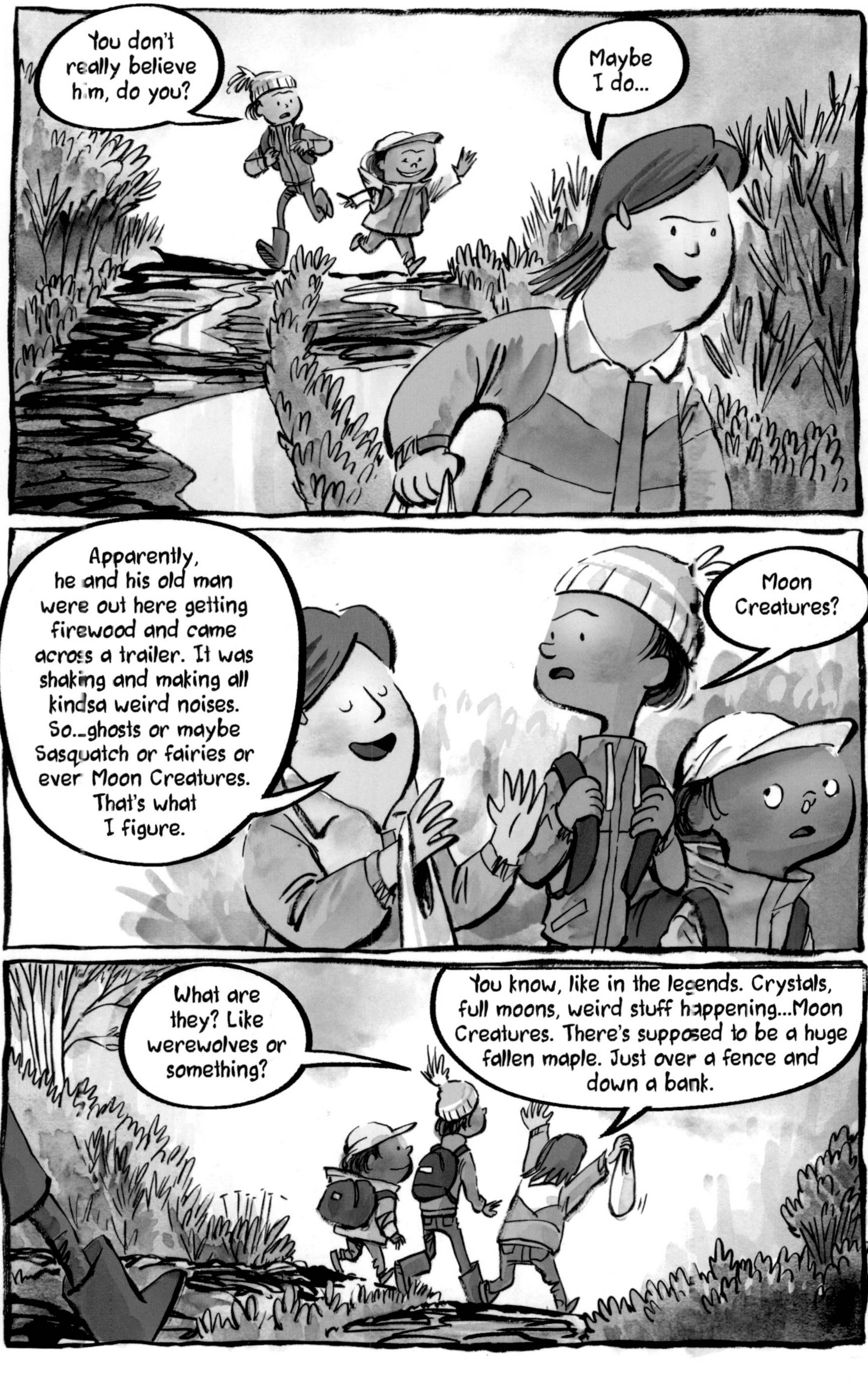
You don't really believe him, do you?
Maybe I do...
Apparently, he and his old man were out here getting firewood and came across a trailer. It was shaking and making all kindsa weird noises. So...ghosts or maybe Sasquatch or fairies or even Moon Creatures. That's what I figure.
Moon Creatures?
What are they? Like werewolves or something?
You know, like in the legends. Crystals, full moons, weird stuff happening...Moon Creatures. There's supposed to be a huge fallen maple. Just over a fence and down a bank.

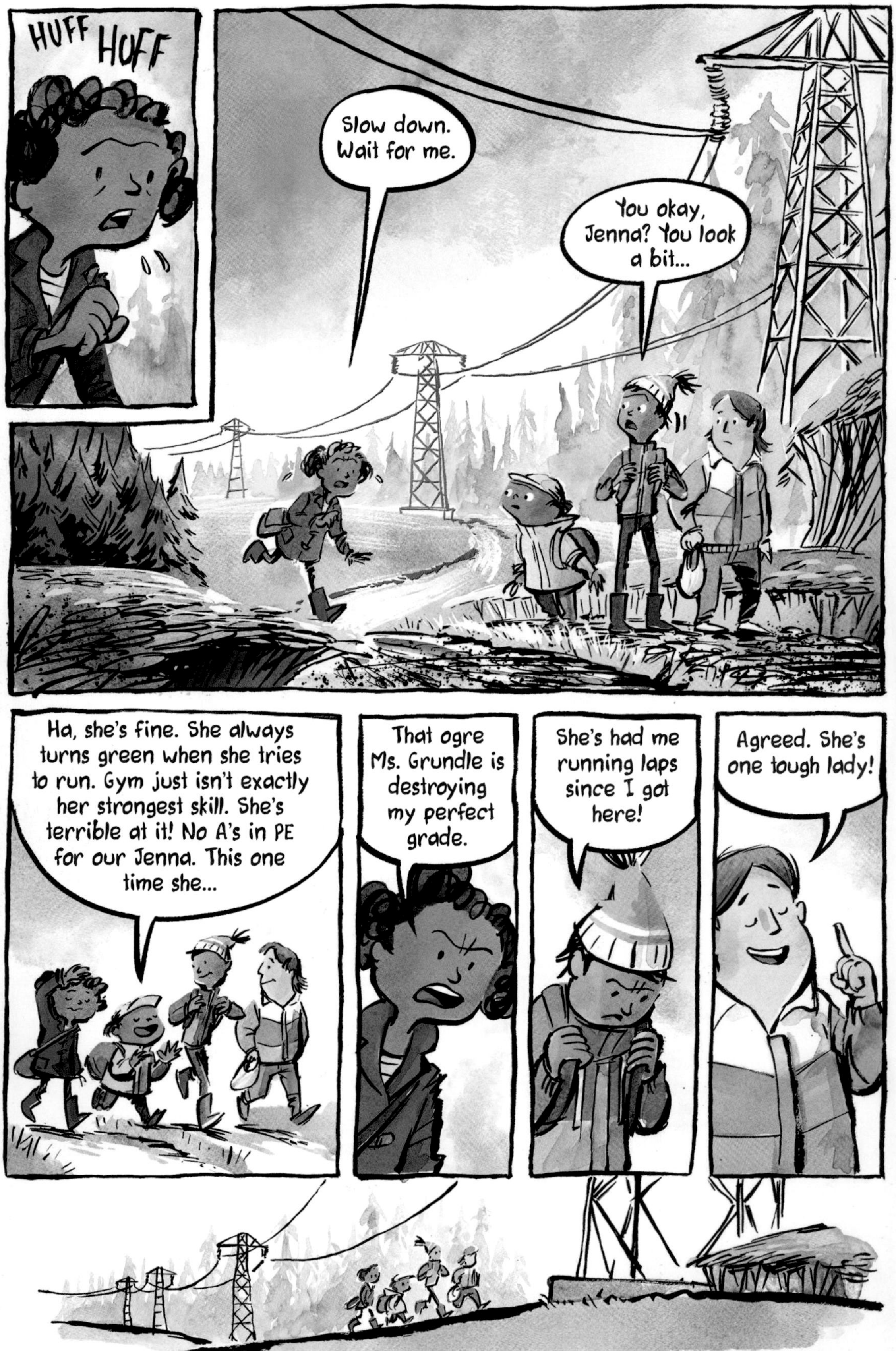

HUFF HUFF
Slow down. Wait for me.
You okay, Jenna? You look a bit...
Ha, she's fine. She always turns green when she tries to run. Gym just isn't exactly her strongest skill. She's terrible at it! No A's in PE for our Jenna. This one time she...
That ogre Ms. Grundle is destroying my perfect grade.
She's had me running laps since I got here!
Agreed. She's one tough lady!

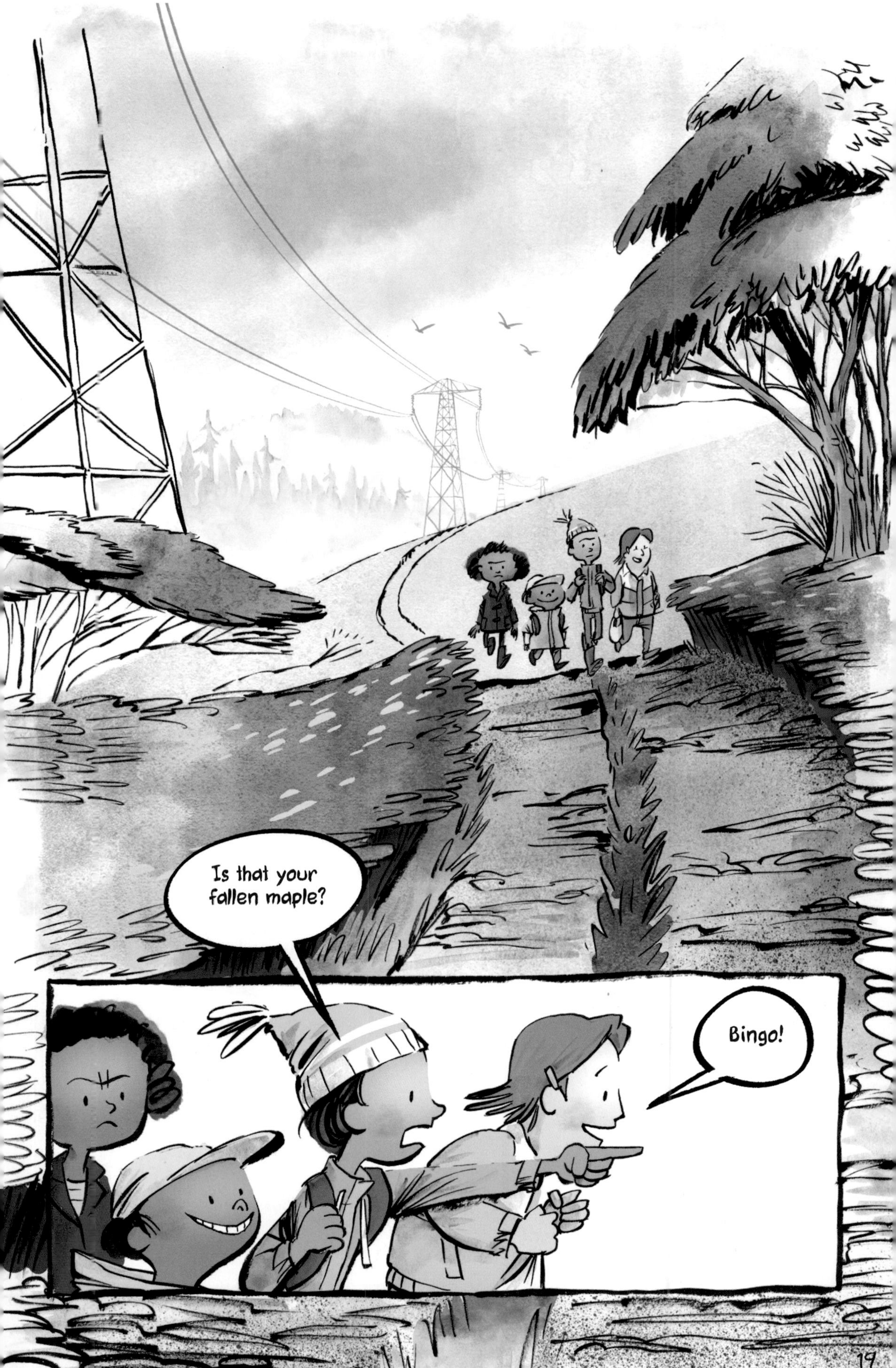
Is that your fallen maple?
Bingo!

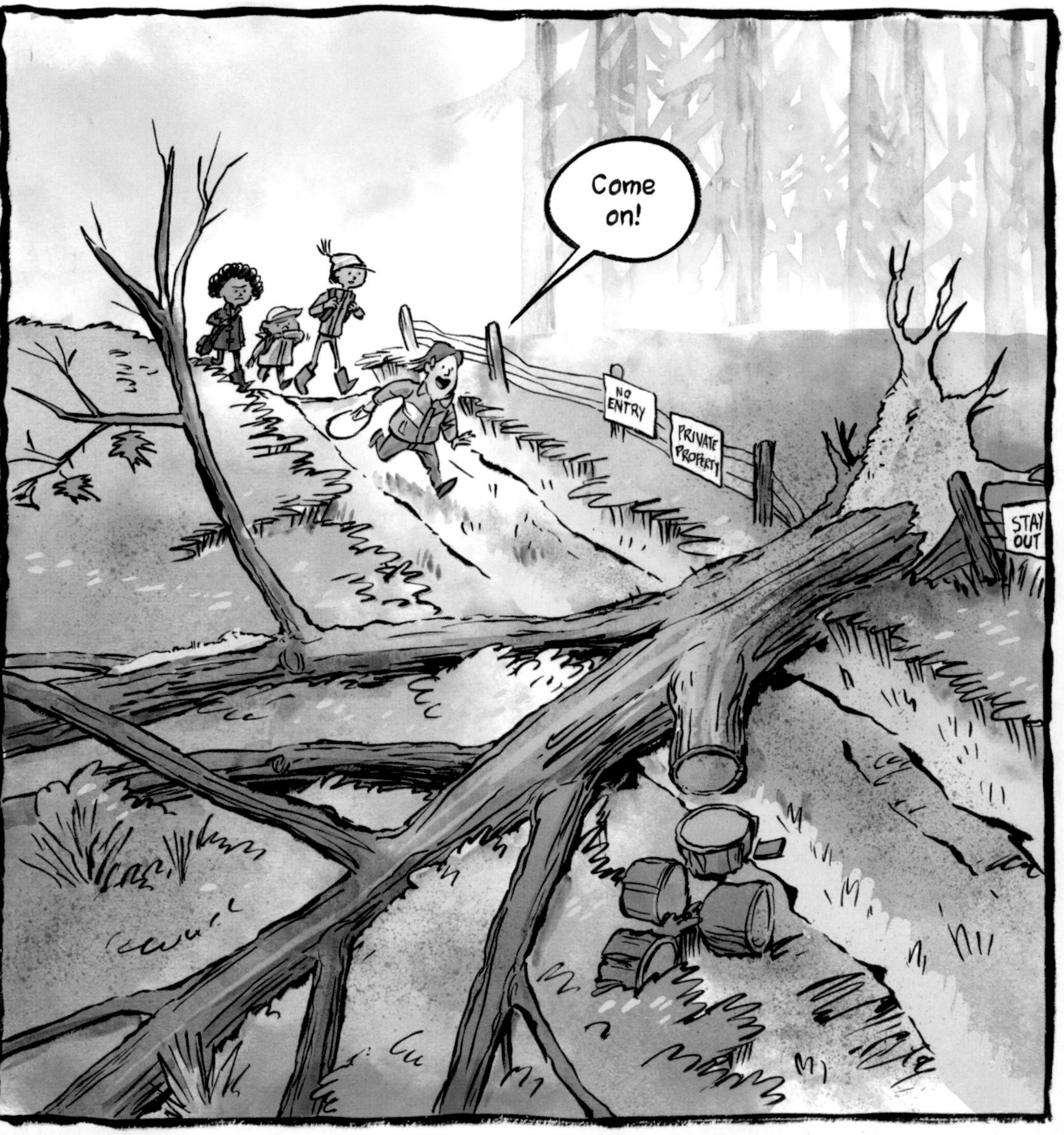
Come on!
NO ENTRY
PRIVATE PROPERTY
STAY OUT

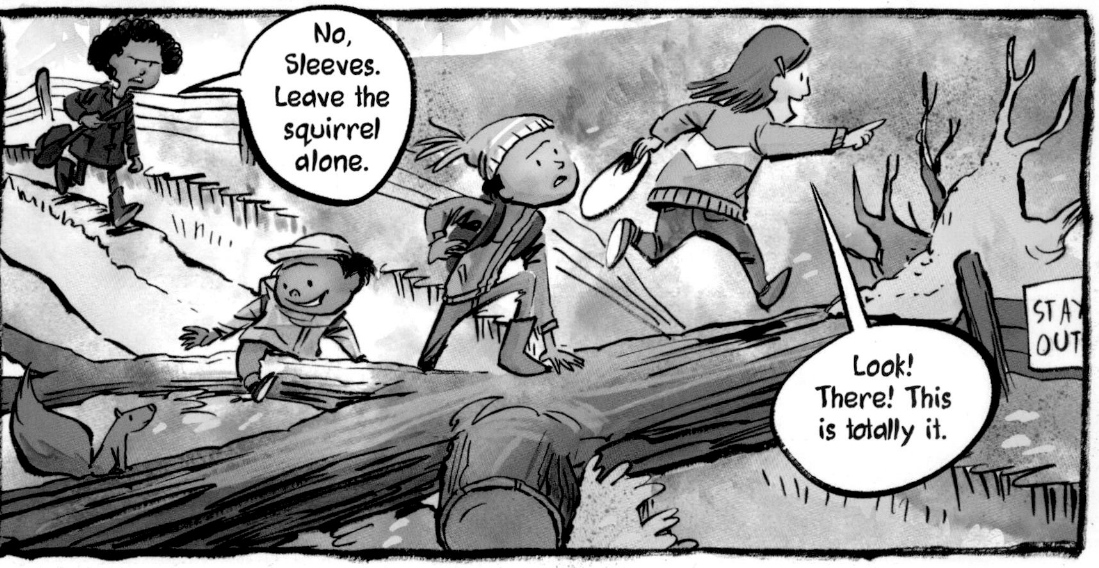
No, Sleeves. Leave the squirrel alone.
Look! There! This is totally it.
STAY OUT

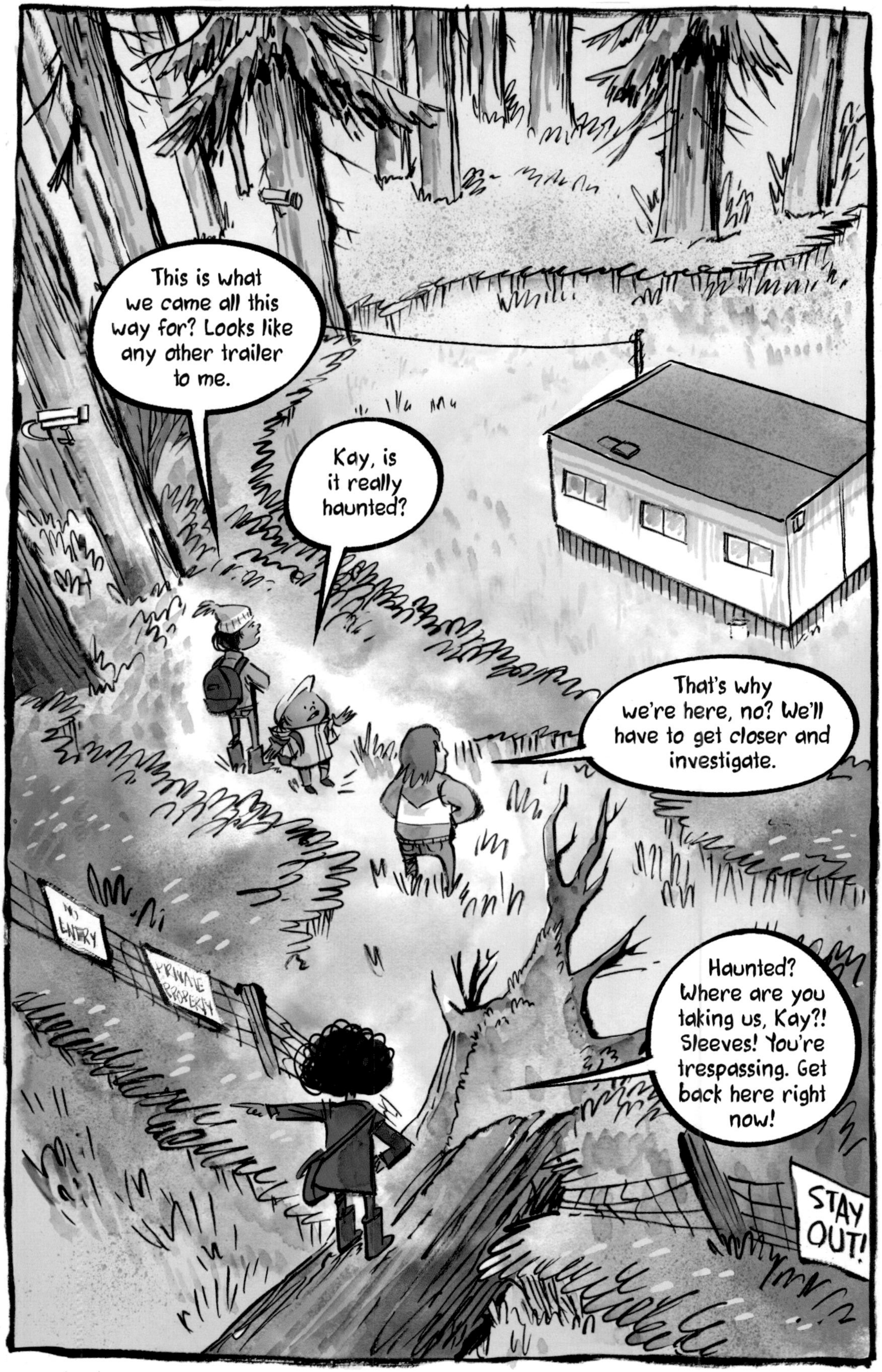
This is what we came all this way for? Looks like any other trailer to me.
Kay, is it really haunted?
That's why we're here, no? We'll have to get closer and investigate.
NO ENTRY
PRIVATE PROPERTY
Haunted? Where are you taking us, Kay?! Sleeves! You're trespassing. Get back here right now!
STAY OUT!

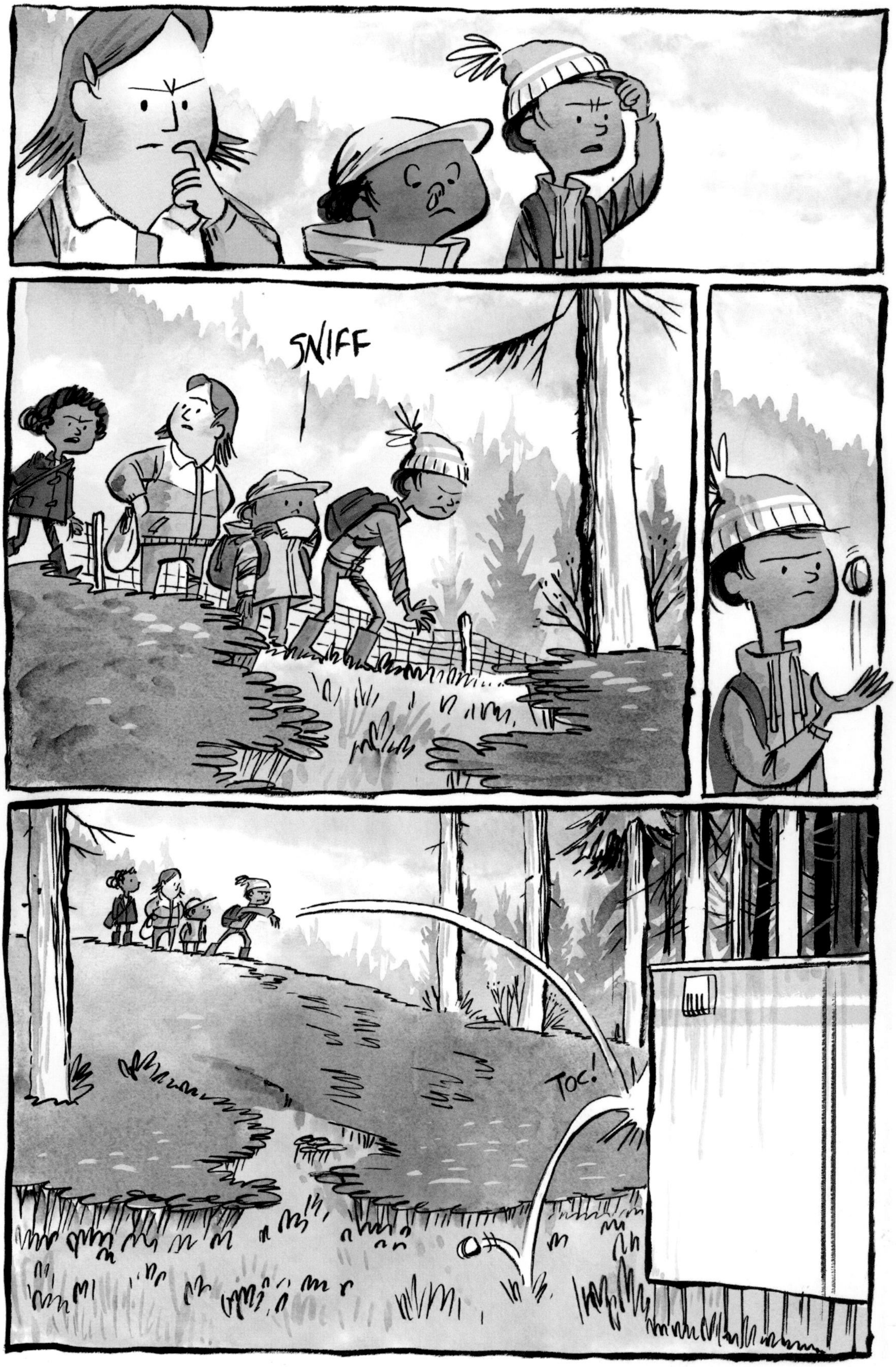
SNIFF
TOC!

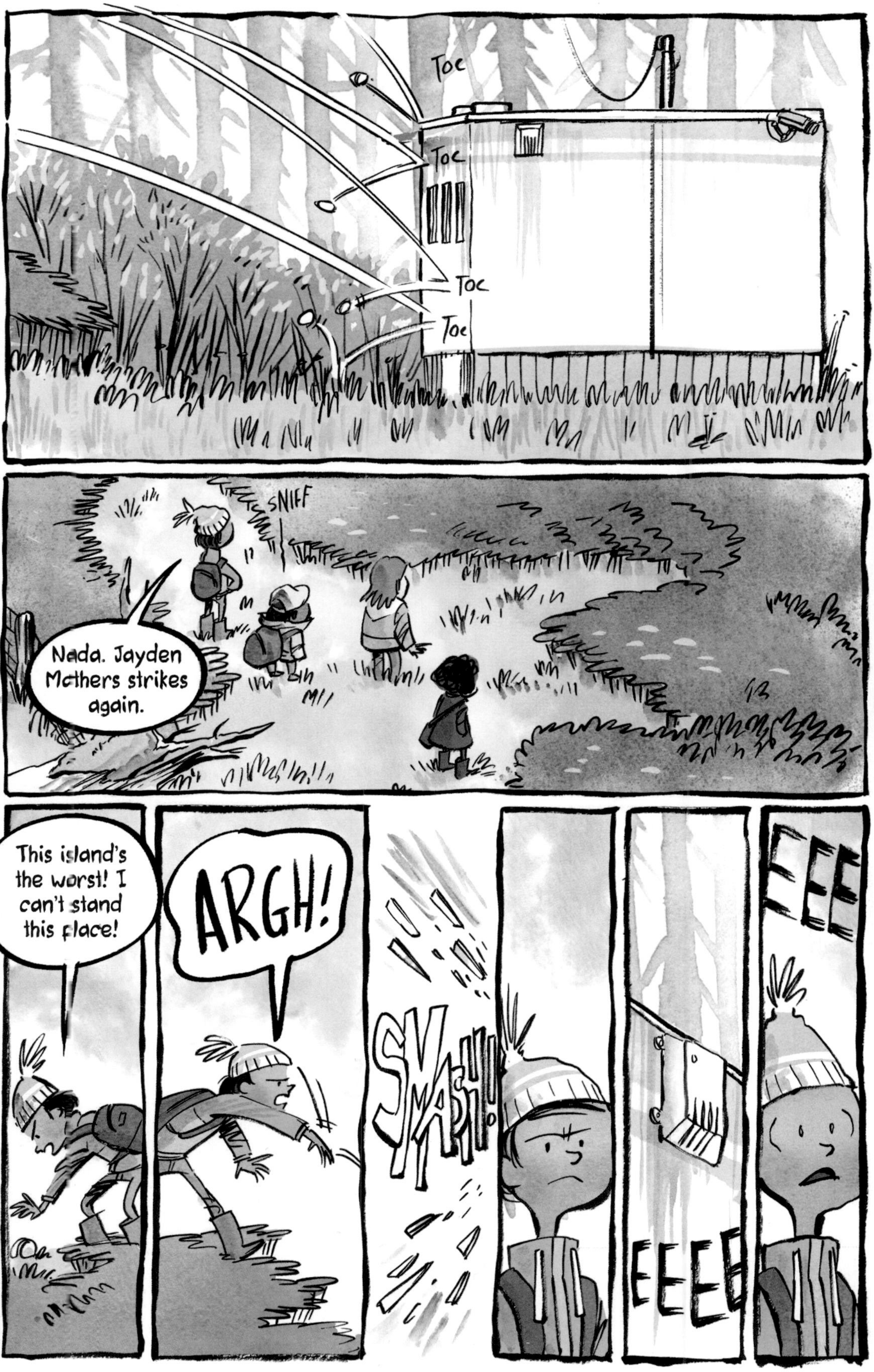

Toc
Toc
Toc
Toc
SNIFF
Nada. Jayden Mathers strikes again.
This island's the worst! I can't stand this place!
ARGH!
SMASH!
EEEE
EEE

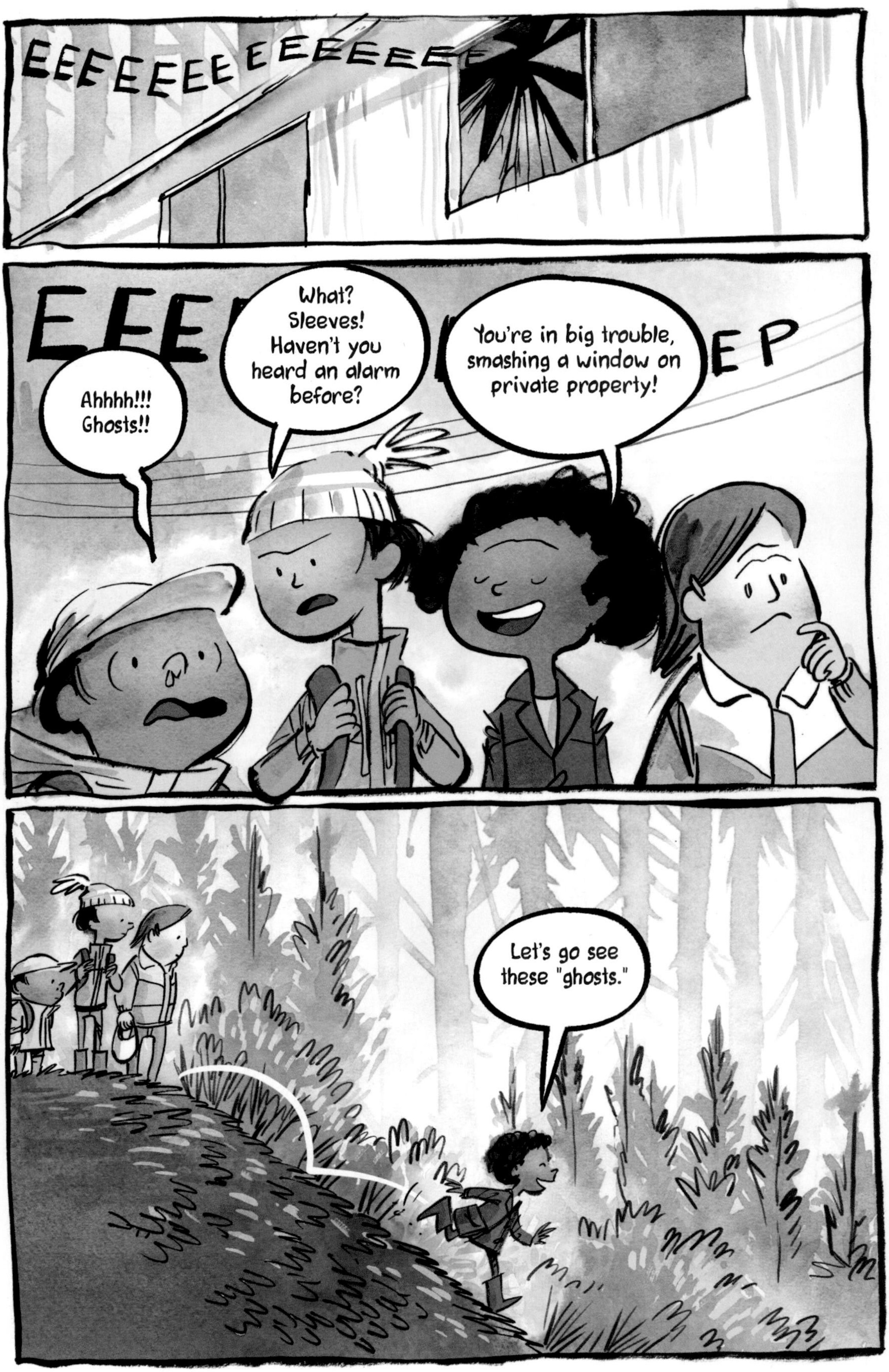
EEEEEEEEEEEEEE
EEE
EP
Ahhhh!!! Ghosts!!
What? Sleeves! Haven't you heard an alarm before?
You're in big trouble, smashing a window on private property!
Let's go see these "ghosts."

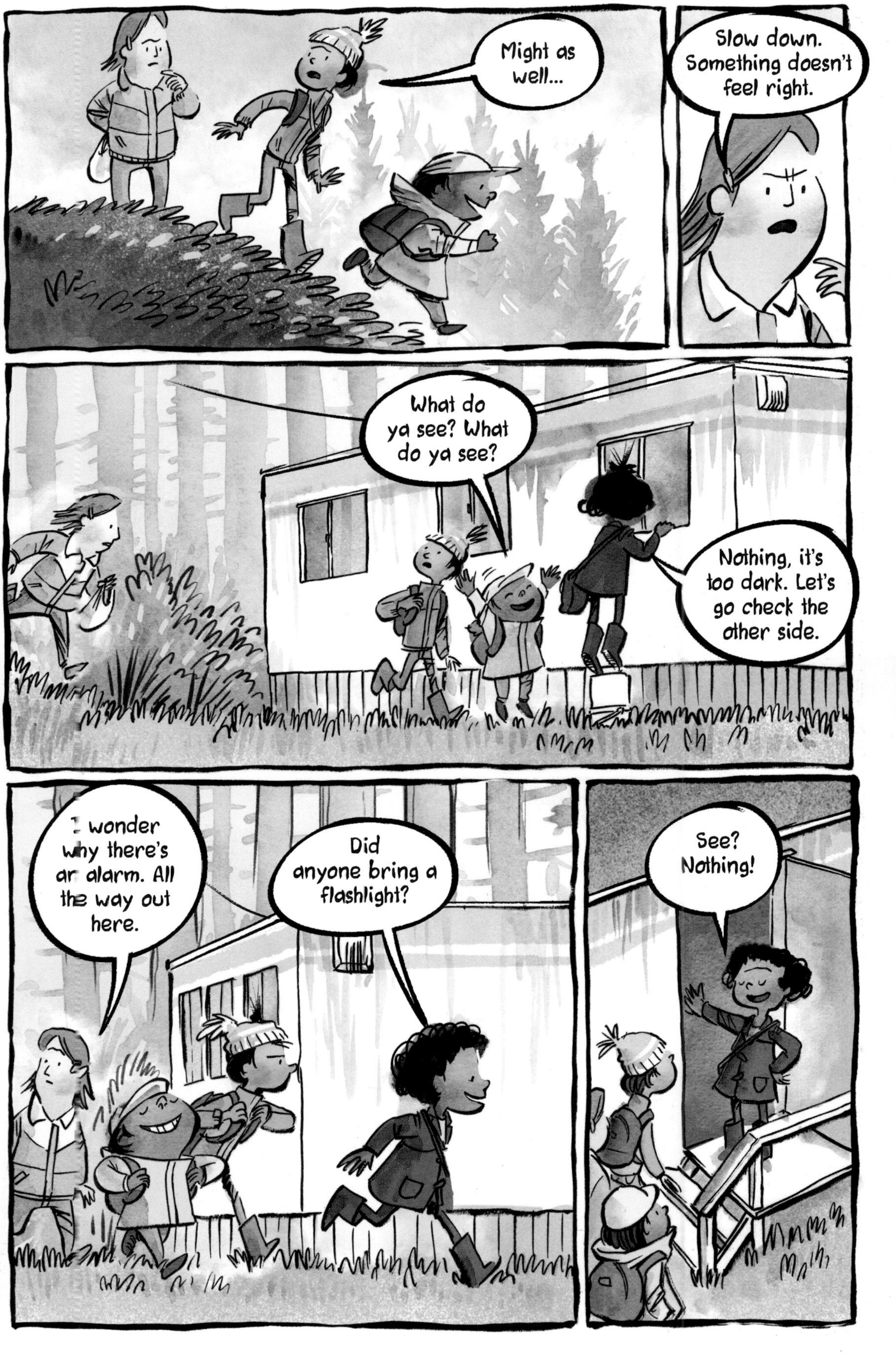
Might as well...
Slow down. Something doesn't feel right.
What do ya see? What do ya see?
Nothing, it's too dark. Let's go check the other side.
I wonder why there's an alarm. All the way out here.
Did anyone bring a flashlight?
See? Nothing!

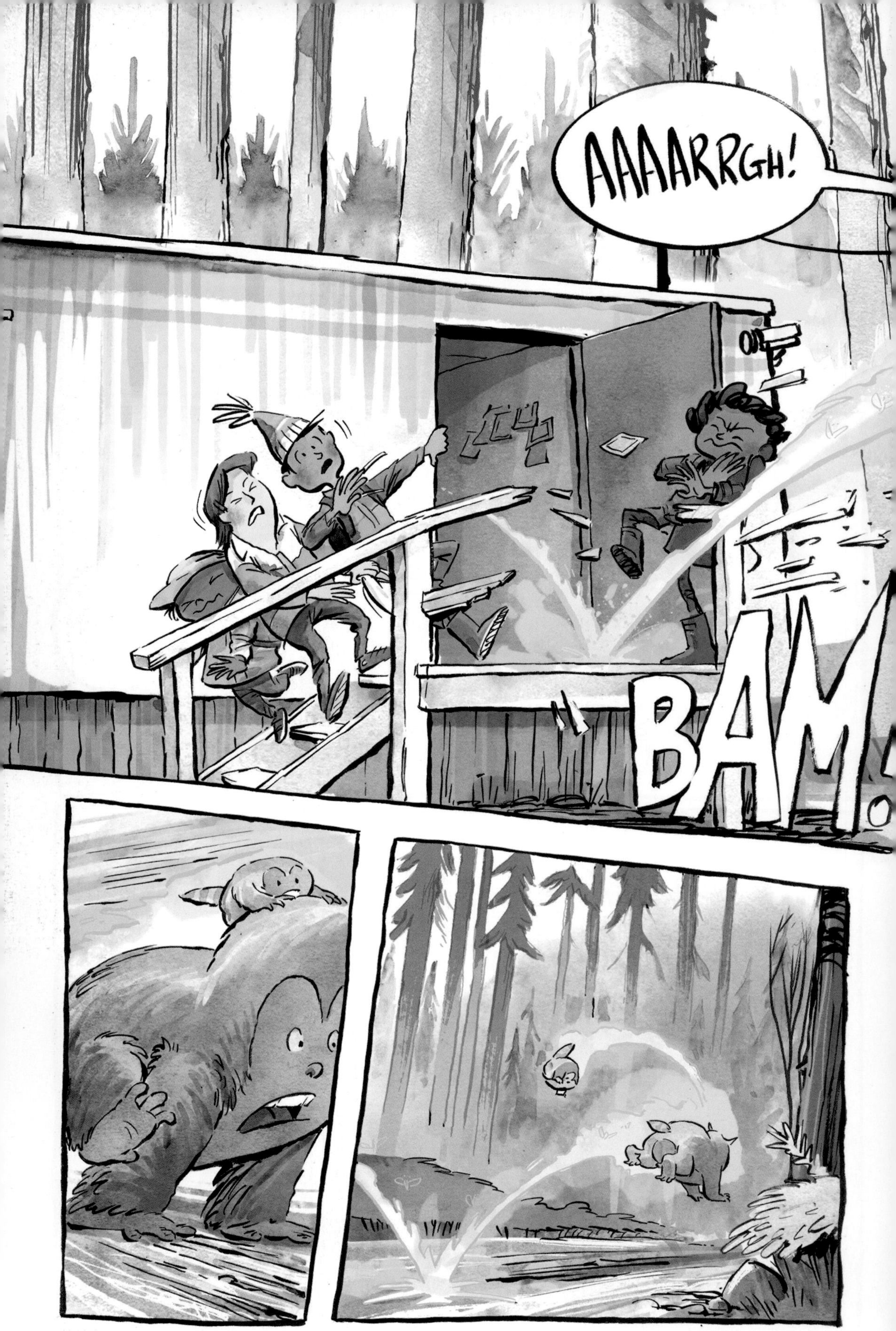
AAAARRGH!
BAM!

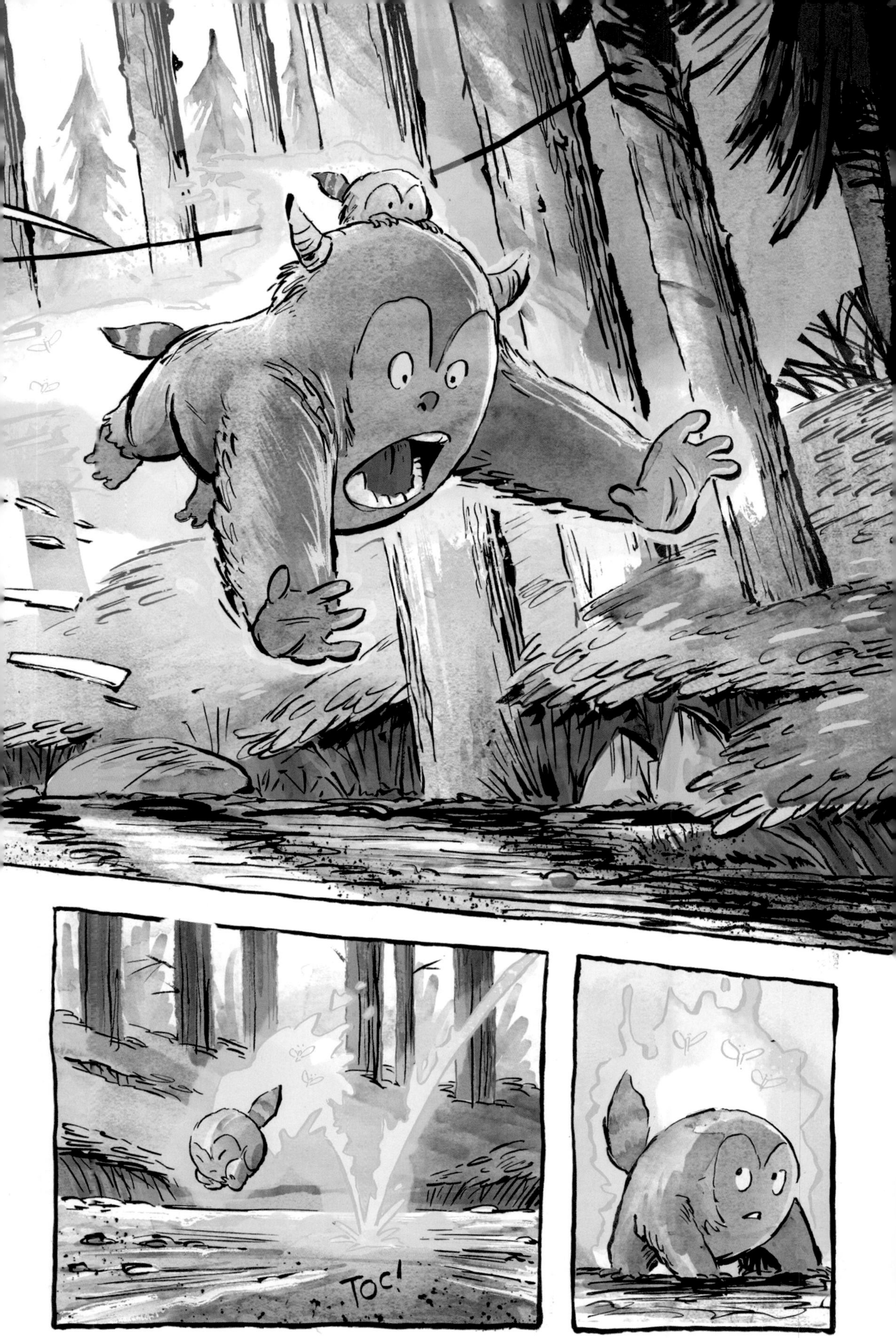
TOC!

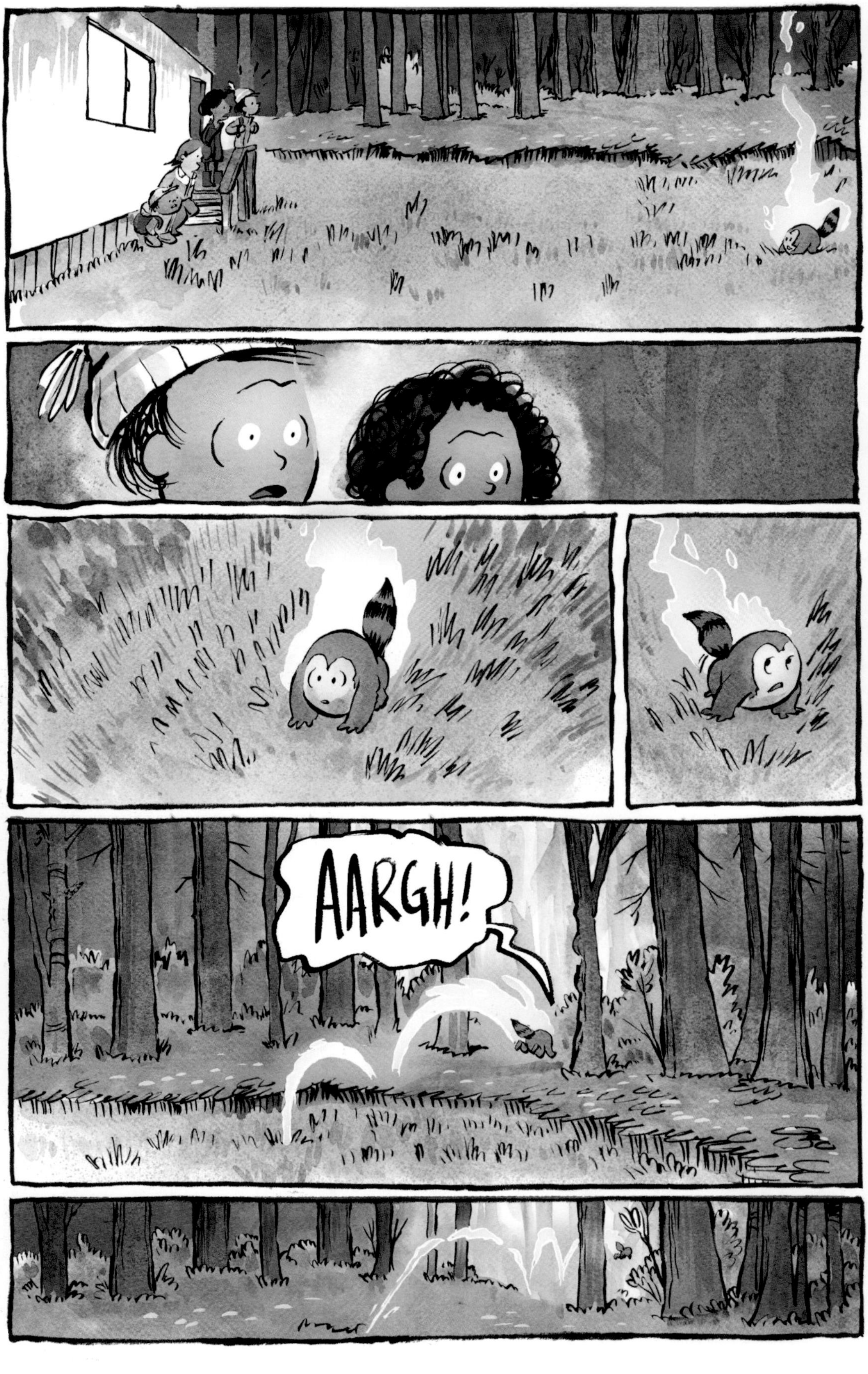
AARGH!

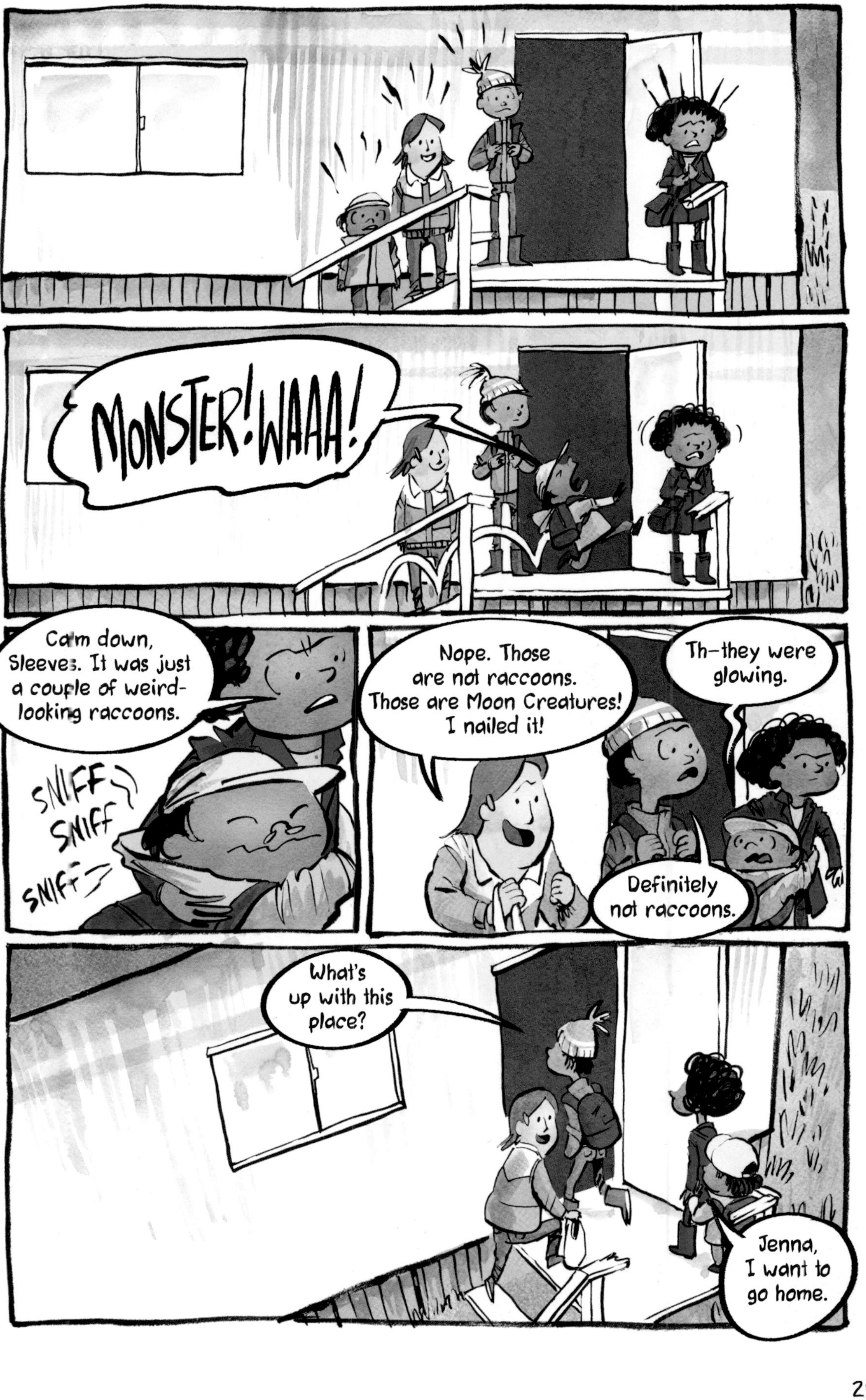
MONSTER! WAAA!
Calm down, Sleeves. It was just a couple of weird-looking raccoons.
SNIFF SNIFF SNIFF
Nope. Those are not raccoons. Those are Moon Creatures! I nailed it!
Th—they were glowing.
Definitely not raccoons.
What's up with this place?
Jenna, I want to go home.

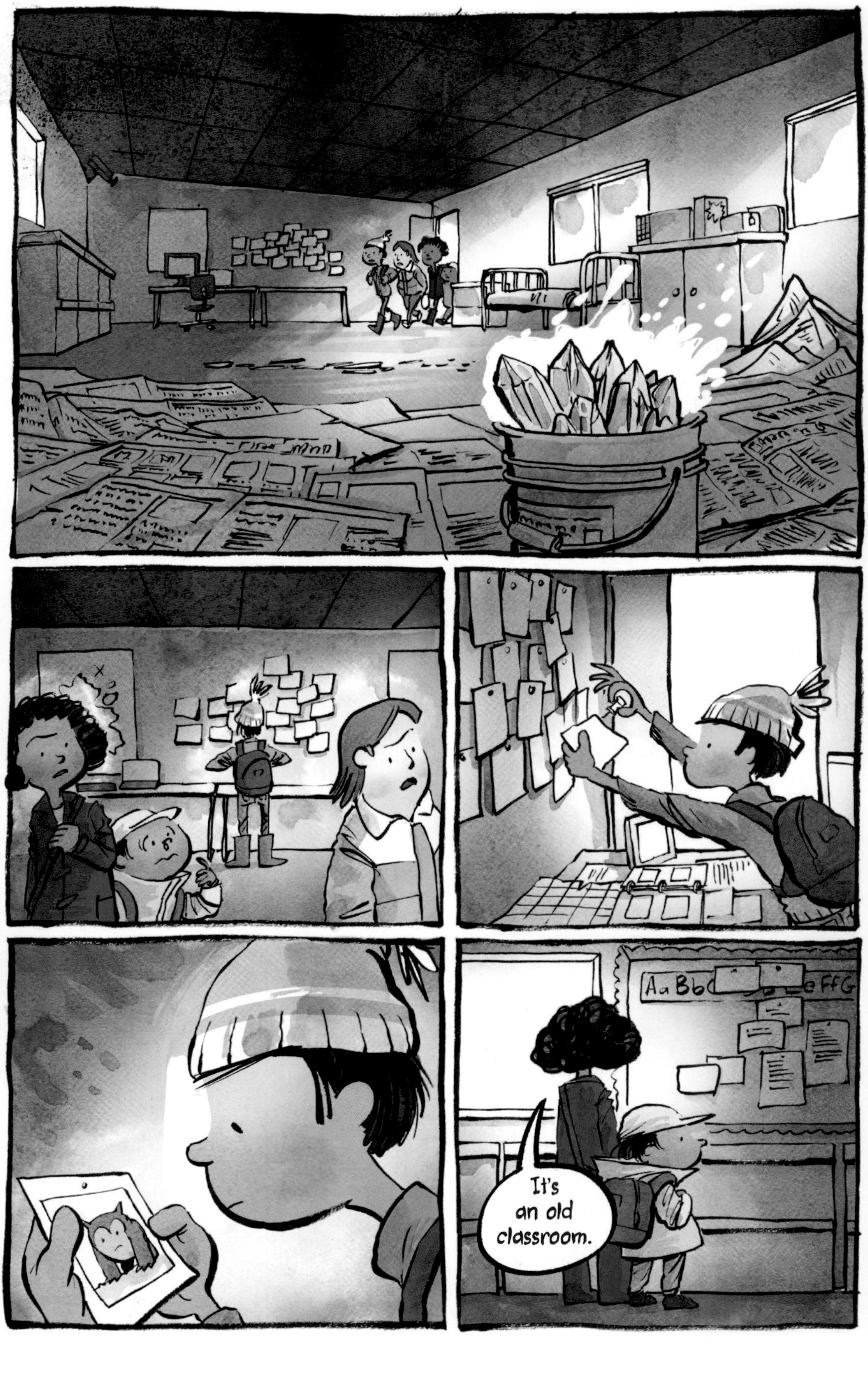
It's an old classroom.

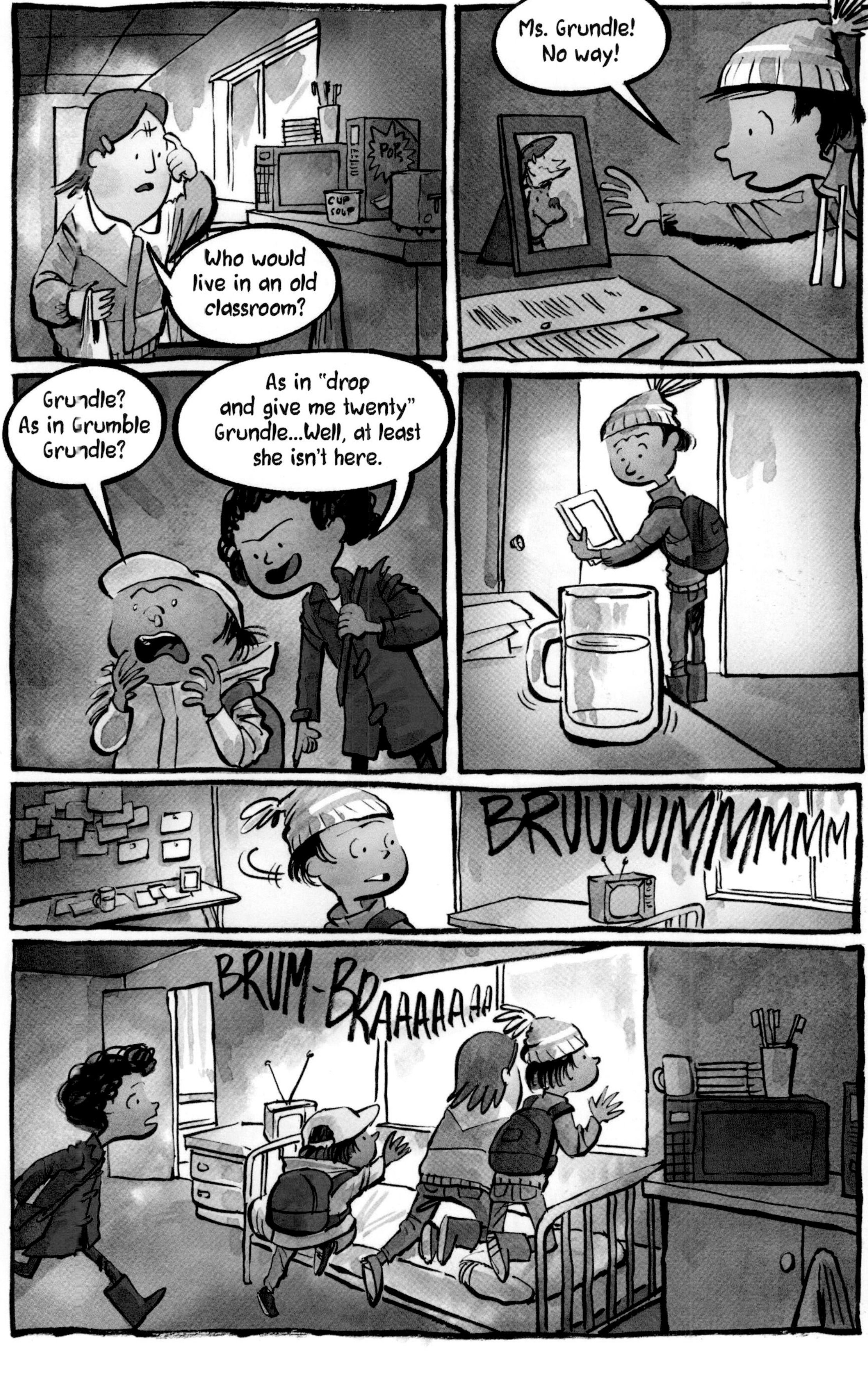
Who would live in an old classroom?
Ms. Grundle! No way!
Grundle? As in Grumble Grundle?
As in "drop and give me twenty" Grundle...Well, at least she isn't here.
CUP SOUP
BRUUUUMMMMM
BRUM-BRAAAAAA

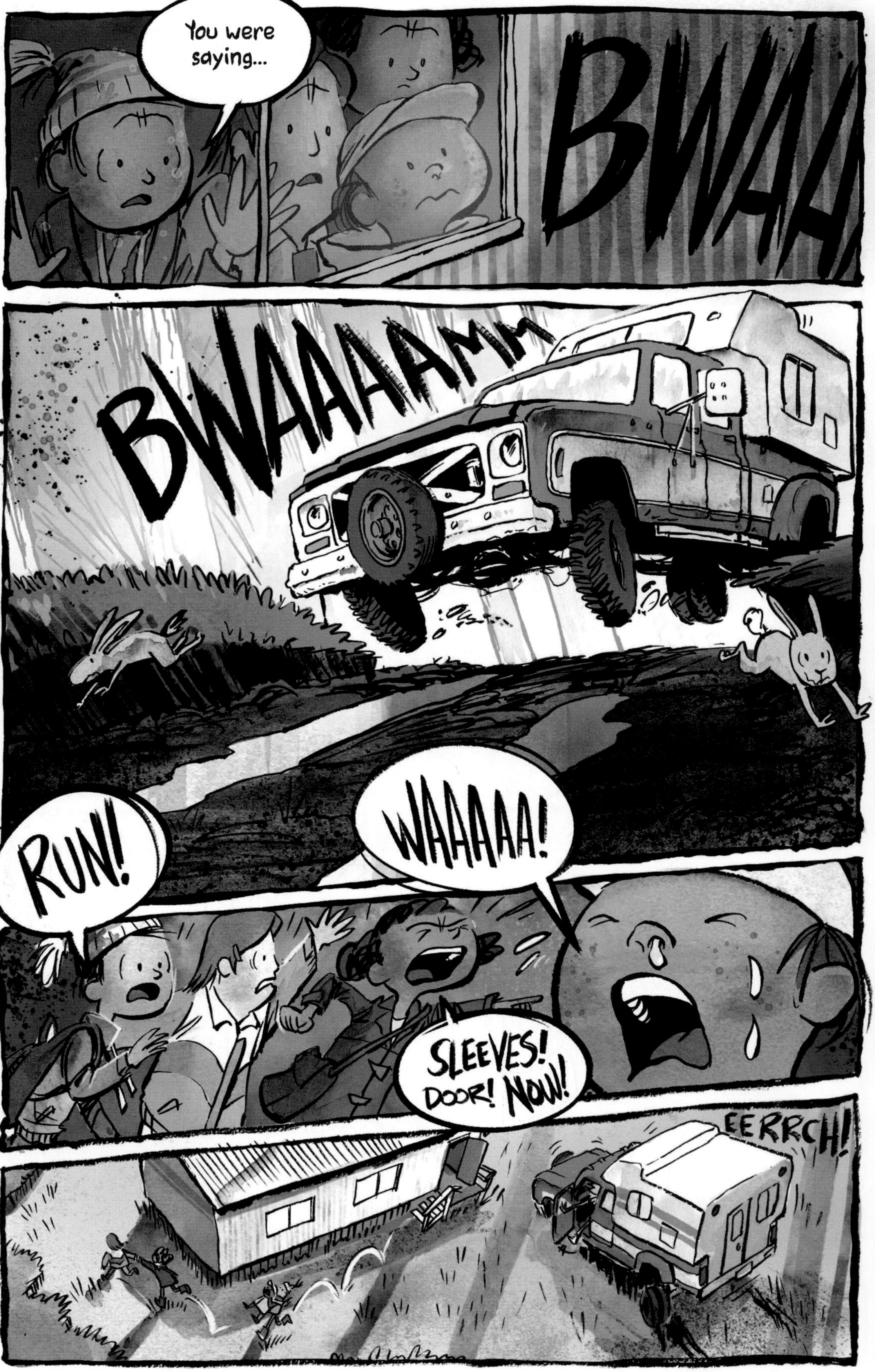
You were saying...
BWAA
BWAAAAAMM
RUN!
WAAAAA!
SLEEVES! DOOR! NOW!
EERRCH!

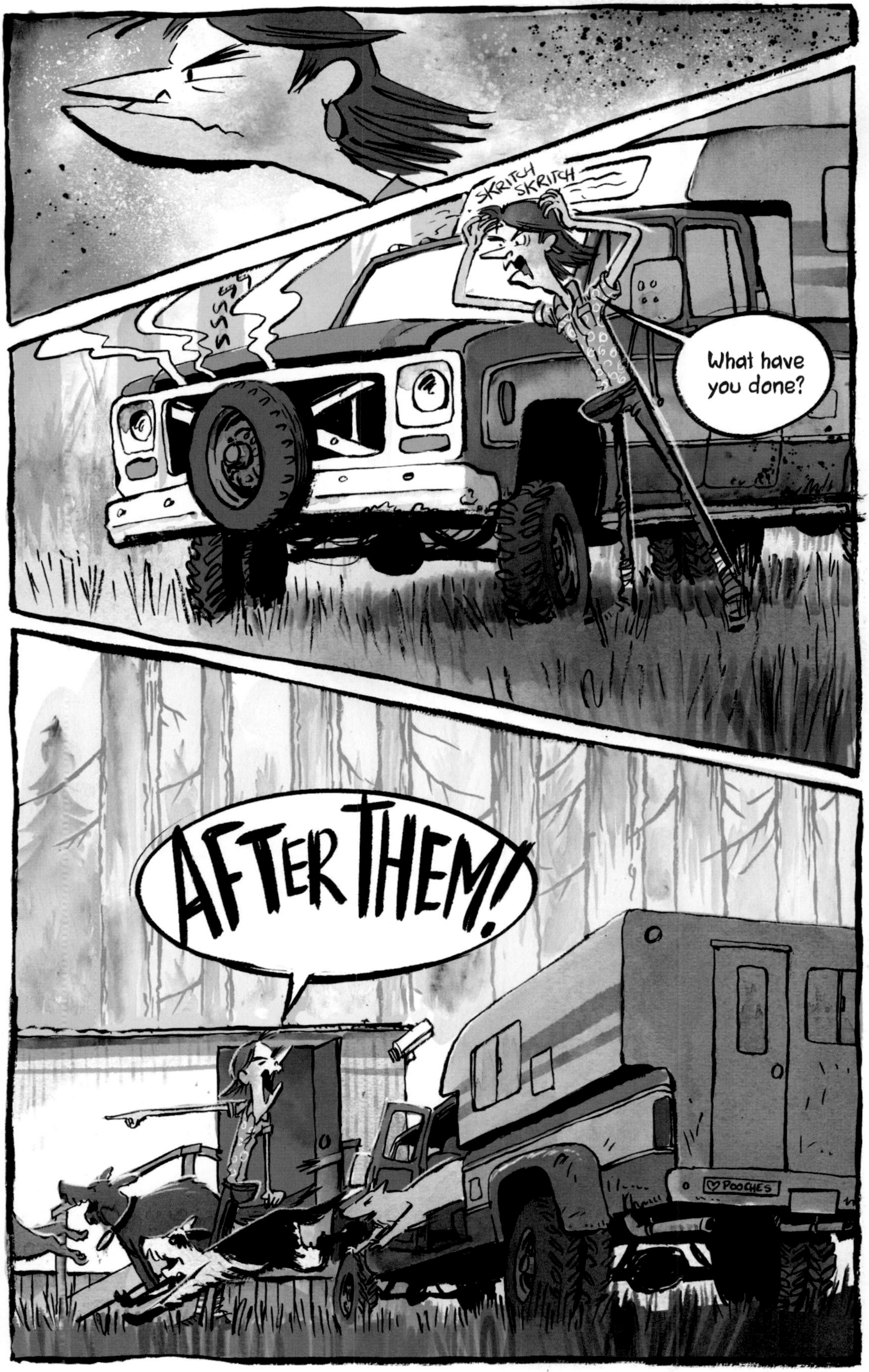
SKRITCH SKRITCH
What have you done?
AFTER THEM!
POOCHES

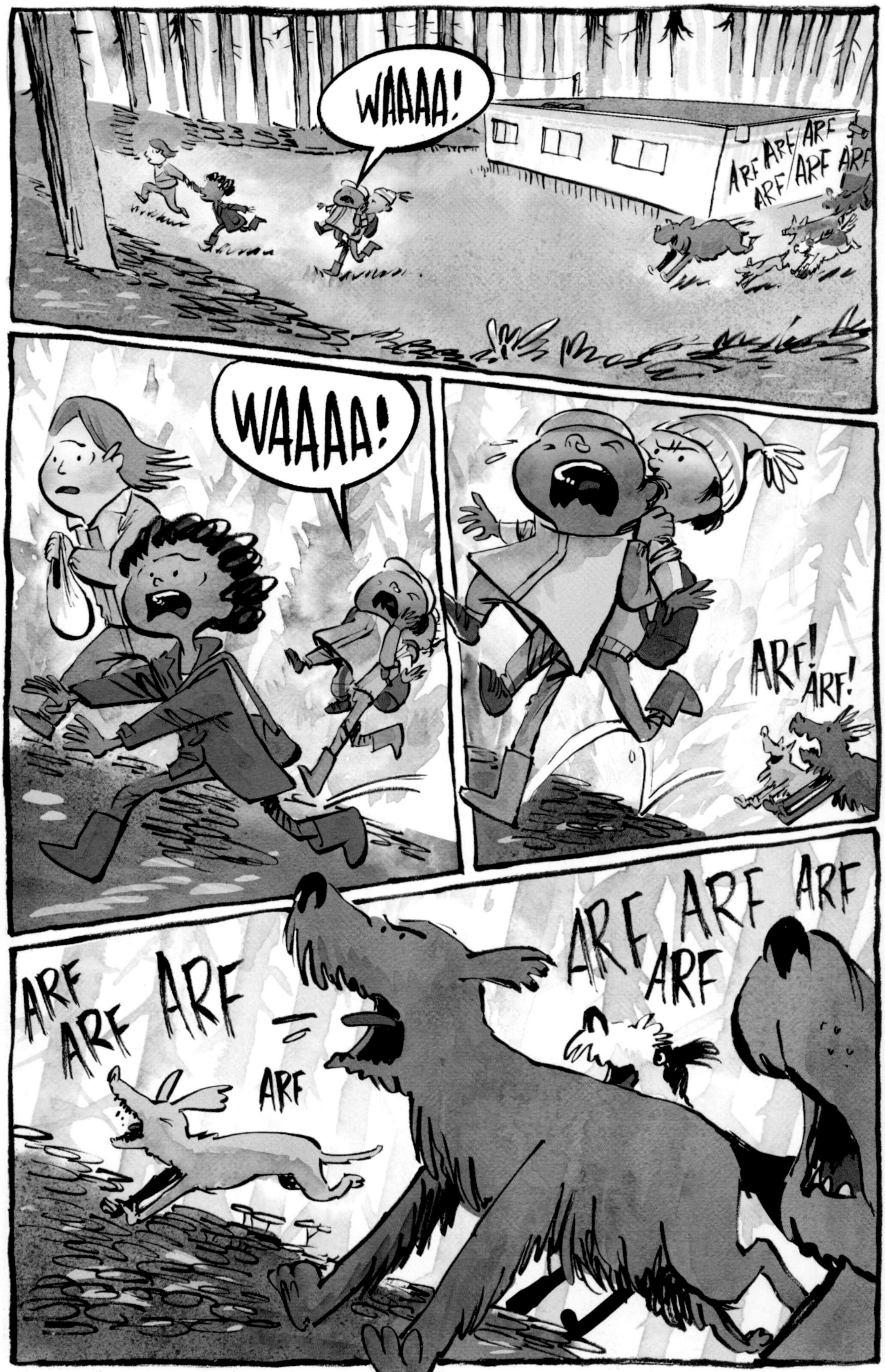
WAAAA!
ARF ARF ARF
ARF ARF ARF
WAAAA!
ARF! ARF!
ARF ARF ARF ARF
ARF ARF ARF
ARF

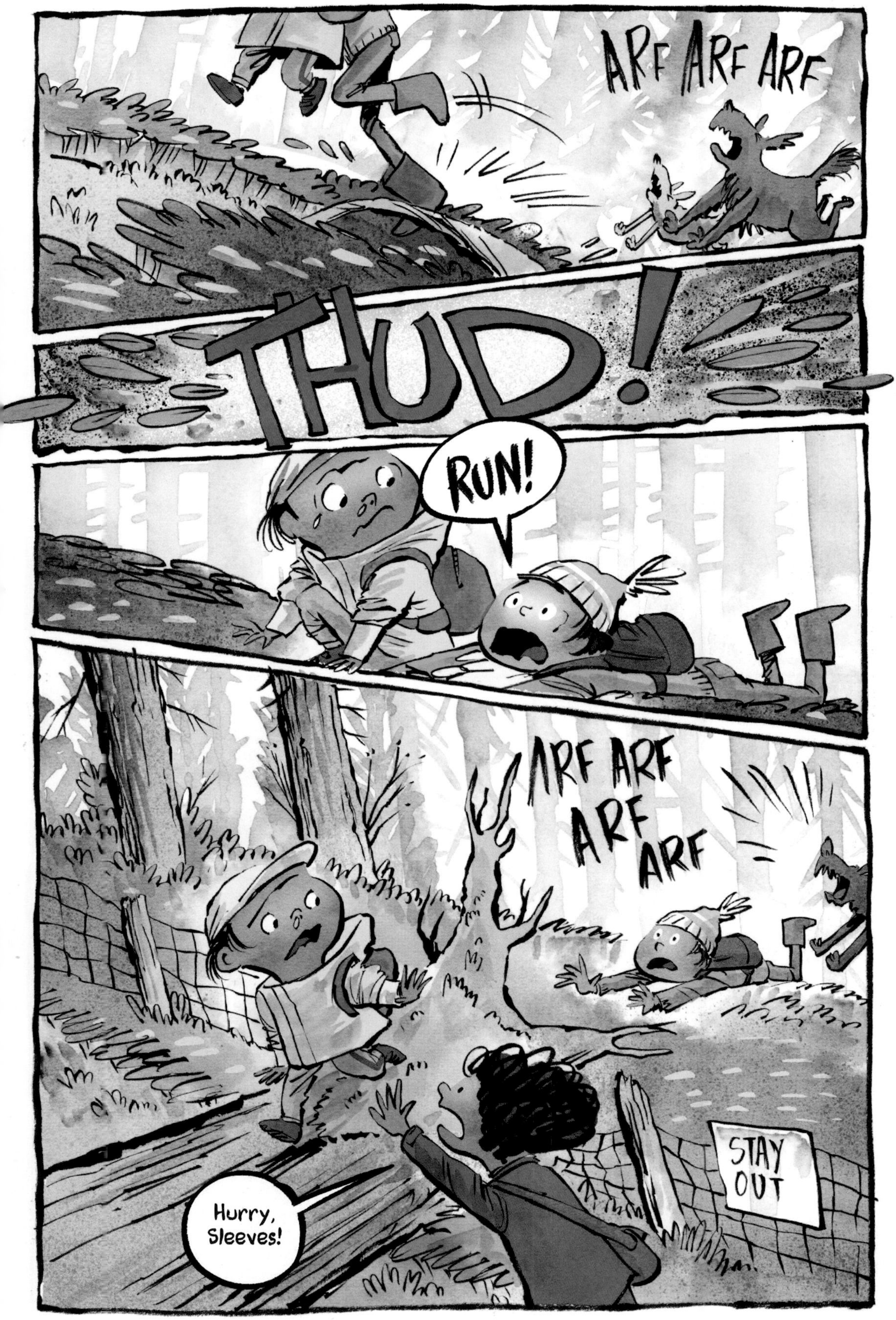
ARF ARF ARF
THUD!
RUN!
ARF ARF ARF ARF
STAY OUT
Hurry, Sleeves!

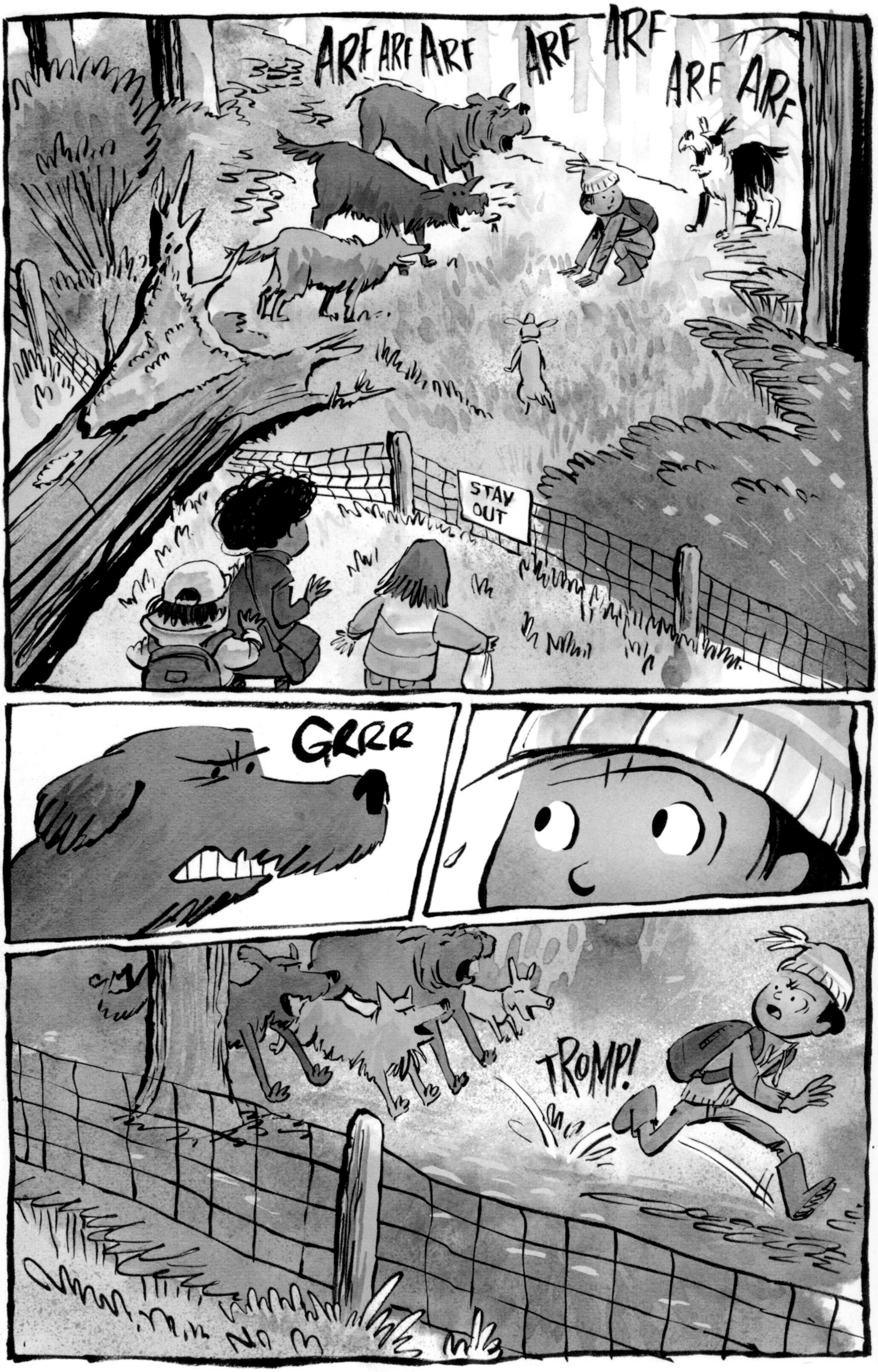
ARF ARF ARF
ARF
ARF
ARF ARF
STAY OUT
GRRR
TROMP!

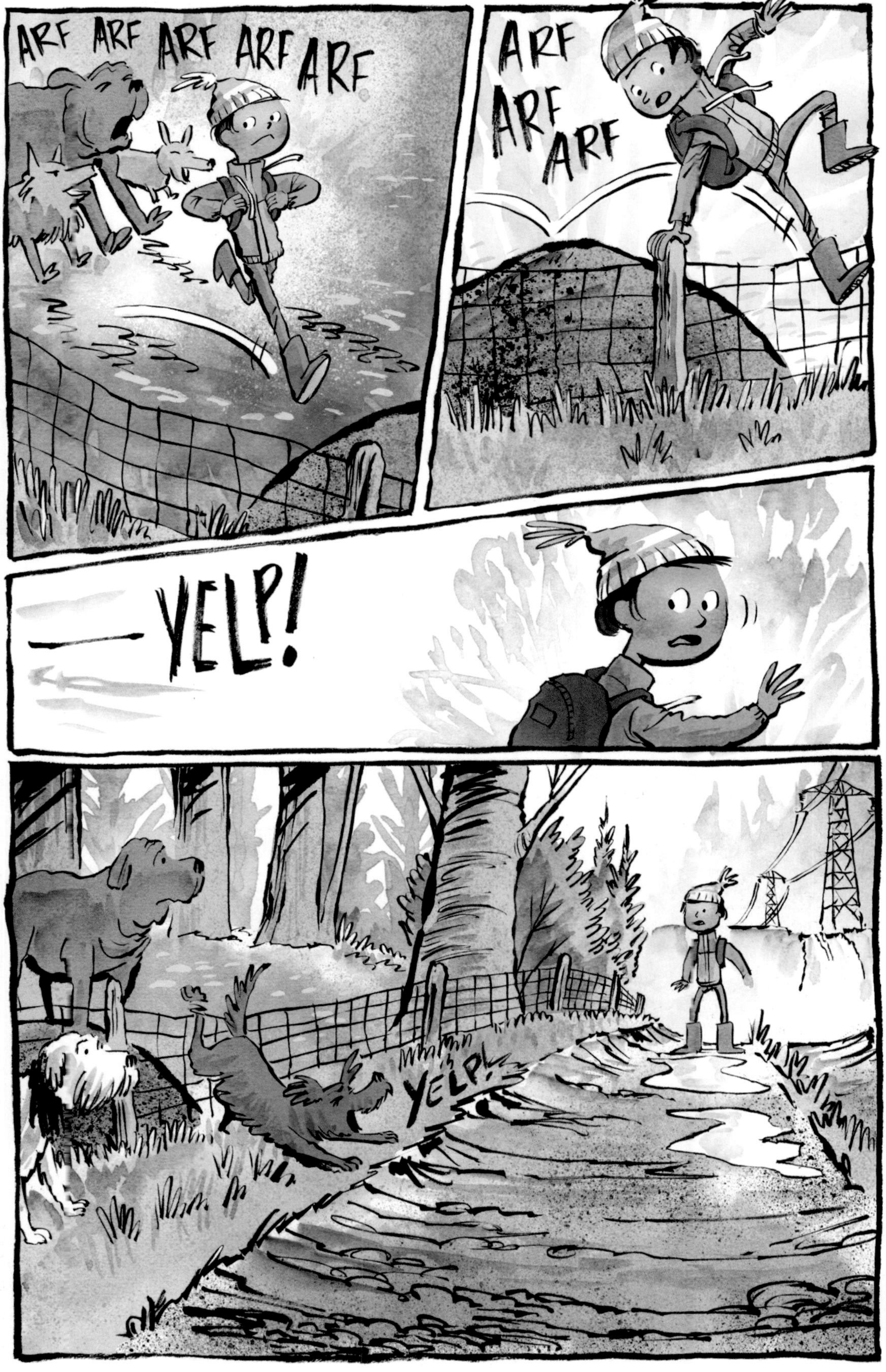
ARF ARF ARF ARF ARF
ARF ARF ARF
YELP!
YELP!

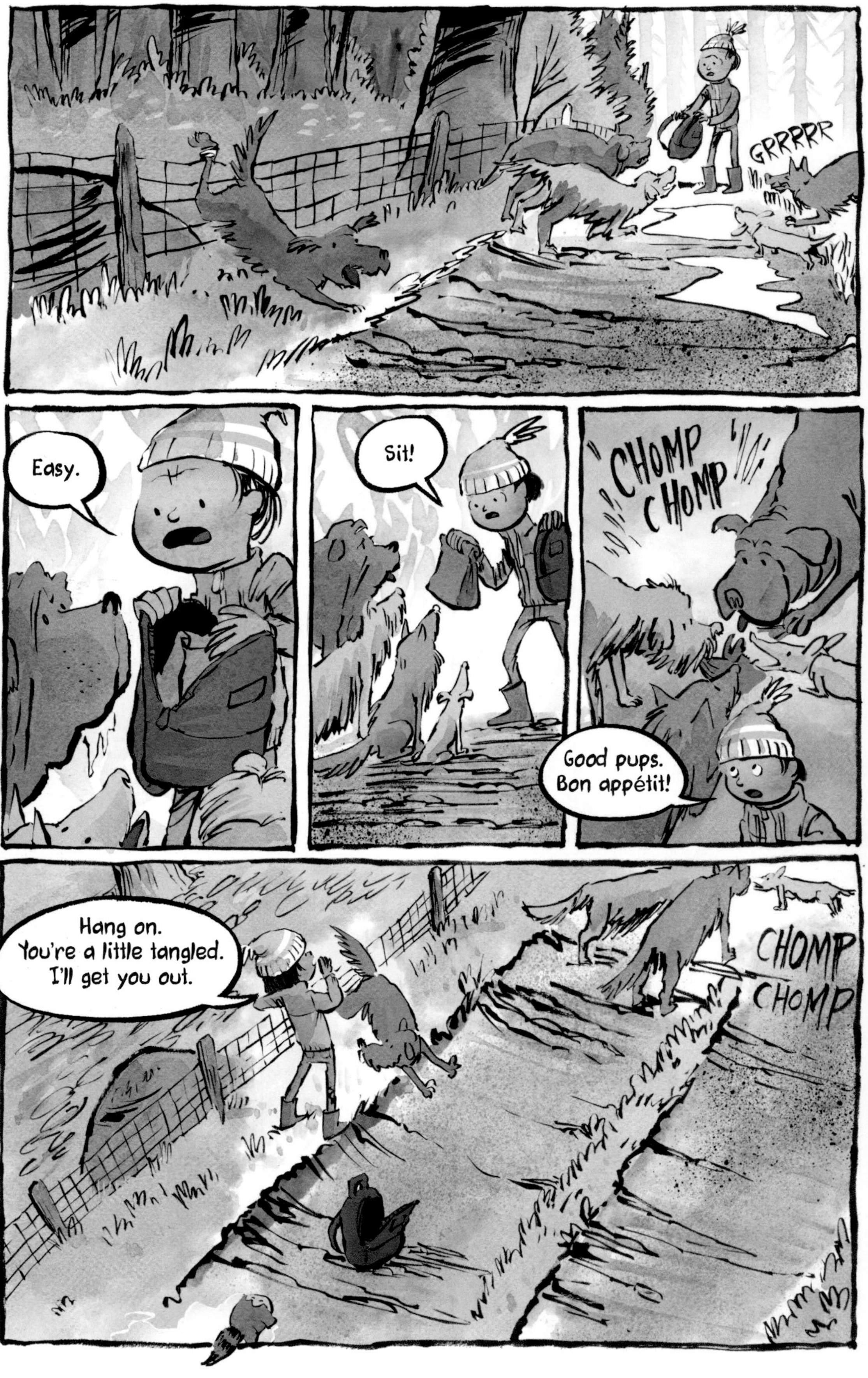
GRRRRR
Easy.
Sit!
CHOMP CHOMP
Good pups. Bon appétit!
Hang on. You're a little tangled. I'll get you out.
CHOMP CHOMP

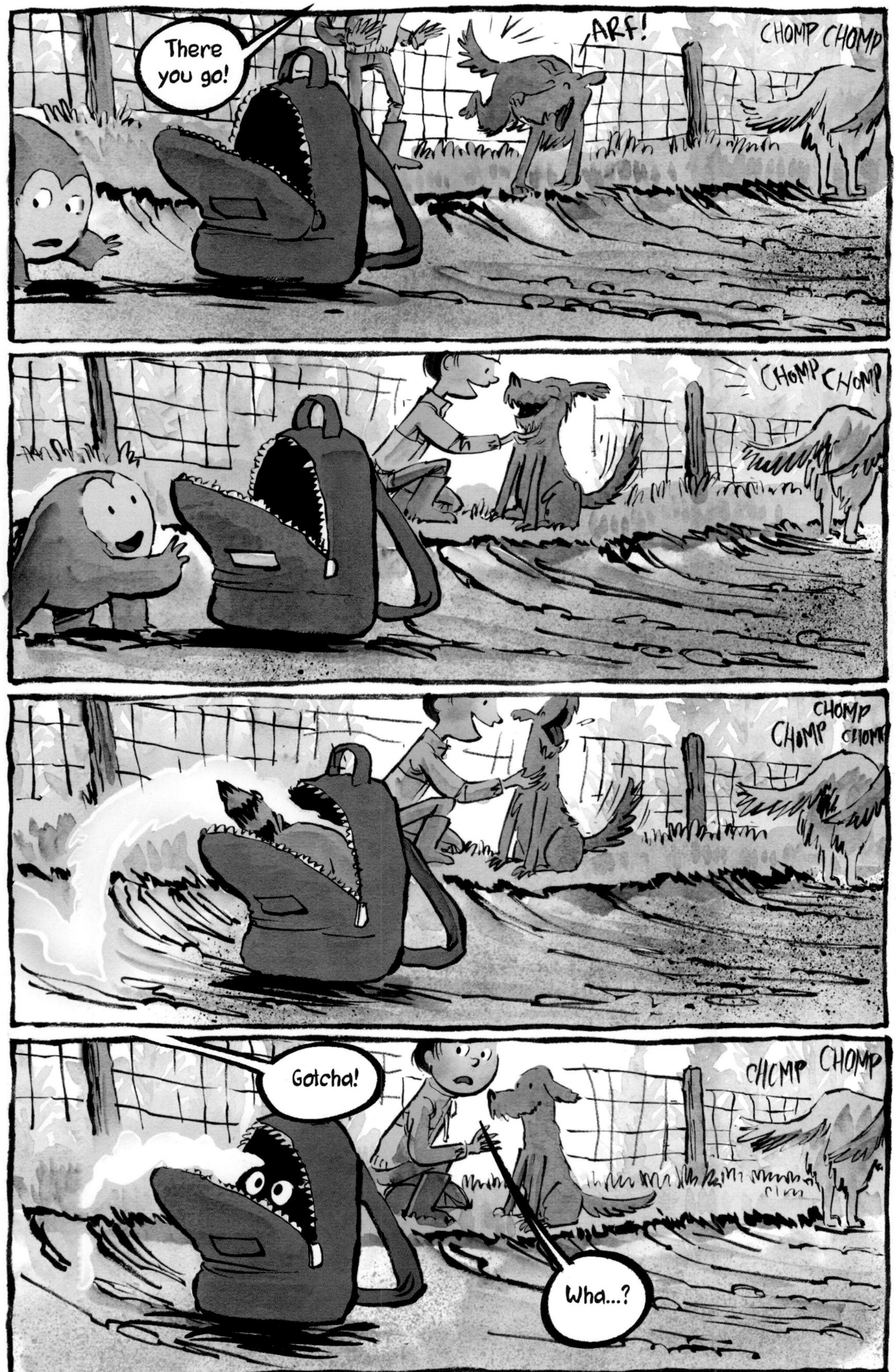
There you go!
ARF!
CHOMP CHOMP
CHOMP CHOMP
CHOMP
CHOMP
Gotcha!
CHOMP CHOMP
Wha...?

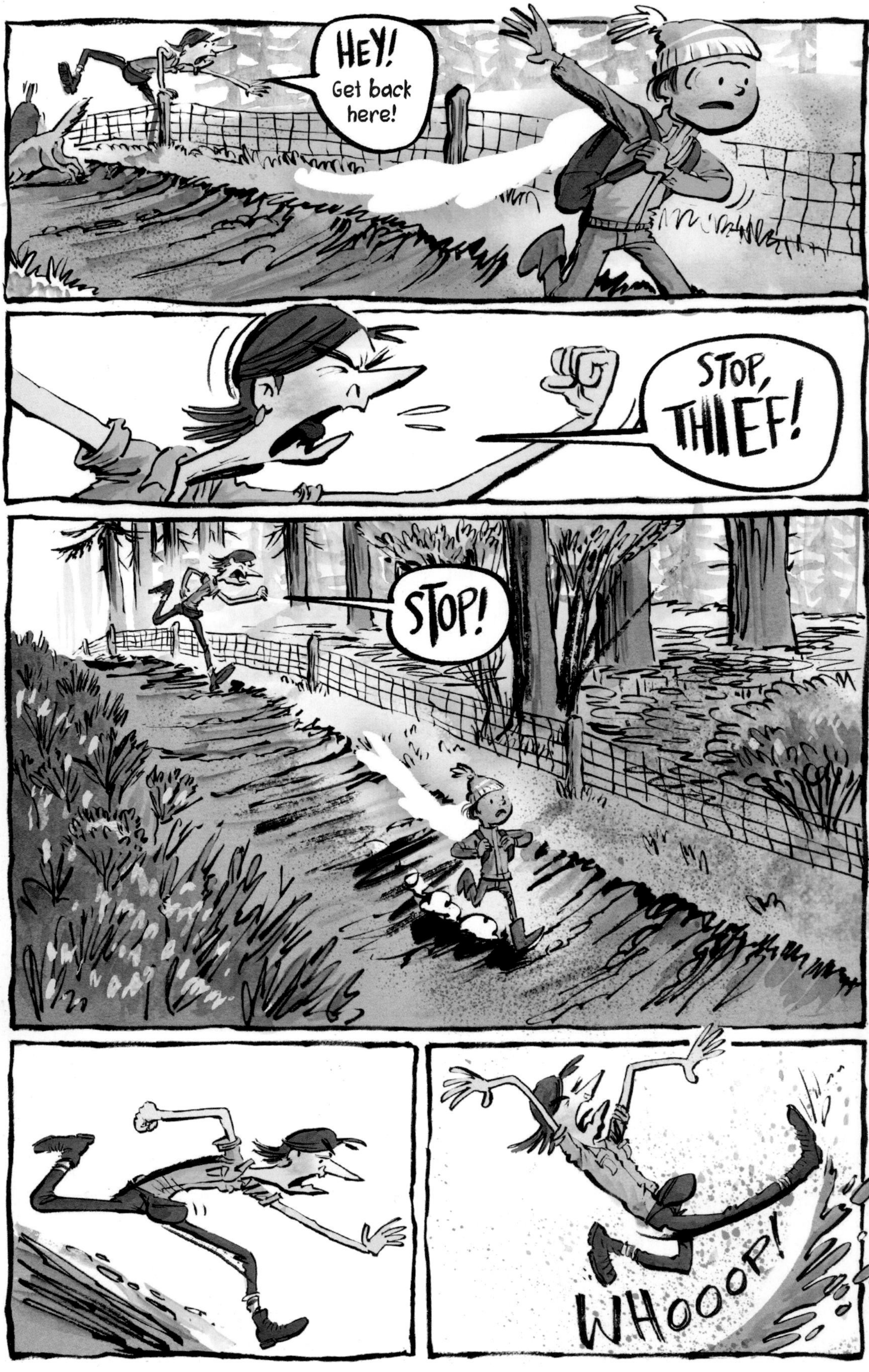
HEY! Get back here!
STOP, THIEF!
STOP!
WHOOOP!

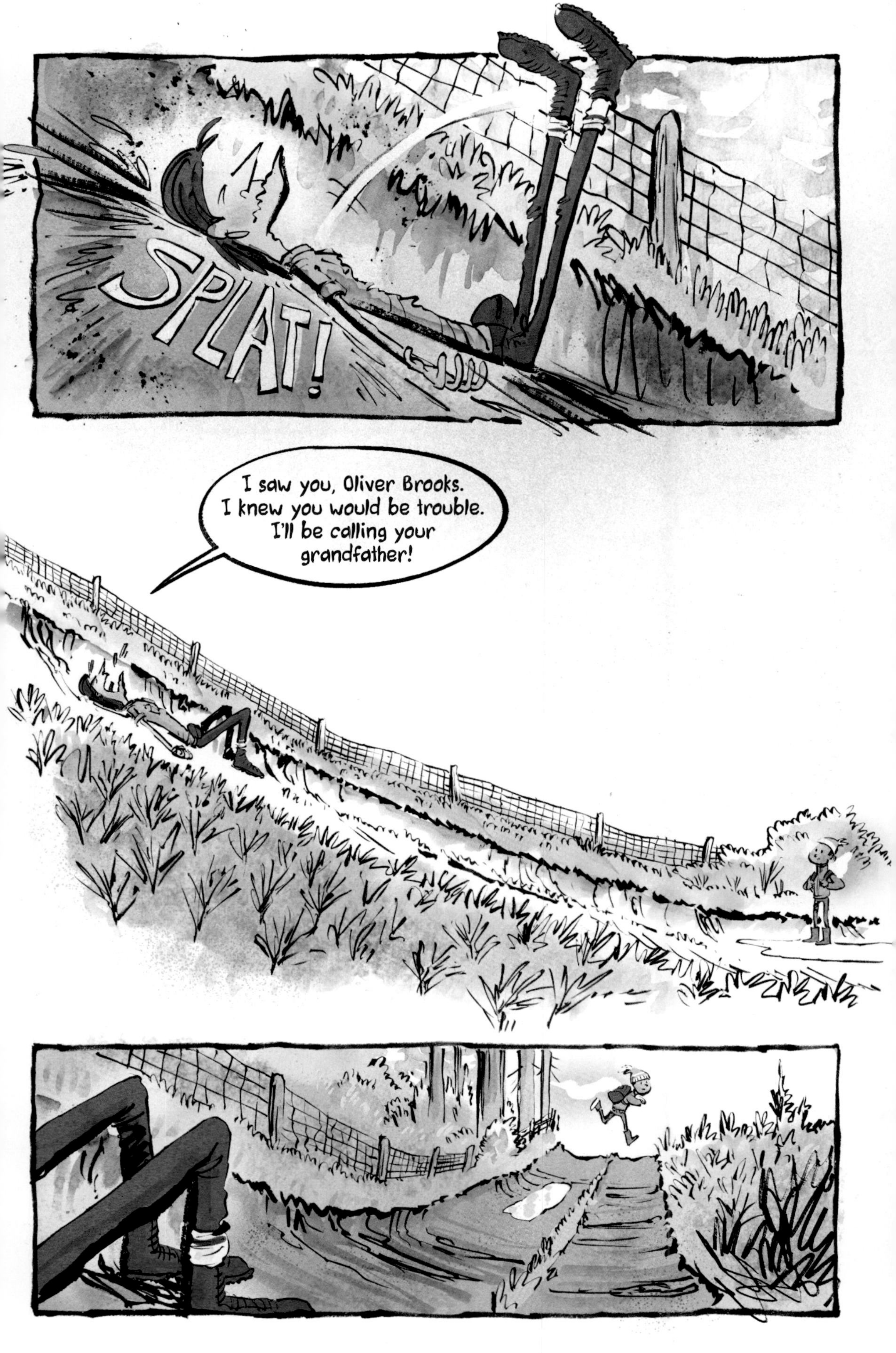
SPLAT!
I saw you, Oliver Brooks. I knew you would be trouble. I'll be calling your grandfather!

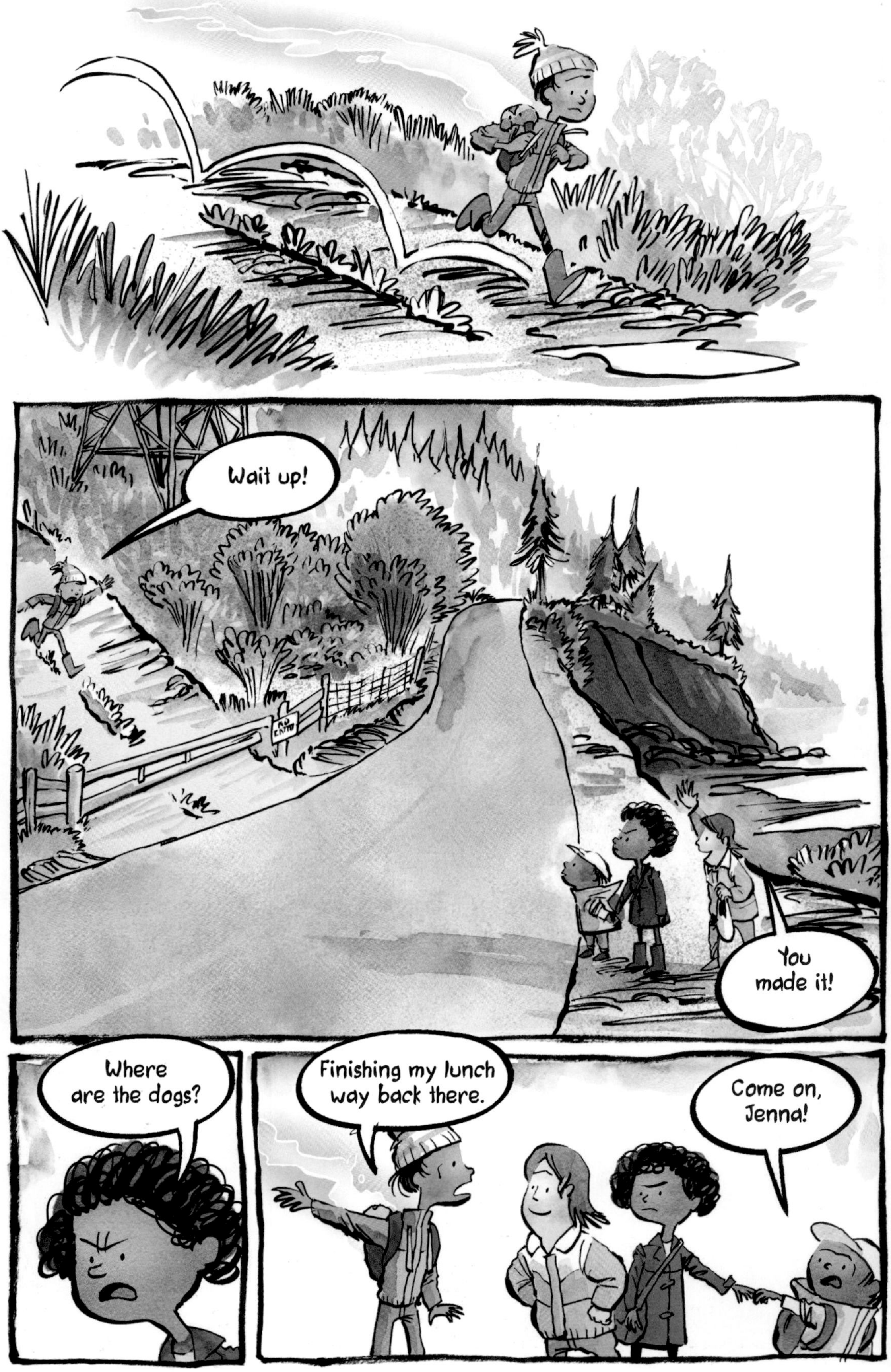

Wait up!
You made it!
Where are the dogs?
Finishing my lunch way back there.
Come on, Jenna!

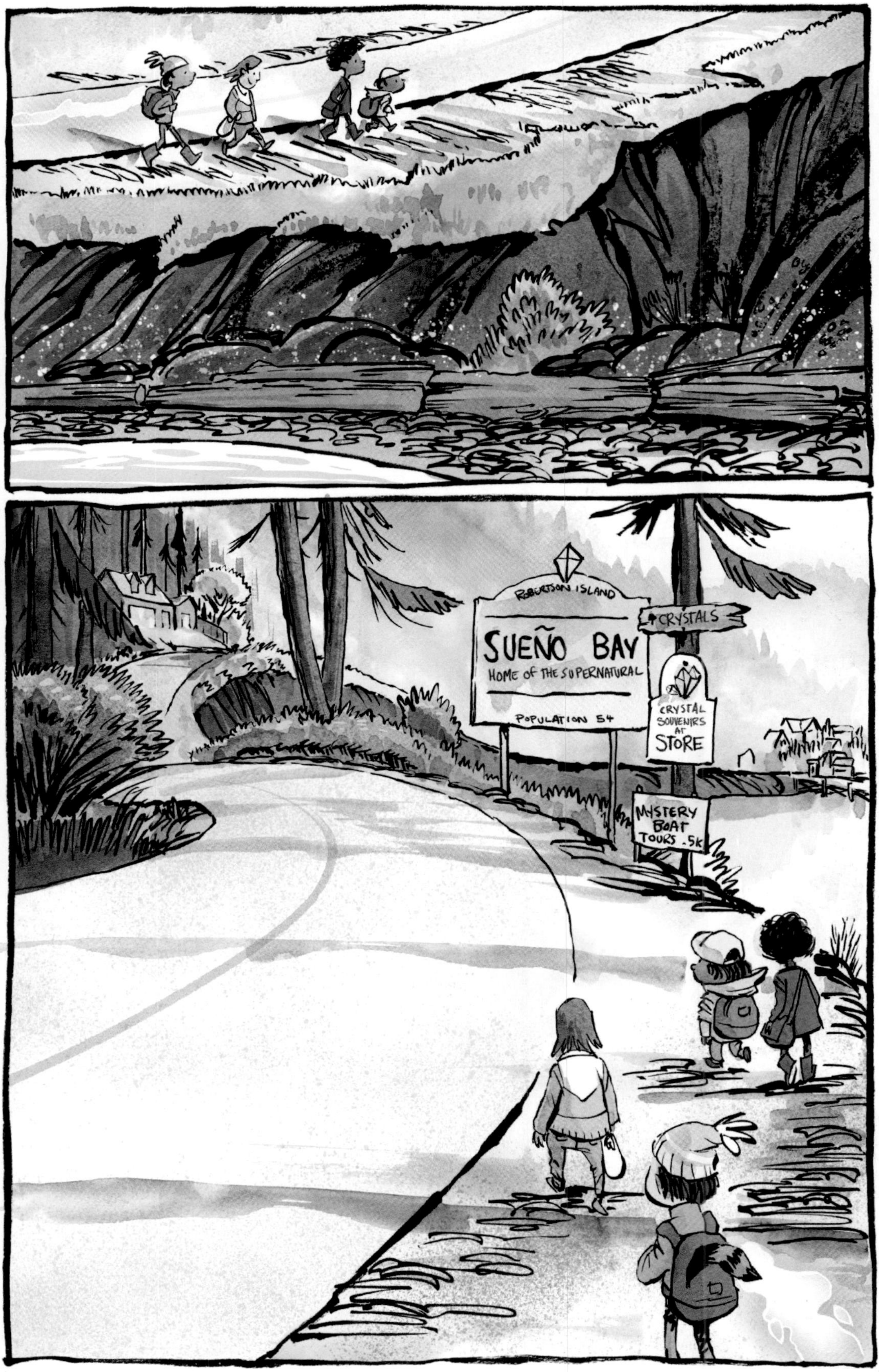
ROBERTSON ISLAND
SUEÑO BAY
HOME OF THE SUPERNATURAL
POPULATION 54
CRYSTALS
CRYSTAL SOUVENIRS AT STORE
MYSTERY BOAT TOURS .5K

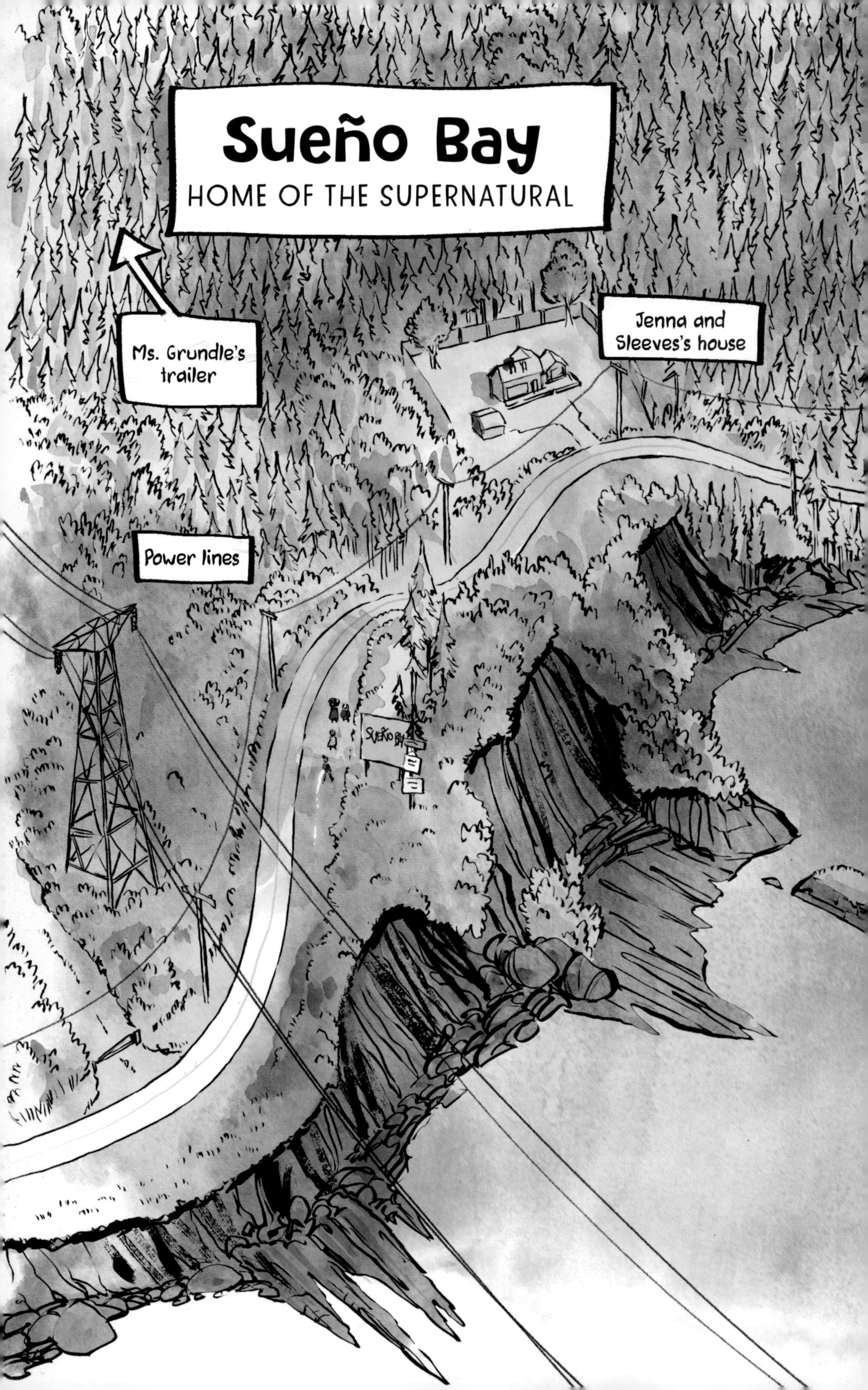
Sueño Bay
HOME OF THE SUPERNATURAL
Ms. Grundle's trailer
Jenna and Sleeves's house
Power lines
SUEÑO BAY

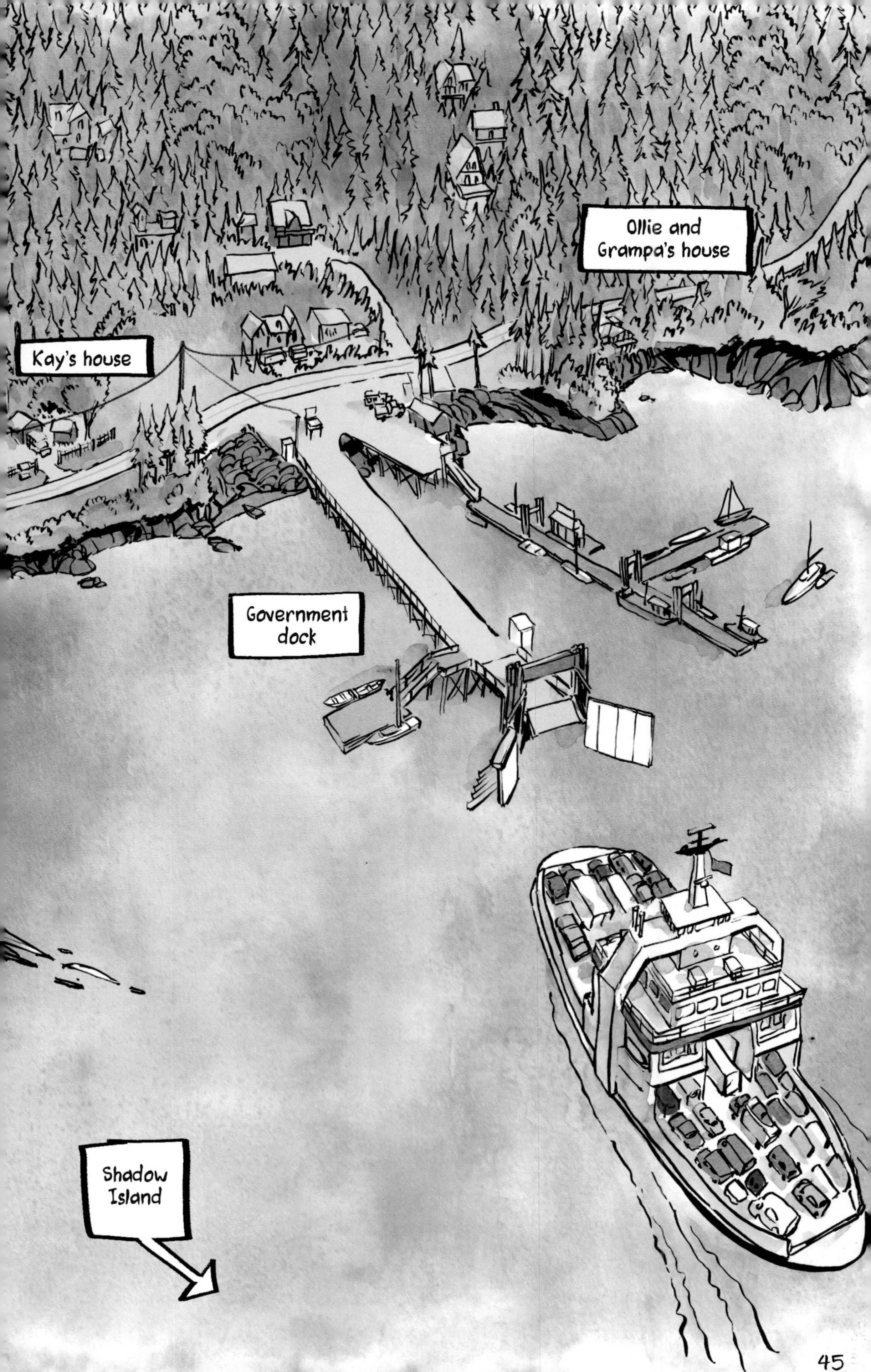
Ollie and Grampa's house
Kay's house
Government dock
Shadow Island

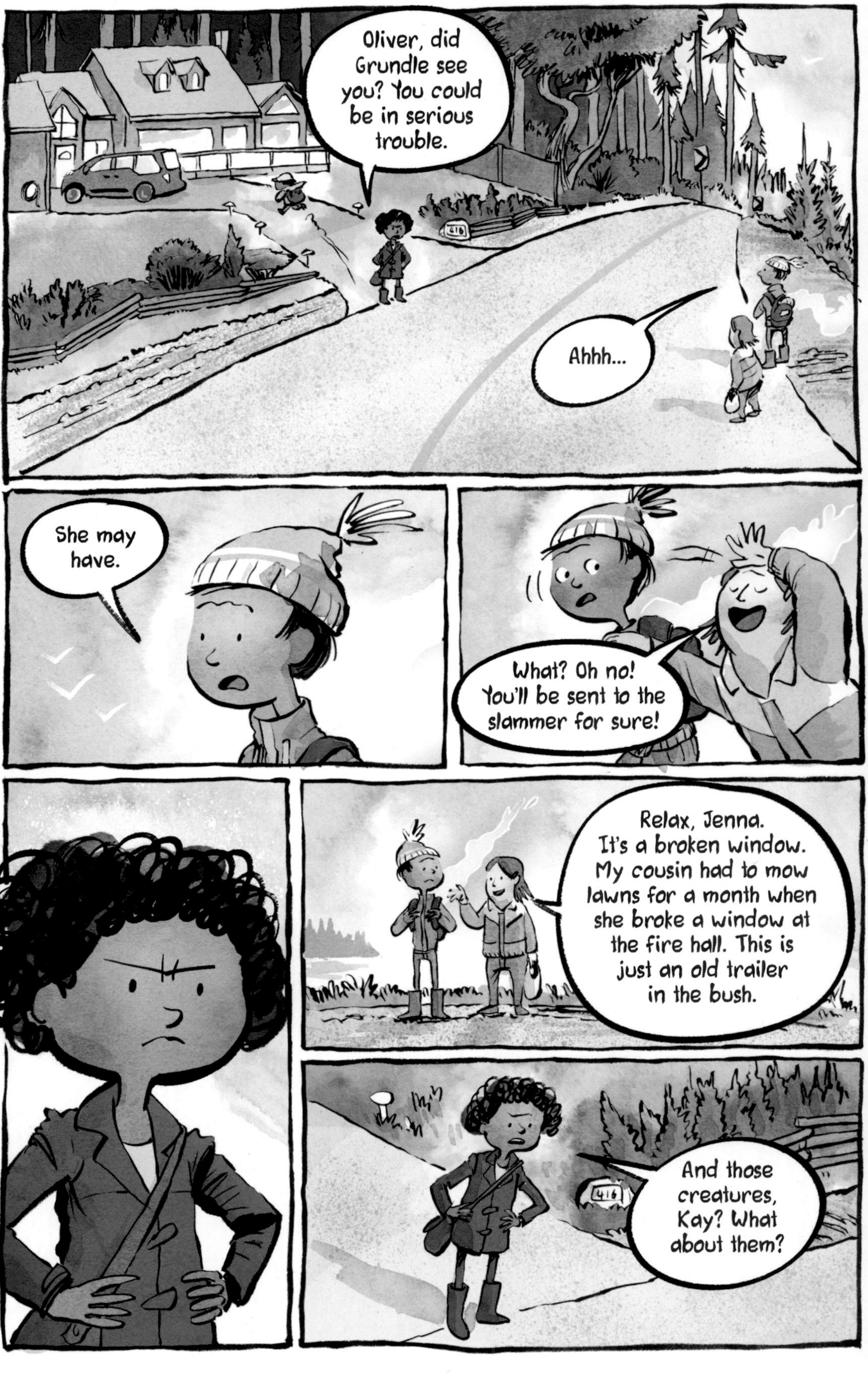
Oliver, did Grundle see you? You could be in serious trouble.
Ahhh...
She may have.
What? Oh no! You'll be sent to the slammer for sure!
Relax, Jenna. It's a broken window. My cousin had to mow lawns for a month when she broke a window at the fire hall. This is just an old trailer in the bush.
And those creatures, Kay? What about them?

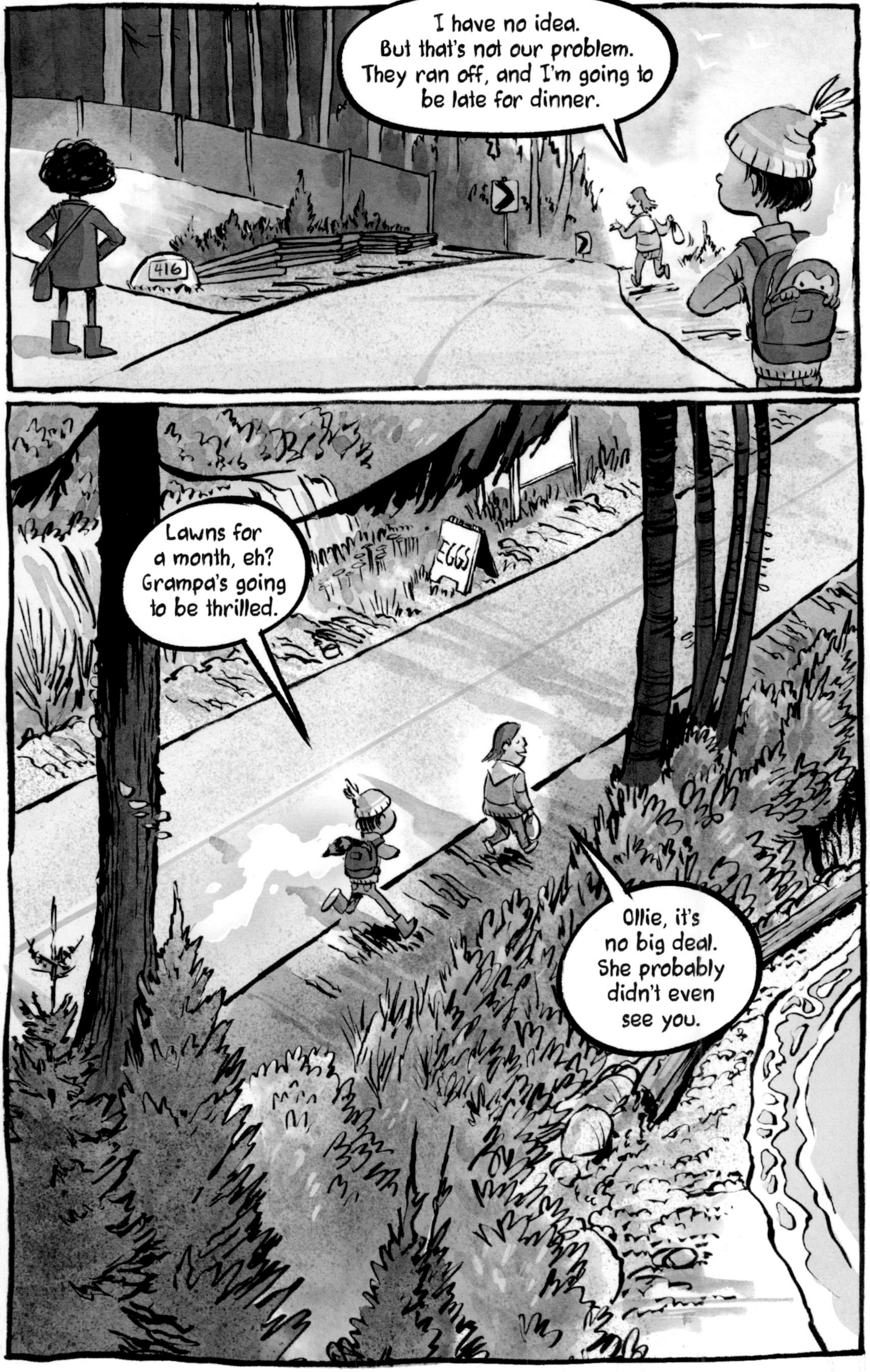
I have no idea. But that's not our problem. They ran off, and I'm going to be late for dinner.
416
EGGS
Lawns for a month, eh? Grampa's going to be thrilled.
Ollie, it's no big deal. She probably didn't even see you.

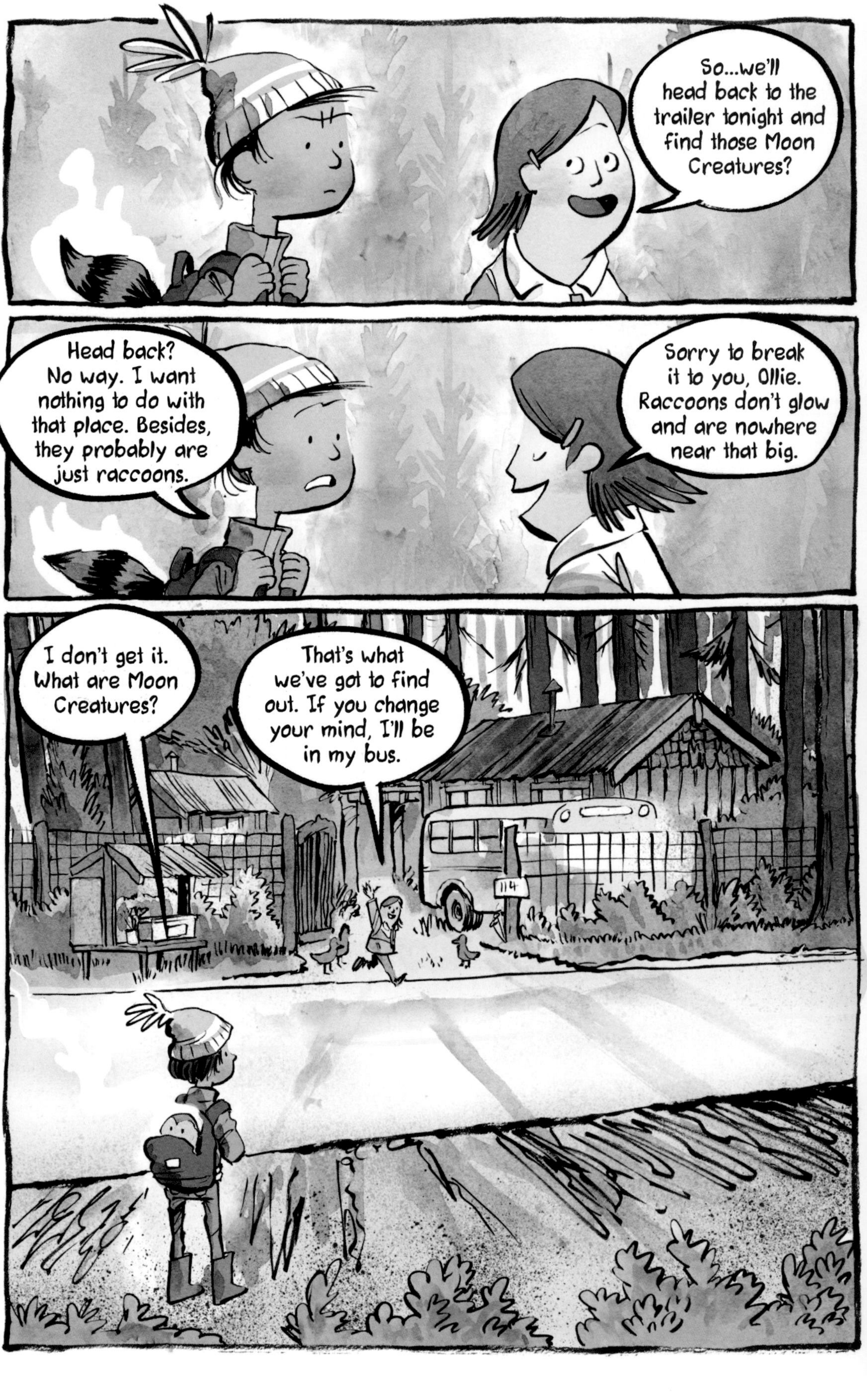
So...we'll head back to the trailer tonight and find those Moon Creatures?
Head back? No way. I want nothing to do with that place. Besides, they probably are just raccoons.
Sorry to break it to you, Ollie. Raccoons don't glow and are nowhere near that big.
I don't get it. What are Moon Creatures?
That's what we've got to find out. If you change your mind, I'll be in my bus.
114

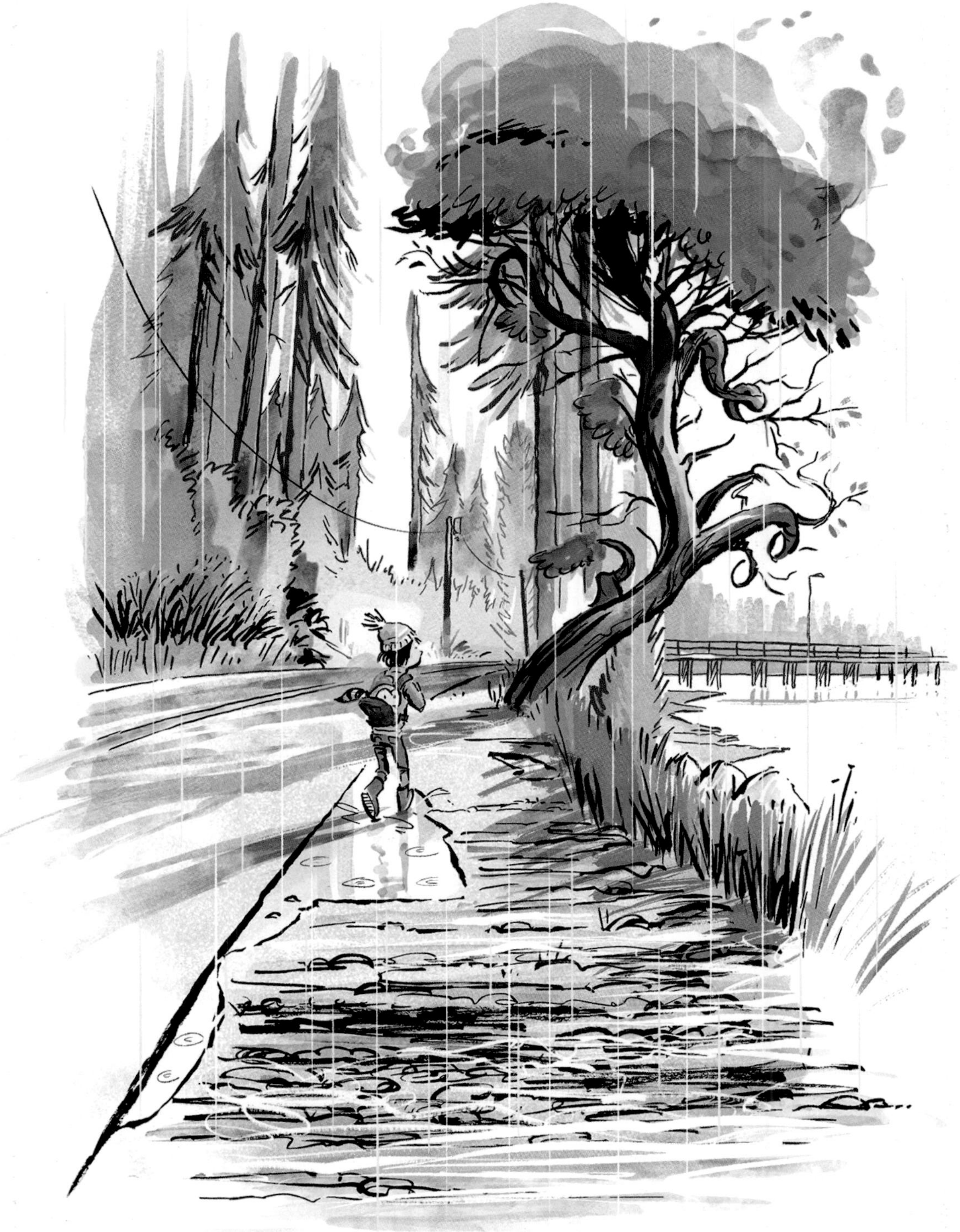

And it's raining again.

CHAPTER TWO

Conkers

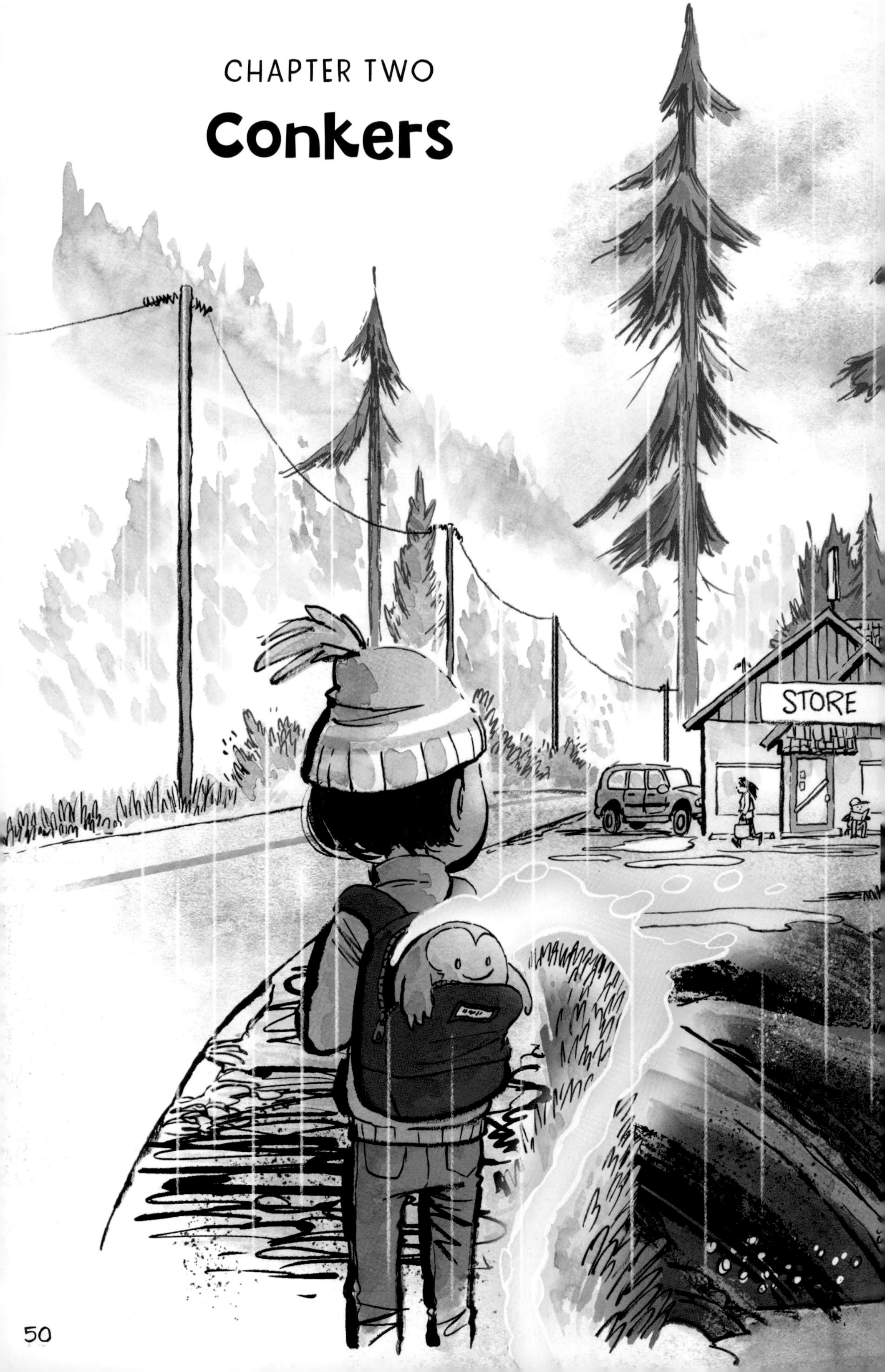
STORE

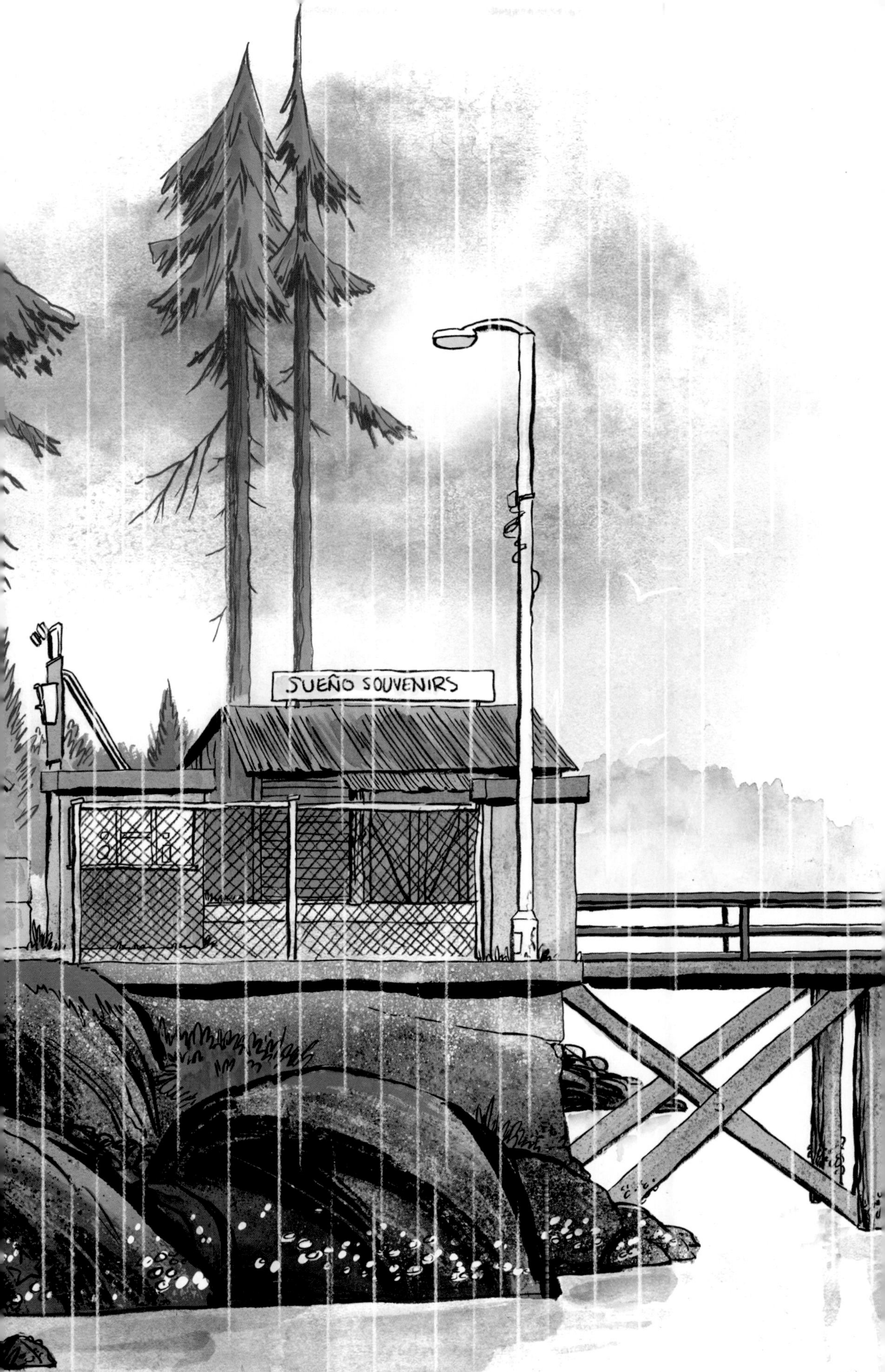
SUEÑO SOUVENIRS

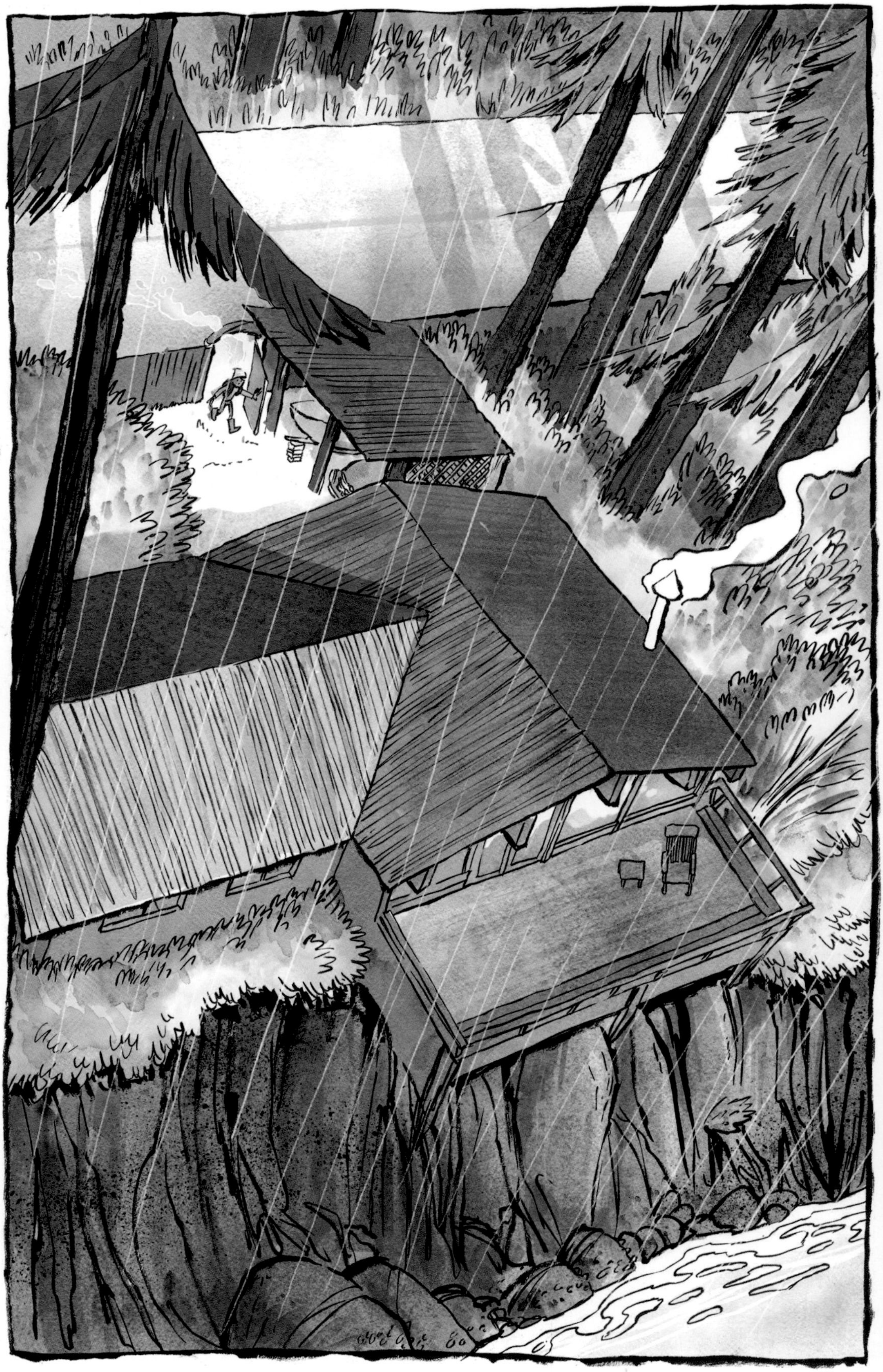

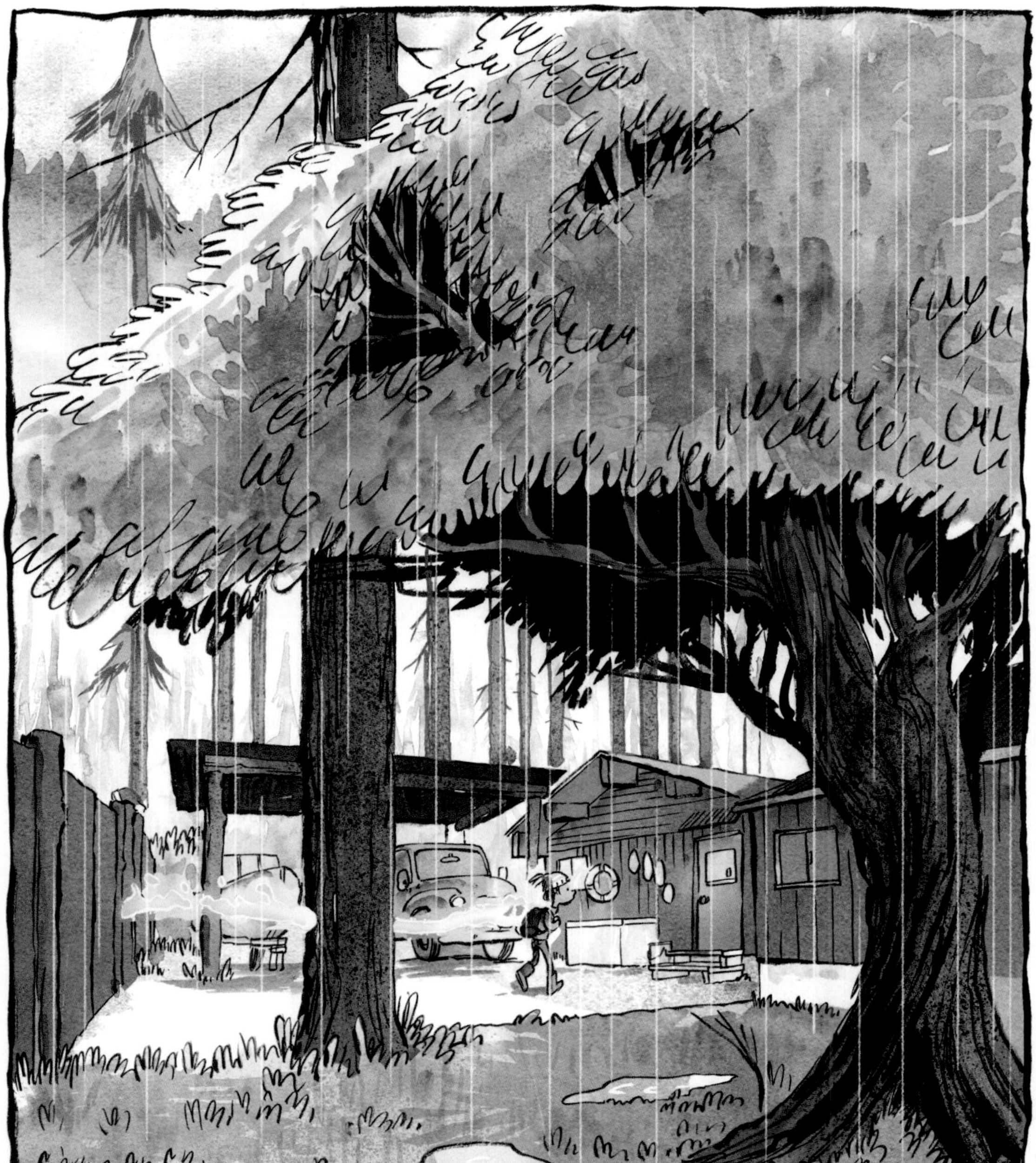

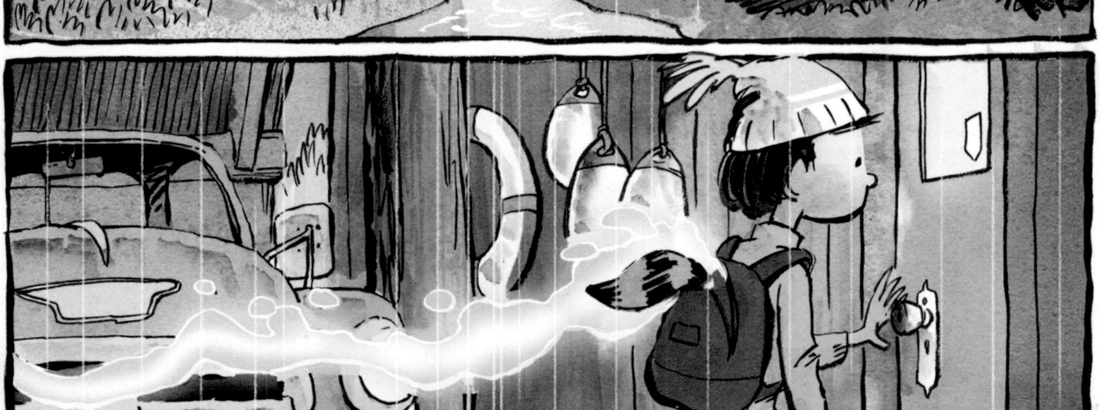

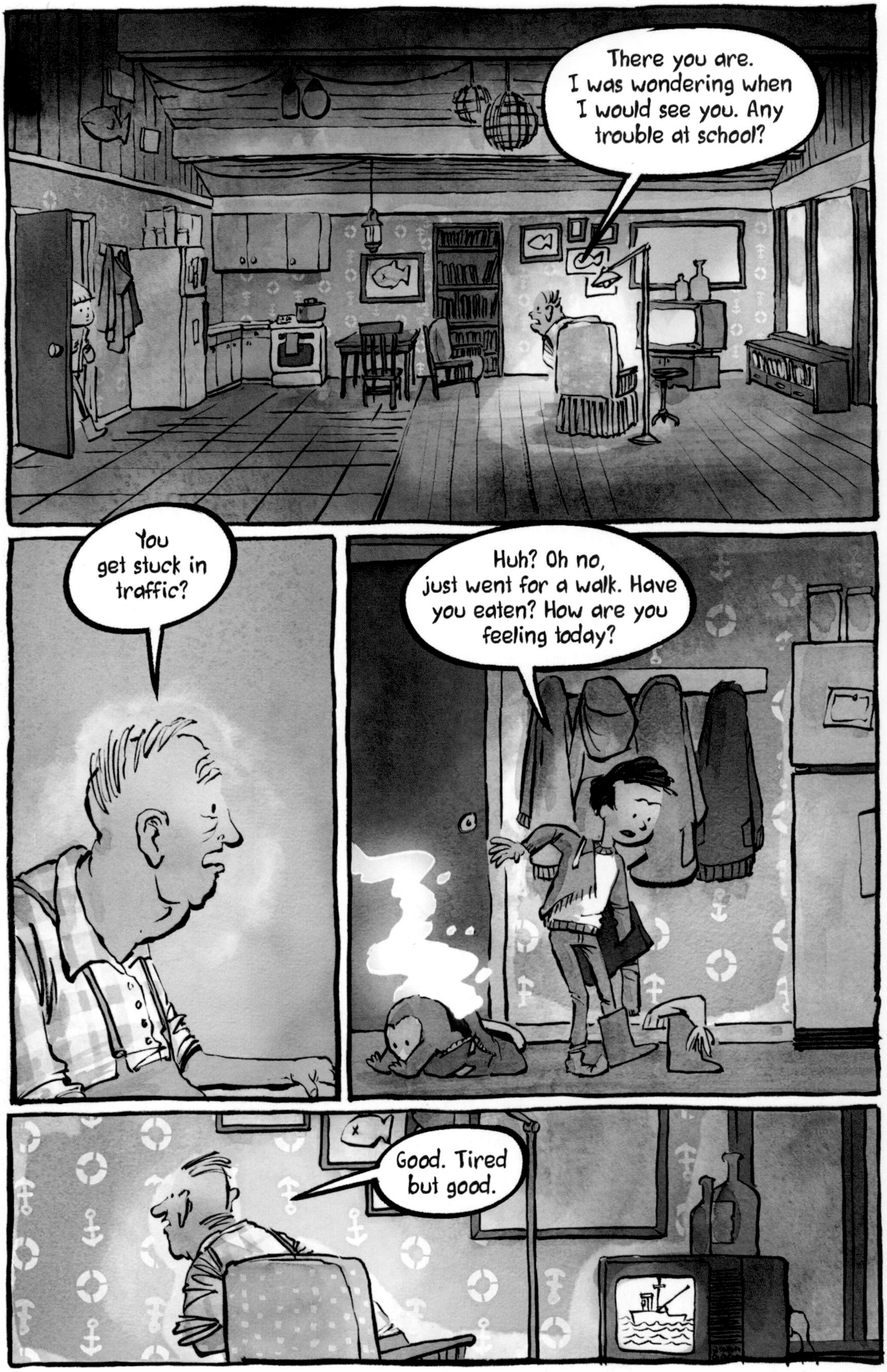
There you are. I was wondering when I would see you. Any trouble at school?
You get stuck in traffic?
Huh? Oh no, just went for a walk. Have you eaten? How are you feeling today?
Good. Tired but good.

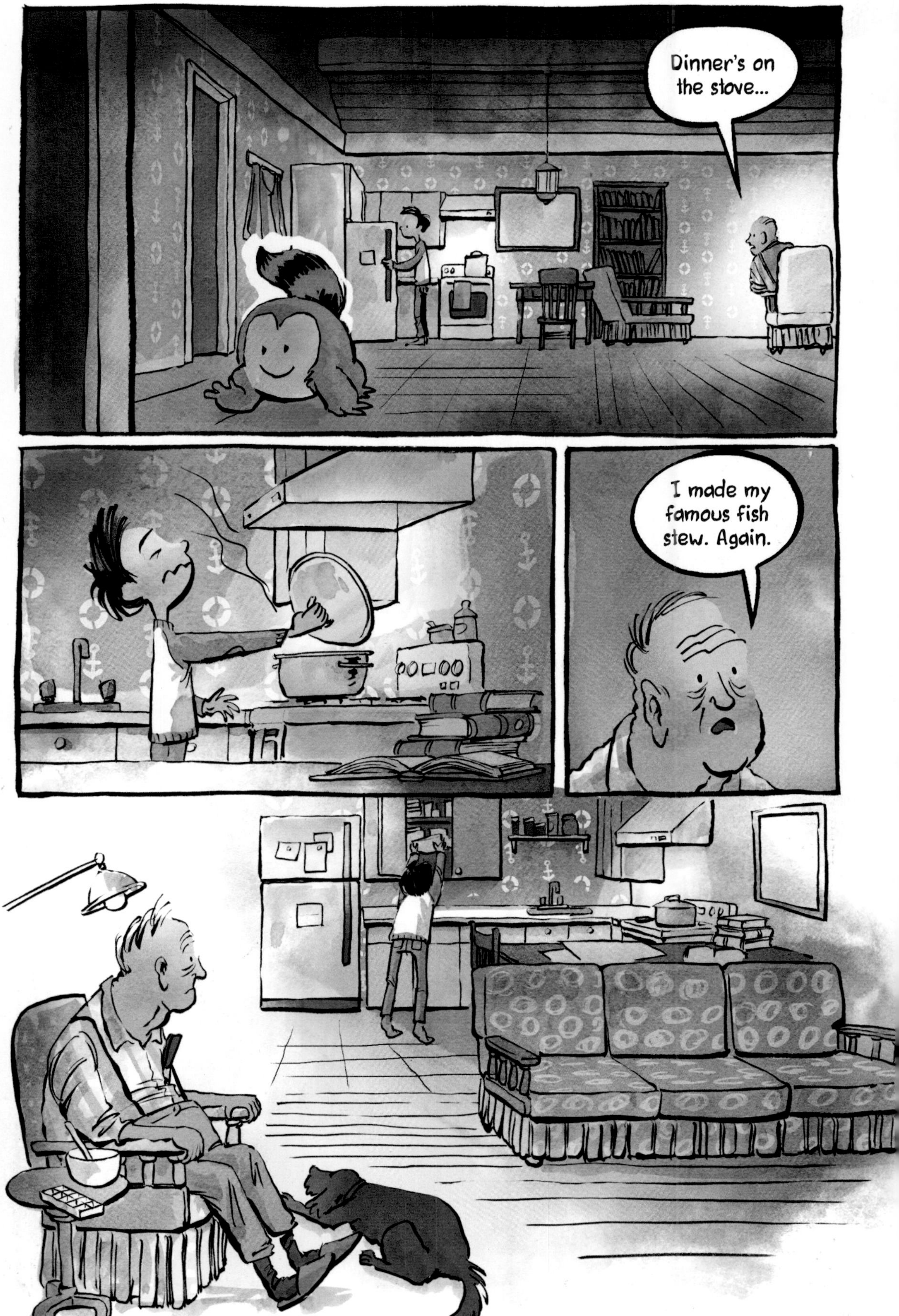
Dinner's on the stove...
I made my famous fish stew. Again.

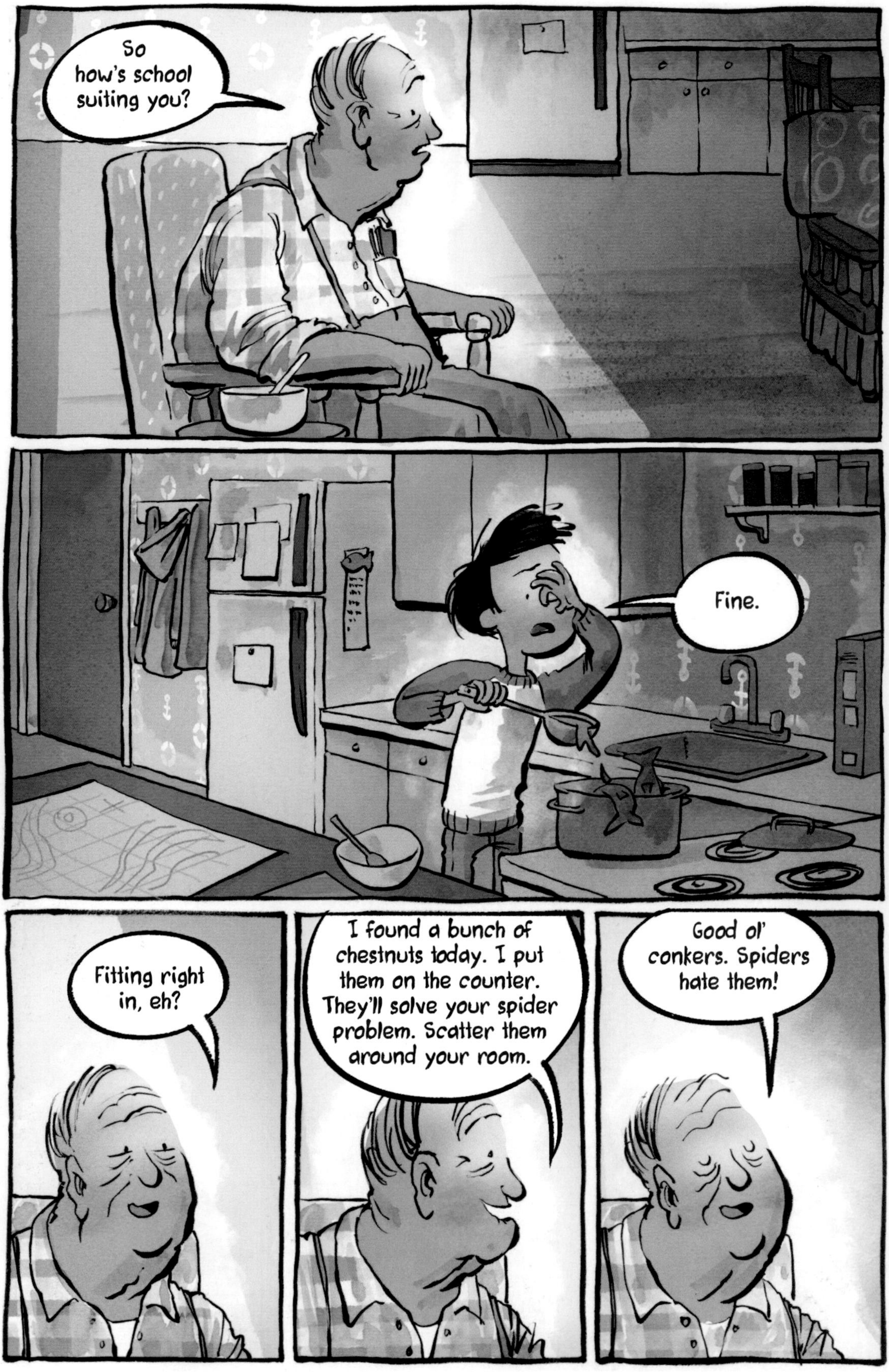
So how's school suiting you?
Fine.
Fitting right in, eh?
I found a bunch of chestnuts today. I put them on the counter. They'll solve your spider problem. Scatter them around your room.
Good ol' conkers. Spiders hate them!

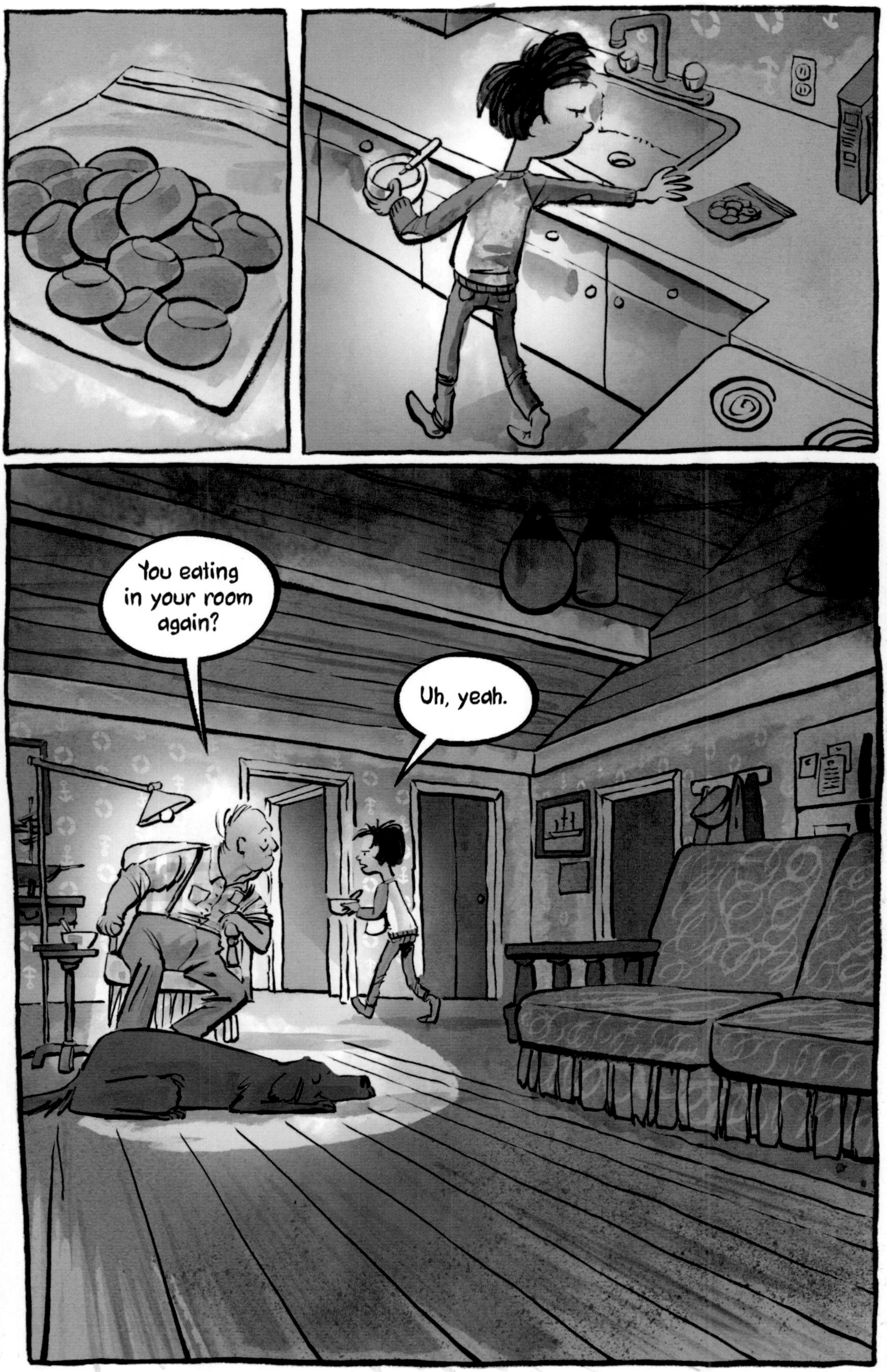
You eating in your room again?
Uh, yeah.

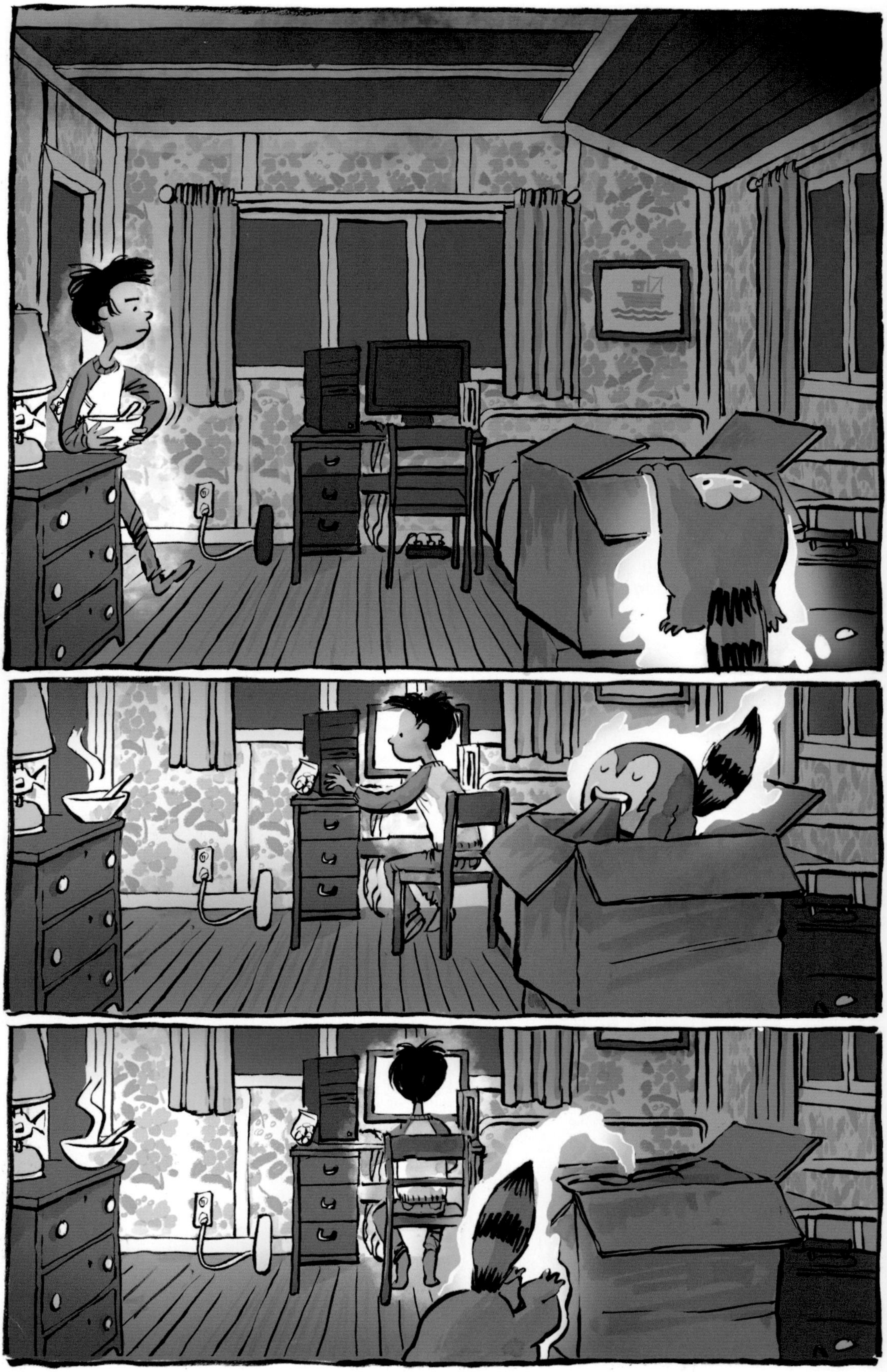

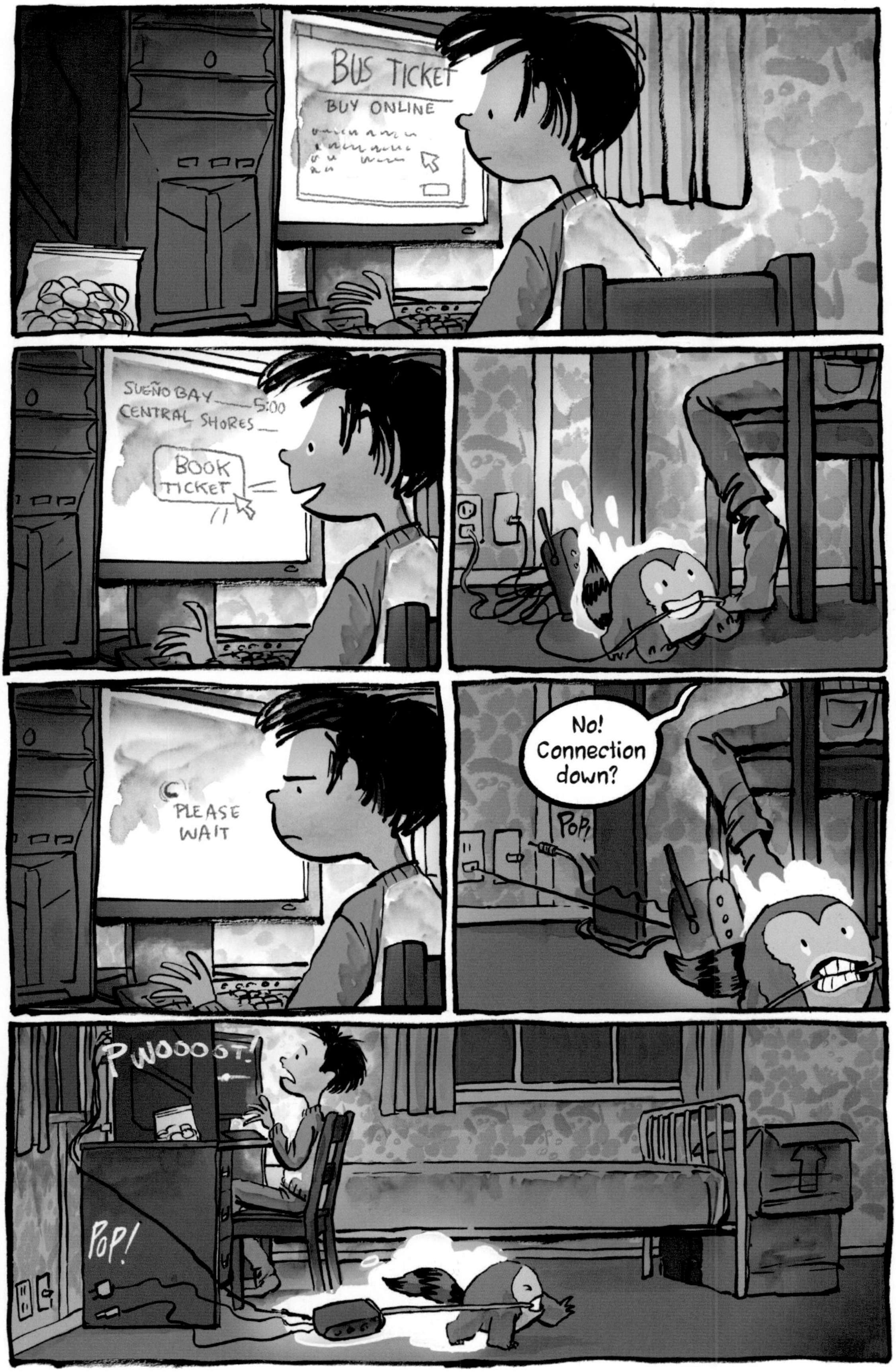
BUS TICKET
BUY ONLINE
SUEÑO BAY 5:00
CENTRAL SHORES
BOOK TICKET
PLEASE WAIT
No! Connection down?
POP!
PWOOOOT!
POP!

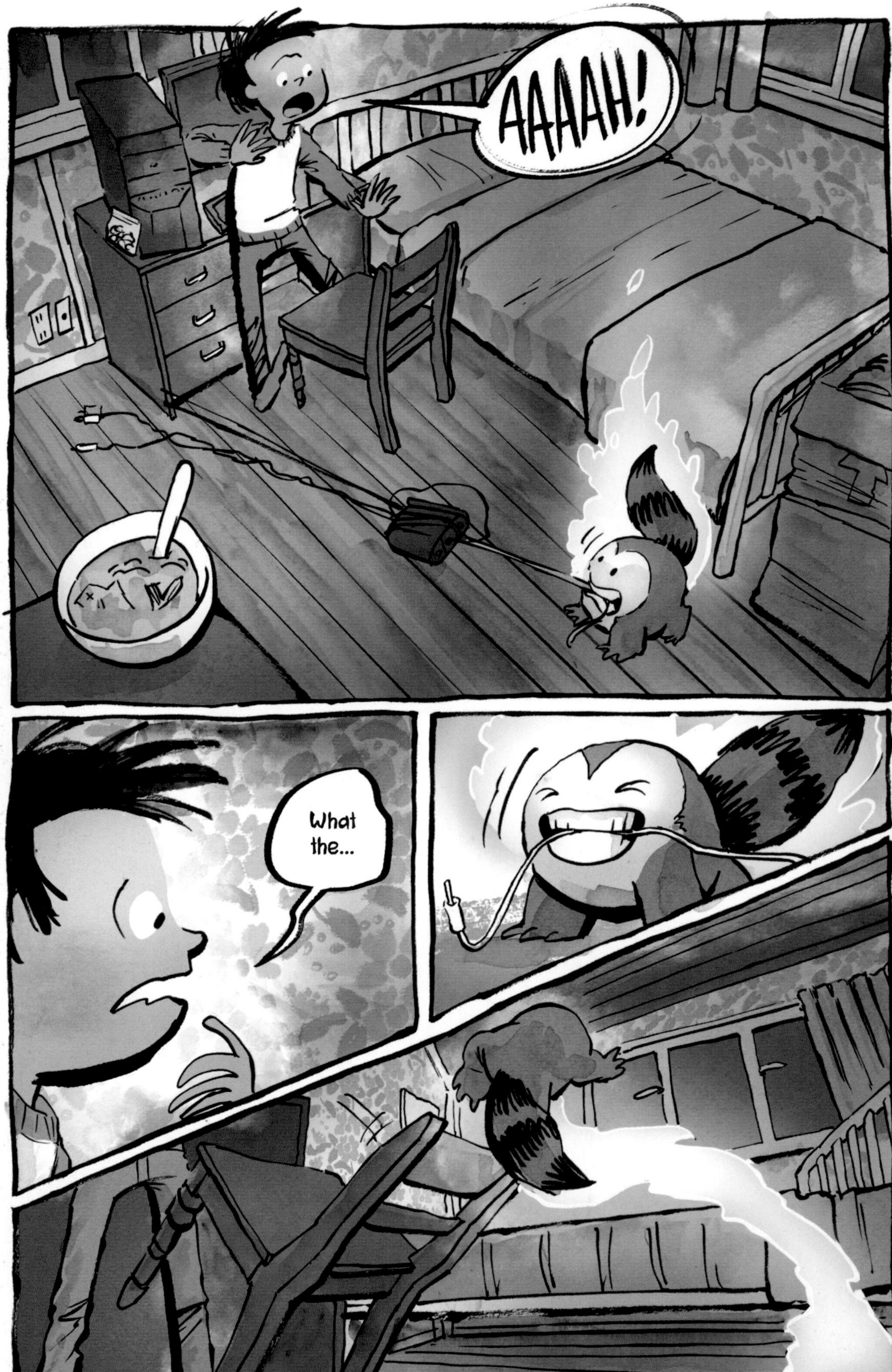
AAAAH!
What the...

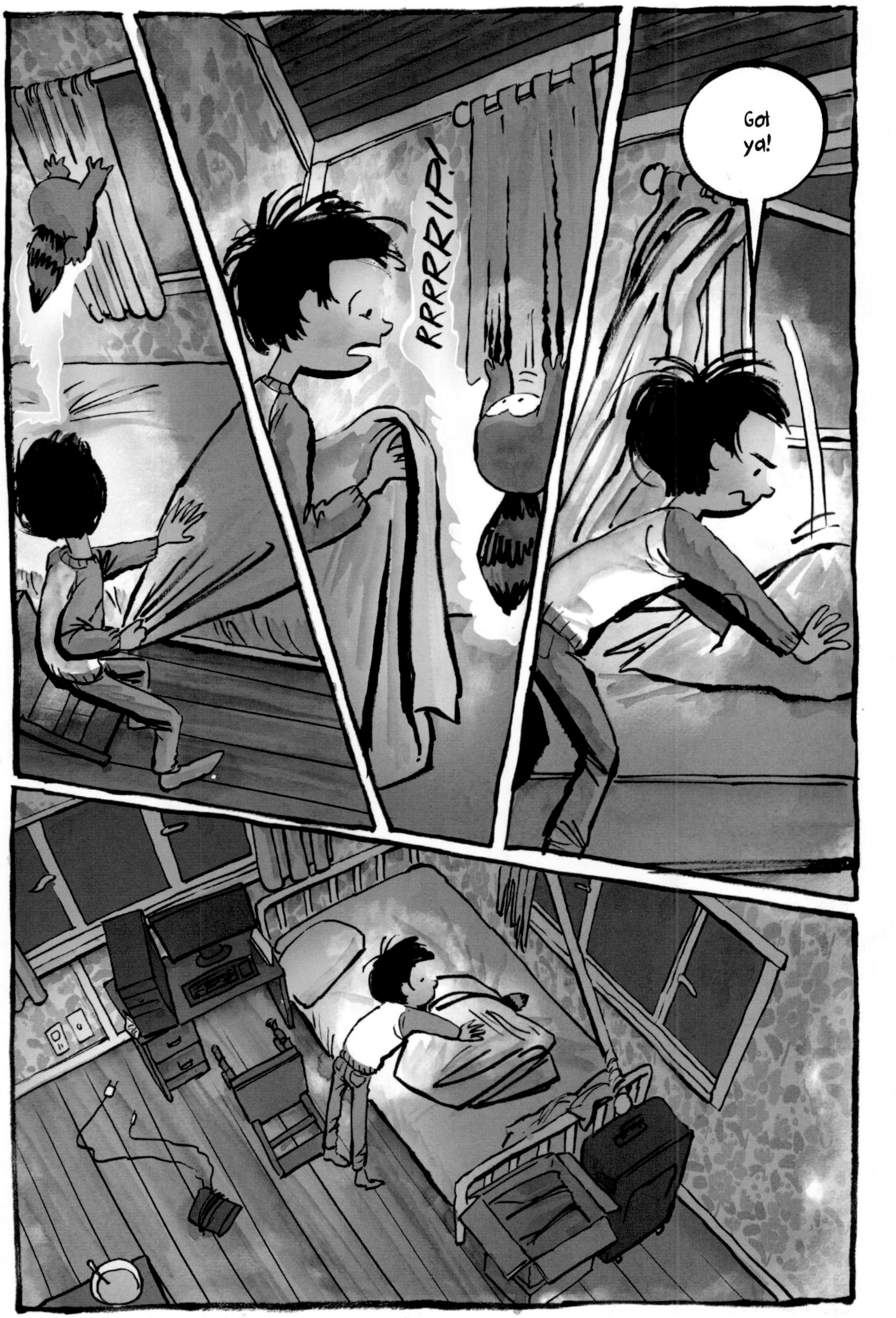
RRRRRIP!
Got ya!

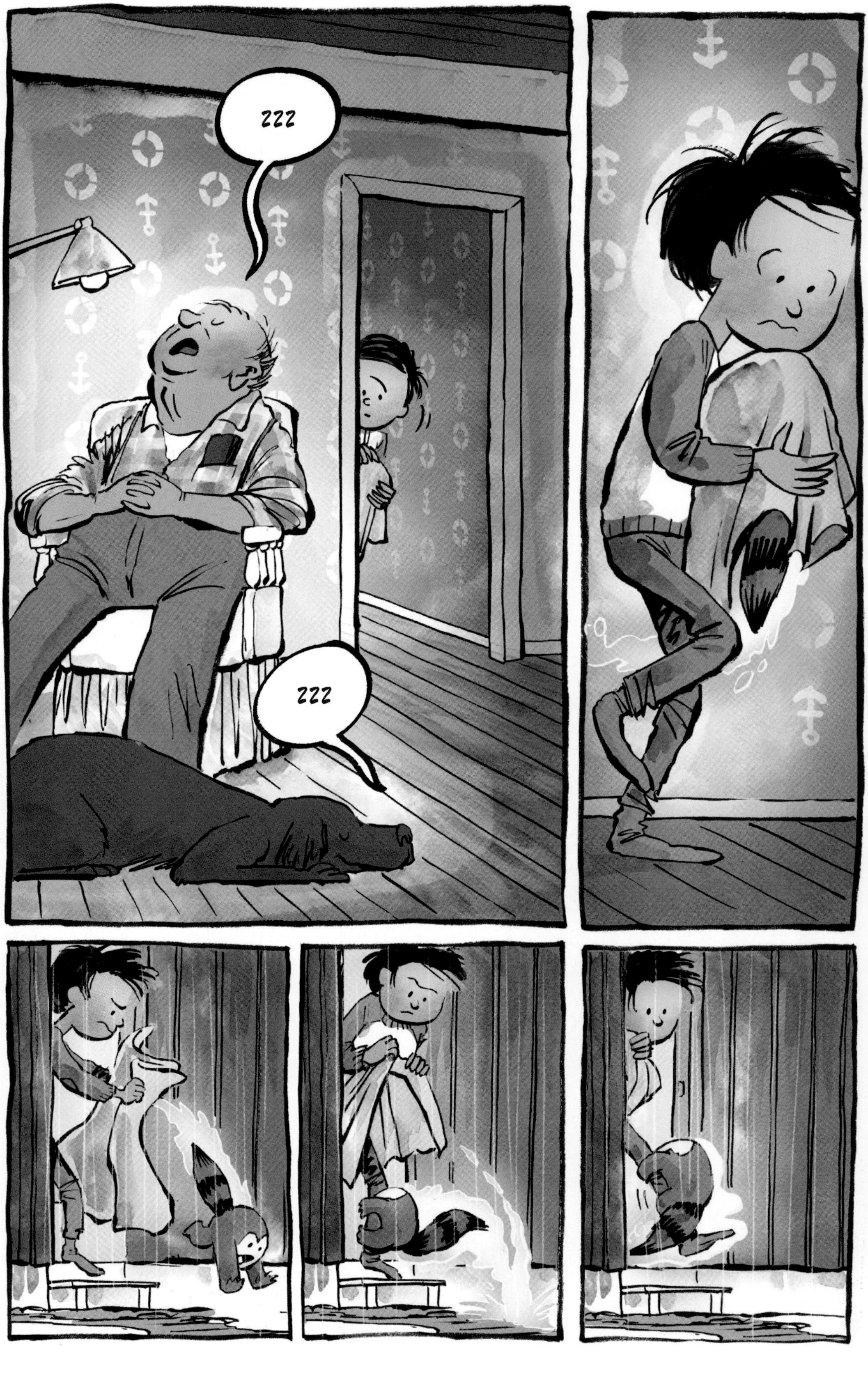
ZZZ
ZZZ

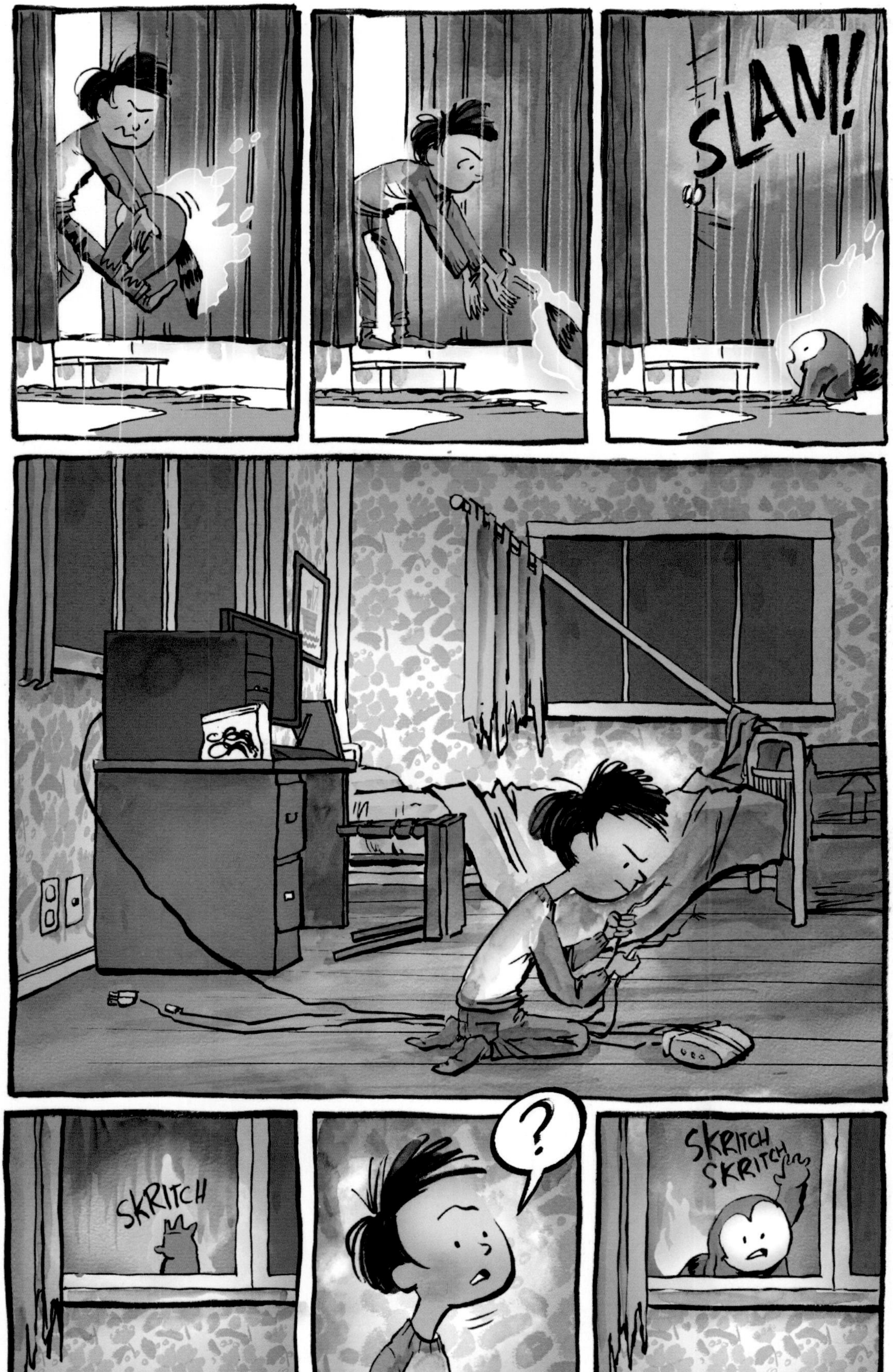
SLAM!
SKRITCH
?
SKRITCH
SKRITCH

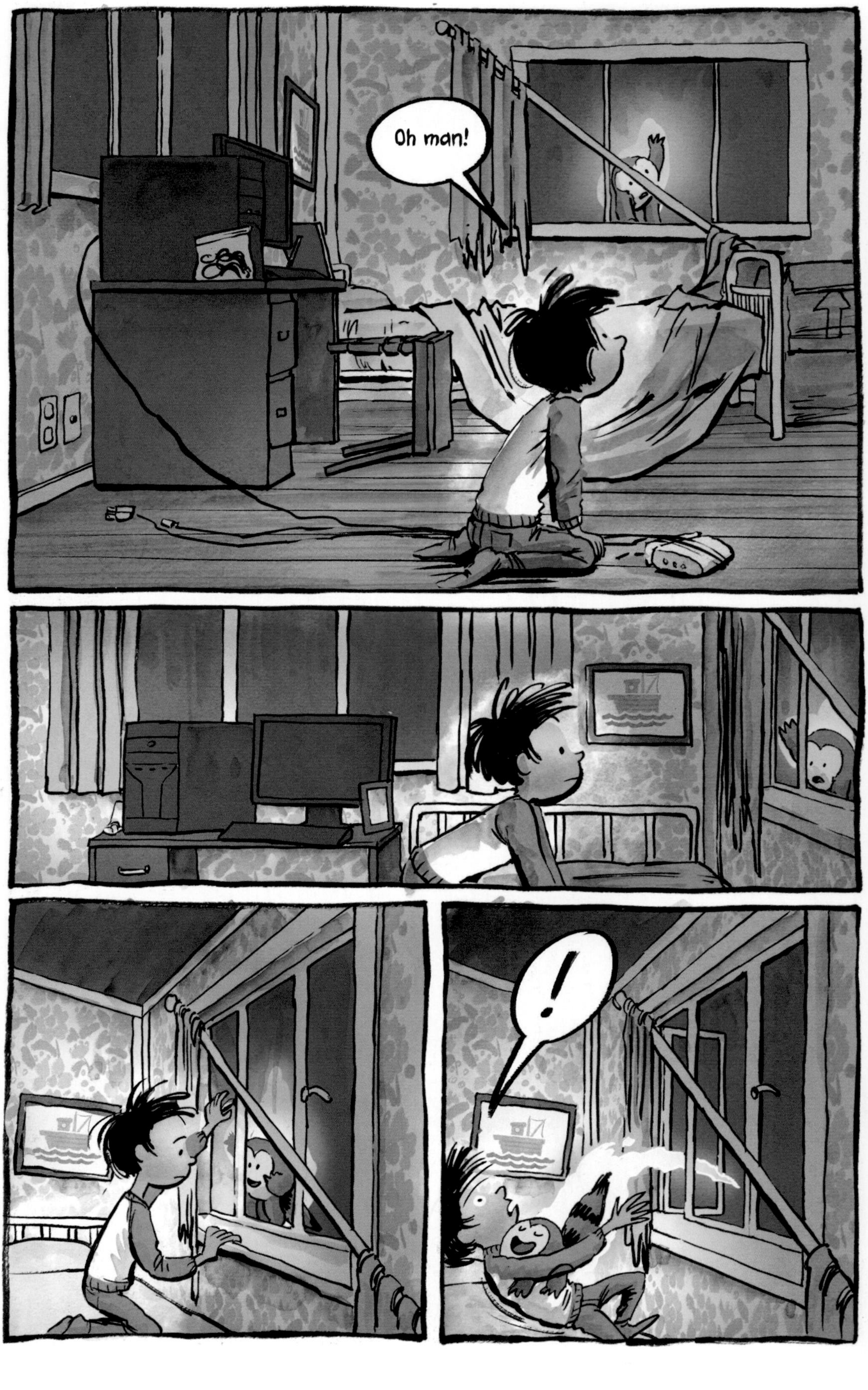
Oh man!
!

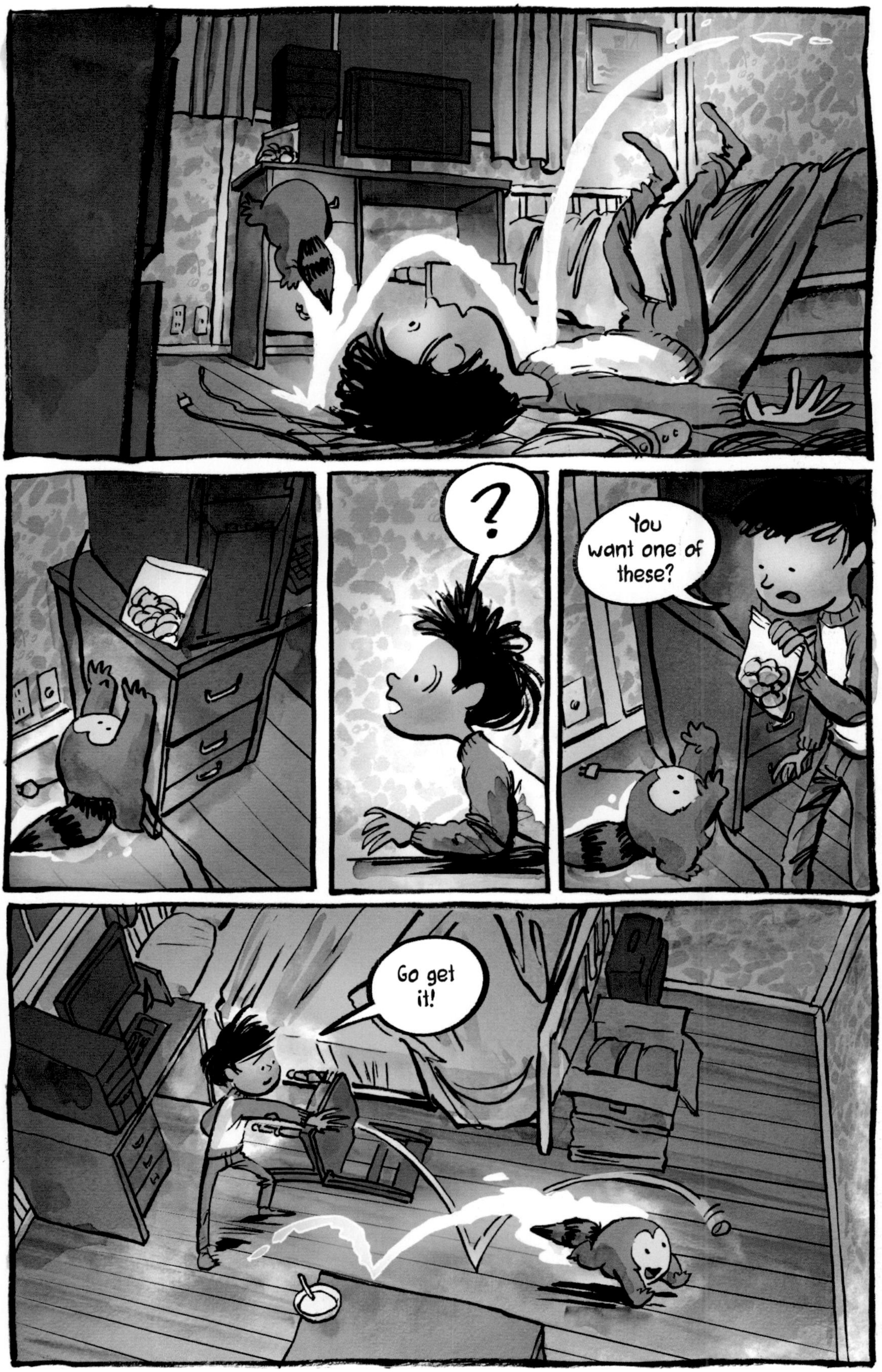
?
You want one of these?
Go get it!

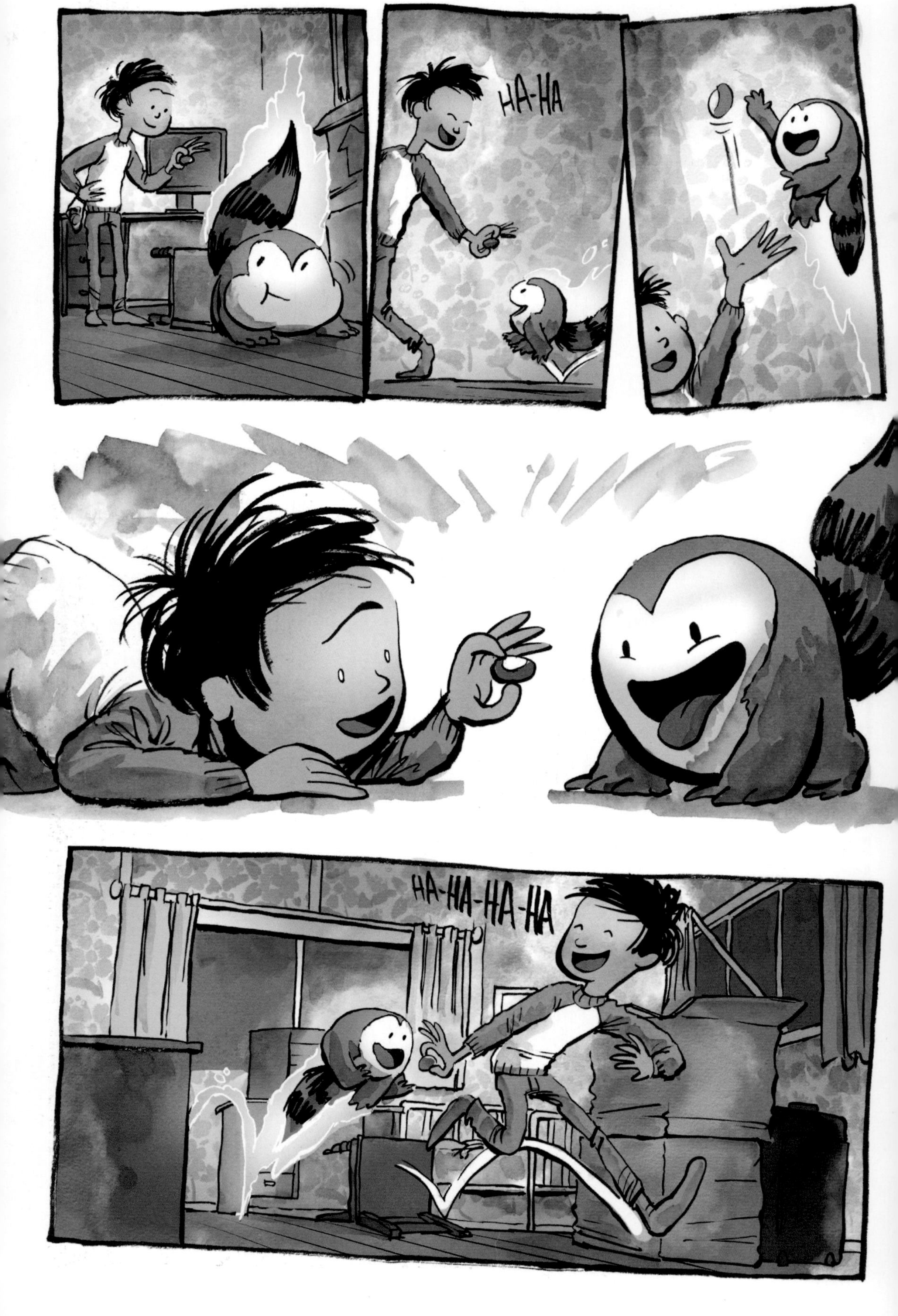
HA-HA
HA-HA-HA-HA

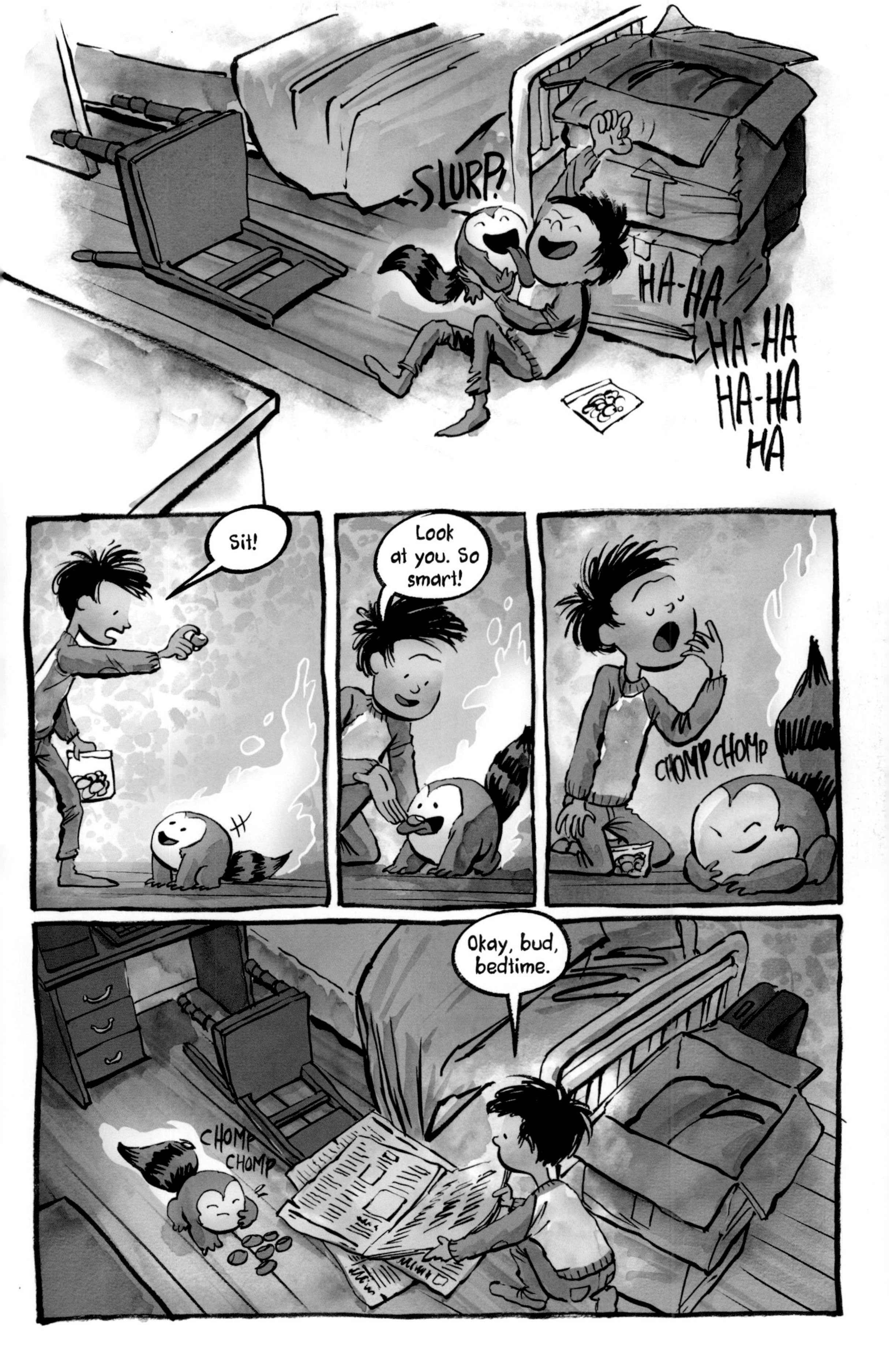
SLURP!
HA-HA
HA-HA
HA-HA
HA
Sit!
Look at you. So smart!
CHOMP CHOMP
Okay, bud, bedtime.
CHOMP
CHOMP

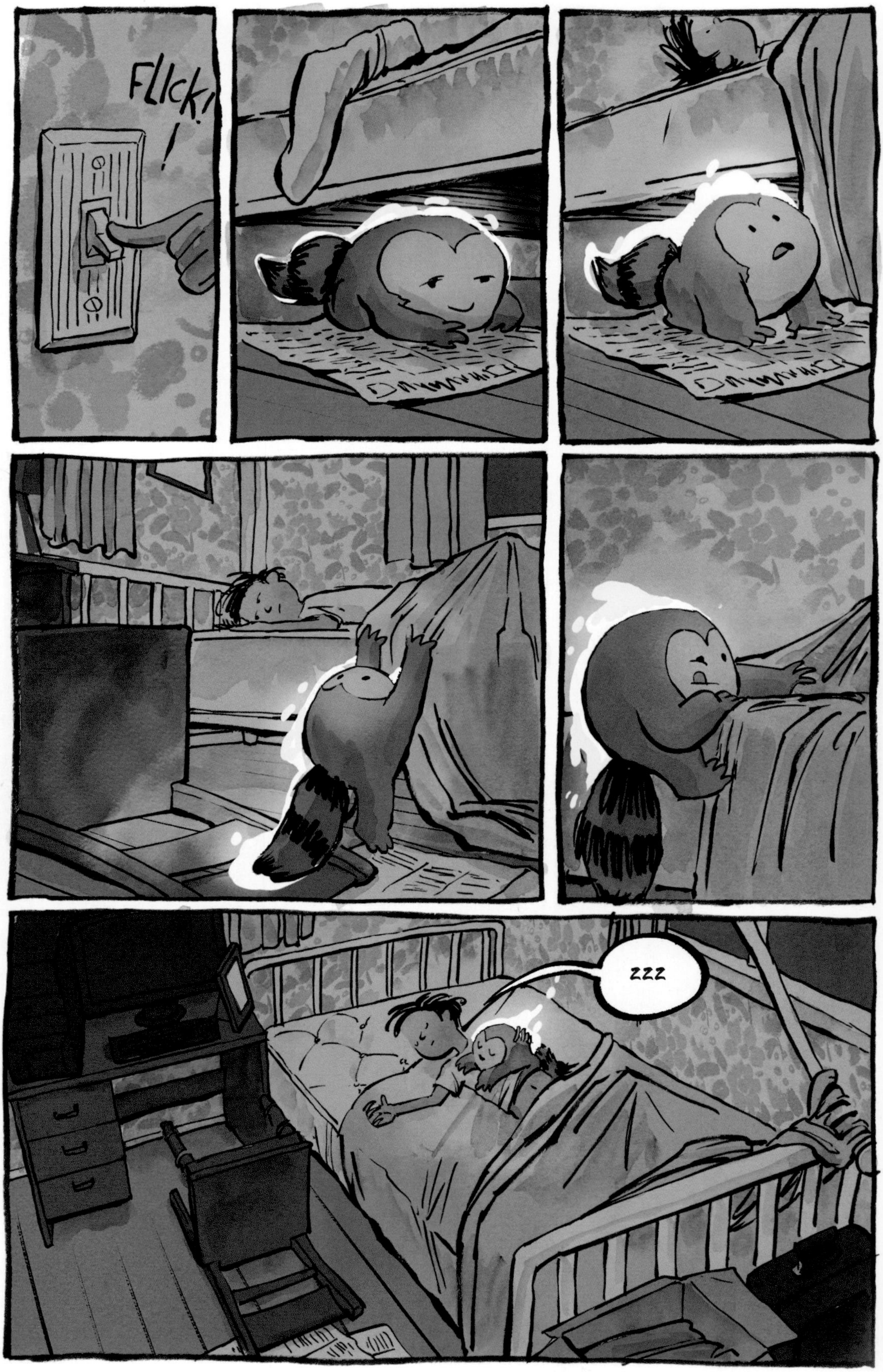
FLICK!
ZZZ

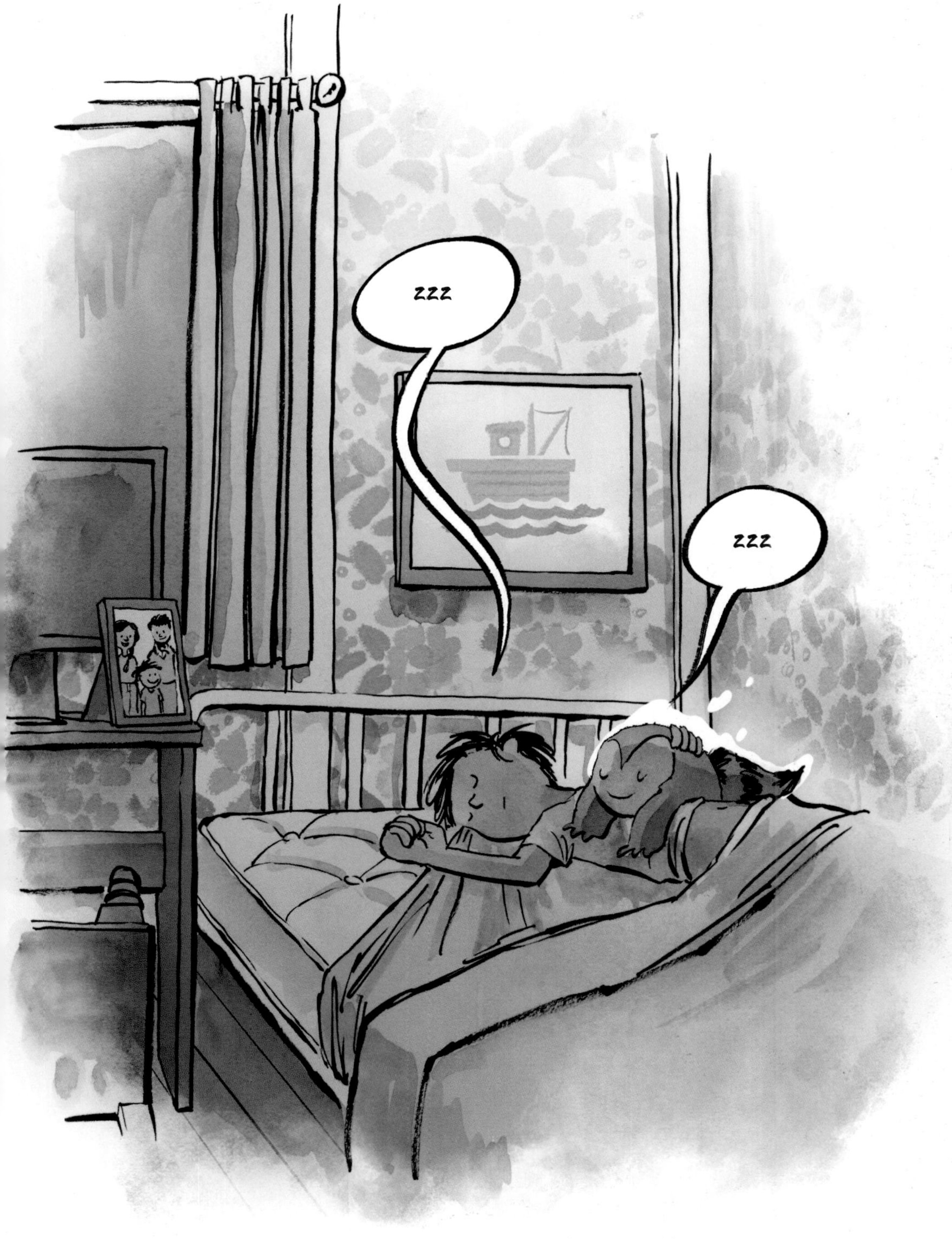
ZZZ
ZZZ

CHAPTER THREE

It's These Crazy Crystals

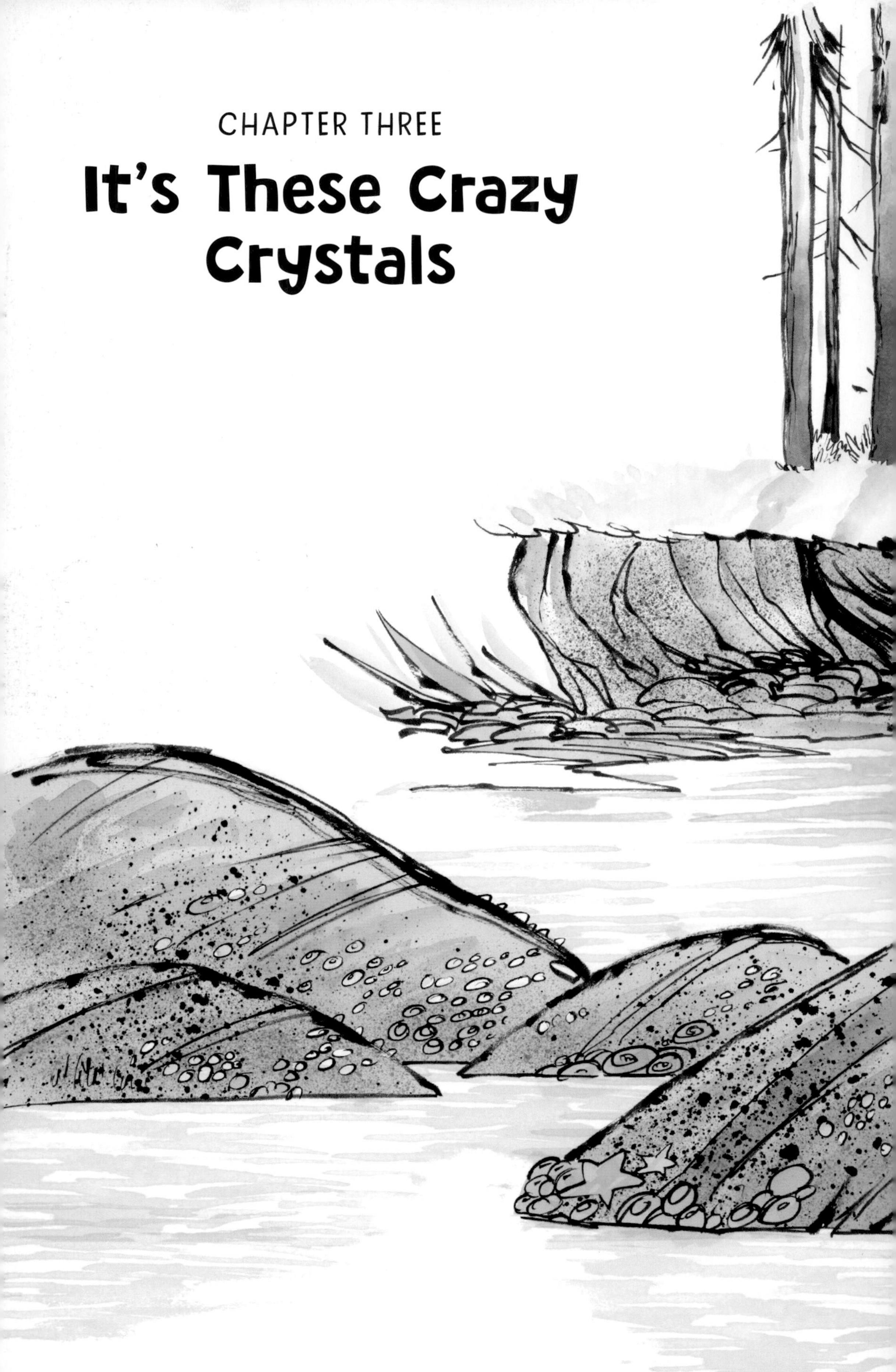

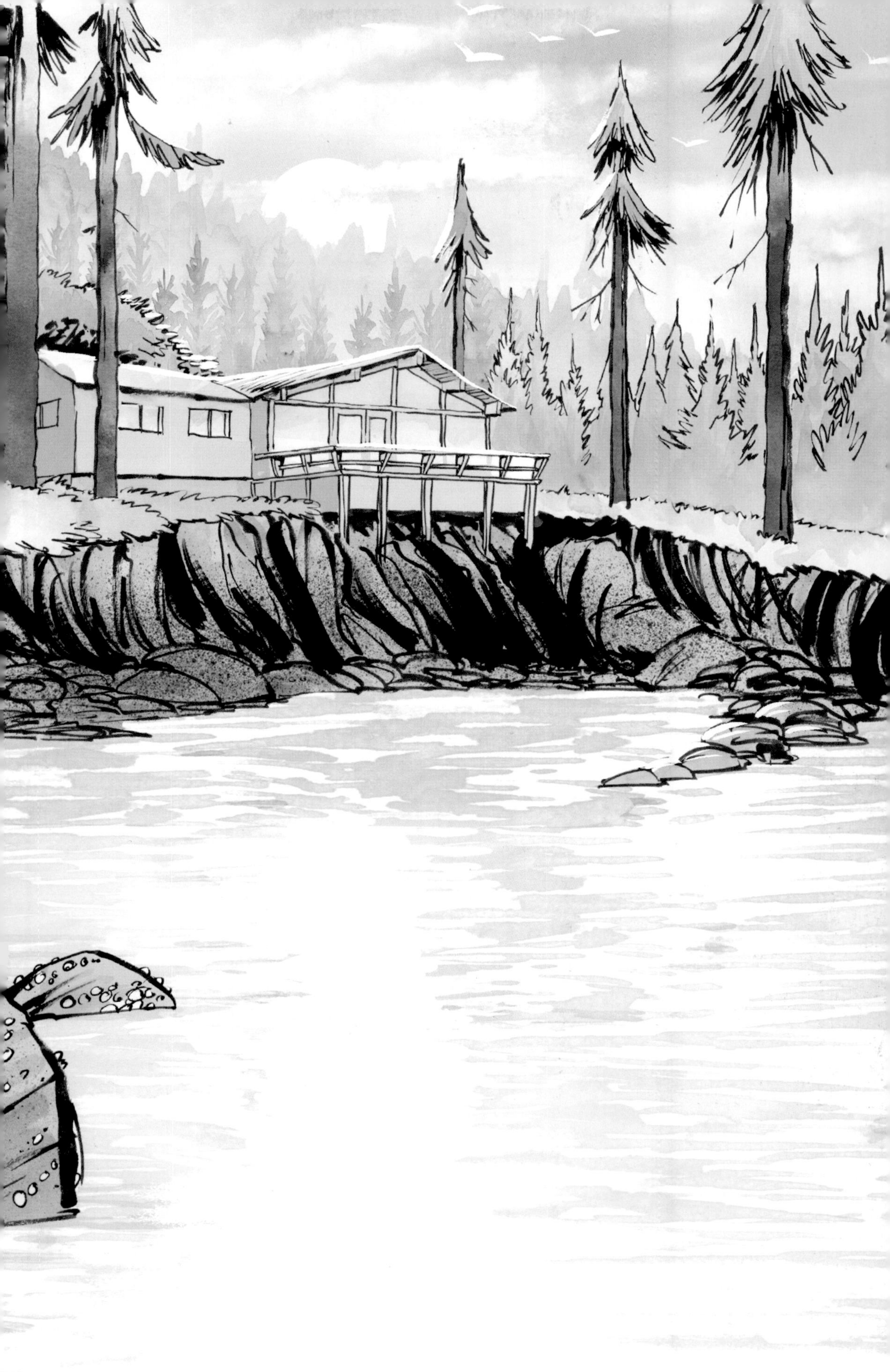

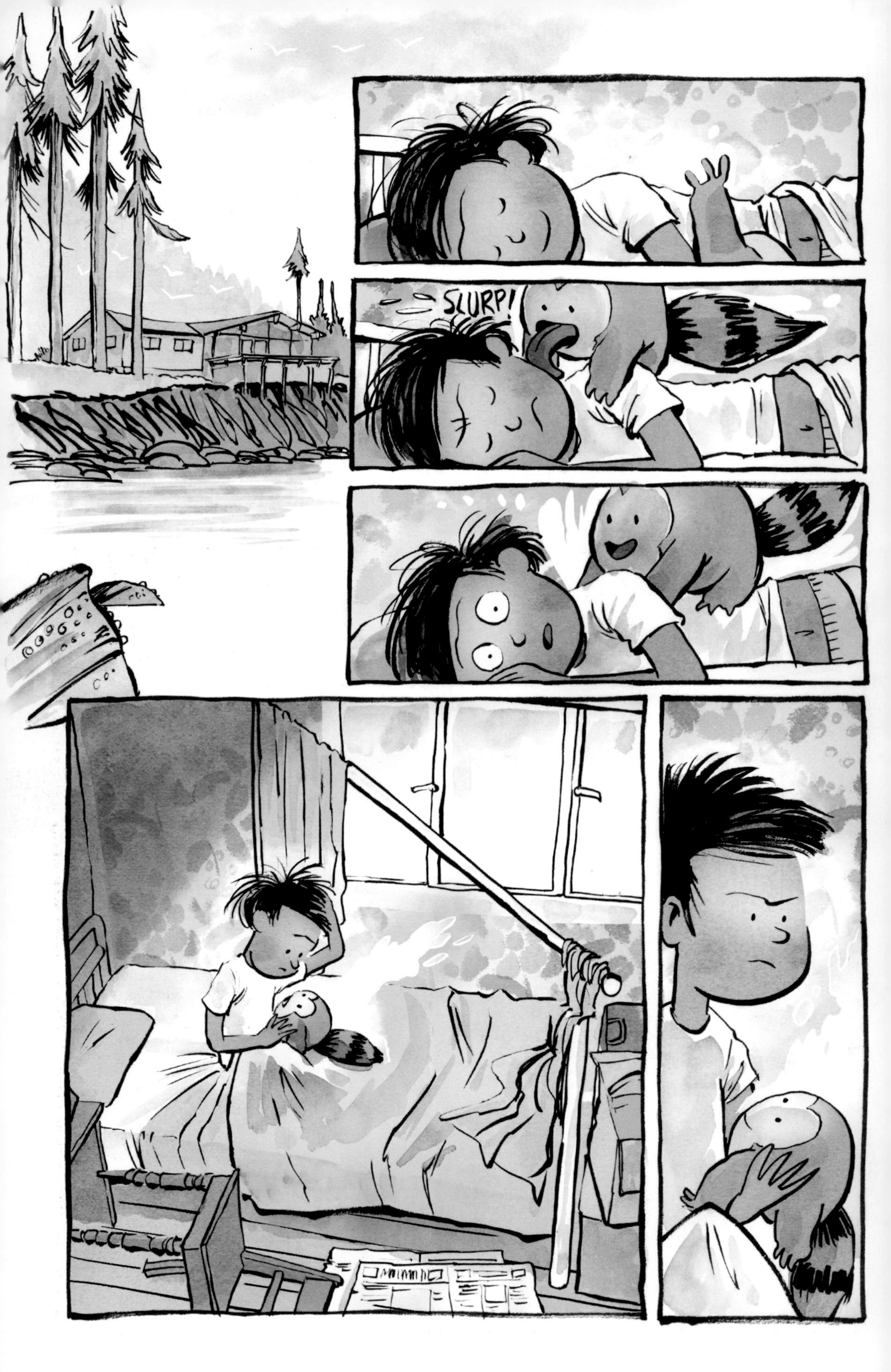
SLURP!

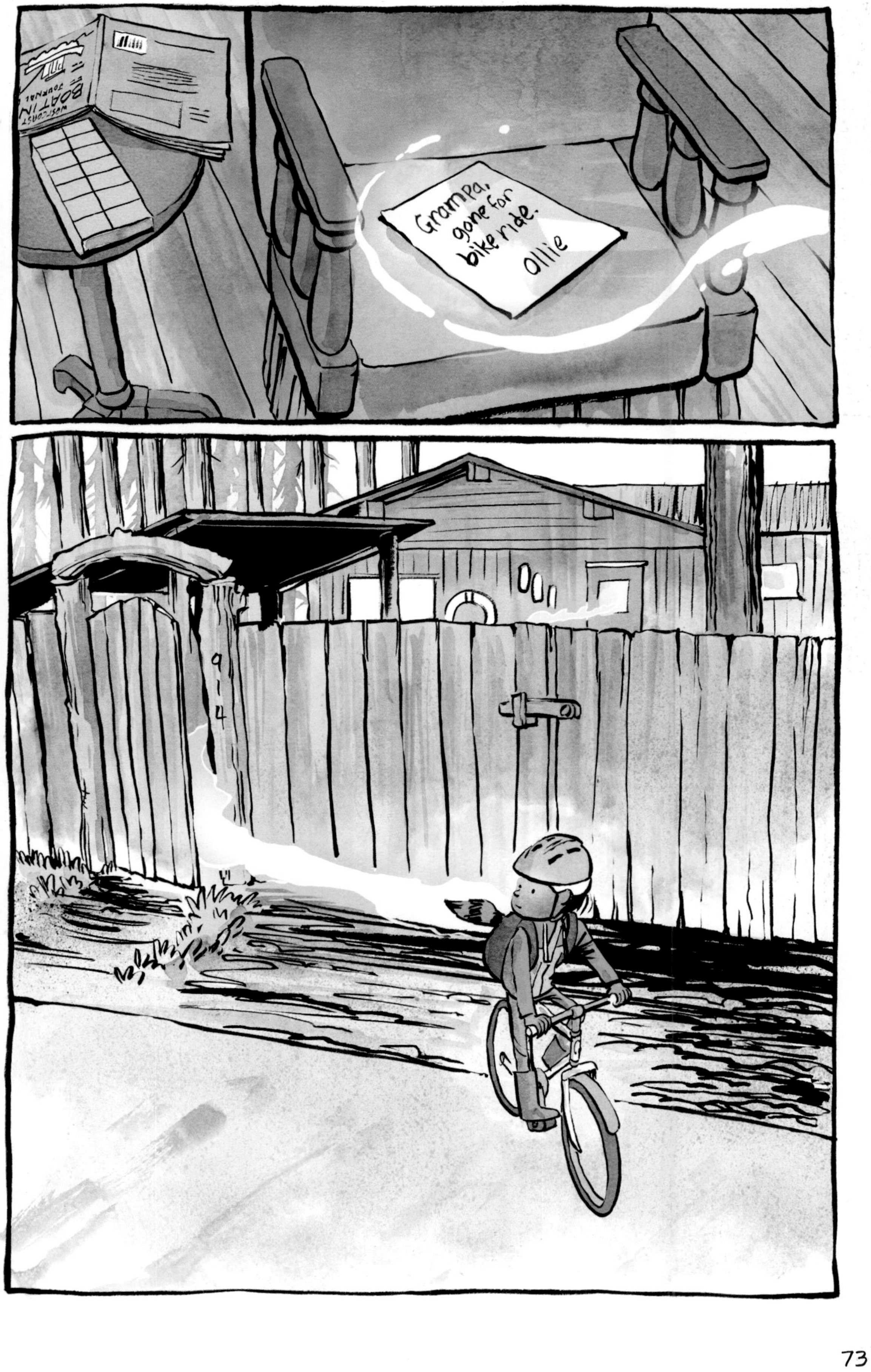
Grampa, gone for bike ride. Ollie

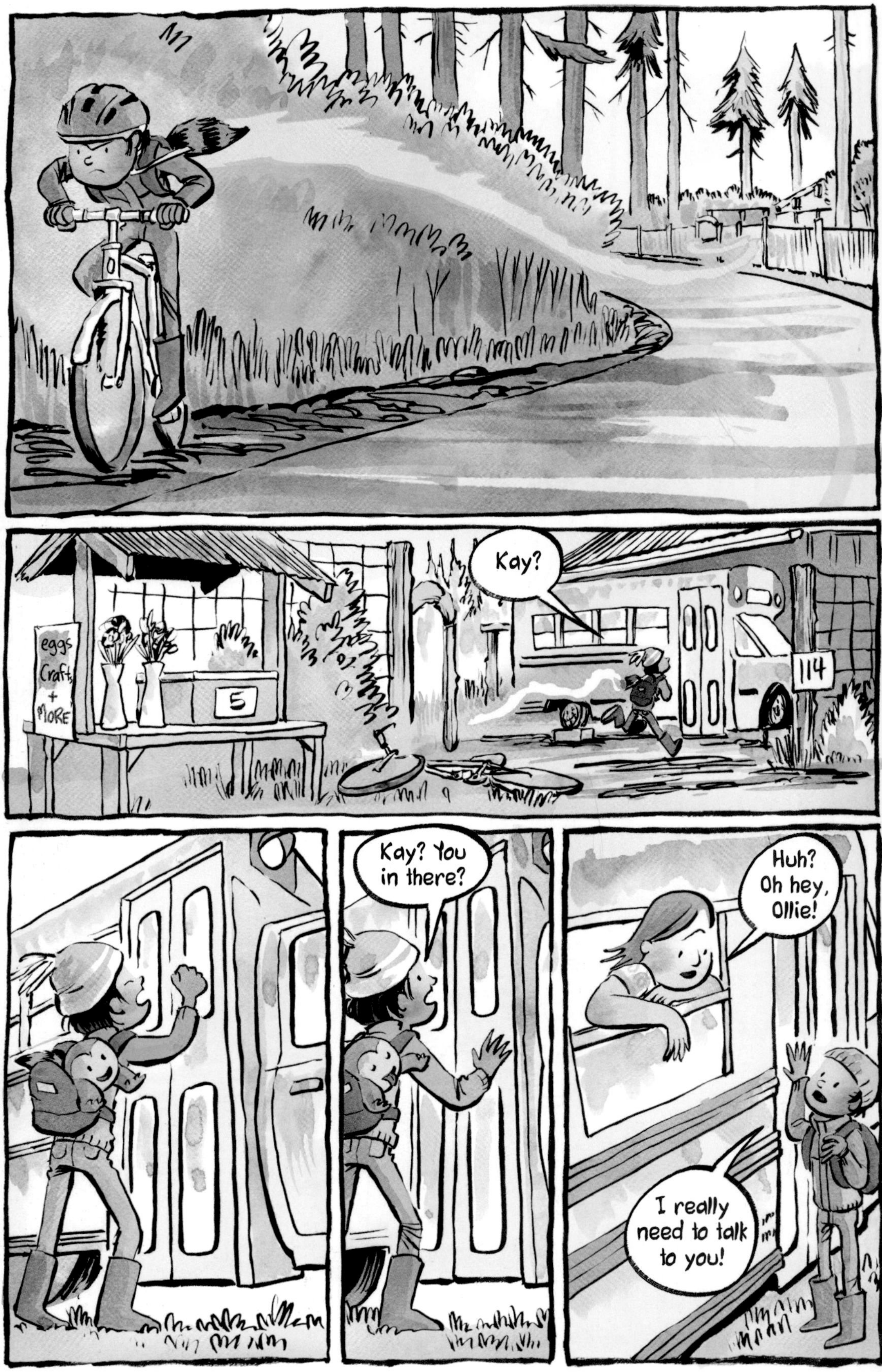

eggs Crafts + MORE
5
Kay?
114
Kay? You in there?
Huh? Oh hey, Ollie!
I really need to talk to you!

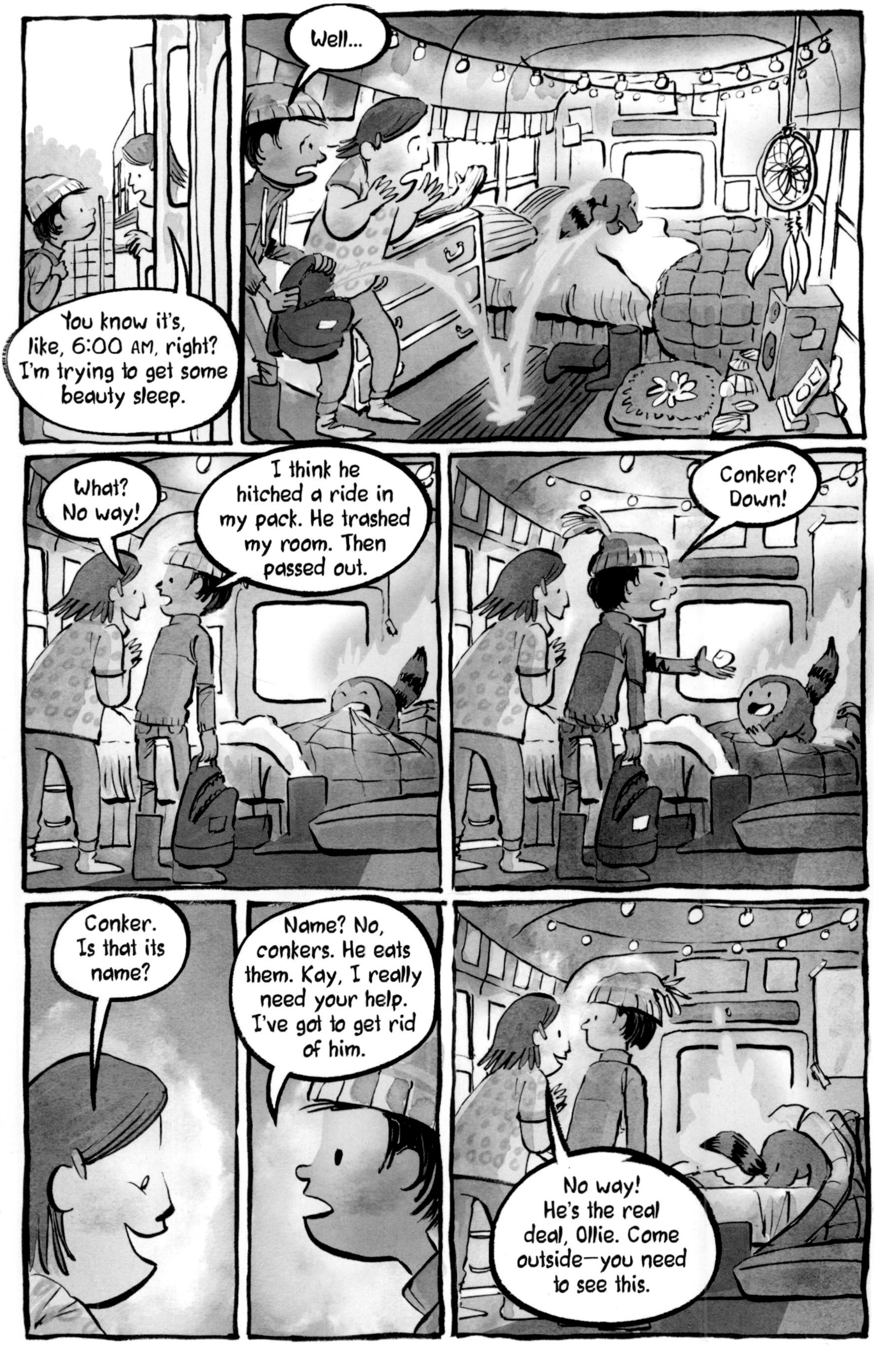
You know it's, like, 6:00 AM, right? I'm trying to get some beauty sleep.
Well...
What? No way!
I think he hitched a ride in my pack. He trashed my room. Then passed out.
Conker? Down!
Conker. Is that its name?
Name? No, conkers. He eats them. Kay, I really need your help. I've got to get rid of him.
No way! He's the real deal, Ollie. Come outside—you need to see this.

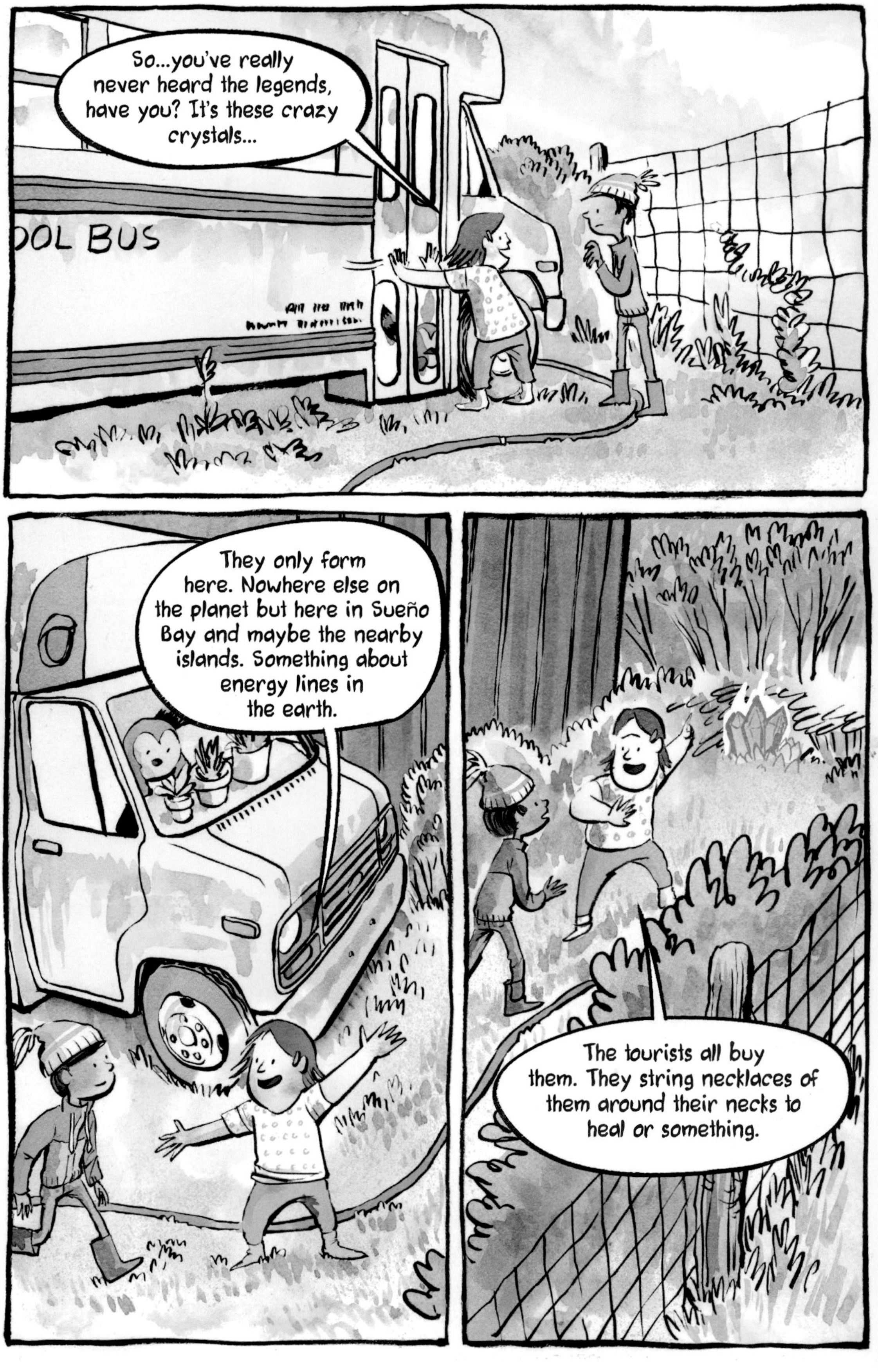
So...you've really never heard the legends, have you? It's these crazy crystals...
They only form here. Nowhere else on the planet but here in Sueño Bay and maybe the nearby islands. Something about energy lines in the earth.
The tourists all buy them. They string necklaces of them around their necks to heal or something.

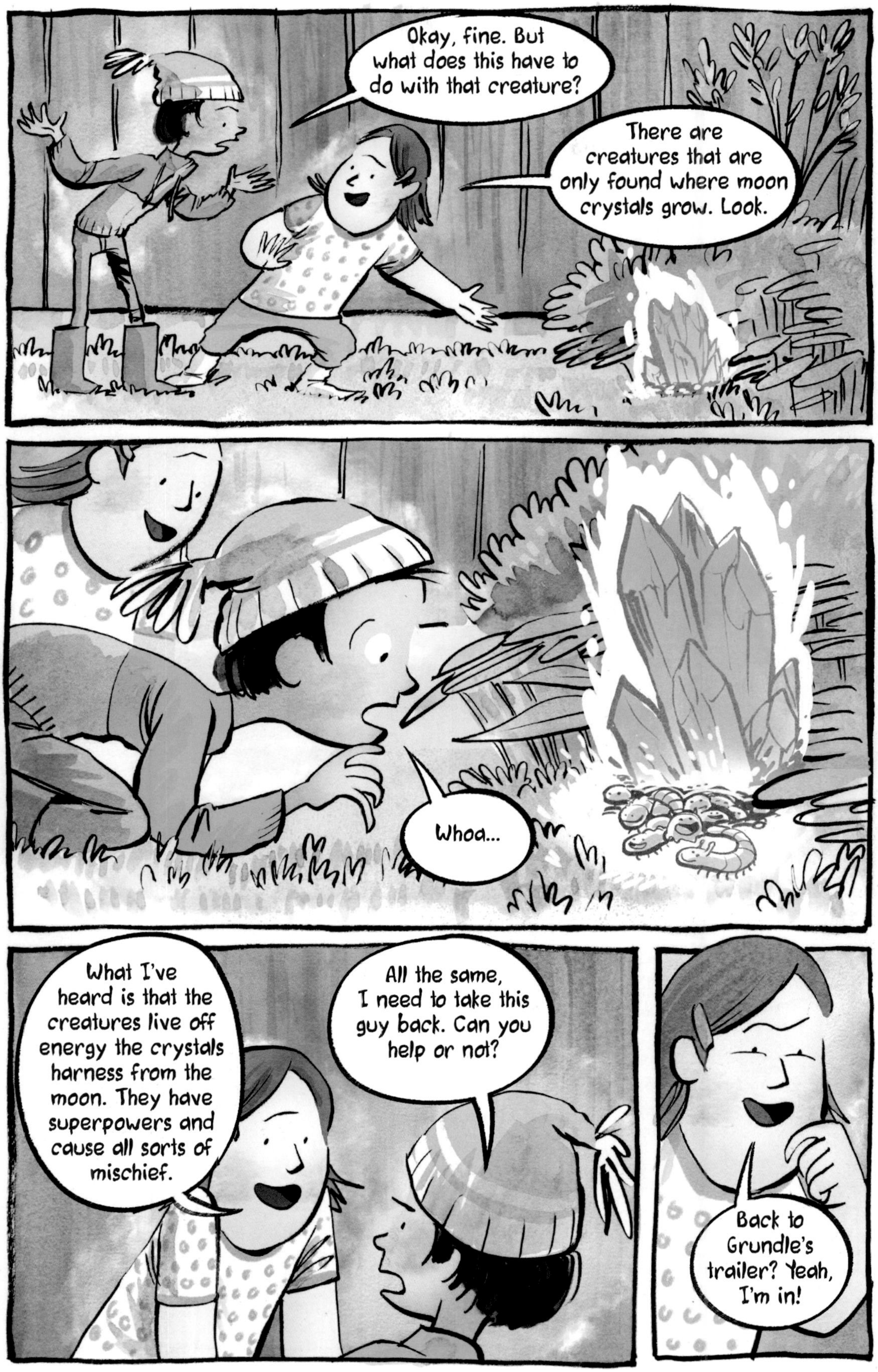

Okay, fine. But what does this have to do with that creature?
There are creatures that are only found where moon crystals grow. Look.
Whoa...
What I've heard is that the creatures live off energy the crystals harness from the moon. They have superpowers and cause all sorts of mischief.
All the same, I need to take this guy back. Can you help or not?
Back to Grundle's trailer? Yeah, I'm in!

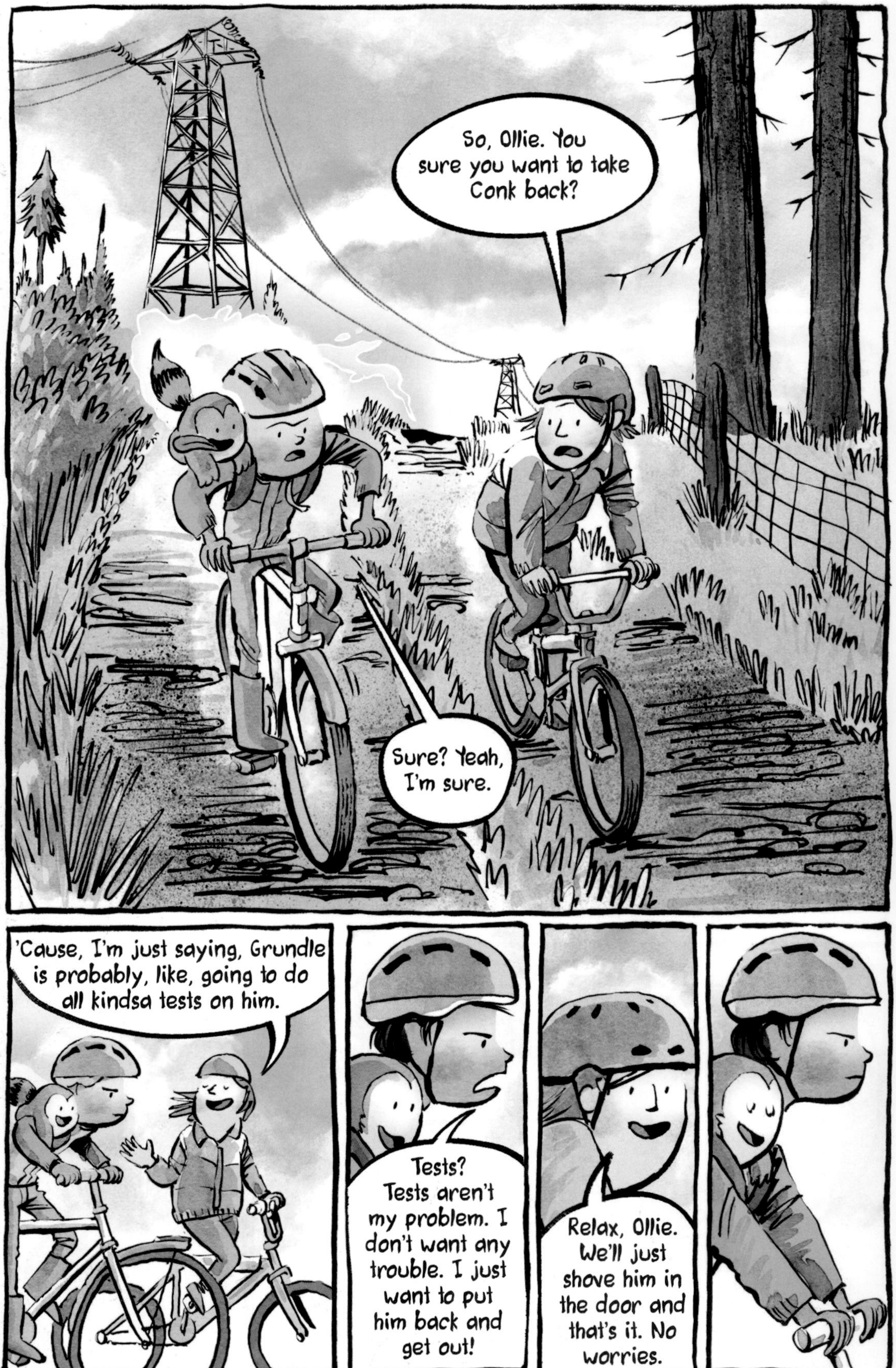
So, Ollie. You sure you want to take Conk back?
Sure? Yeah, I'm sure.
'Cause, I'm just saying, Grundle is probably, like, going to do all kindsa tests on him.
Tests? Tests aren't my problem. I don't want any trouble. I just want to put him back and get out!
Relax, Ollie. We'll just shove him in the door and that's it. No worries.

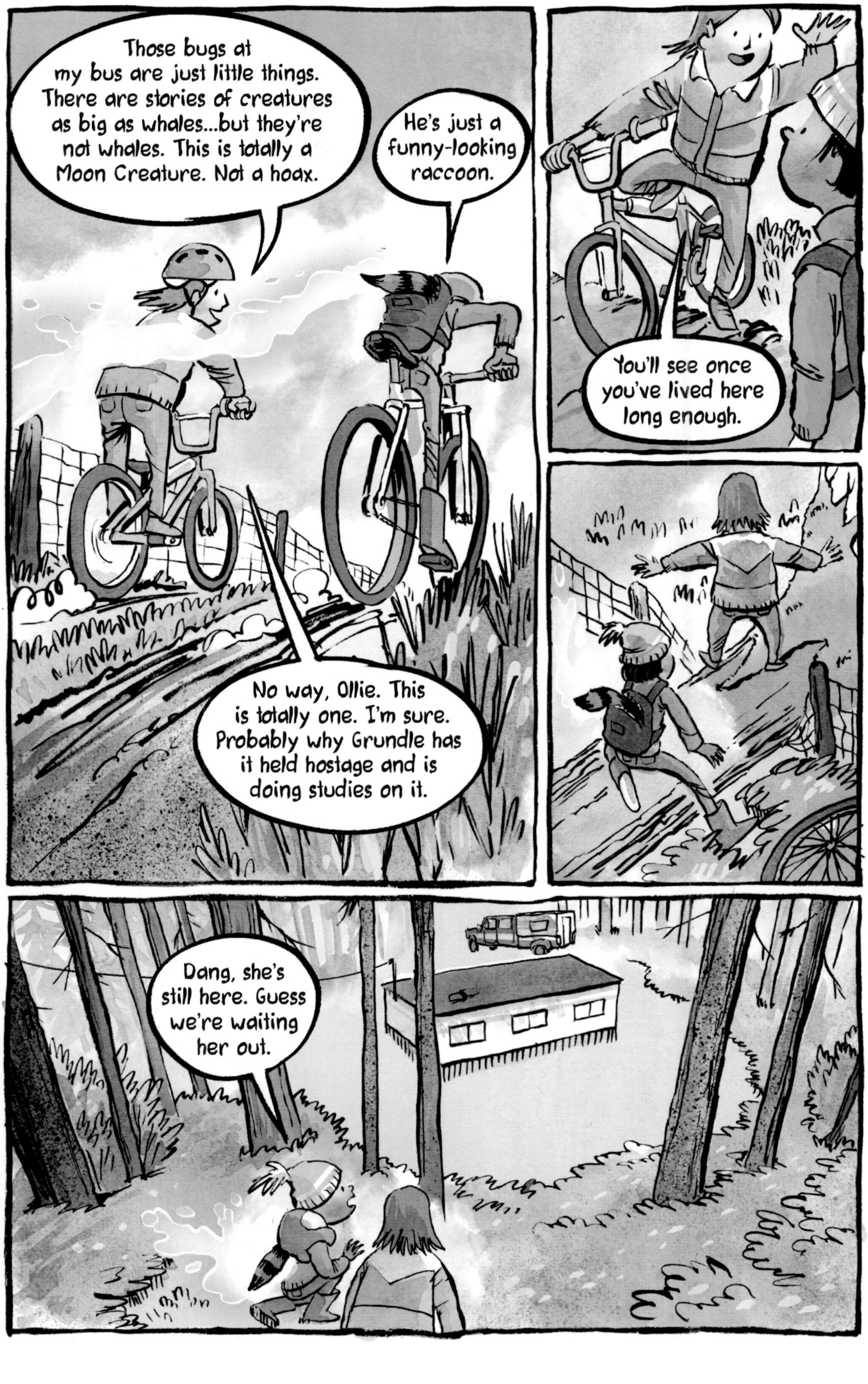
Those bugs at my bus are just little things. There are stories of creatures as big as whales...but they're not whales. This is totally a Moon Creature. Not a hoax.
He's just a funny-looking raccoon.
No way, Ollie. This is totally one. I'm sure. Probably why Grundle has it held hostage and is doing studies on it.
You'll see once you've lived here long enough.
Dang, she's still here. Guess we're waiting her out.

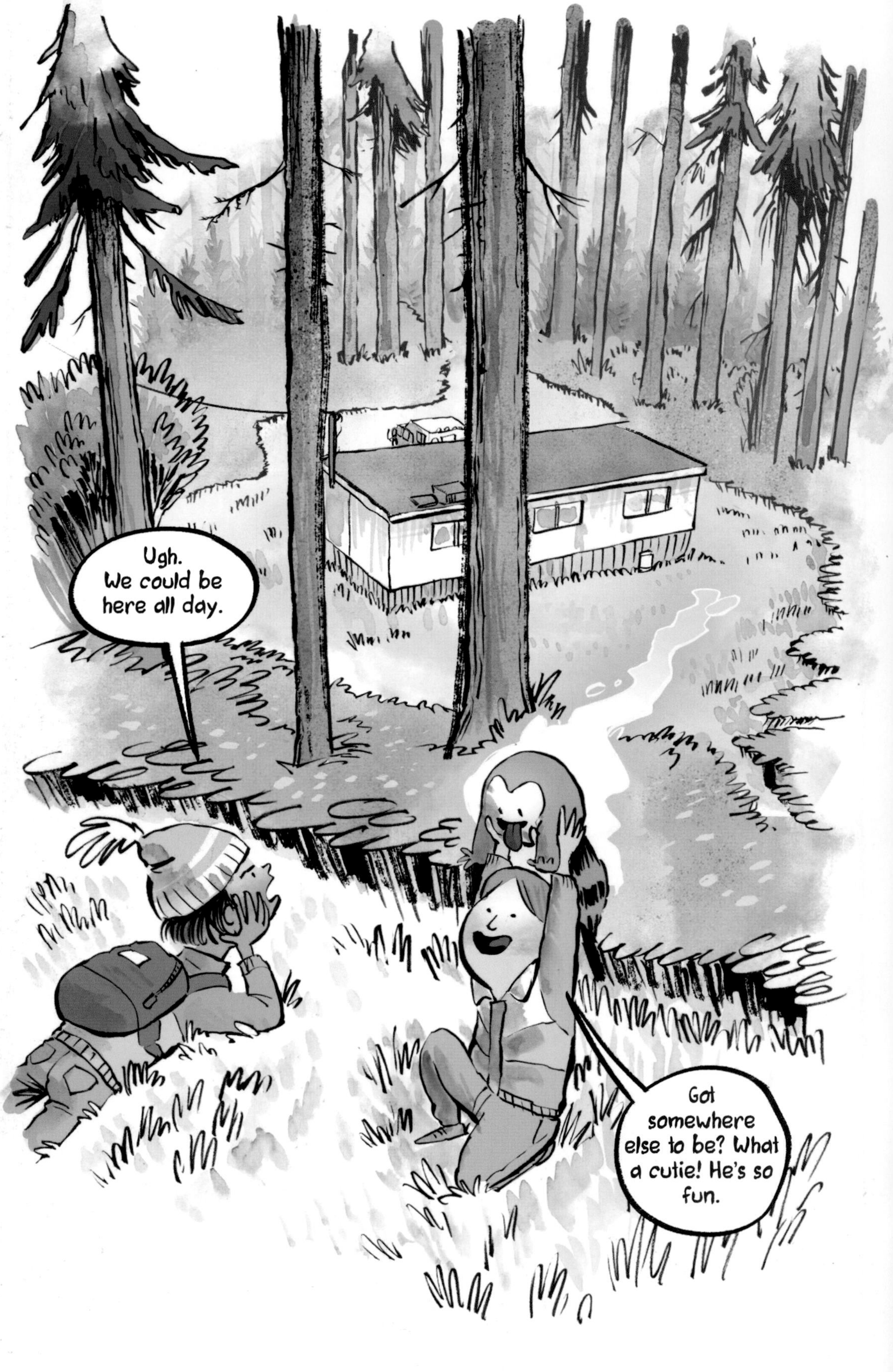
Ugh. We could be here all day.
Got somewhere else to be? What a cutie! He's so fun.

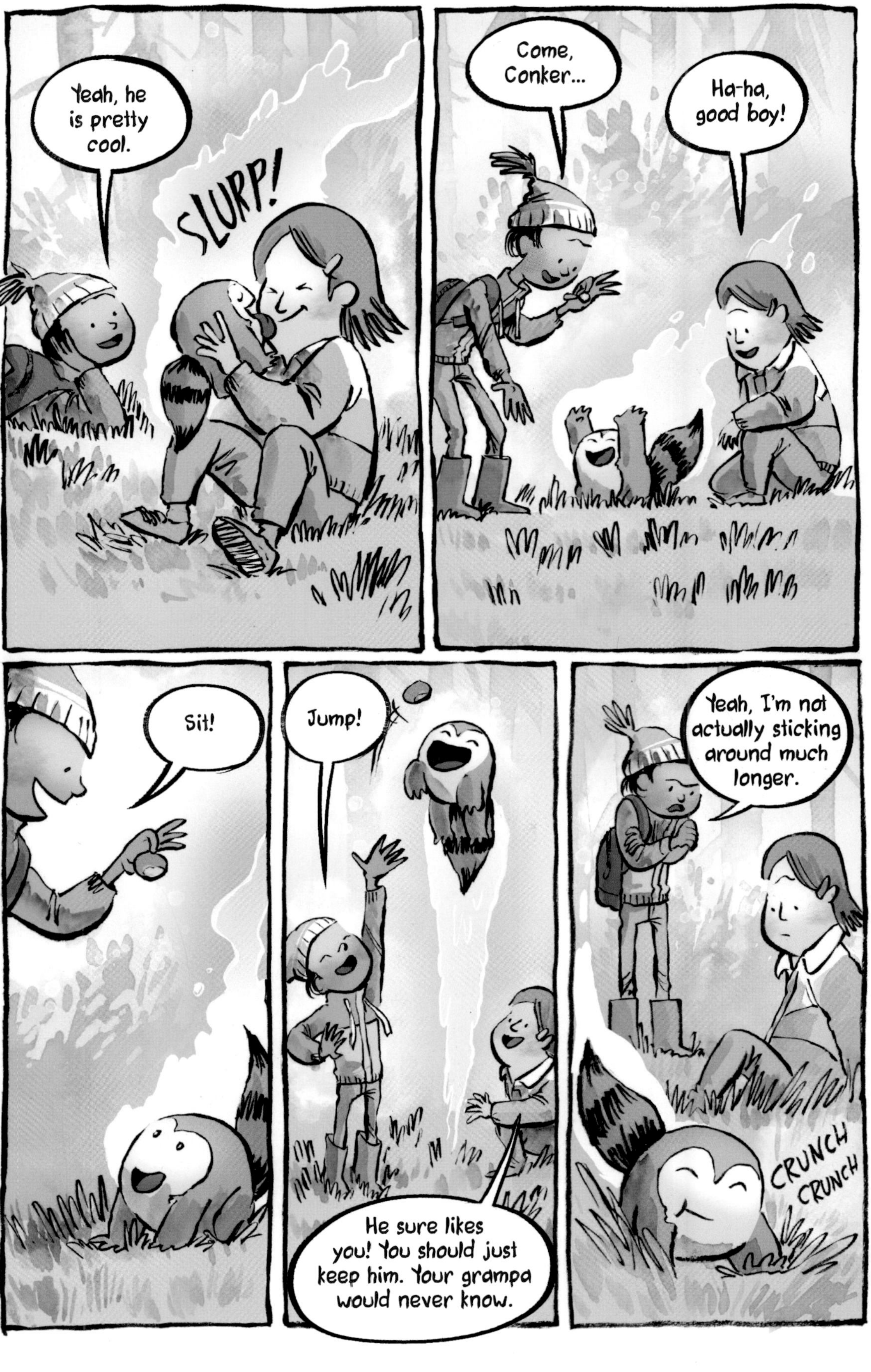
Yeah, he is pretty cool.
SLURP!
Come, Conker...
Ha-ha, good boy!
Sit!
Jump!
He sure likes you! You should just keep him. Your grampa would never know.
Yeah, I'm not actually sticking around much longer.
CRUNCH CRUNCH

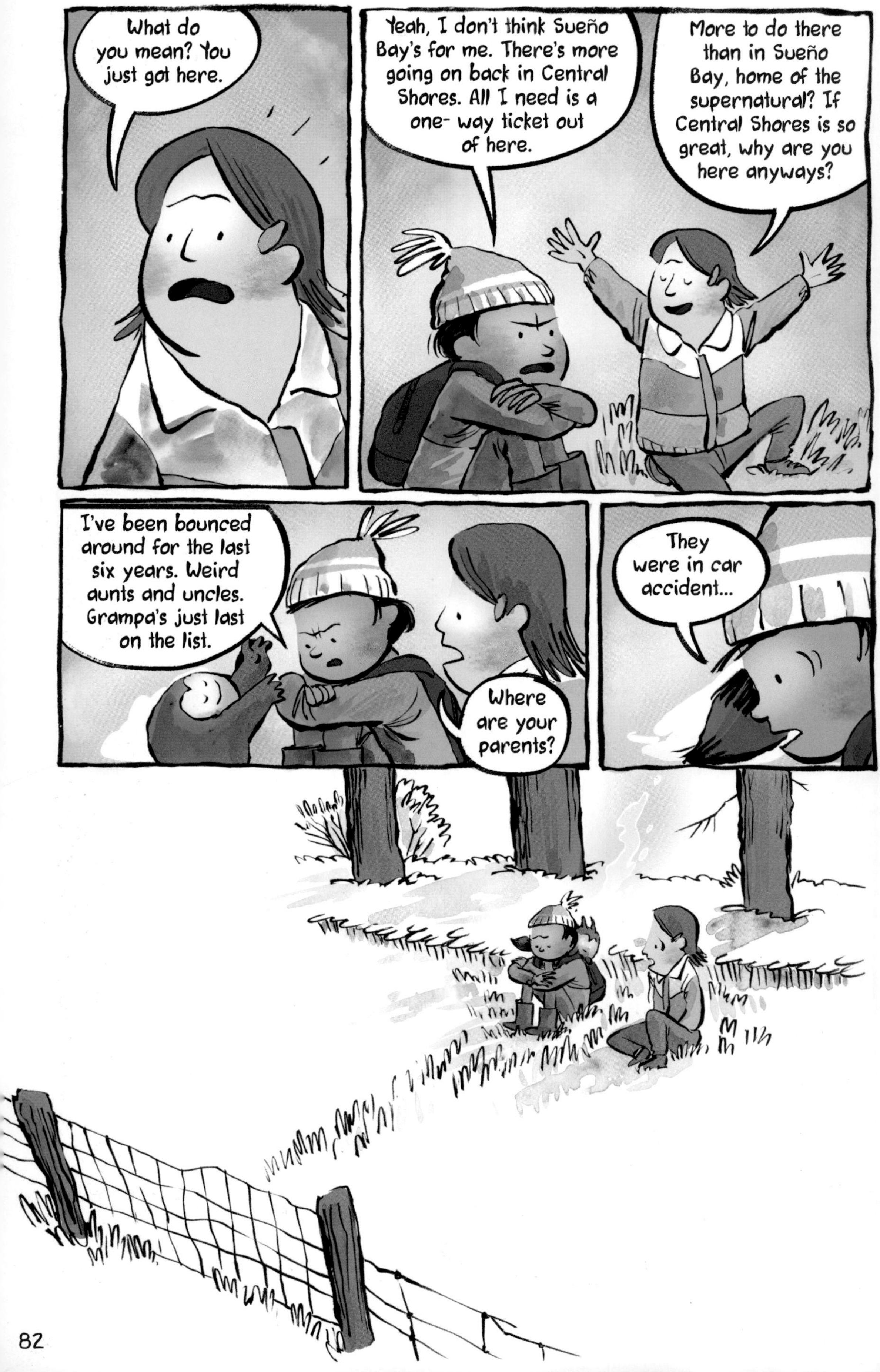
What do you mean? You just got here.
Yeah, I don't think Sueño Bay's for me. There's more going on back in Central Shores. All I need is a one- way ticket out of here.
More to do there than in Sueño Bay, home of the supernatural? If Central Shores is so great, why are you here anyways?
I've been bounced around for the last six years. Weird aunts and uncles. Grampa's just last on the list.
Where are your parents?
They were in car accident...

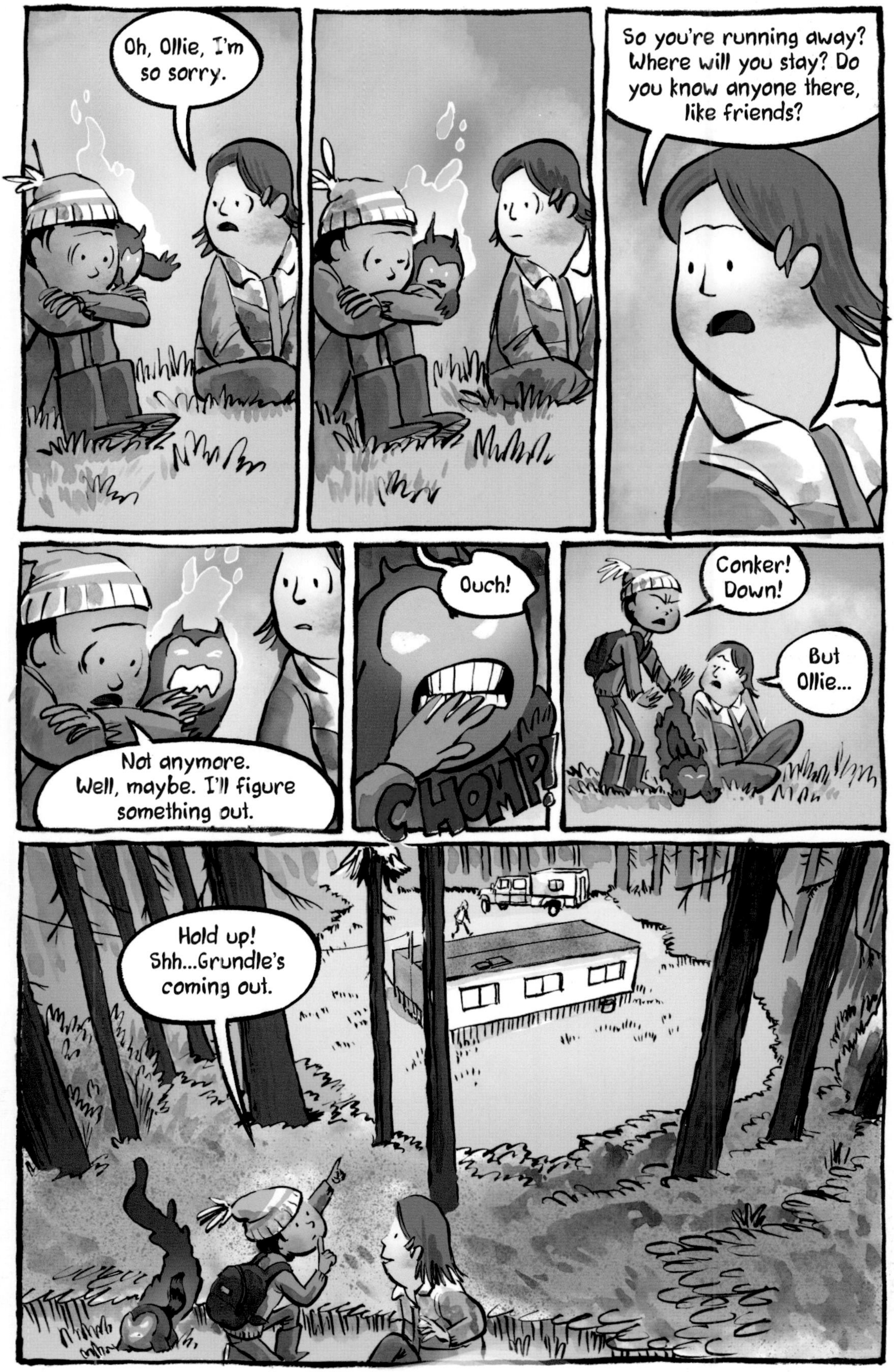
Oh, Ollie, I'm so sorry.
So you're running away? Where will you stay? Do you know anyone there, like friends?
Not anymore. Well, maybe. I'll figure something out.
Ouch!
CHOMP!
Conker! Down!
But Ollie...
Hold up! Shh...Grundle's coming out.

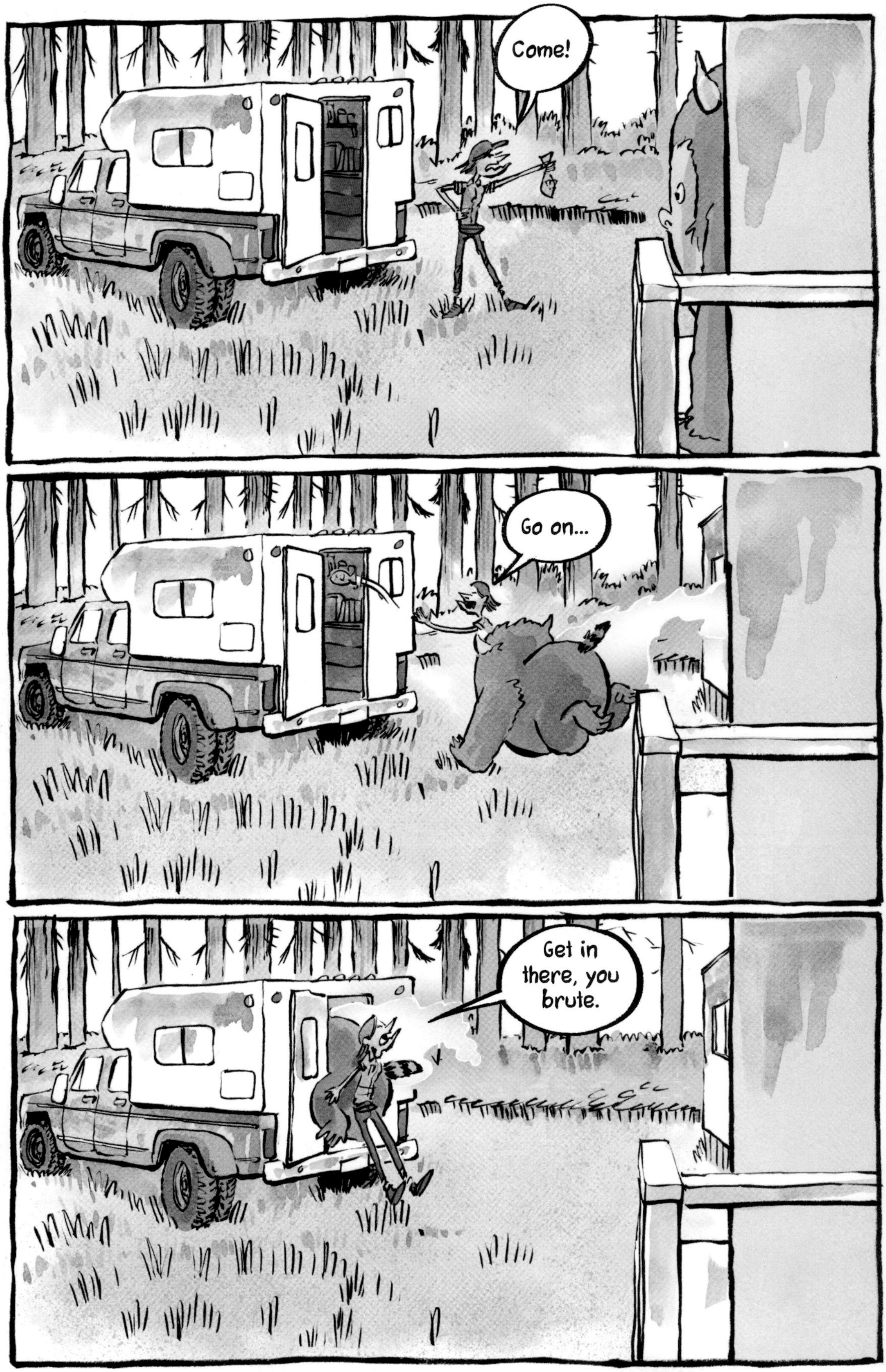
Come!
Go on...
Get in there, you brute.

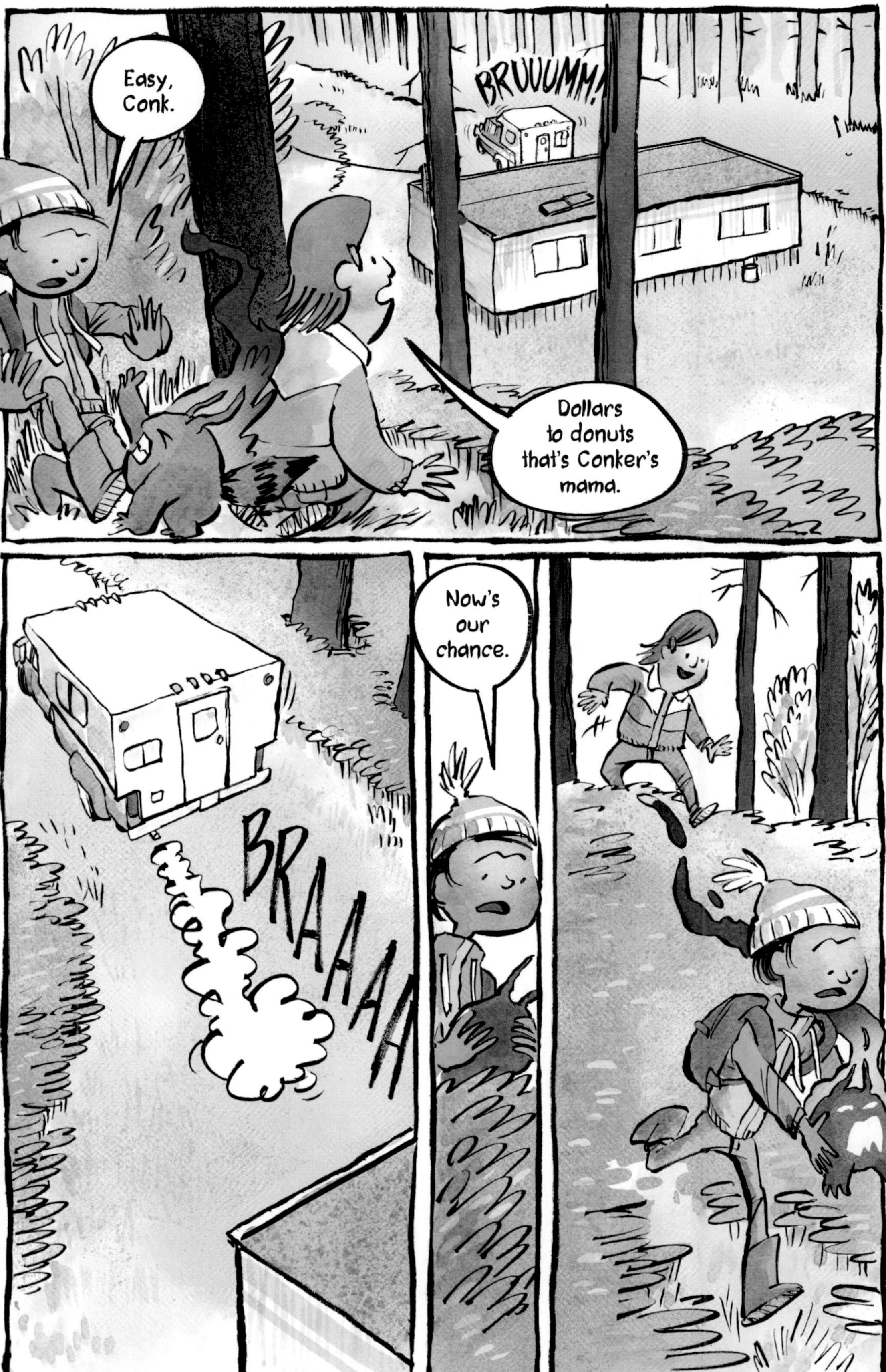
Easy, Conk.
BRUUUMM!
Dollars to donuts that's Conker's mama.
BRAAAA
Now's our chance.

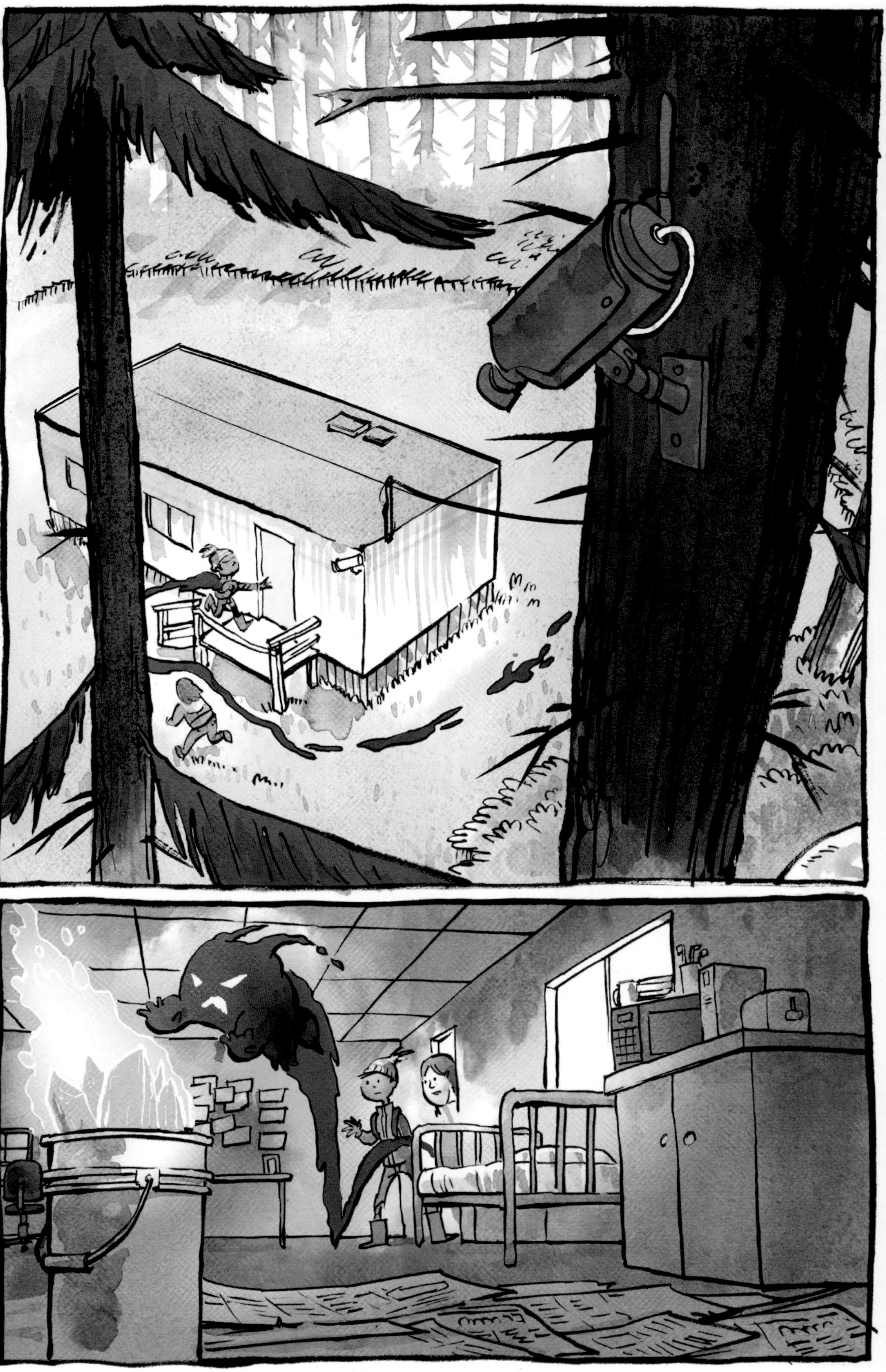

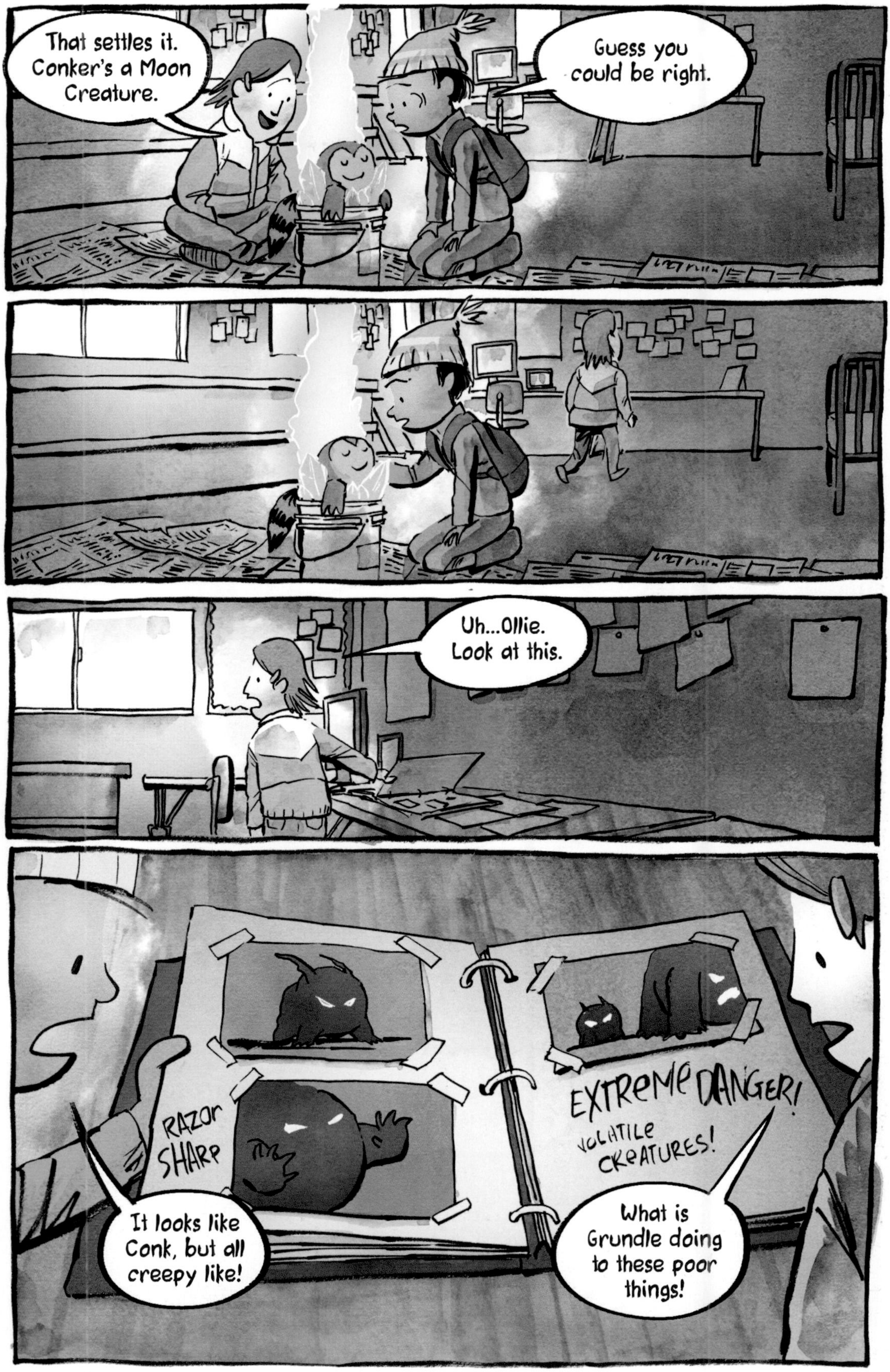
That settles it. Conker's a Moon Creature.
Guess you could be right.
Uh...Ollie. Look at this.
RAZOR SHARP
EXTREME DANGER!
VOLATILE CREATURES!
It looks like Conk, but all creepy like!
What is Grundle doing to these poor things!

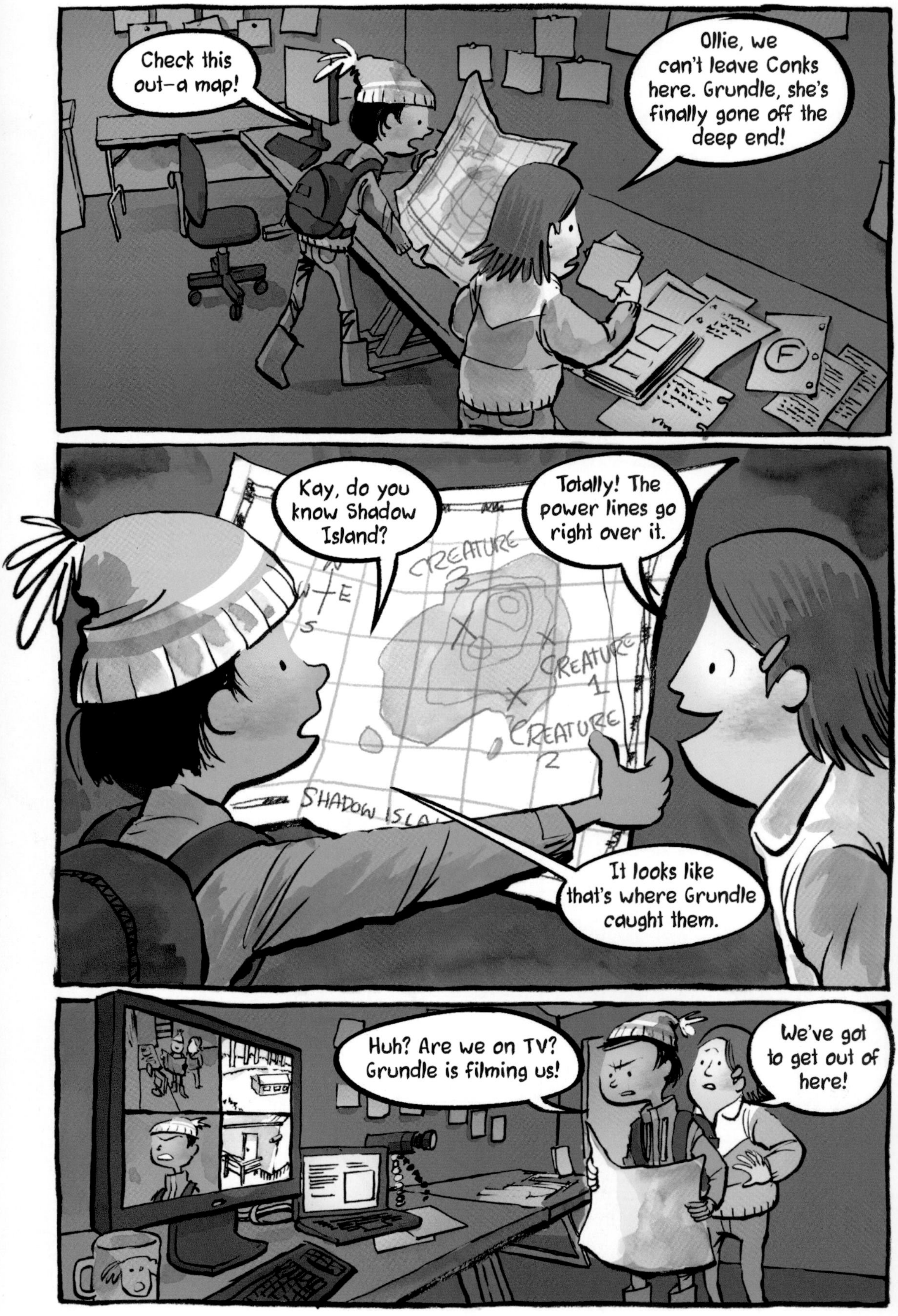
Check this out—a map!
Ollie, we can't leave Conks here. Grundle, she's finally gone off the deep end!
Kay, do you know Shadow Island?
Totally! The power lines go right over it.
CREATURE 3
CREATURE 1
CREATURE 2
SHADOW ISLA
It looks like that's where Grundle caught them.
Huh? Are we on TV? Grundle is filming us!
We've got to get out of here!

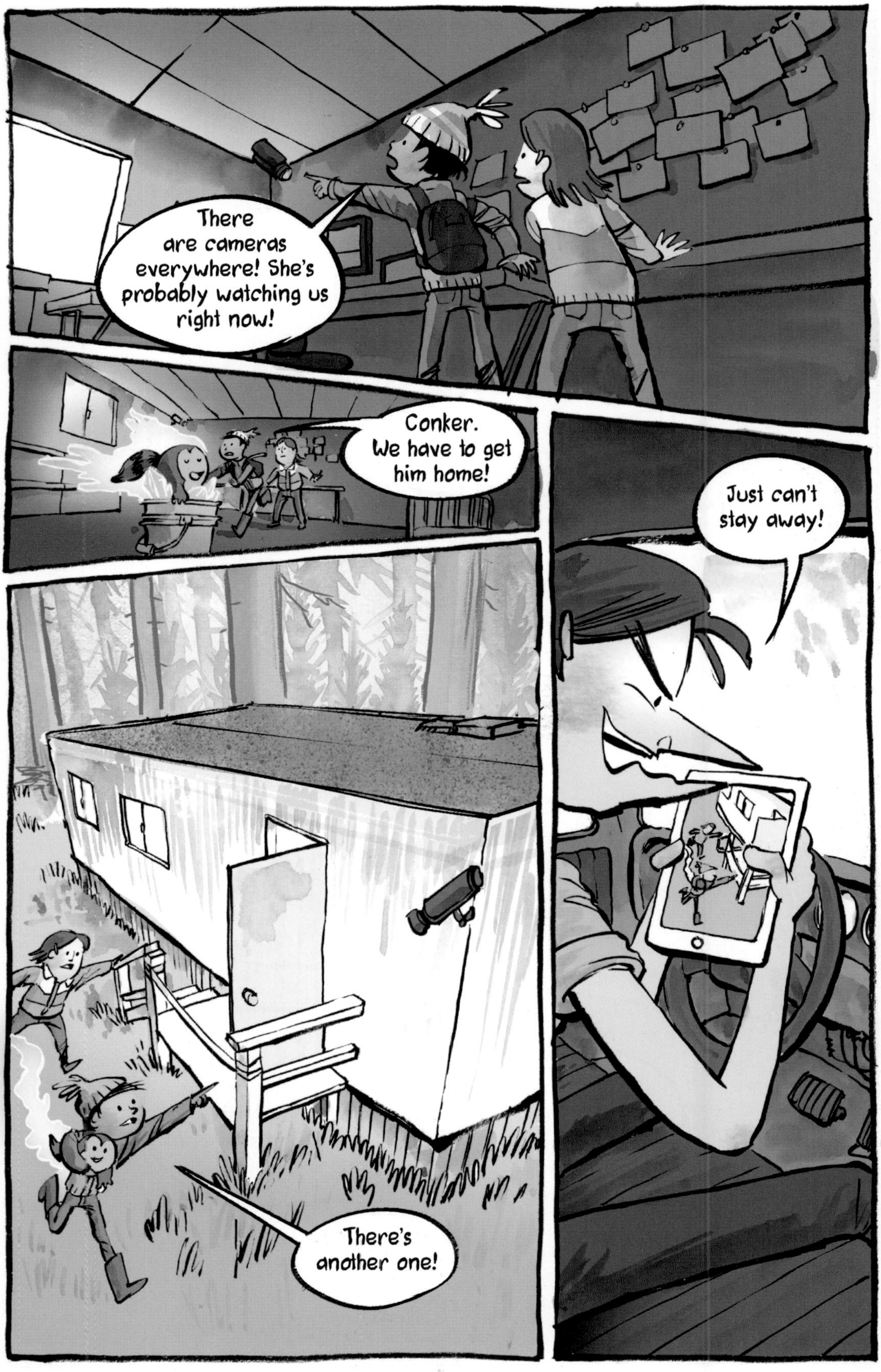
There are cameras everywhere! She's probably watching us right now!
Conker. We have to get him home!
Just can't stay away!
There's another one!

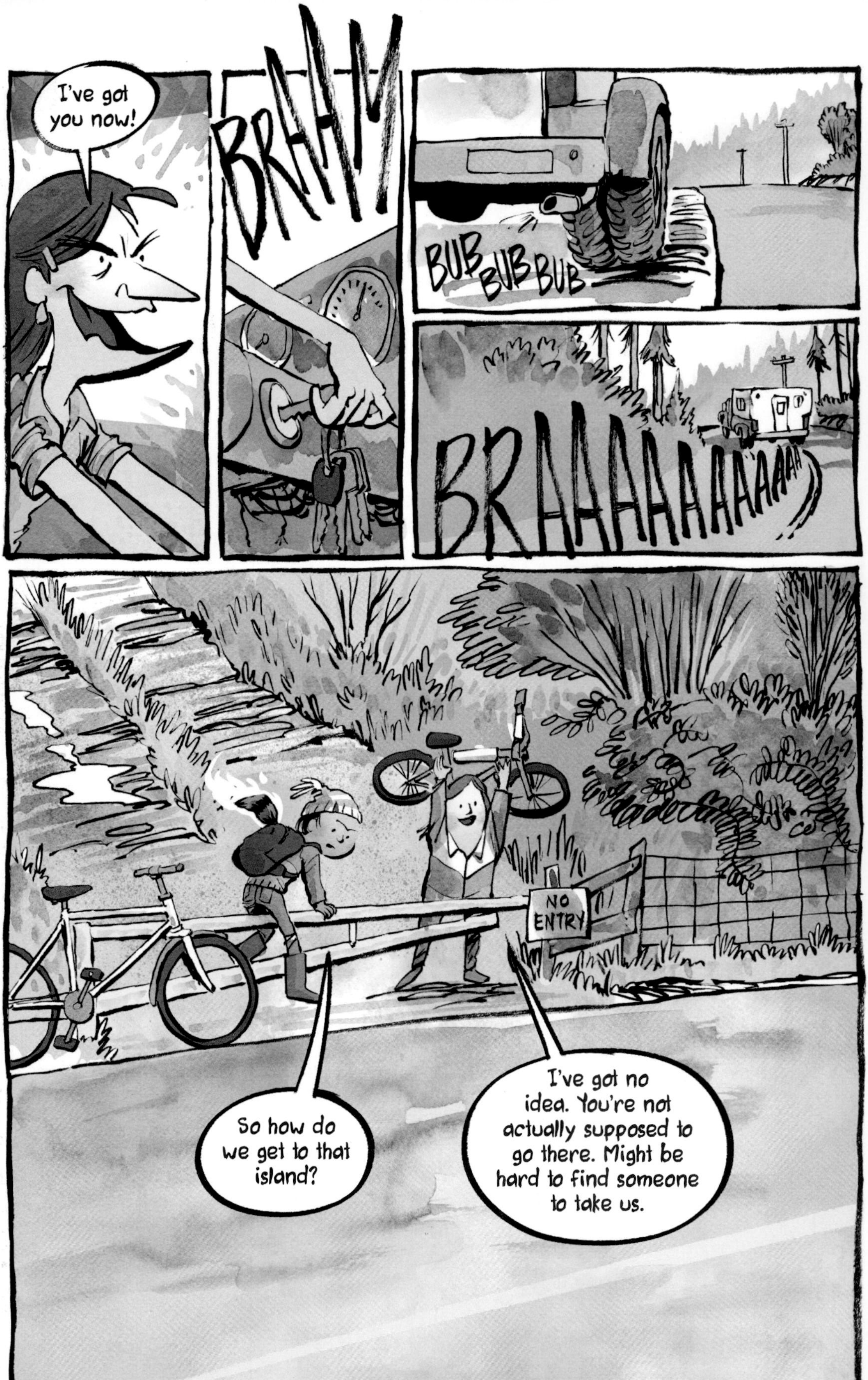
I've got you now!
BRAAM
BUB BUB BUB
BRAAAAAAAAAA
NO ENTRY
So how do we get to that island?
I've got no idea. You're not actually supposed to go there. Might be hard to find someone to take us.

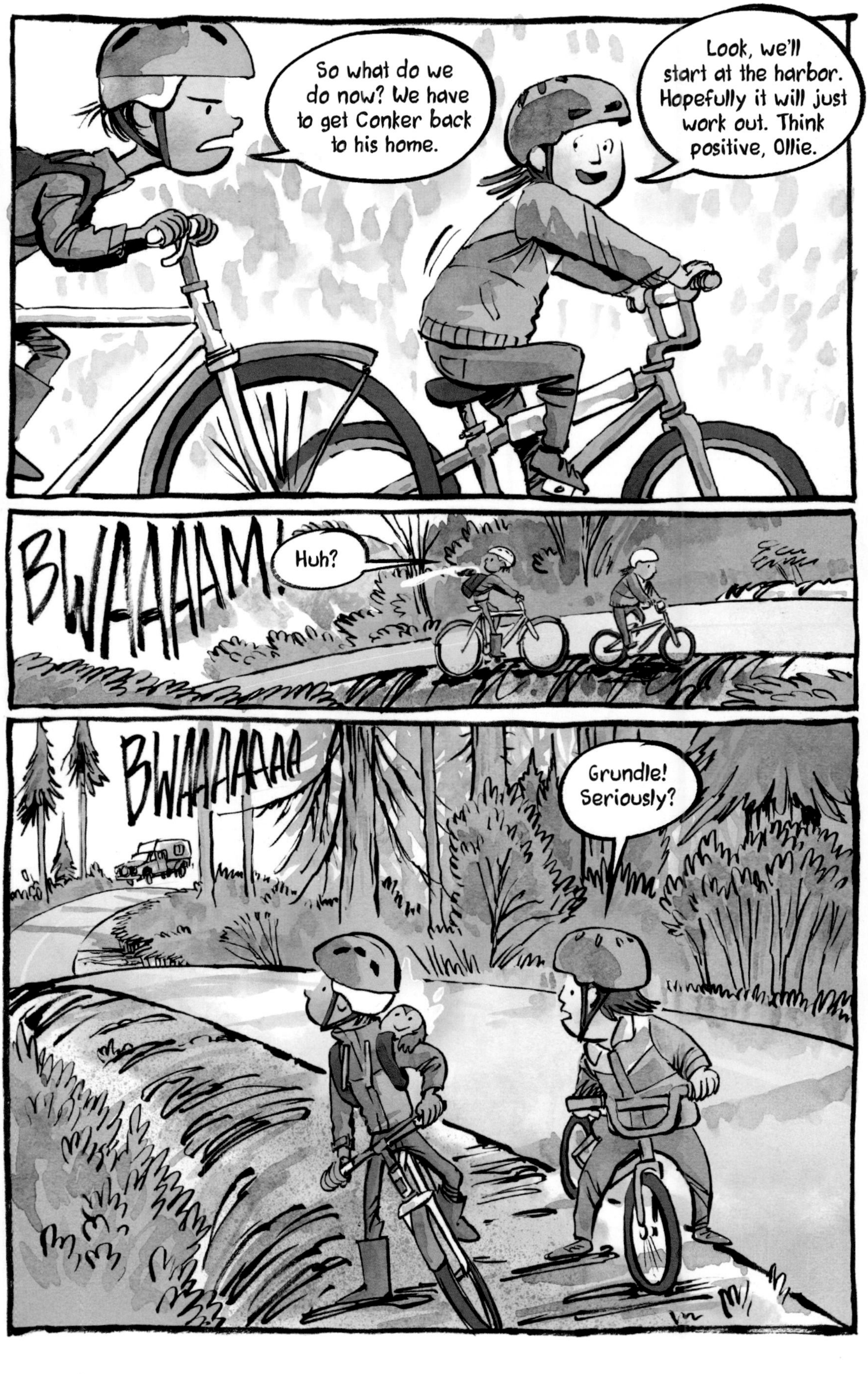
So what do we do now? We have to get Conker back to his home.
Look, we'll start at the harbor. Hopefully it will just work out. Think positive, Ollie.
BWAAAAM!
Huh?
BWAAAAAA
Grundle! Seriously?

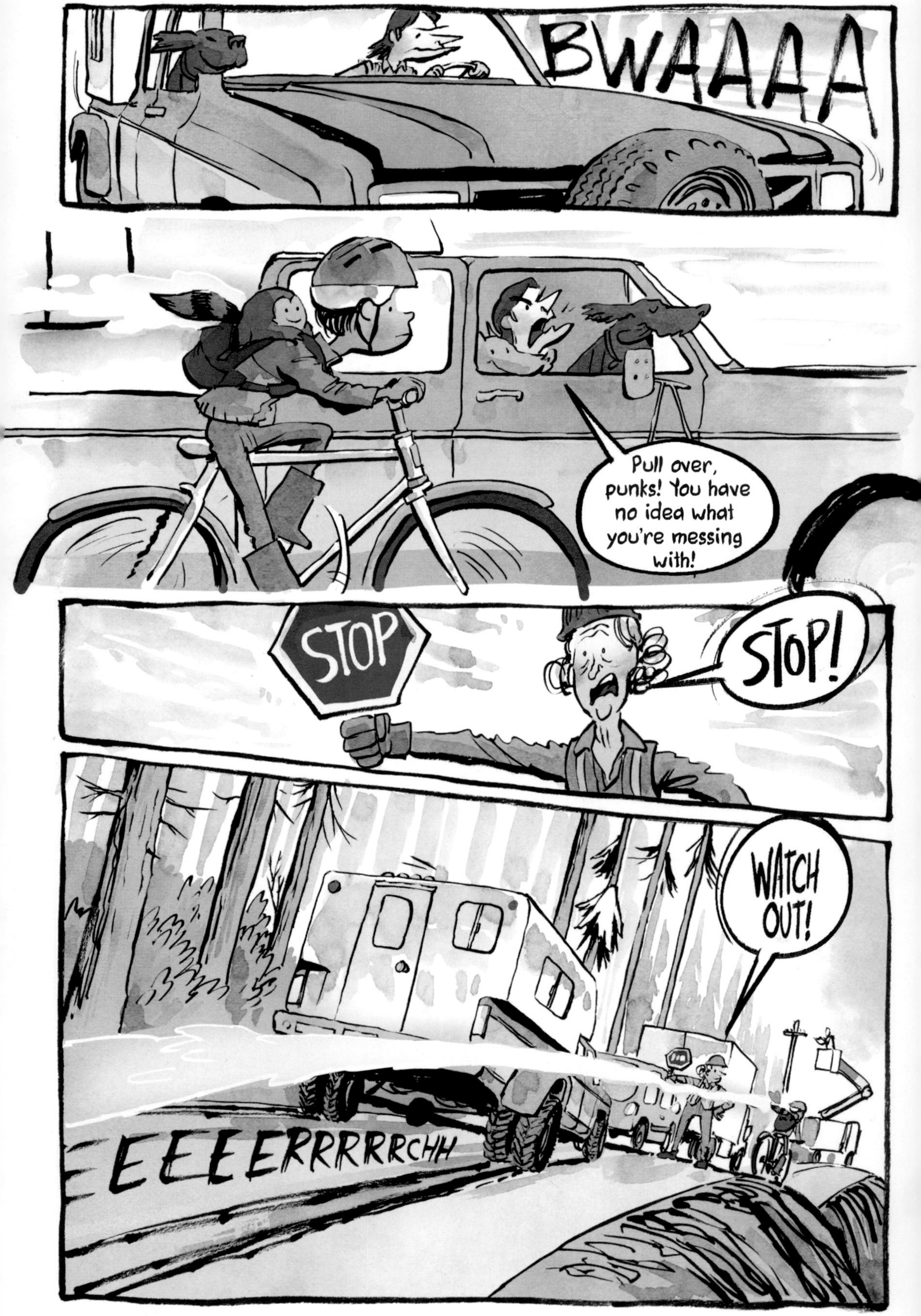

BWAAAA
Pull over, punks! You have no idea what you're messing with!
STOP
STOP!
WATCH OUT!
EEEERRRRRCHH

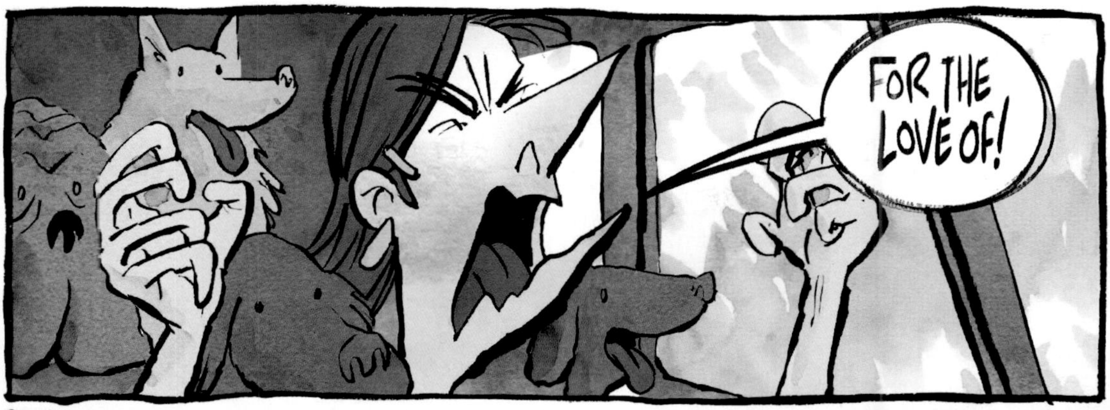
FOR THE LOVE OF!

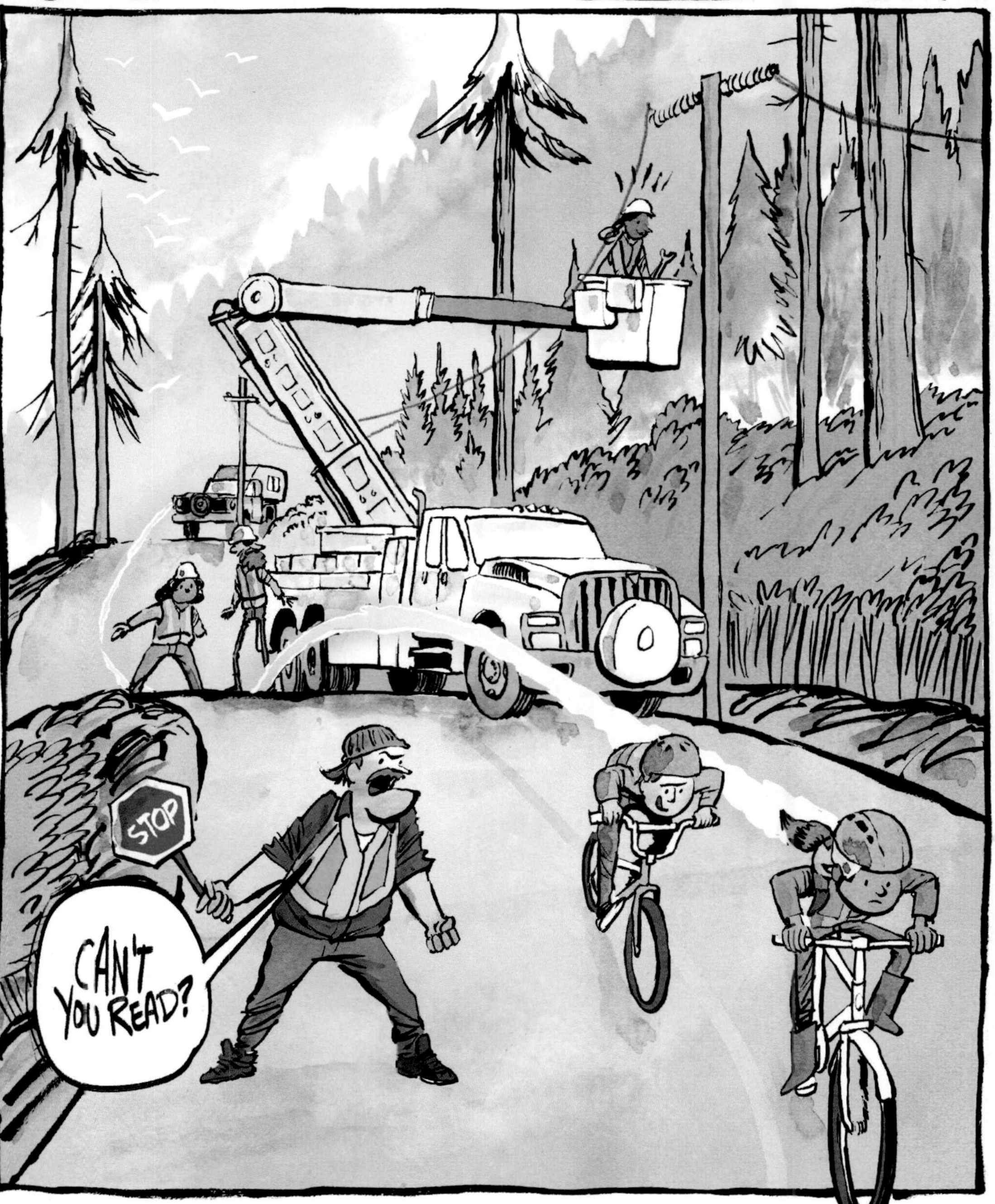
STOP
CAN'T YOU READ?

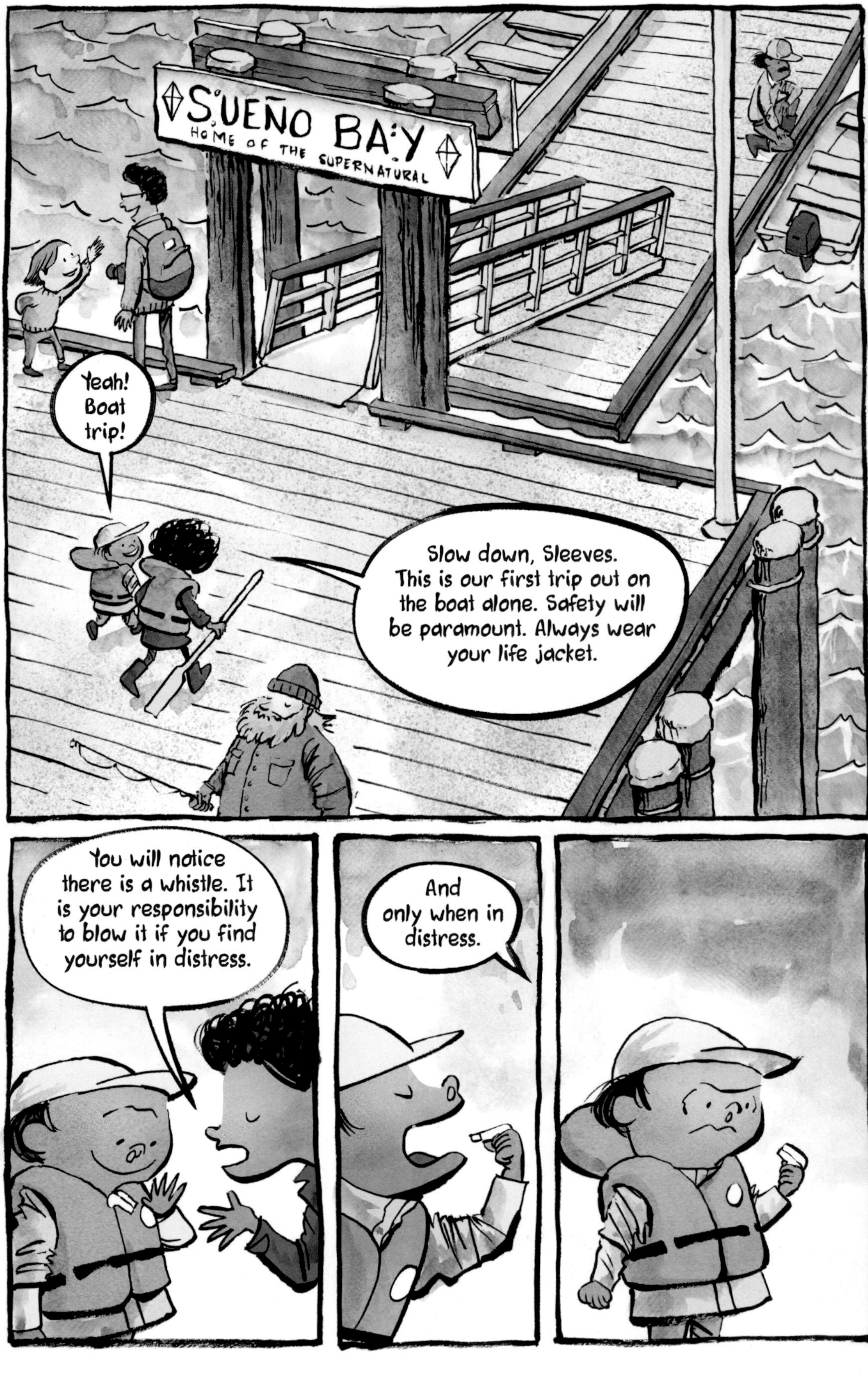
SUEÑO BAY
HOME OF THE SUPERNATURAL
Yeah! Boat trip!
Slow down, Sleeves. This is our first trip out on the boat alone. Safety will be paramount. Always wear your life jacket.
You will notice there is a whistle. It is your responsibility to blow it if you find yourself in distress.
And only when in distress.

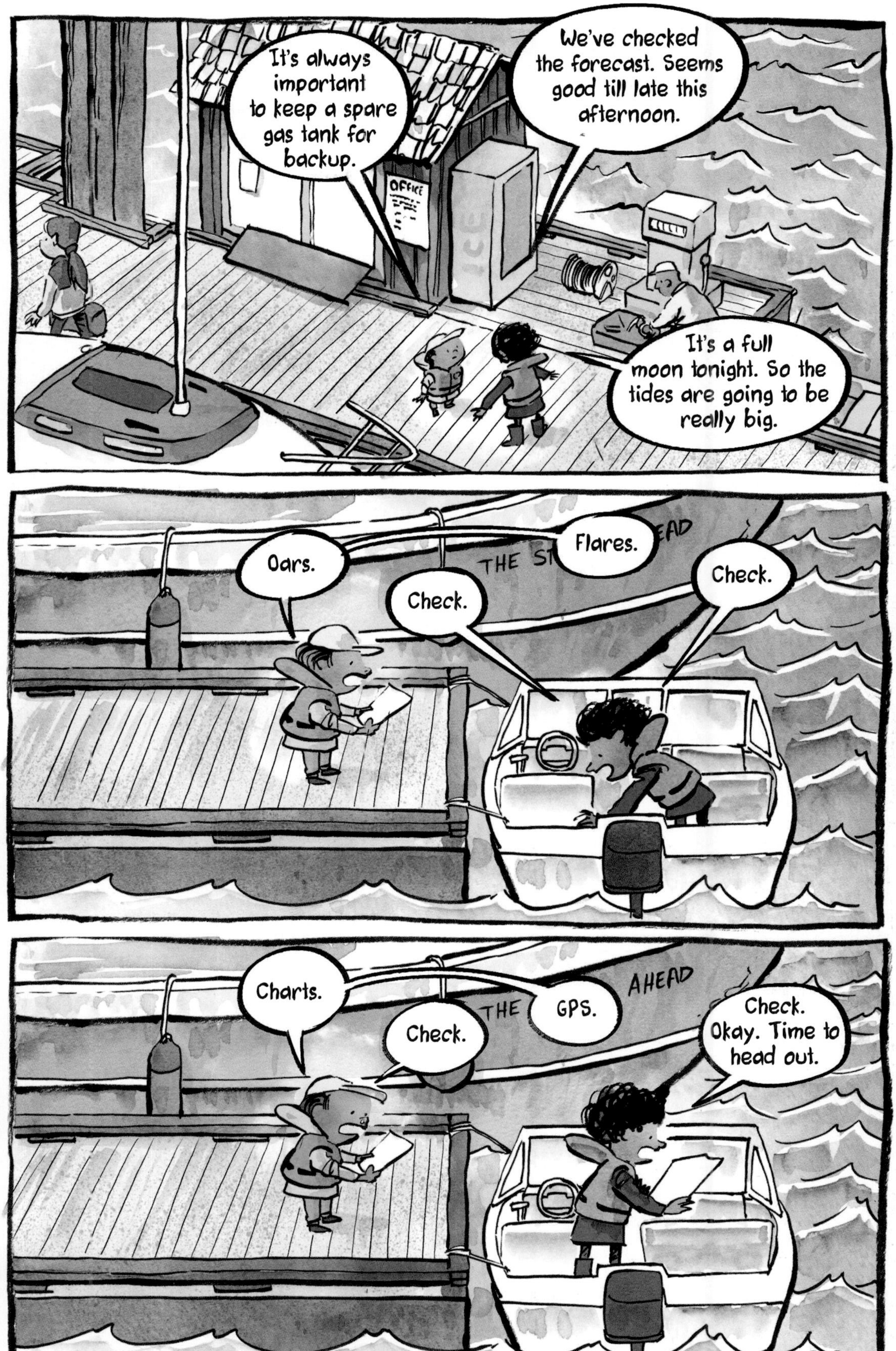
It's always important to keep a spare gas tank for backup.
We've checked the forecast. Seems good till late this afternoon.
OFFICE
ICE
It's a full moon tonight. So the tides are going to be really big.
Oars.
Check.
Flares.
Check.
THE ST
EAD
Charts.
Check.
GPS.
Check. Okay. Time to head out.
THE
AHEAD

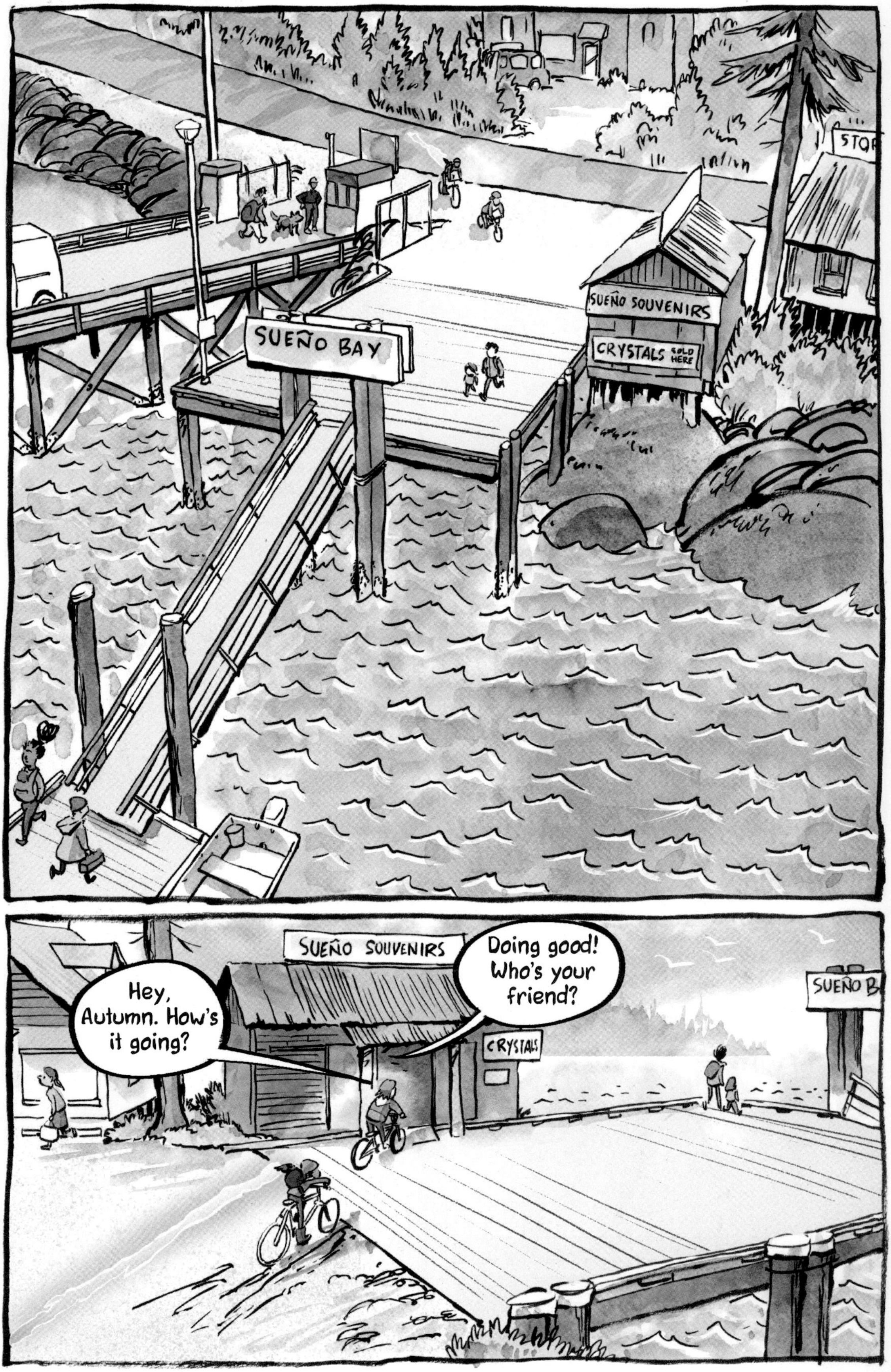
SUEÑO BAY
SUEÑO SOUVENIRS
CRYSTALS SOLD HERE
SUEÑO SOUVENIRS
Hey, Autumn. How's it going?
Doing good! Who's your friend?
CRYSTALS

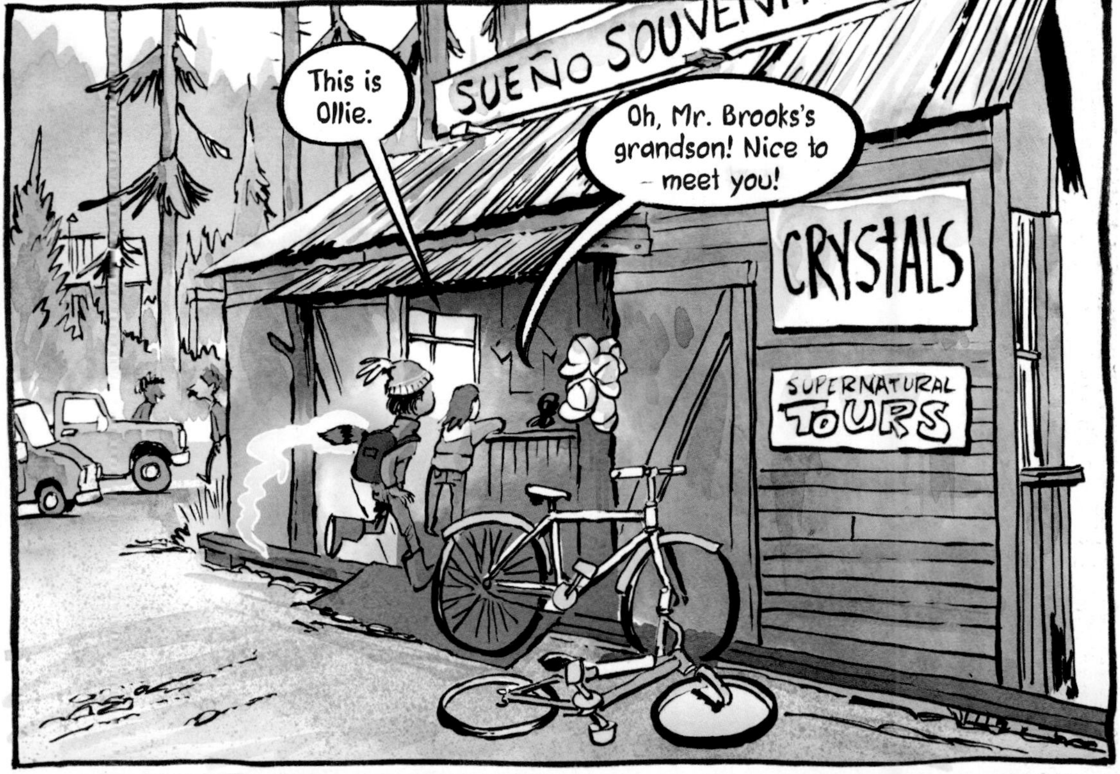
SUEÑO SOUVEN
This is Ollie.
Oh, Mr. Brooks's grandson! Nice to meet you!
CRYSTALS
SUPERNATURAL TOURS

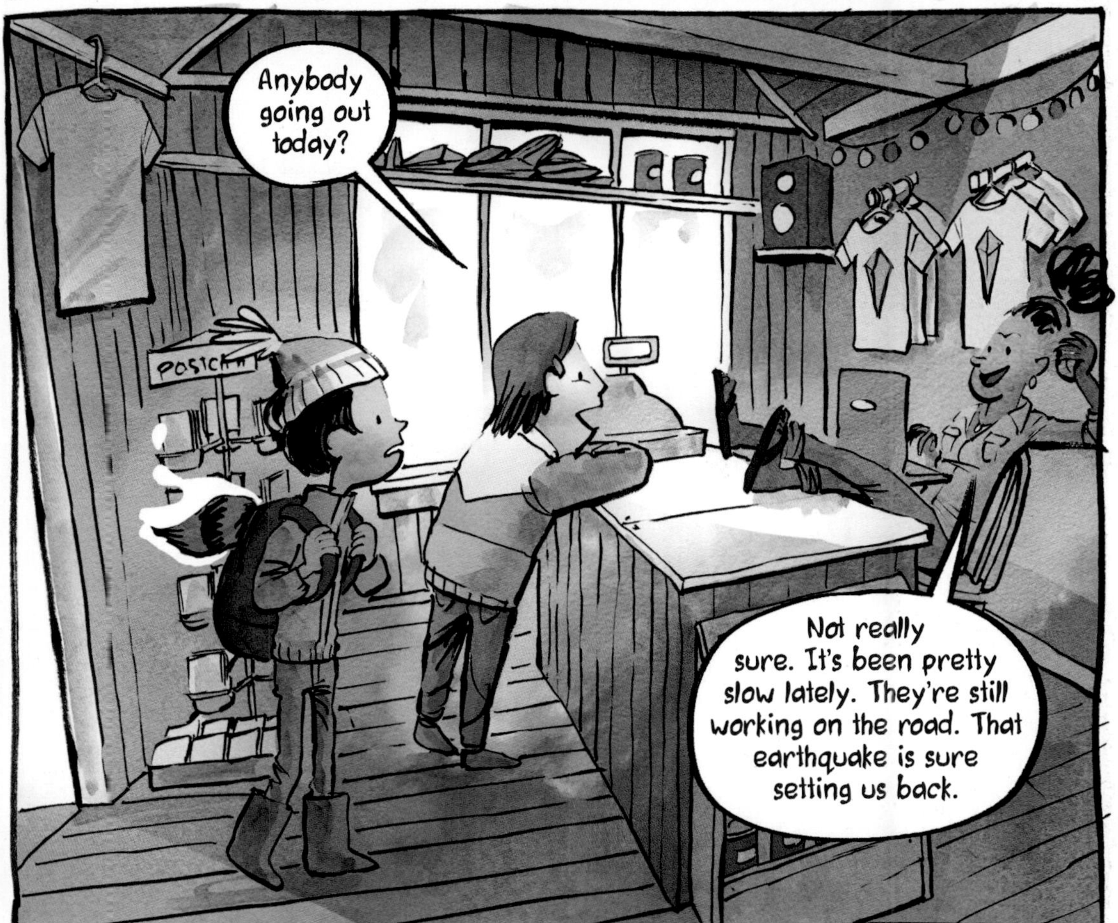
Anybody going out today?
Not really sure. It's been pretty slow lately. They're still working on the road. That earthquake is sure setting us back.

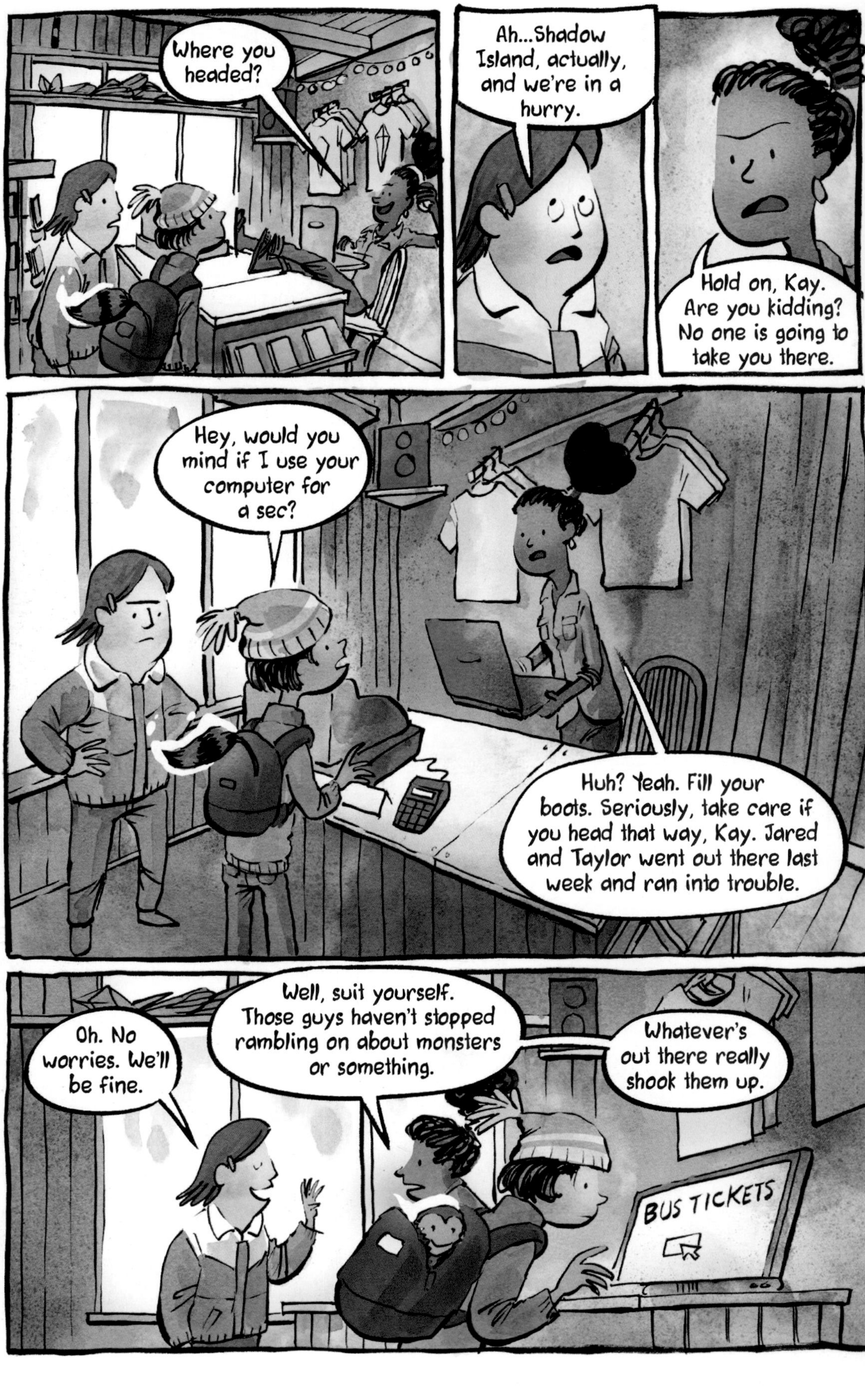

Where you headed?
Ah...Shadow Island, actually, and we're in a hurry.
Hold on, Kay. Are you kidding? No one is going to take you there.
Hey, would you mind if I use your computer for a sec?
Huh? Yeah. Fill your boots. Seriously, take care if you head that way, Kay. Jared and Taylor went out there last week and ran into trouble.
Oh. No worries. We'll be fine.
Well, suit yourself. Those guys haven't stopped rambling on about monsters or something.
Whatever's out there really shook them up.
BUS TICKETS

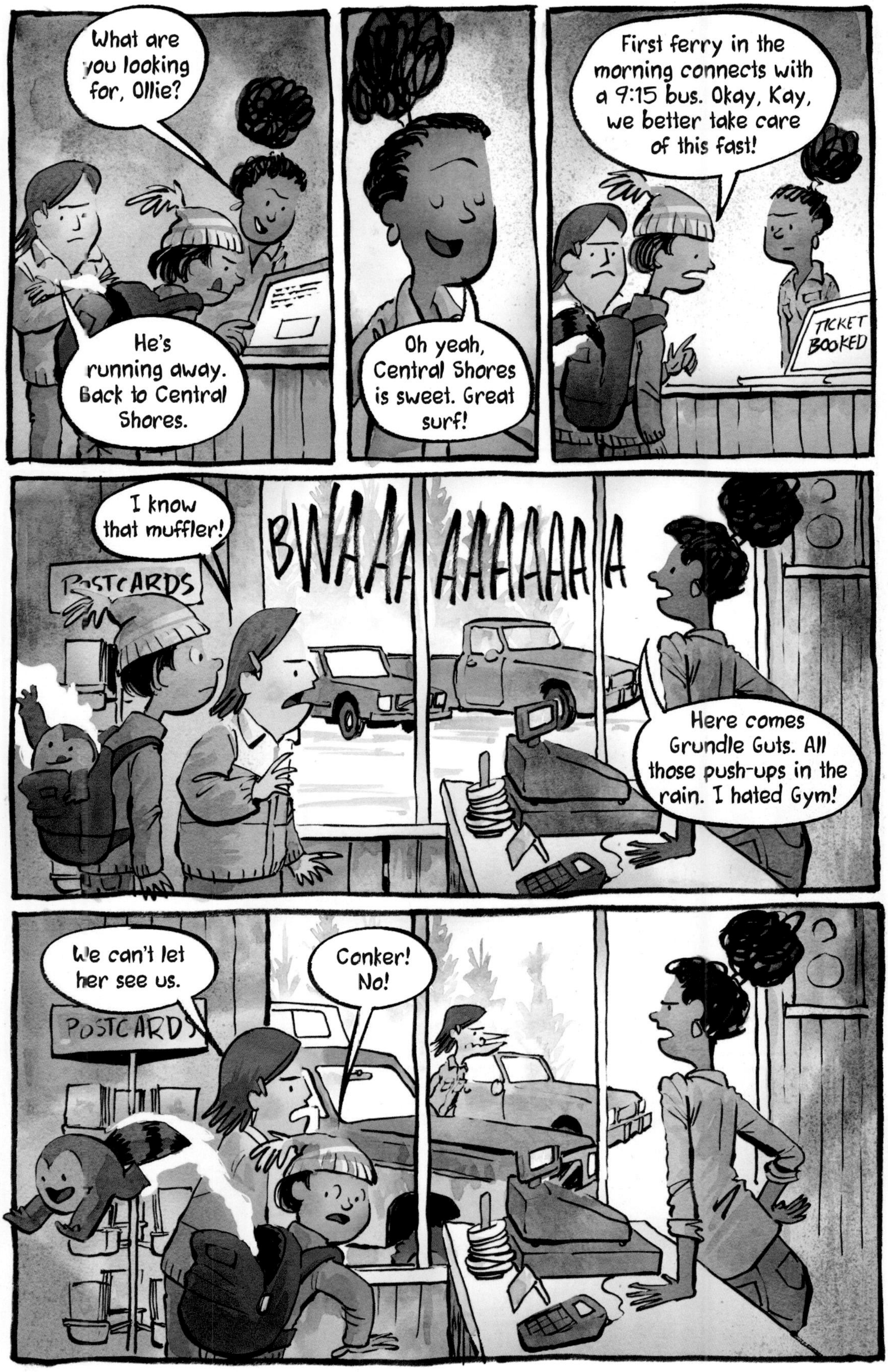
What are you looking for, Ollie?
He's running away. Back to Central Shores.
Oh yeah, Central Shores is sweet. Great surf!
First ferry in the morning connects with a 9:15 bus. Okay, Kay, we better take care of this fast!
TICKET BOOKED
I know that muffler!
POSTCARDS
BWAAAAAAAAAA
Here comes Grundle Guts. All those push-ups in the rain. I hated Gym!
We can't let her see us.
Conker! No!
POSTCARDS

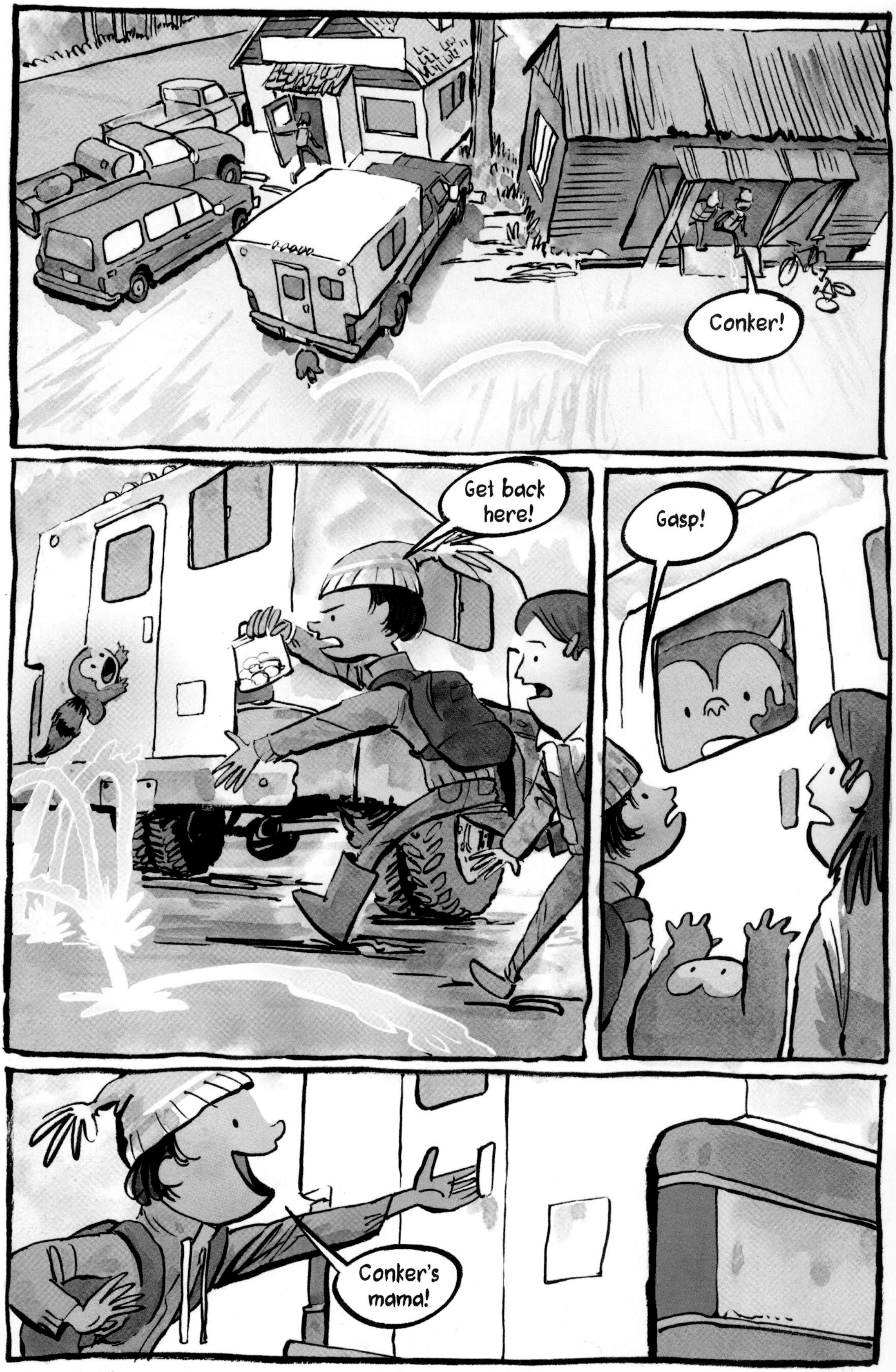
Conker!
Get back here!
Gasp!
Conker's mama!

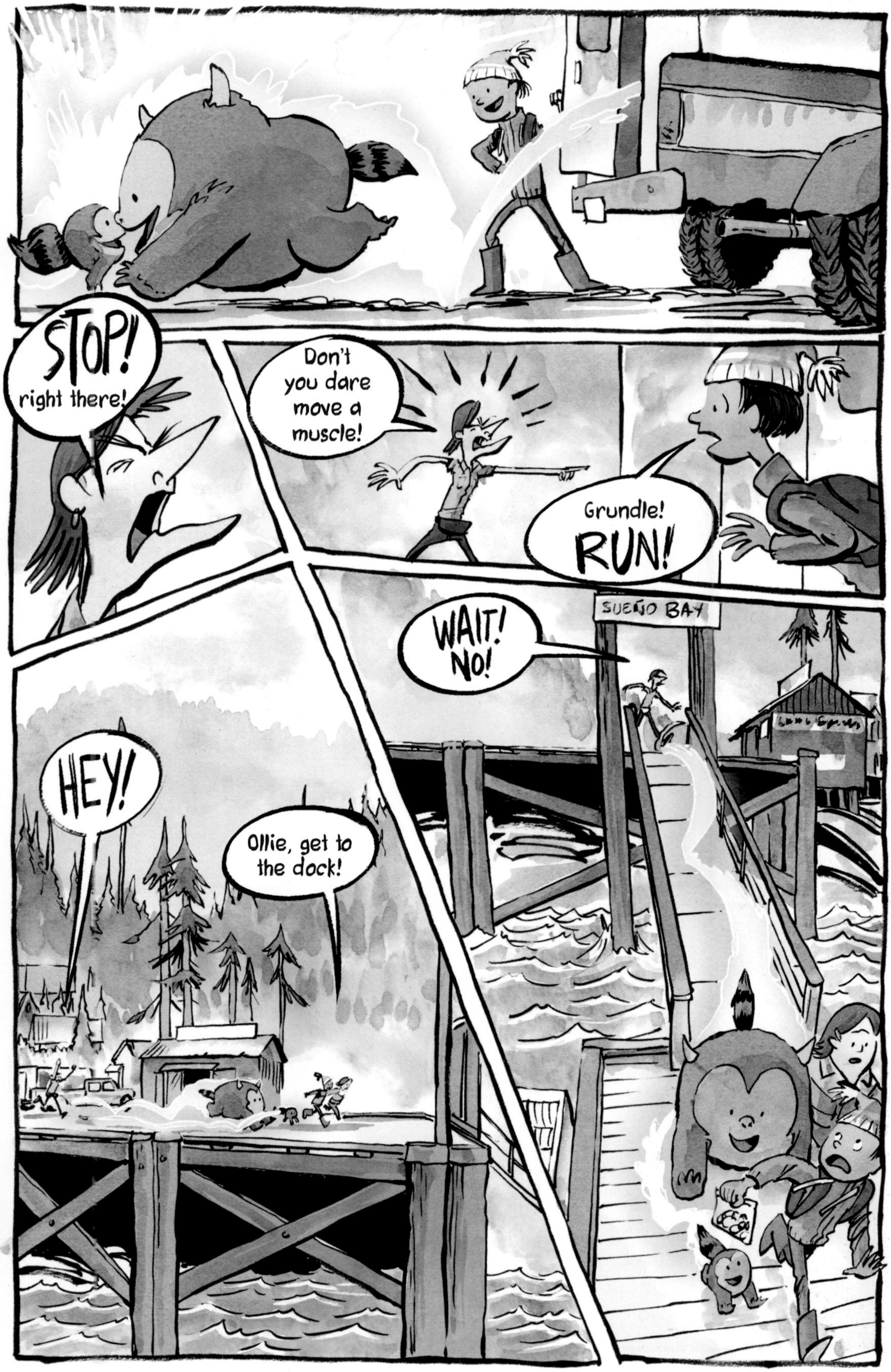

STOP! right there!
Don't you dare move a muscle!
Grundle! RUN!
HEY!
Ollie, get to the dock!
WAIT! NO!
SUEÑO BAY

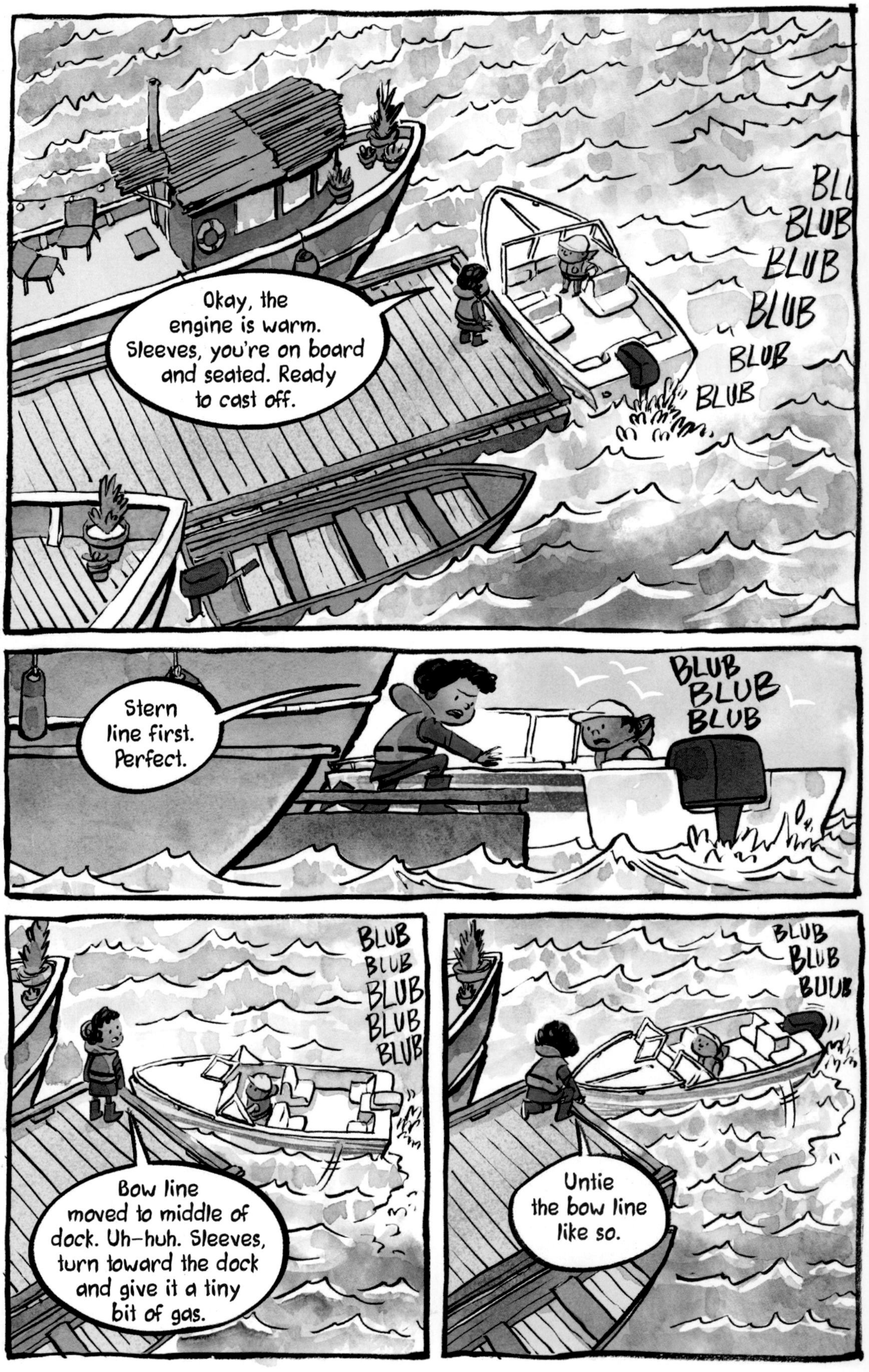
Okay, the engine is warm. Sleeves, you're on board and seated. Ready to cast off.
BLU
BLUB
BLUB
BLUB
BLUB
BLUB
Stern line first. Perfect.
BLUB
BLUB
BLUB
BLUB
BLUB
BLUB
BLUB
BLUB
Bow line moved to middle of dock. Uh-huh. Sleeves, turn toward the dock and give it a tiny bit of gas.
BLUB
BLUB
BLUB
Untie the bow line like so.

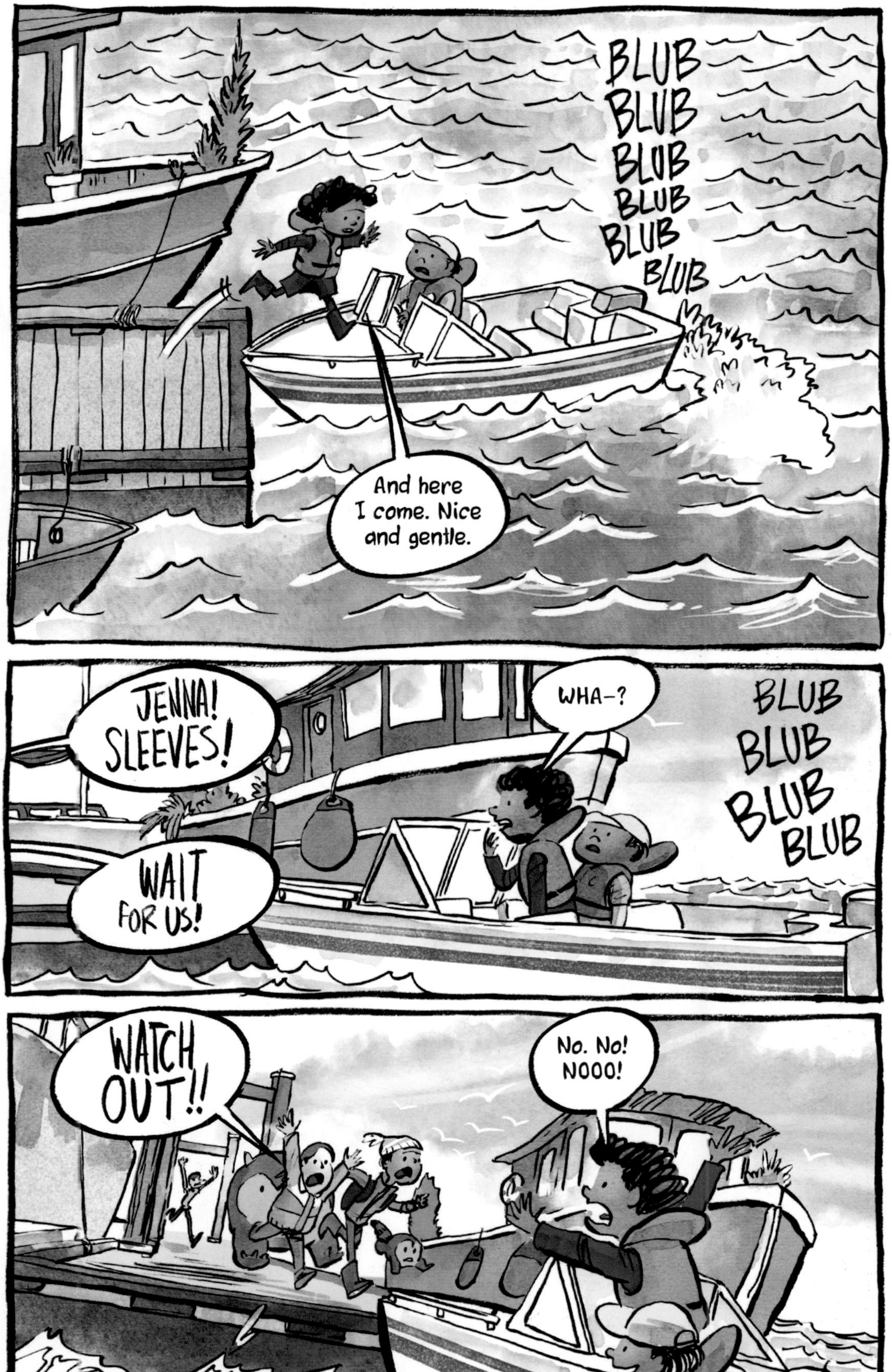
BLUB BLUB BLUB BLUB BLUB BLUB
And here I come. Nice and gentle.
JENNA! SLEEVES!
WAIT FOR US!
WHA-?
BLUB BLUB BLUB BLUB
WATCH OUT!!
No. No! NOOO!

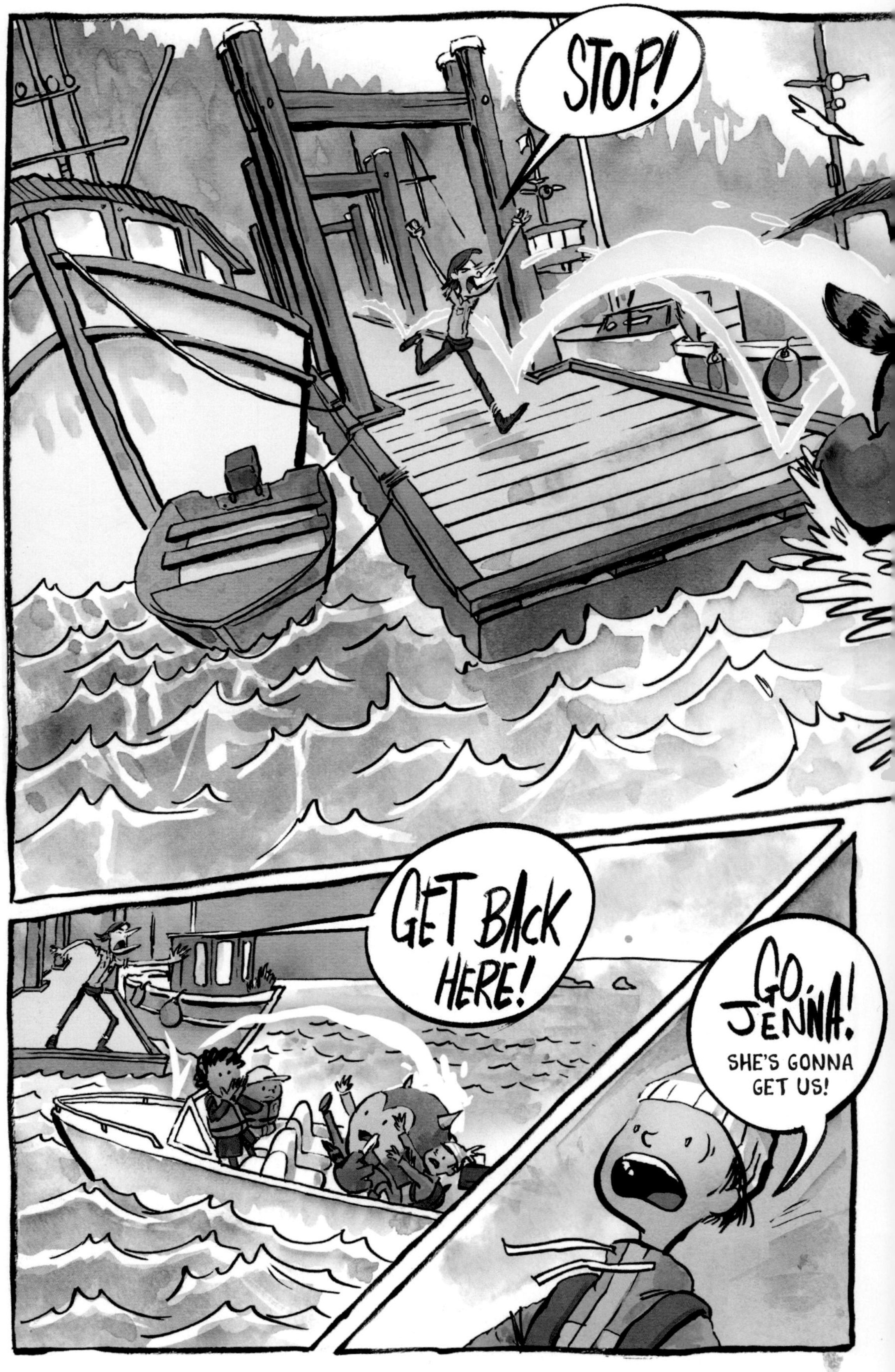
STOP!
GET BACK HERE!
GO, JENNA!
SHE'S GONNA GET US!

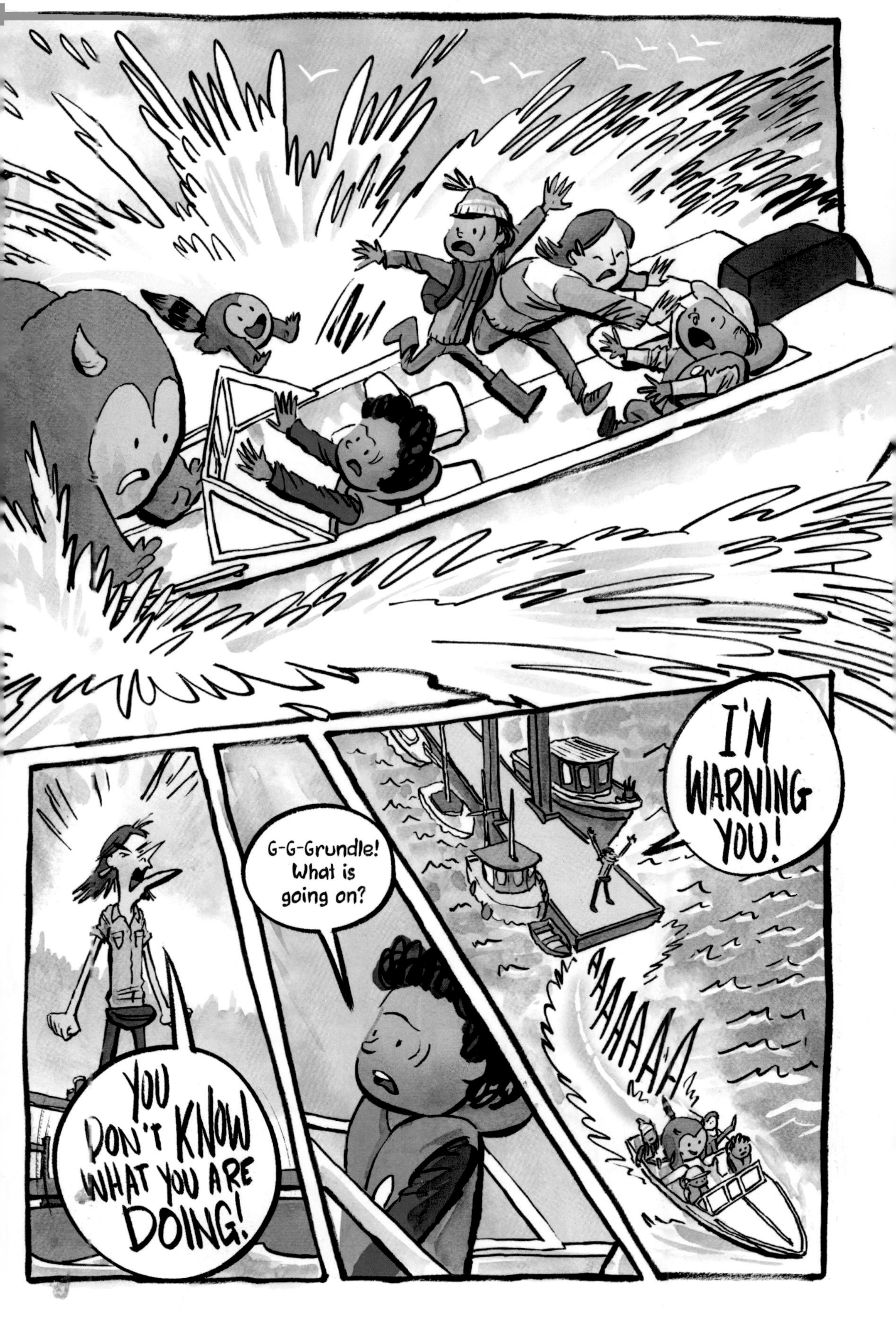
YOU DON'T KNOW WHAT YOU ARE DOING!
G-G-Grundle! What is going on?
I'M WARNING YOU!
AAAAAAA

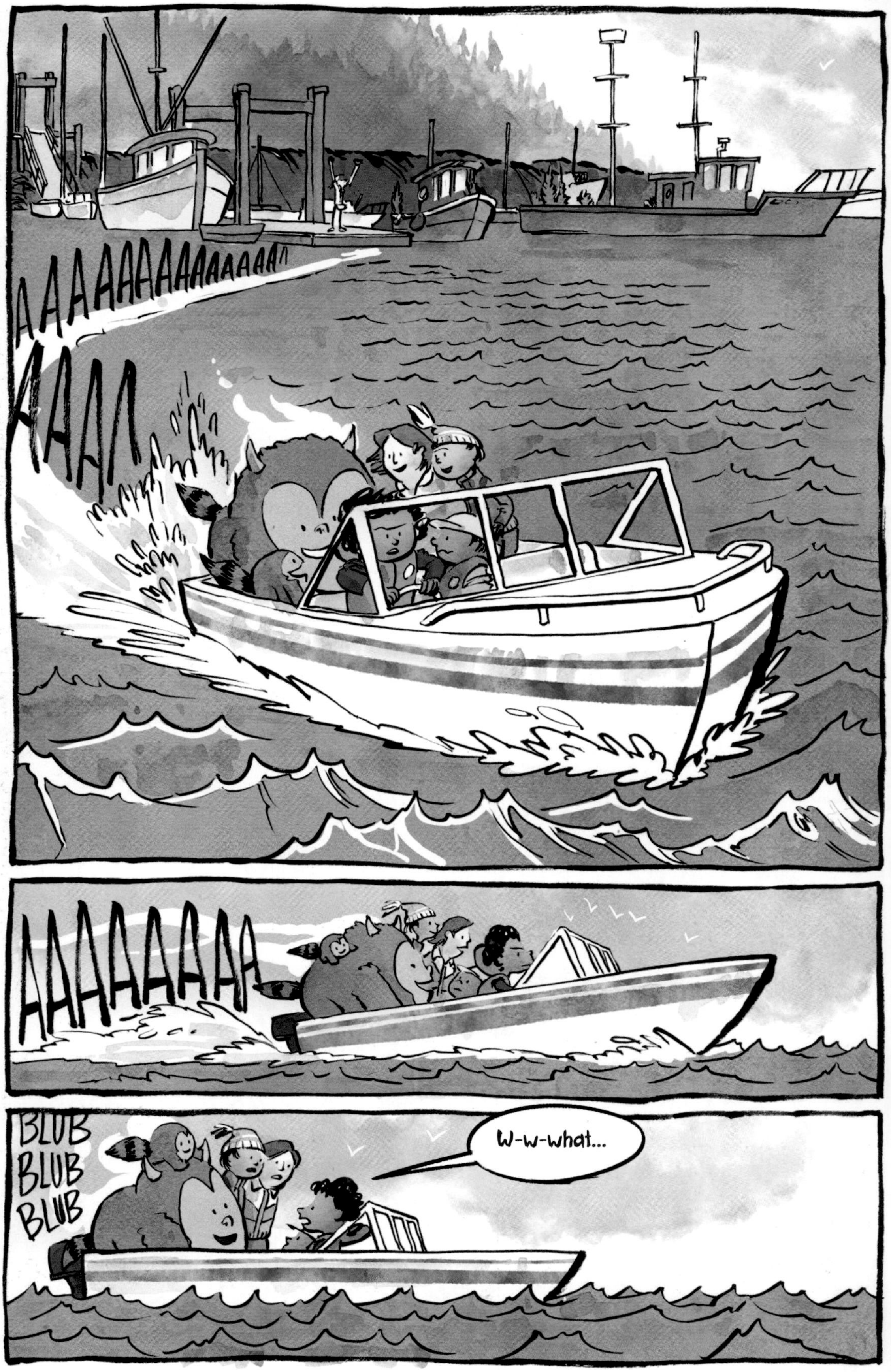
AAAAAAAAAAAAAAAAAAA
AAAAAAAAA
BLUB
BLUB
BLUB
W-w-what...

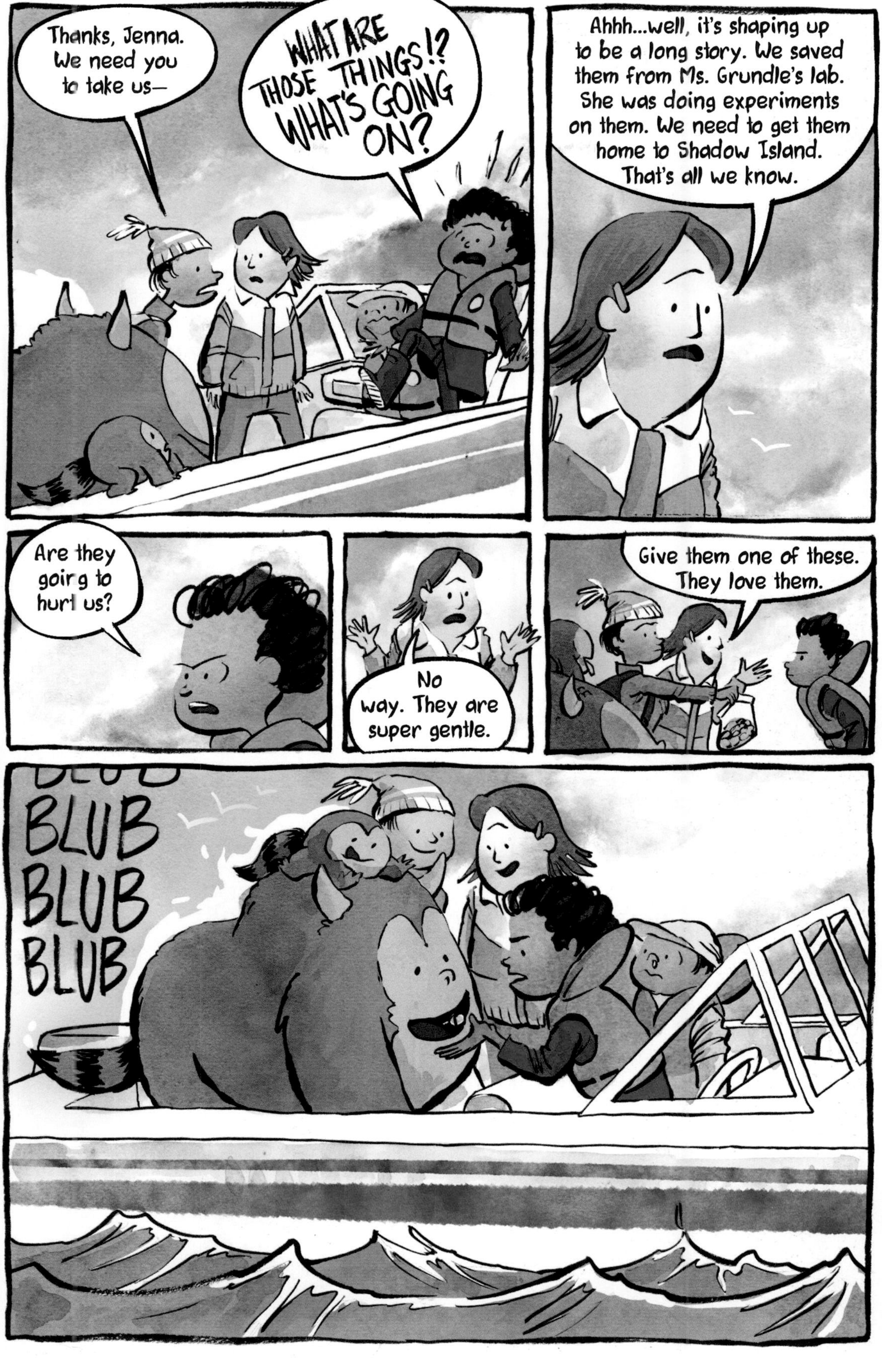
Thanks, Jenna. We need you to take us—
WHAT ARE THOSE THINGS!? WHAT'S GOING ON?
Ahhh...well, it's shaping up to be a long story. We saved them from Ms. Grundle's lab. She was doing experiments on them. We need to get them home to Shadow Island. That's all we know.
Are they going to hurt us?
No way. They are super gentle.
Give them one of these. They love them.
BLUB BLUB BLUB BLUB

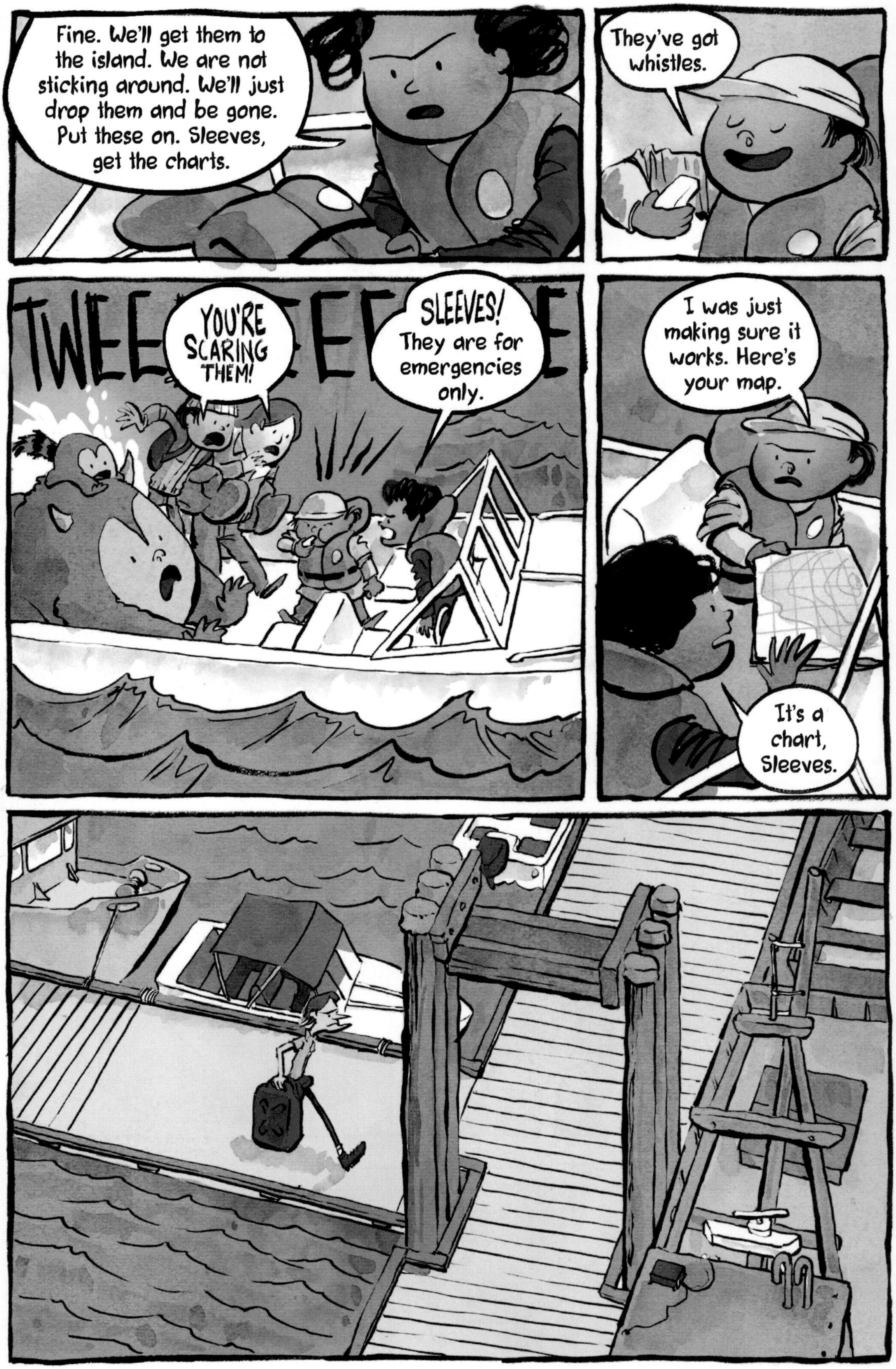
Fine. We'll get them to the island. We are not sticking around. We'll just drop them and be gone. Put these on. Sleeves, get the charts.
They've got whistles.
YOU'RE SCARING THEM!
SLEEVES! They are for emergencies only.
I was just making sure it works. Here's your map.
It's a chart, Sleeves.

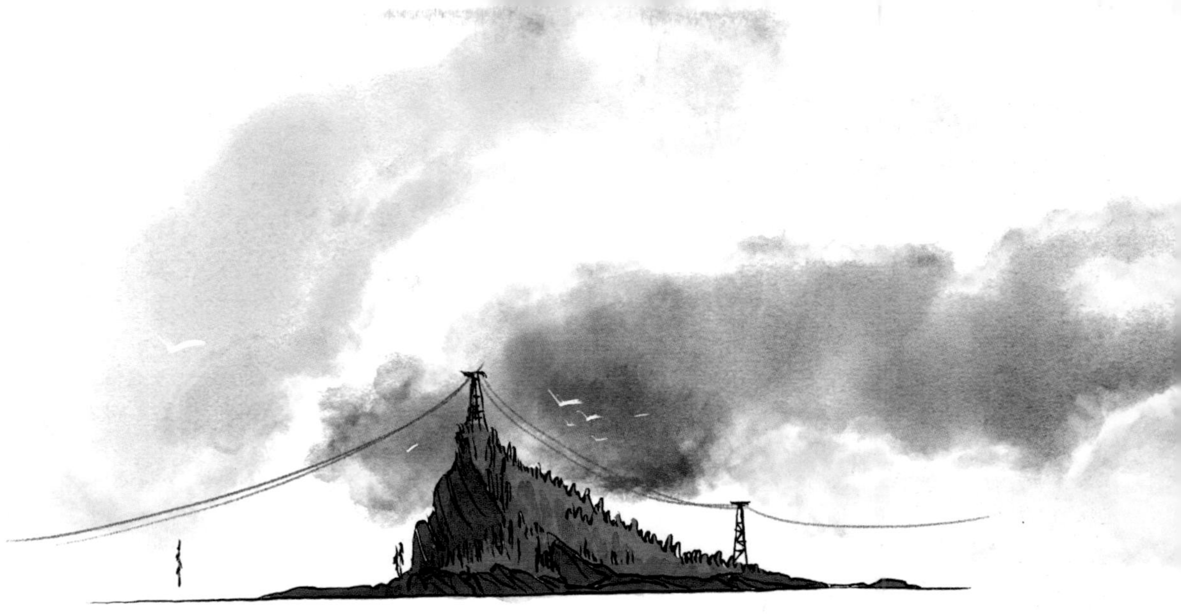

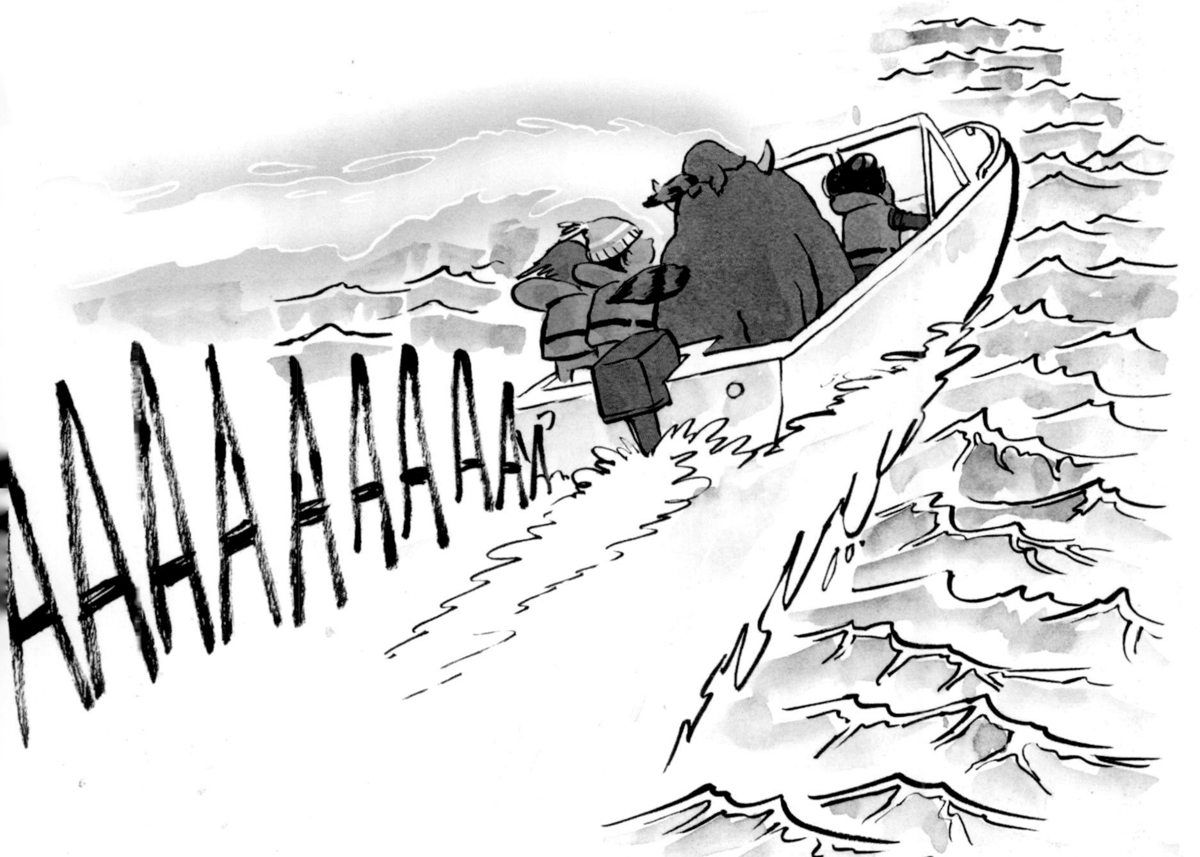
AAAAAAAAAA

CHAPTER FOUR

Wet Socks

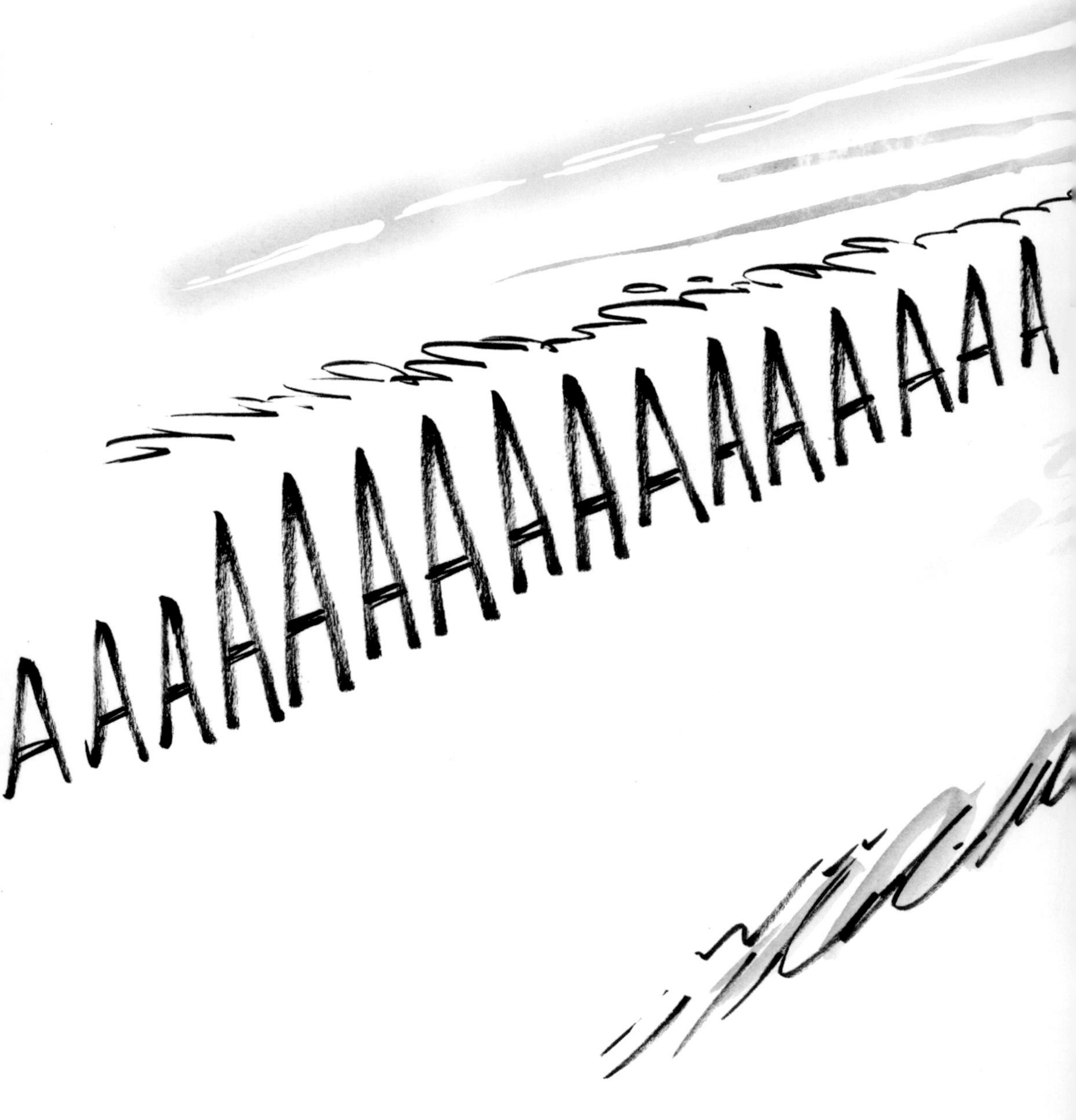

AAAAAAAAAAAAAAAA

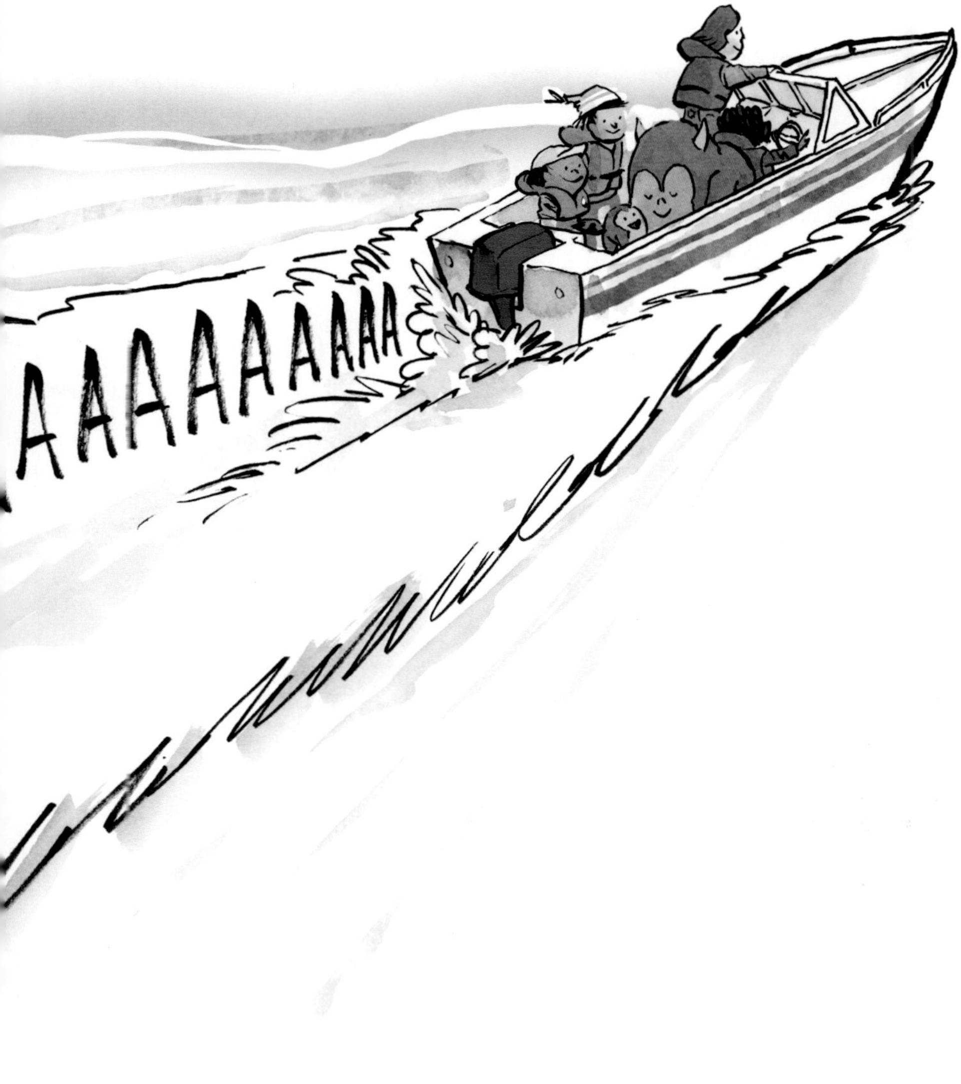
AAAAAAAAAA

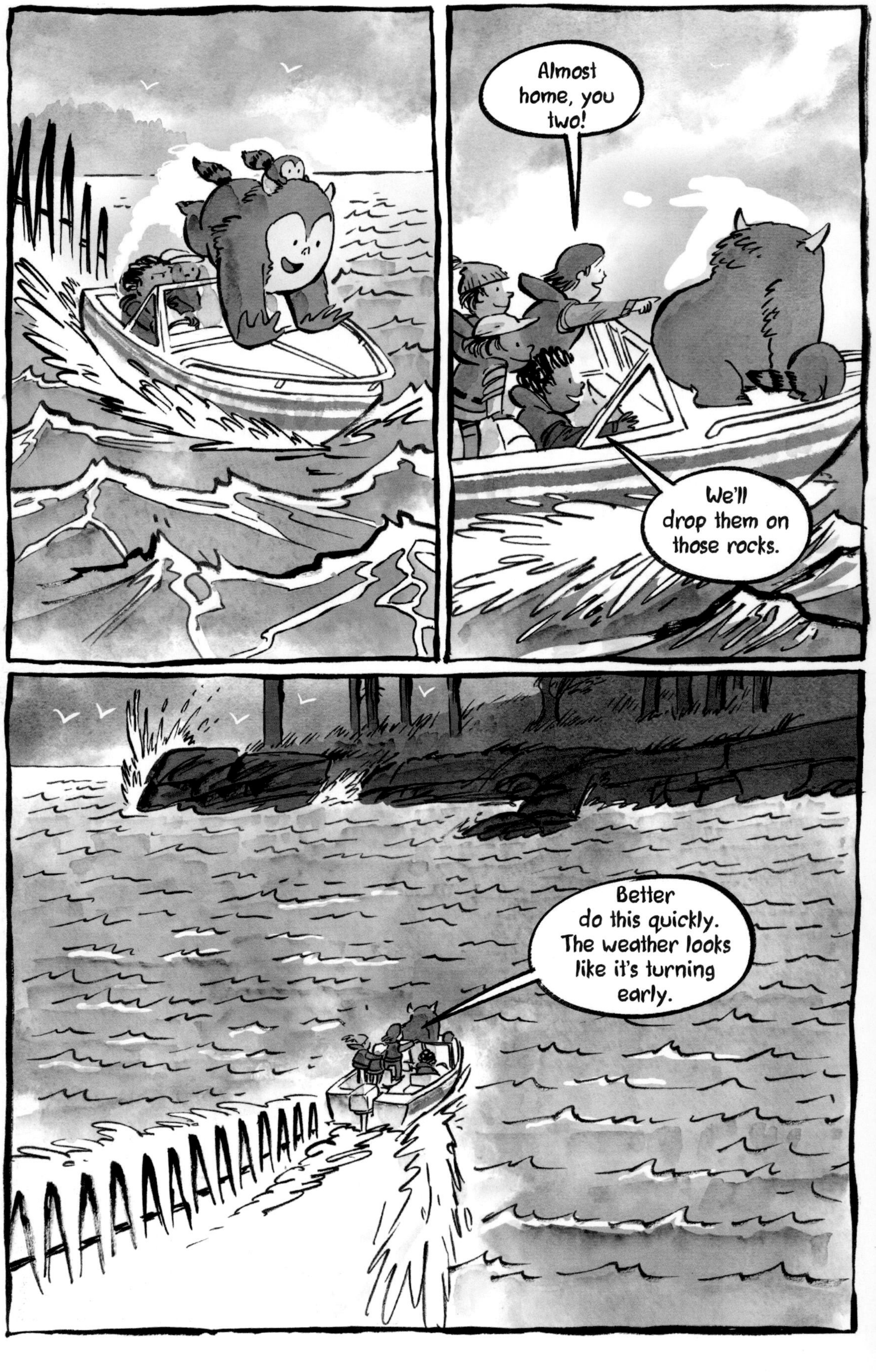
AAAAAA
Almost home, you two!
We'll drop them on those rocks.
Better do this quickly. The weather looks like it's turning early.
AAAAAAAAAAAAAAAAAAAAA

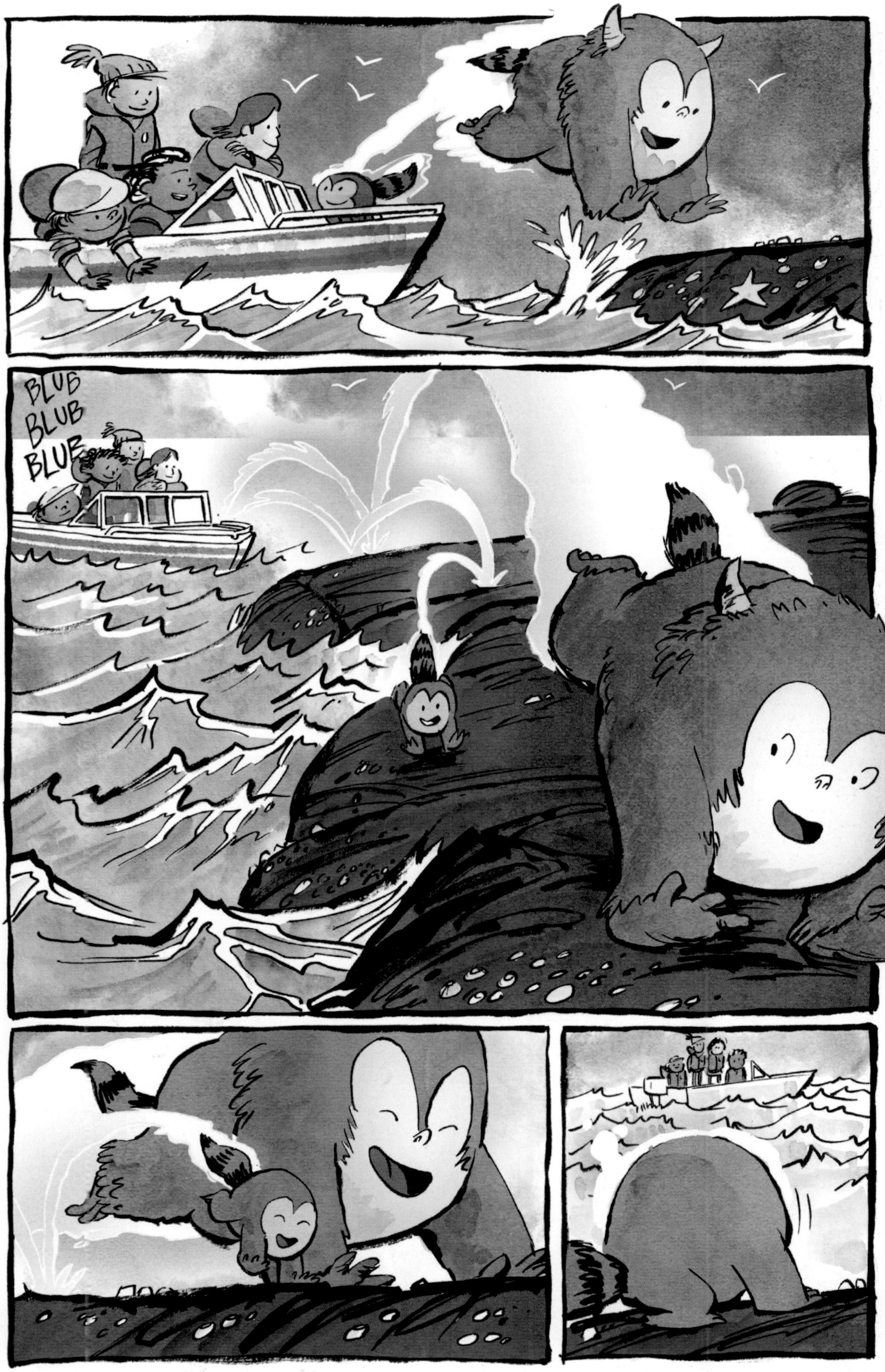
BLUB
BLUB
BLUB

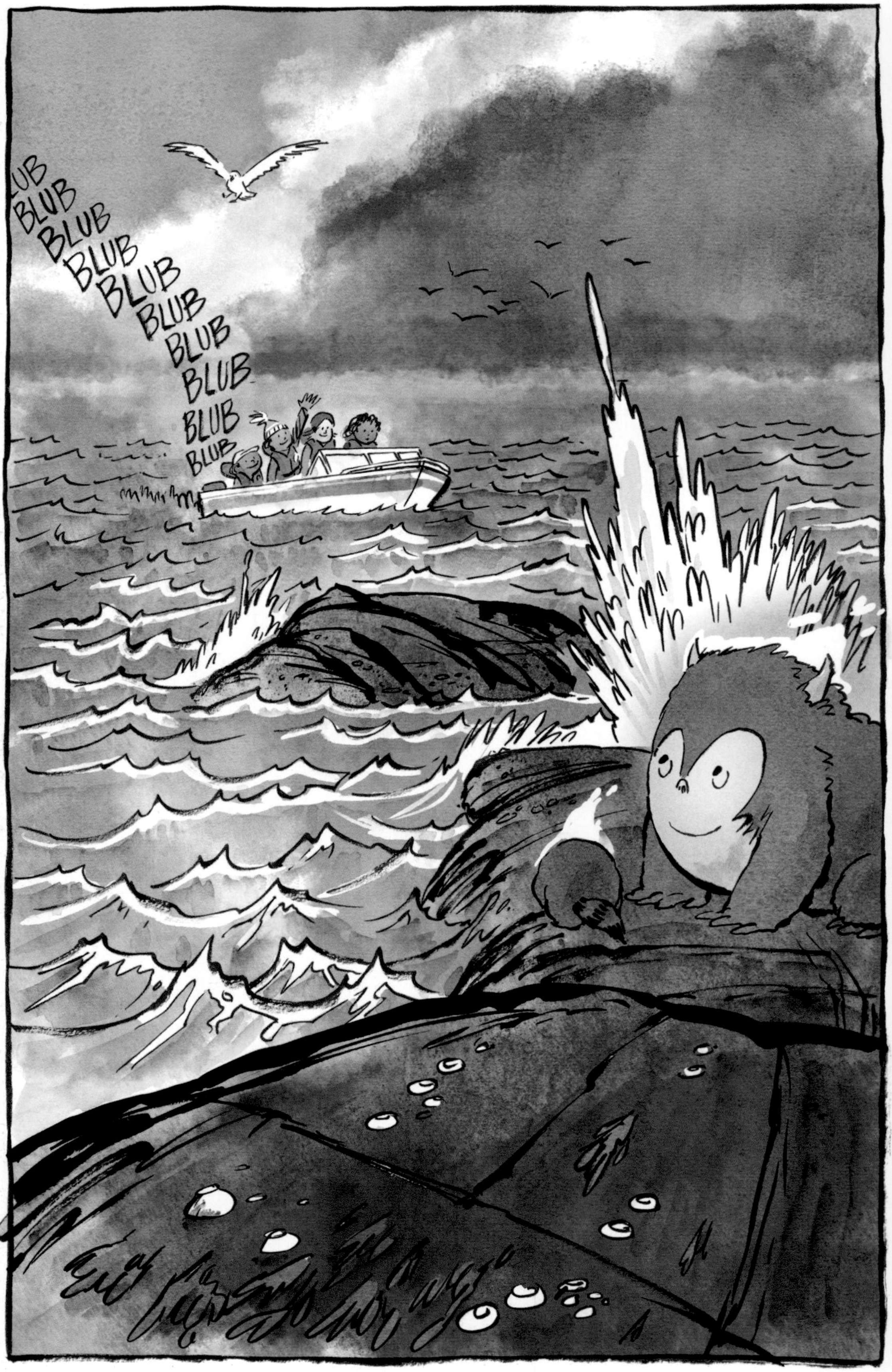
LUB
BLUB
BLUB
BLUB
BLUB
BLUB
BLUB
BLUB
BLUB
BLUB

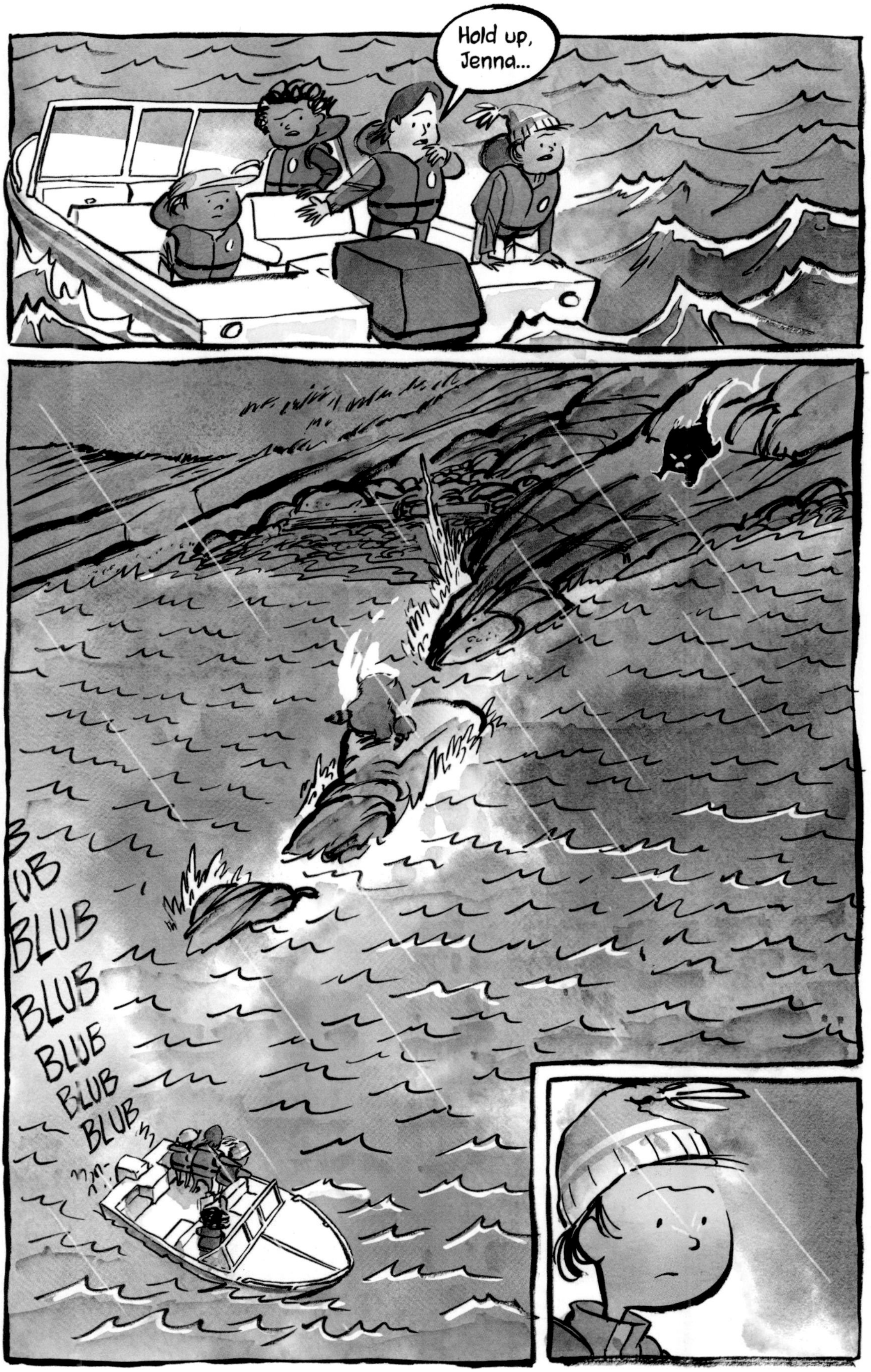
Hold up, Jenna...
BLUB
BLUB
BLUB
BLUB
BLUB
BLUB
BLUB

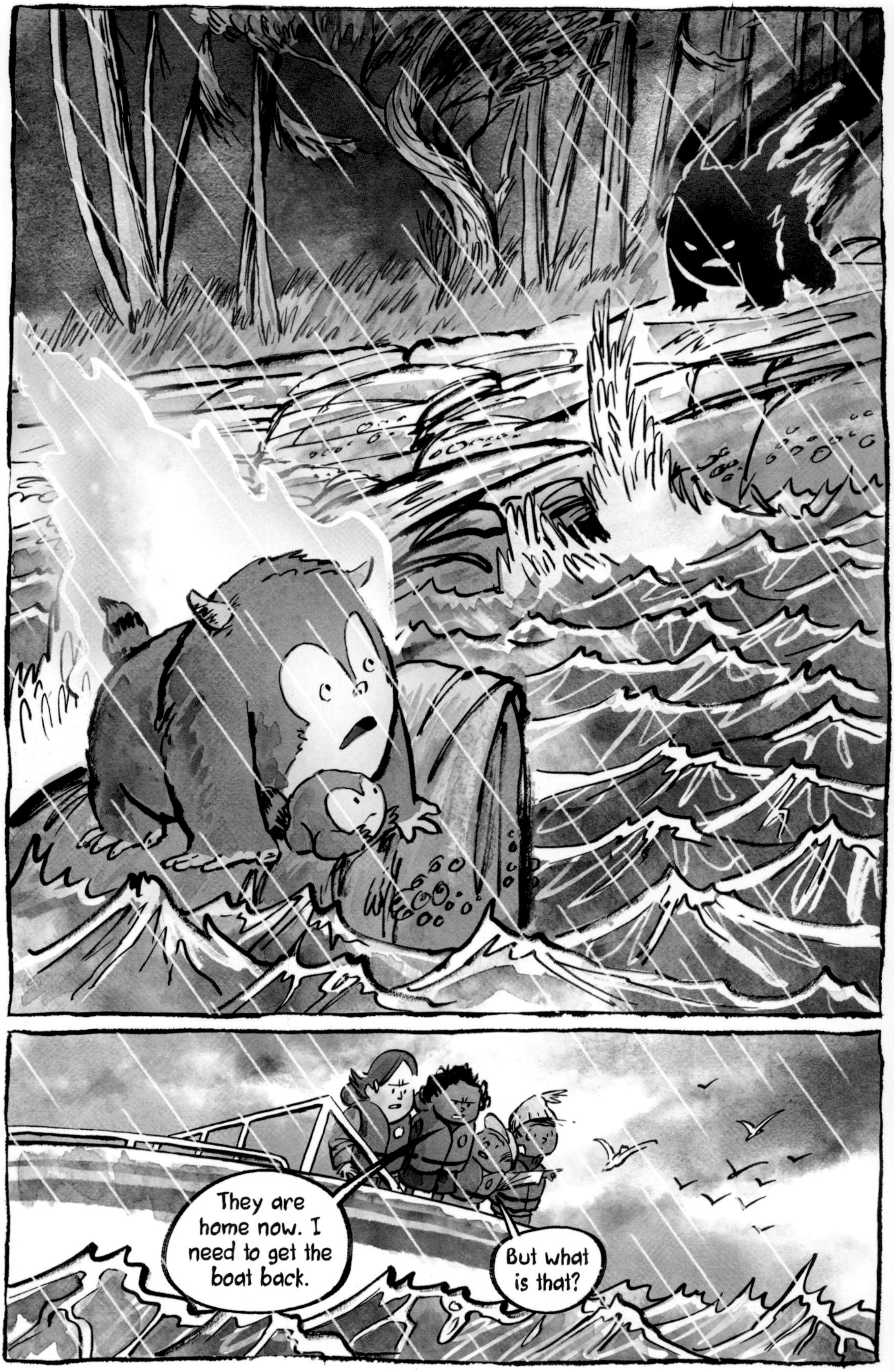
They are home now. I need to get the boat back.
But what is that?

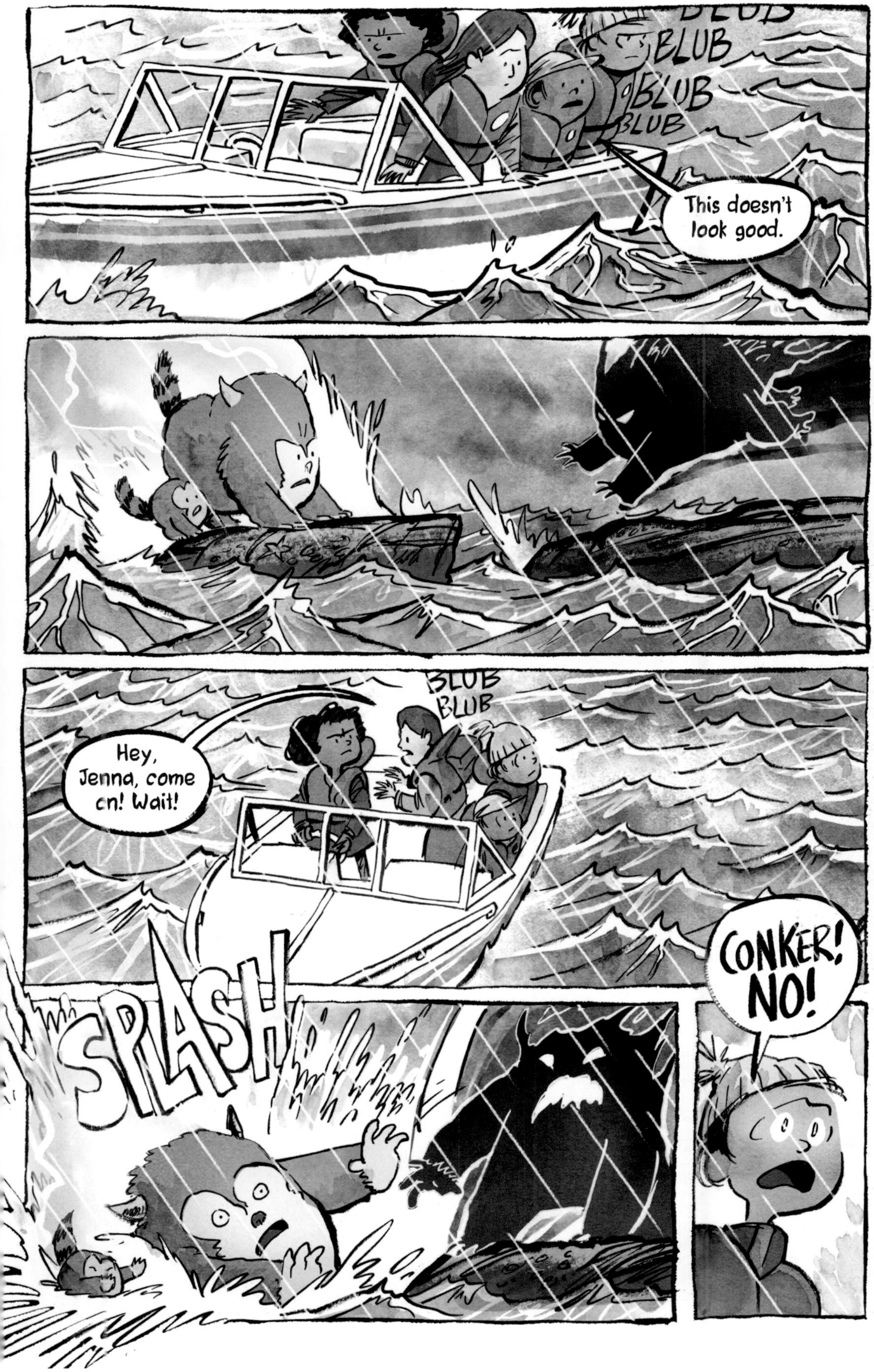
BLUB
BLUB
BLUB
BLUB
This doesn't look good.
BLUB
BLUB
Hey, Jenna, come on! Wait!
SPLASH
CONKER! NO!

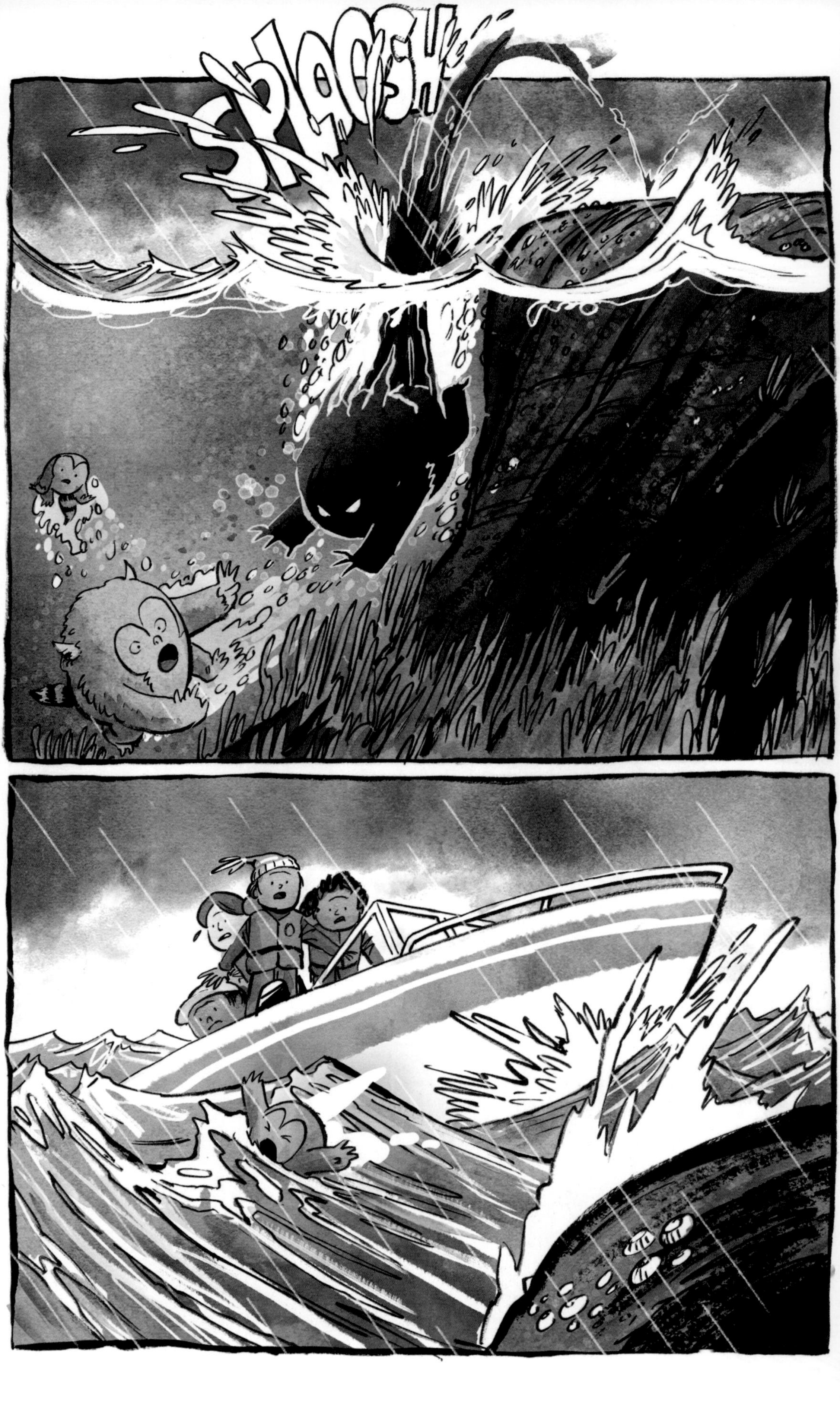
SPLOOSH

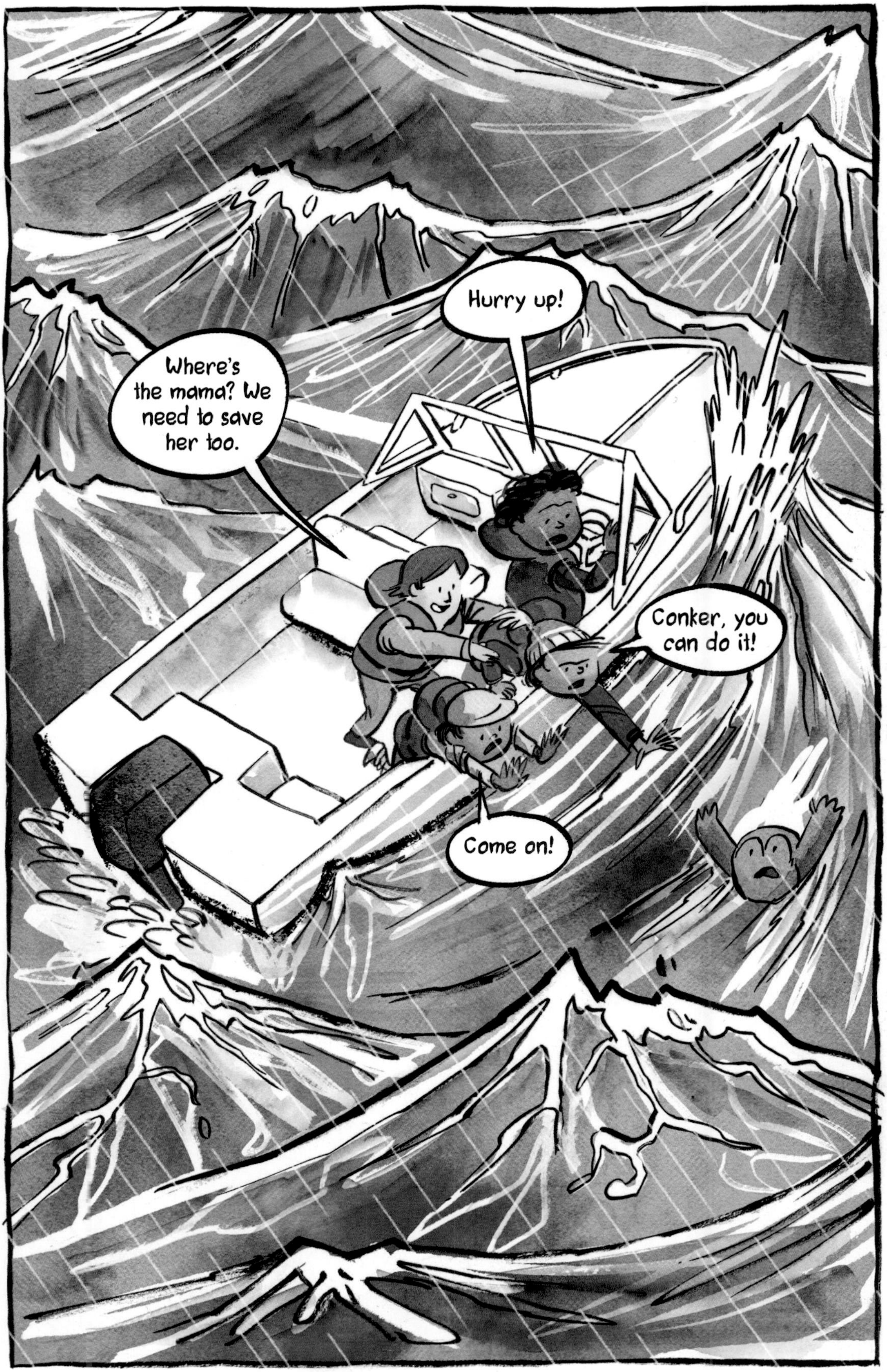
Hurry up!
Where's the mama? We need to save her too.
Conker, you can do it!
Come on!

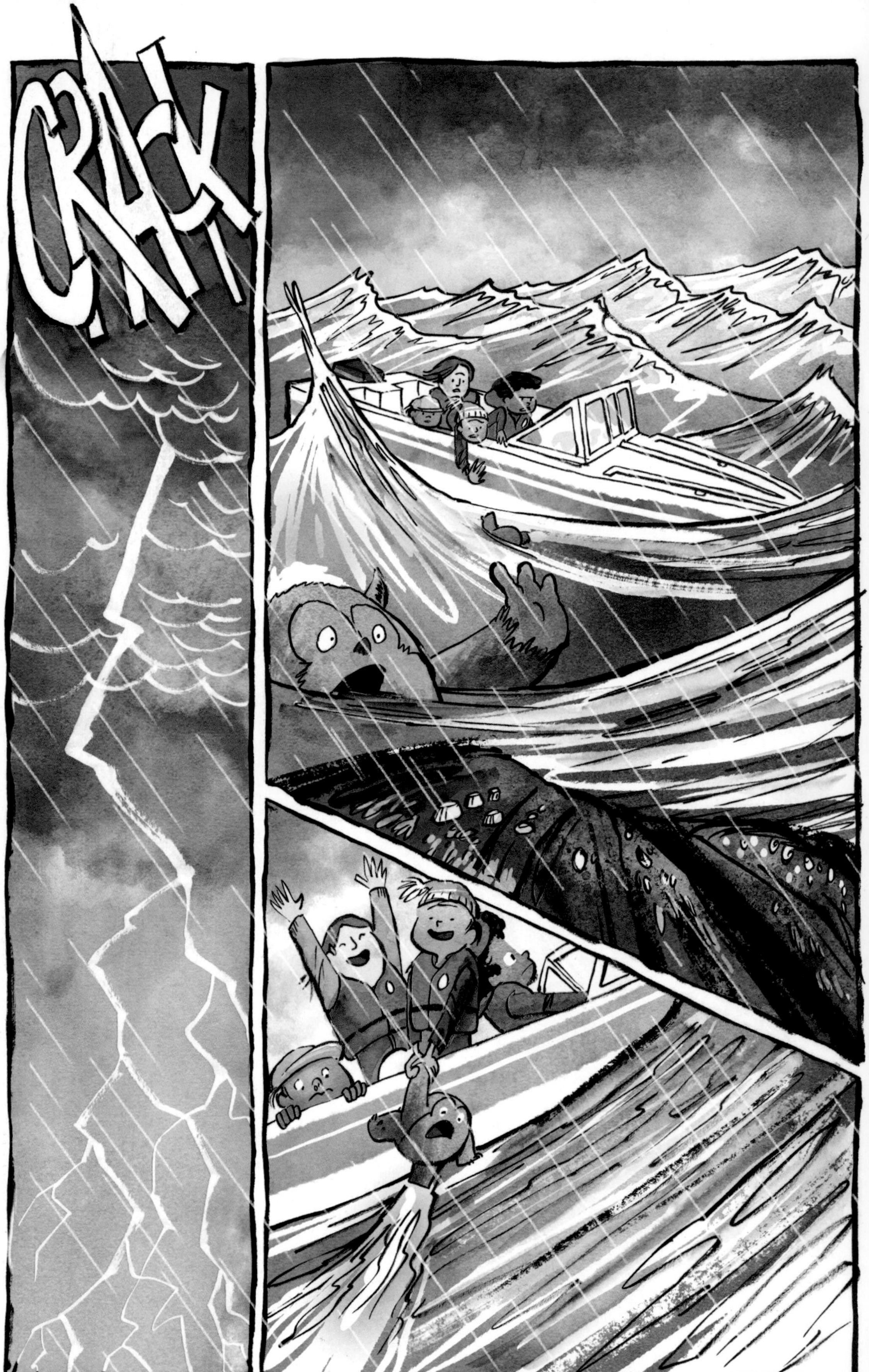
CRACK

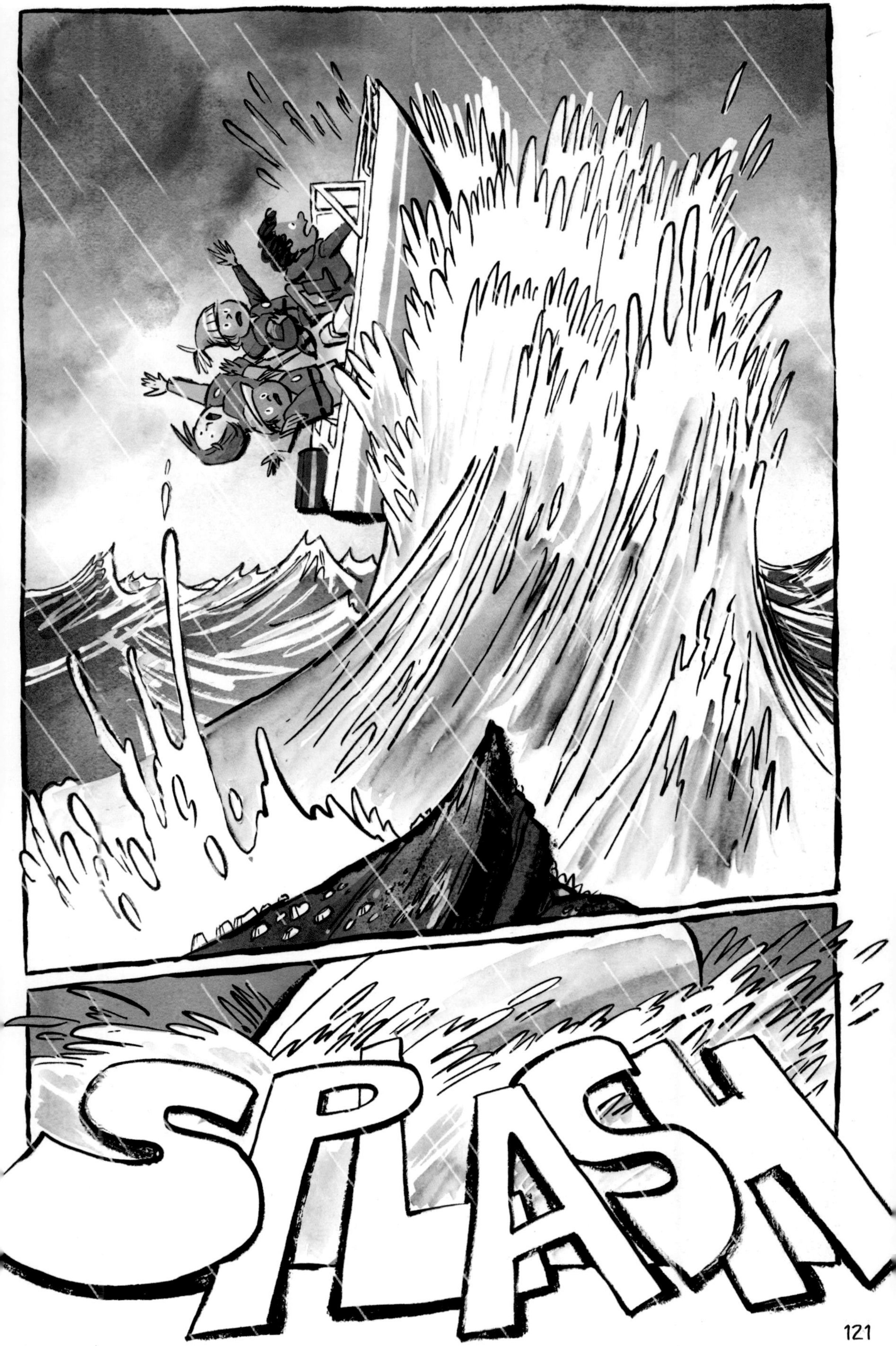
SPLASH

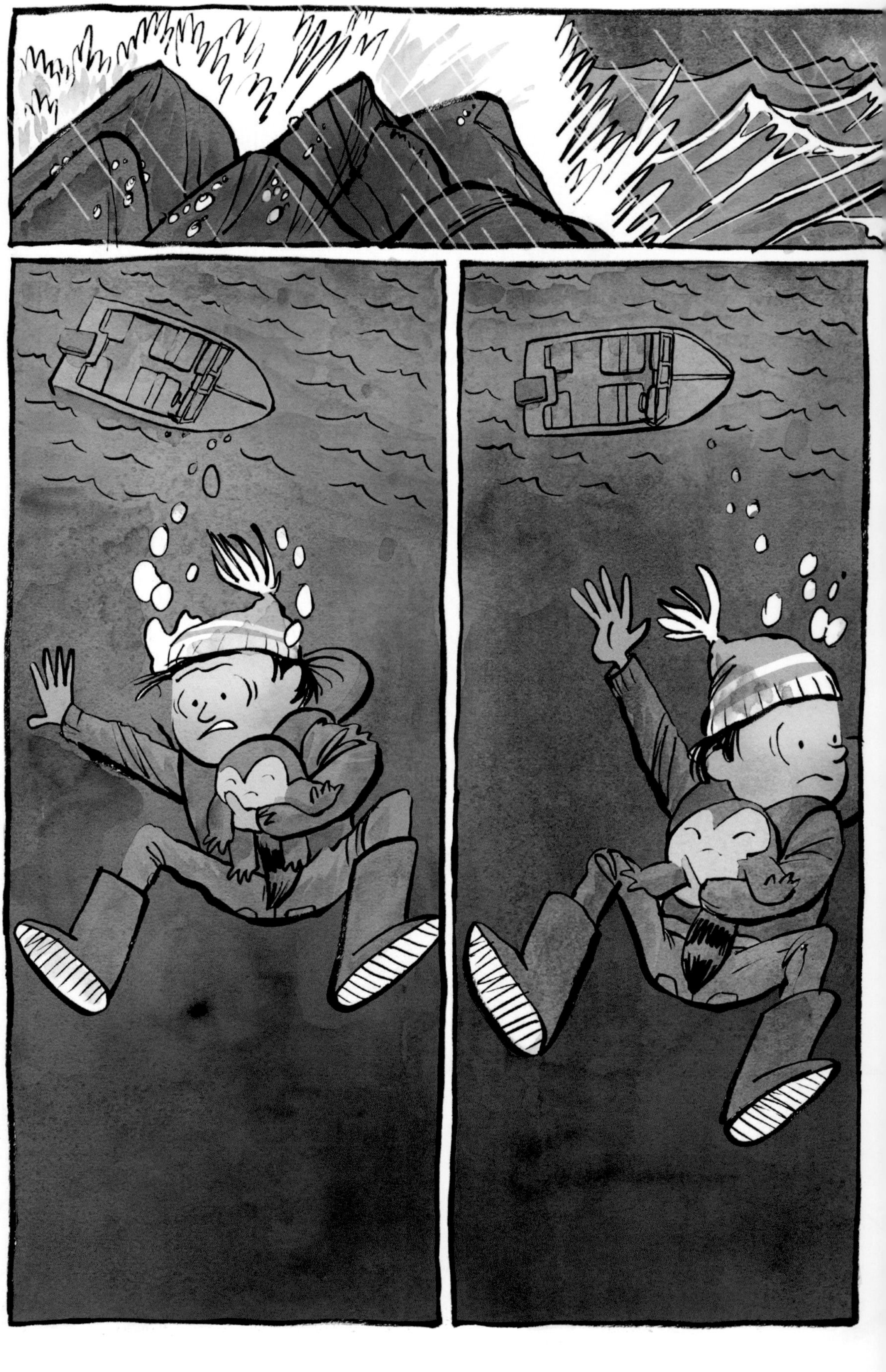

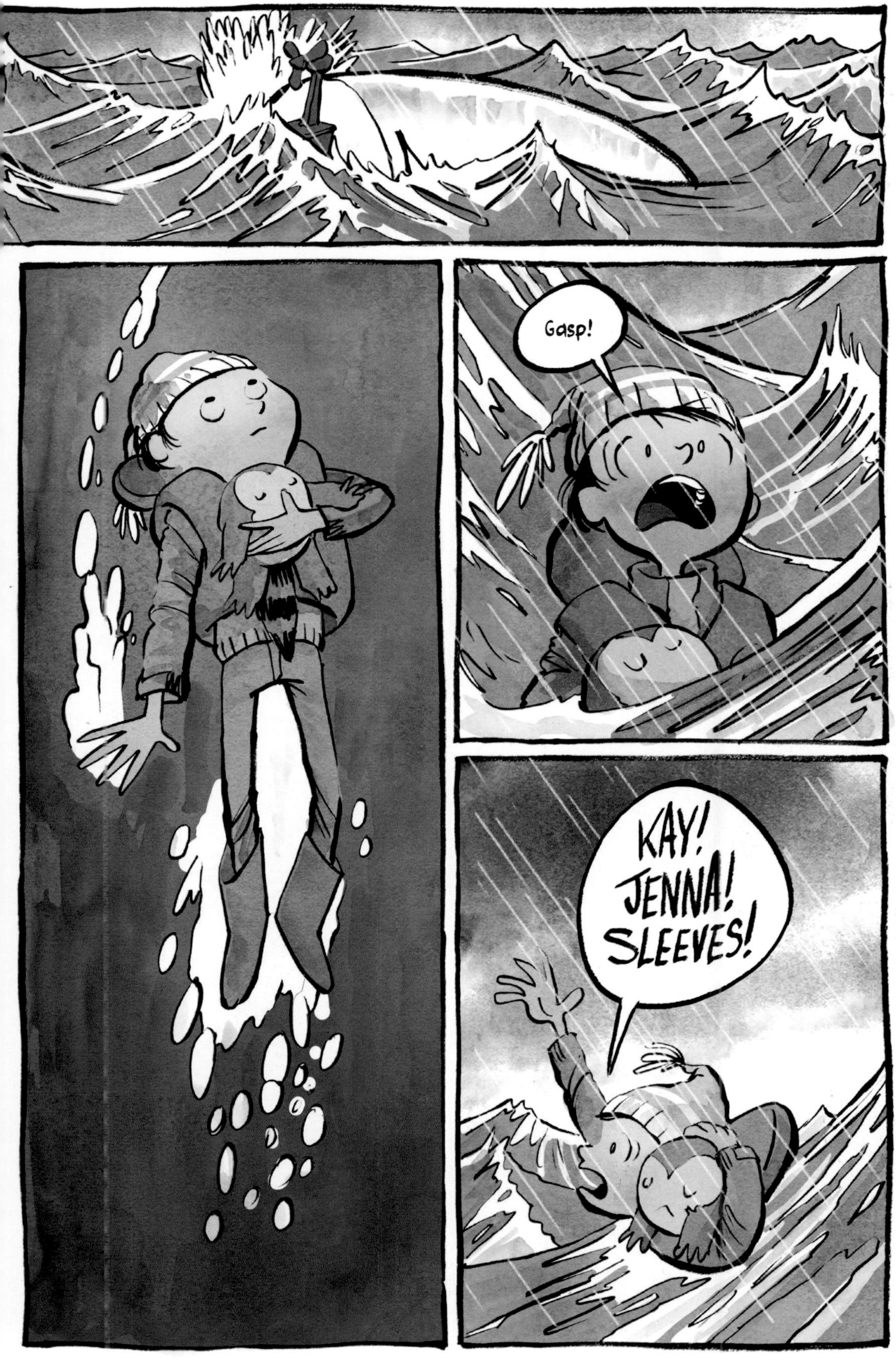
Gasp!
KAY! JENNA! SLEEVES!

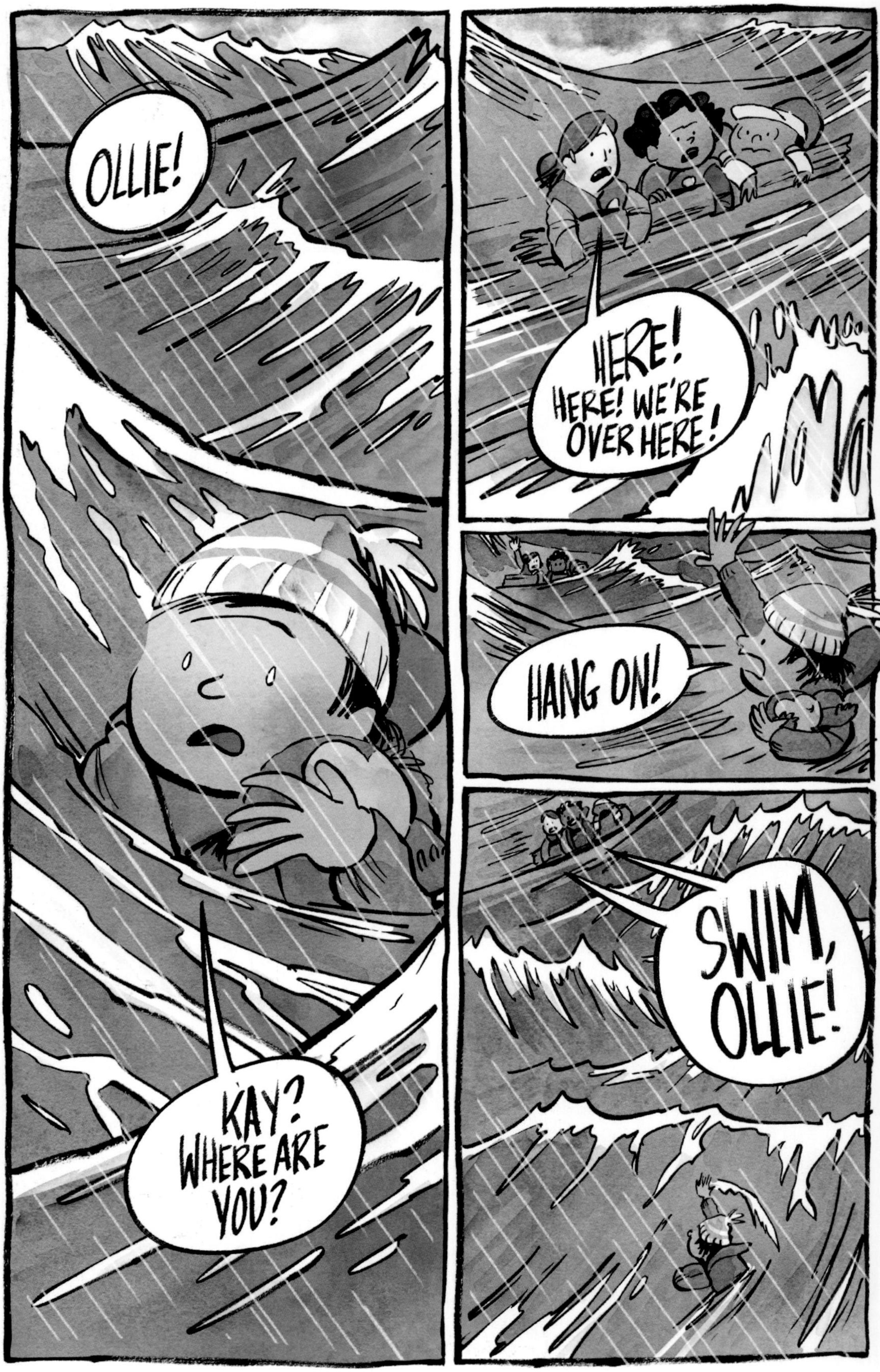
OLLIE!
KAY? WHERE ARE YOU?
HERE! HERE! WE'RE OVER HERE!
HANG ON!
SWIM, OLLIE!

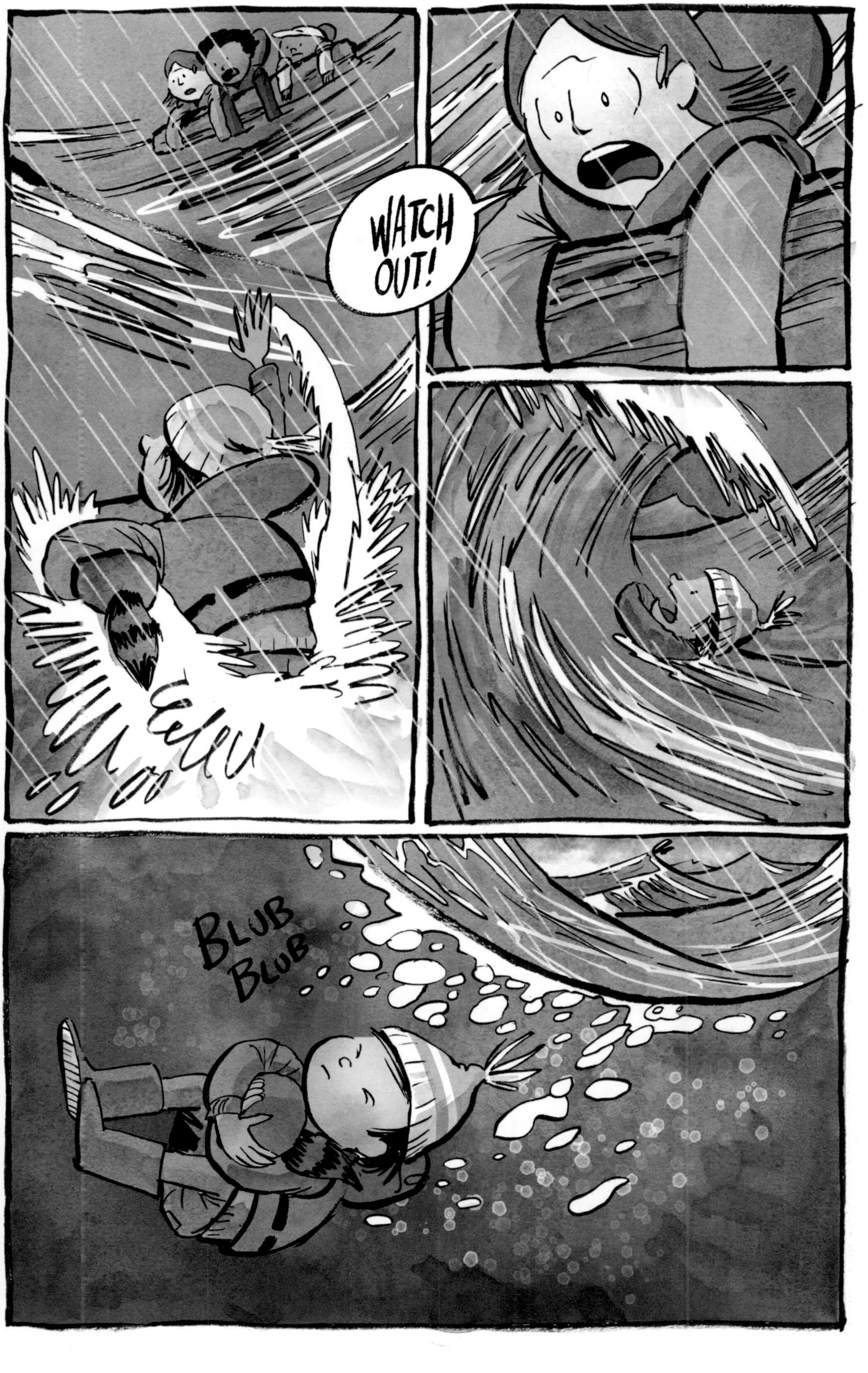
WATCH OUT!
BLUB BLUB

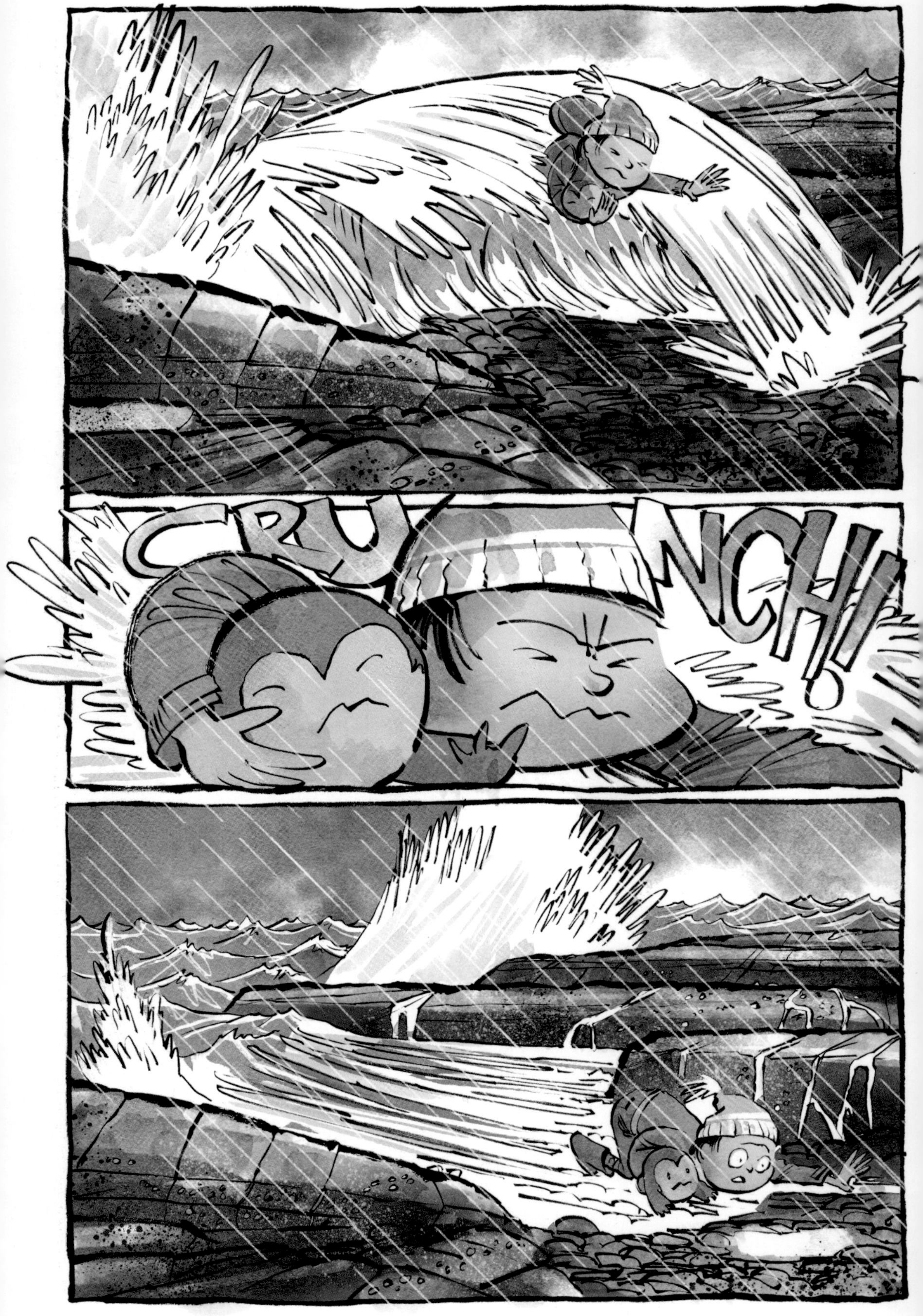
CRUNCH!

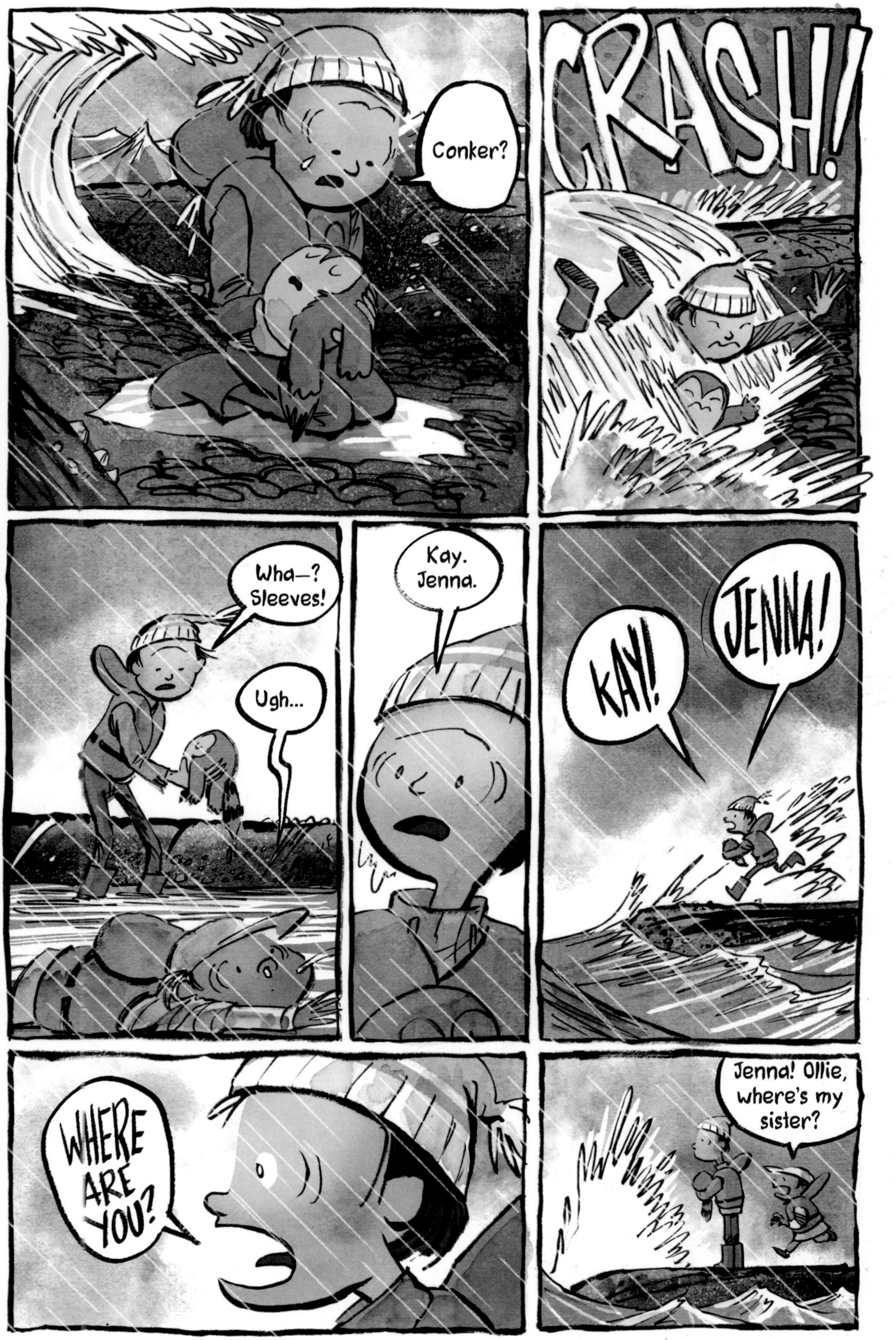
Conker?
CRASH!
Wha—? Sleeves!
Ugh...
Kay. Jenna.
KAY!
JENNA!
WHERE ARE YOU?
Jenna! Ollie, where's my sister?

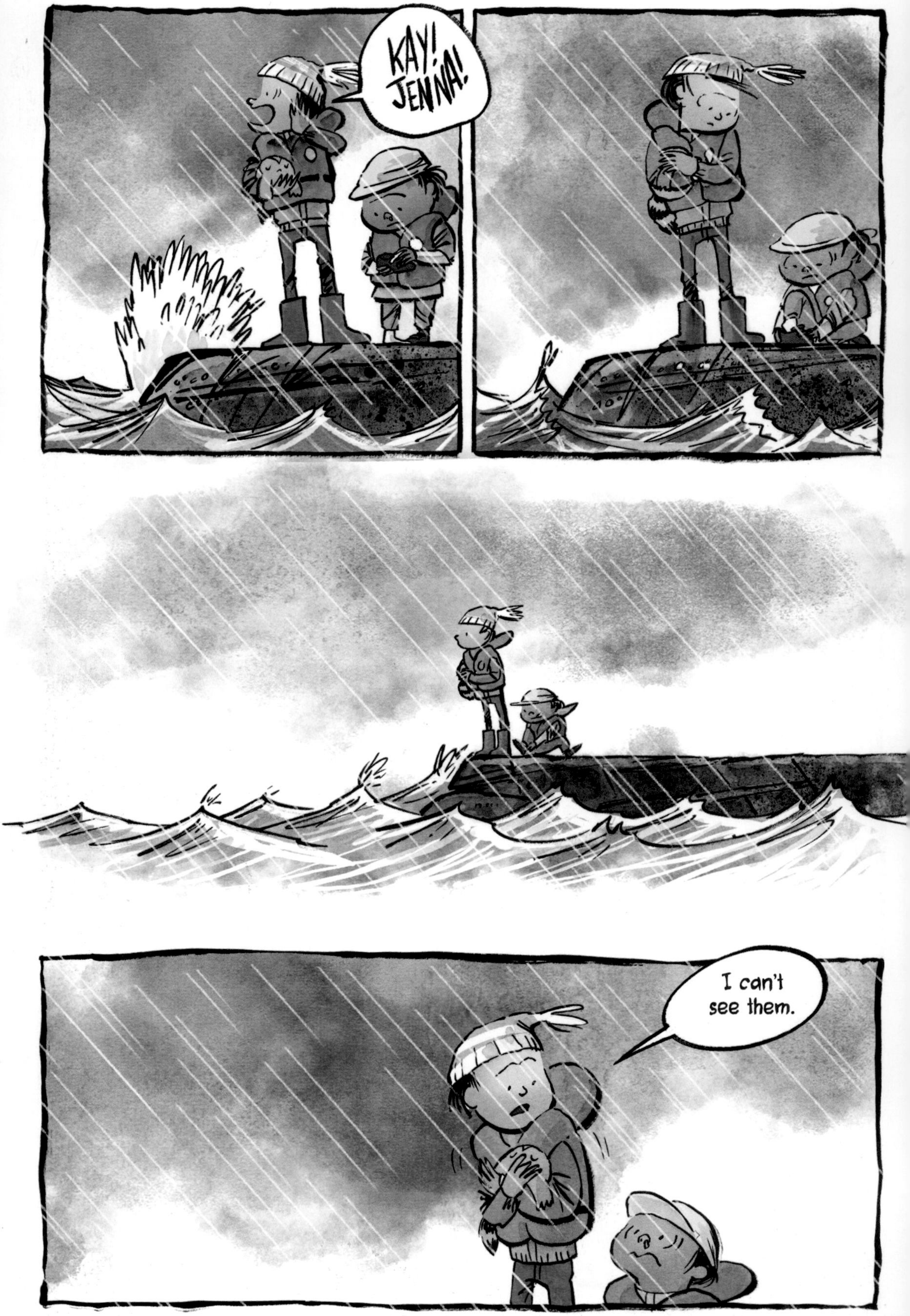
KAY! JENNA!
I can't see them.

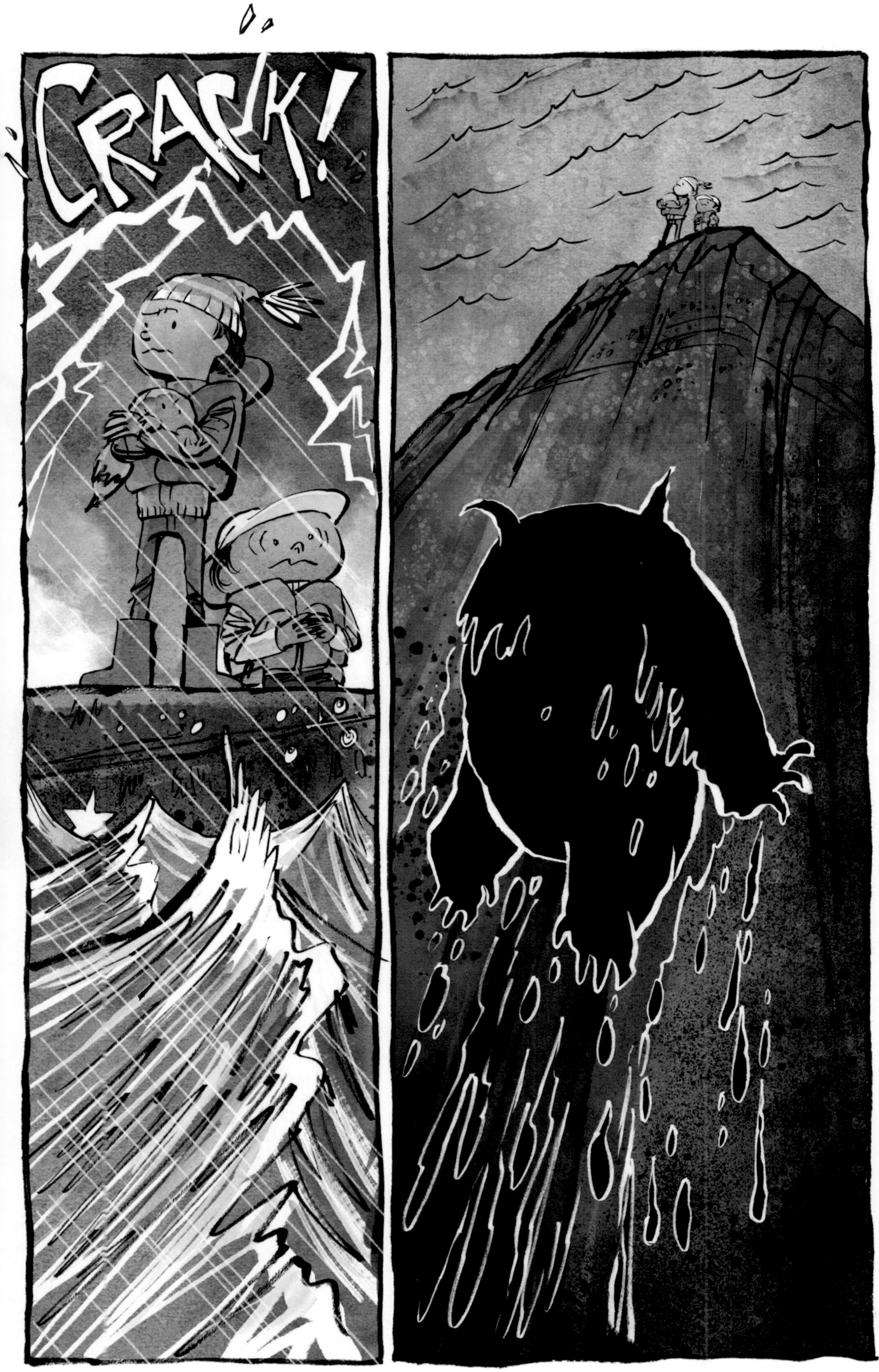
CRACK!

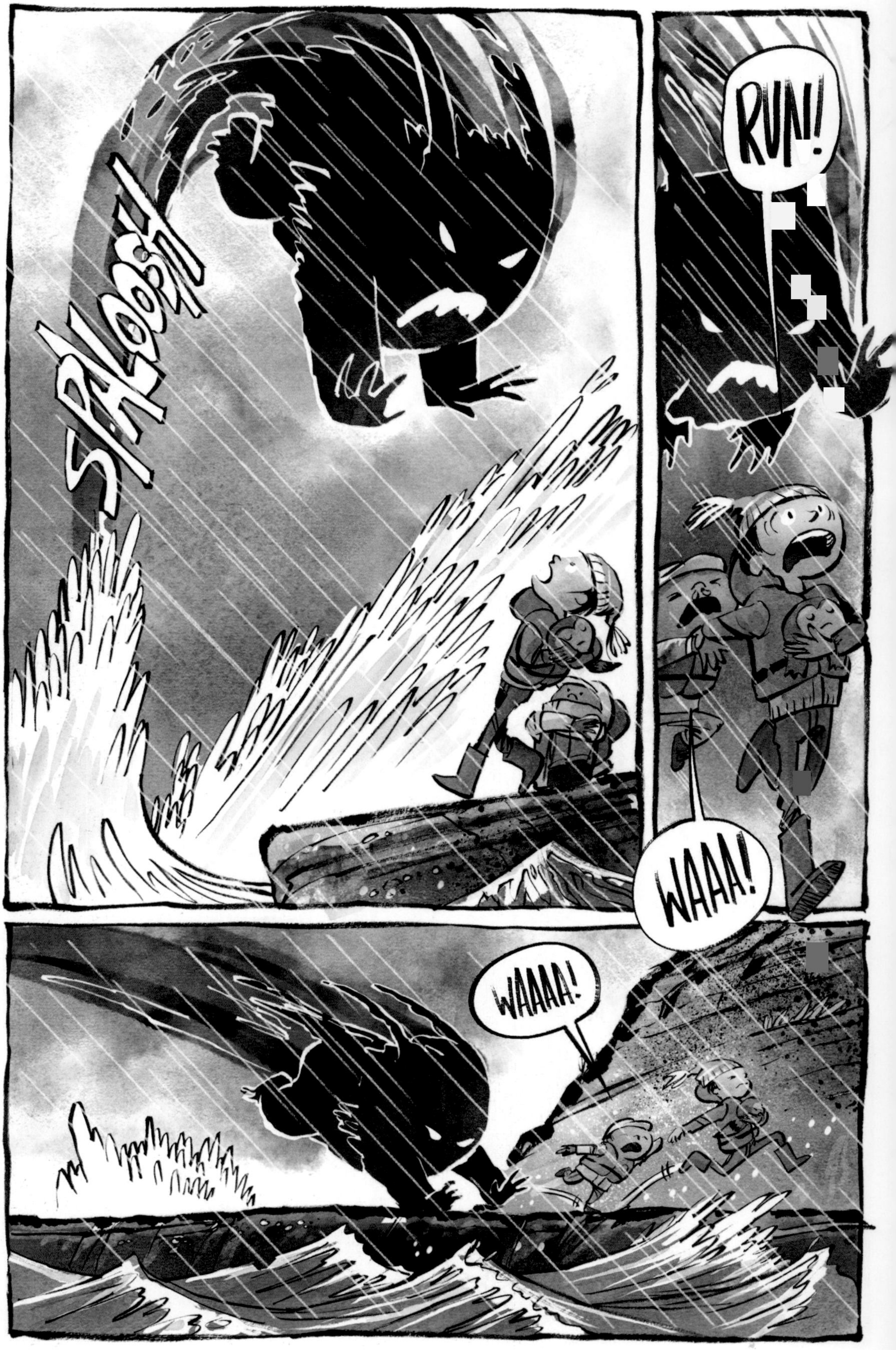
SPLOOSH!
RUN!
WAAA!
WAAAA!

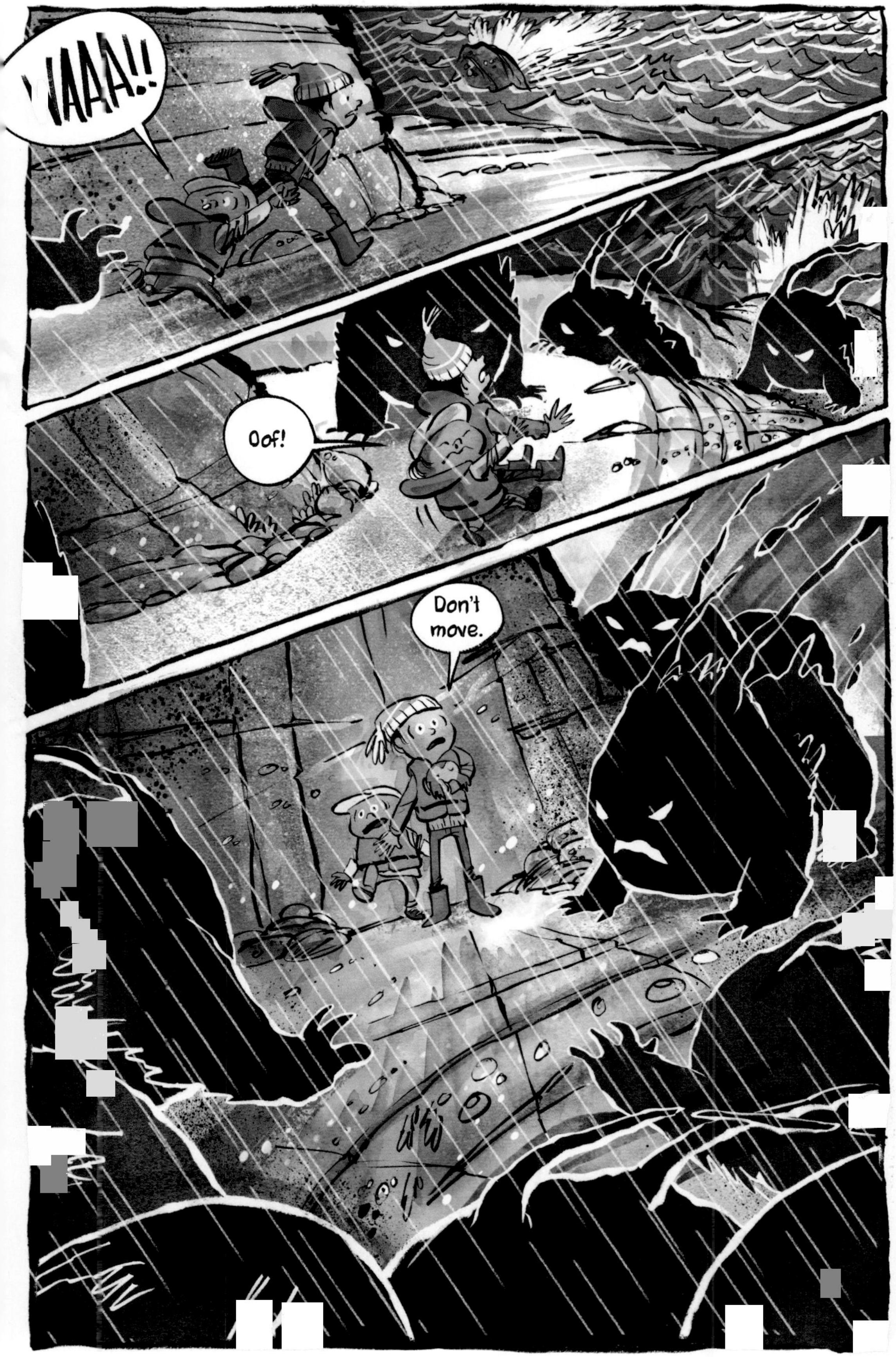
WAAA!!
Oof!
Don't move.

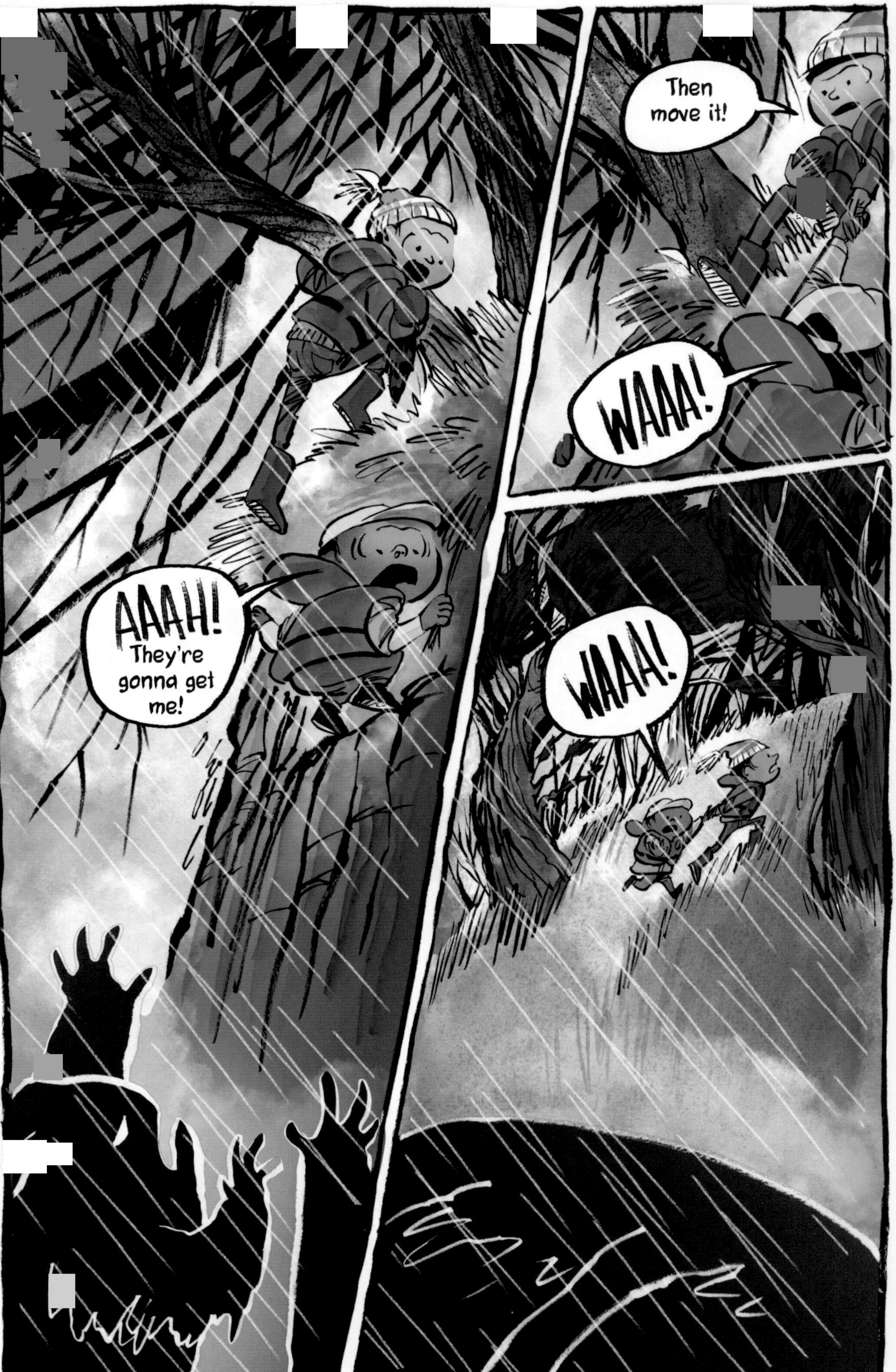
AAAH! They're gonna get me!
Then move it!
WAAA!
WAAA!

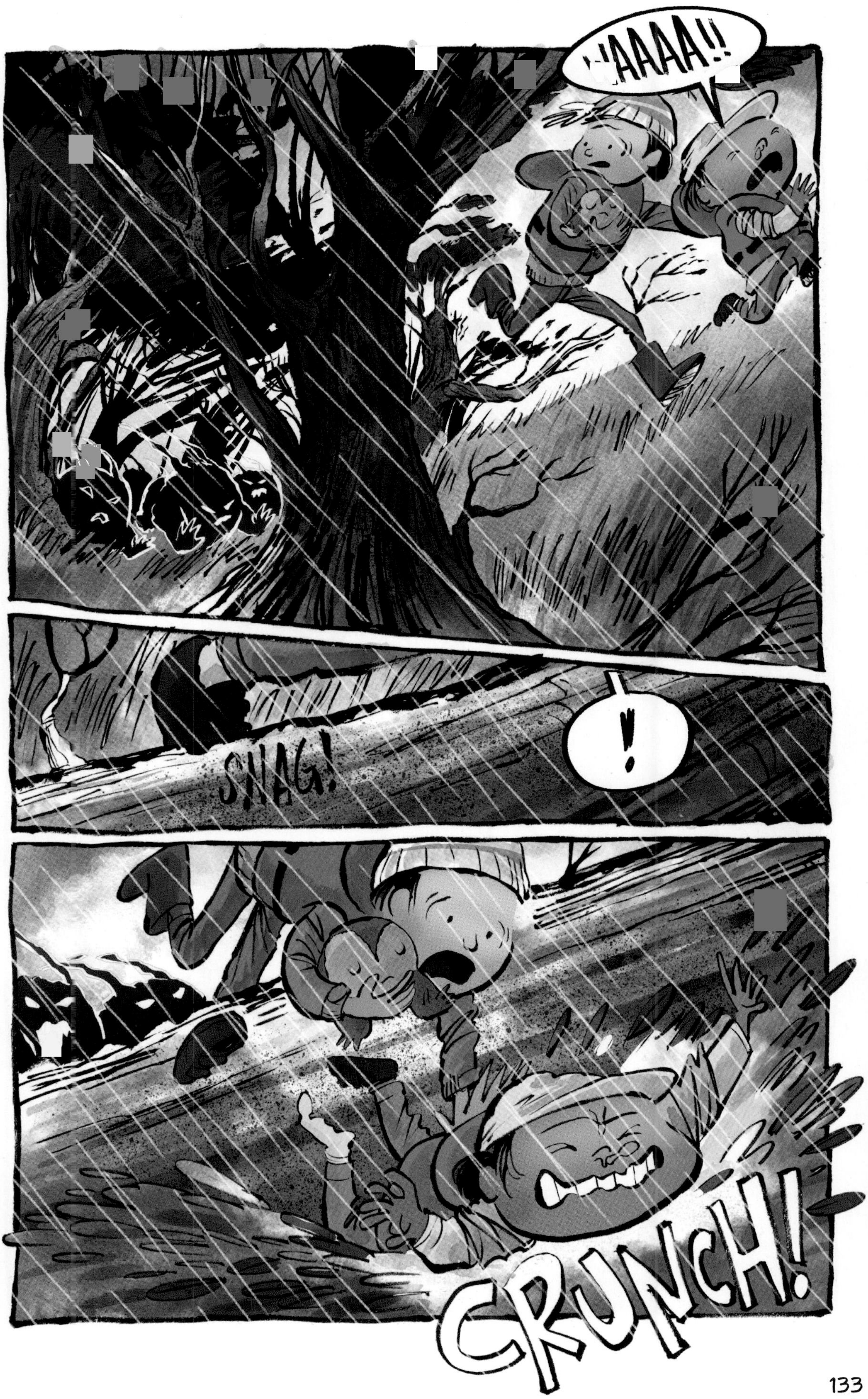
AAAA!!
SNAG!
!
CRUNCH!

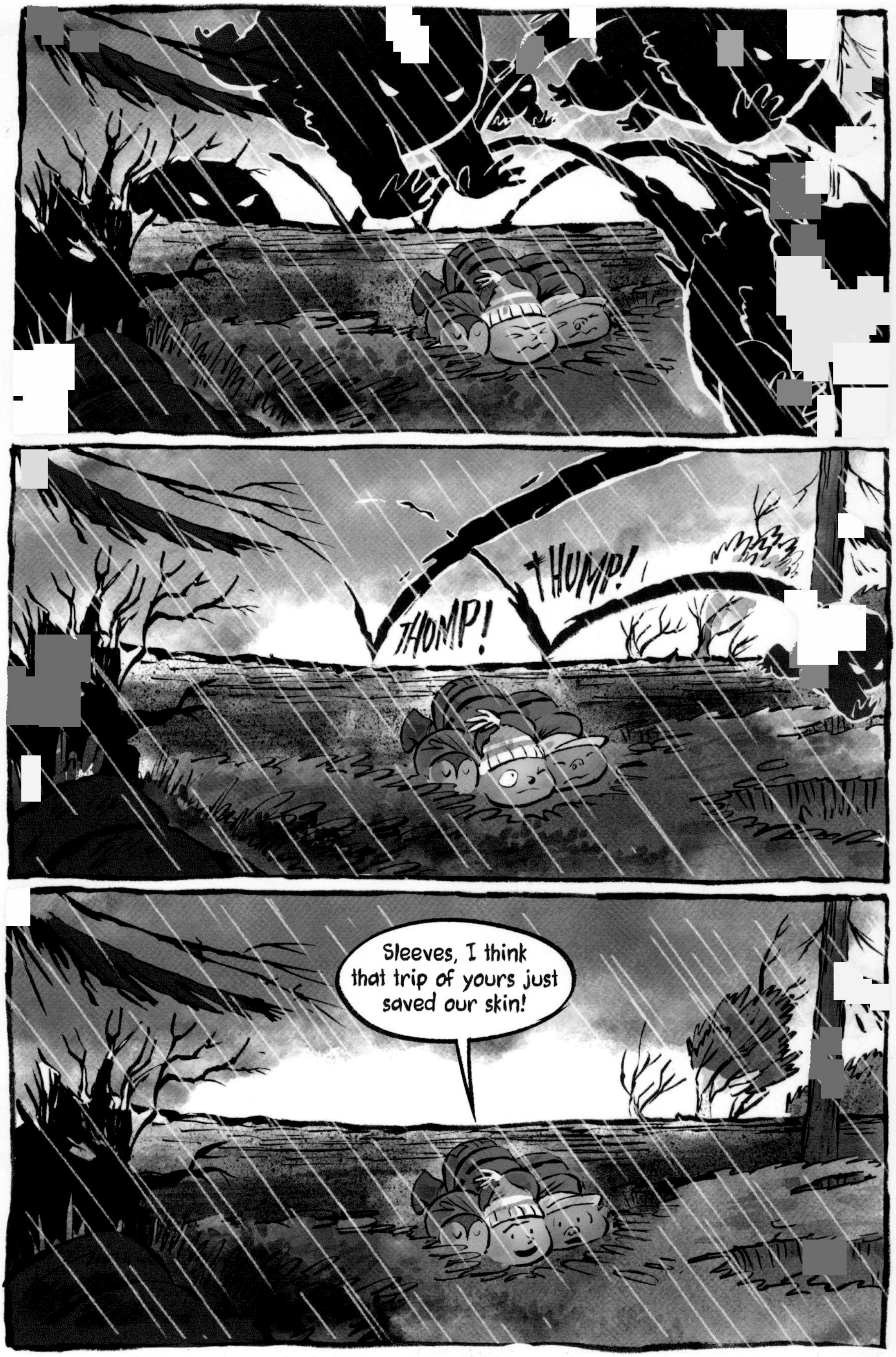
THOMP!
THUMP!
Sleeves, I think that trip of yours just saved our skin!

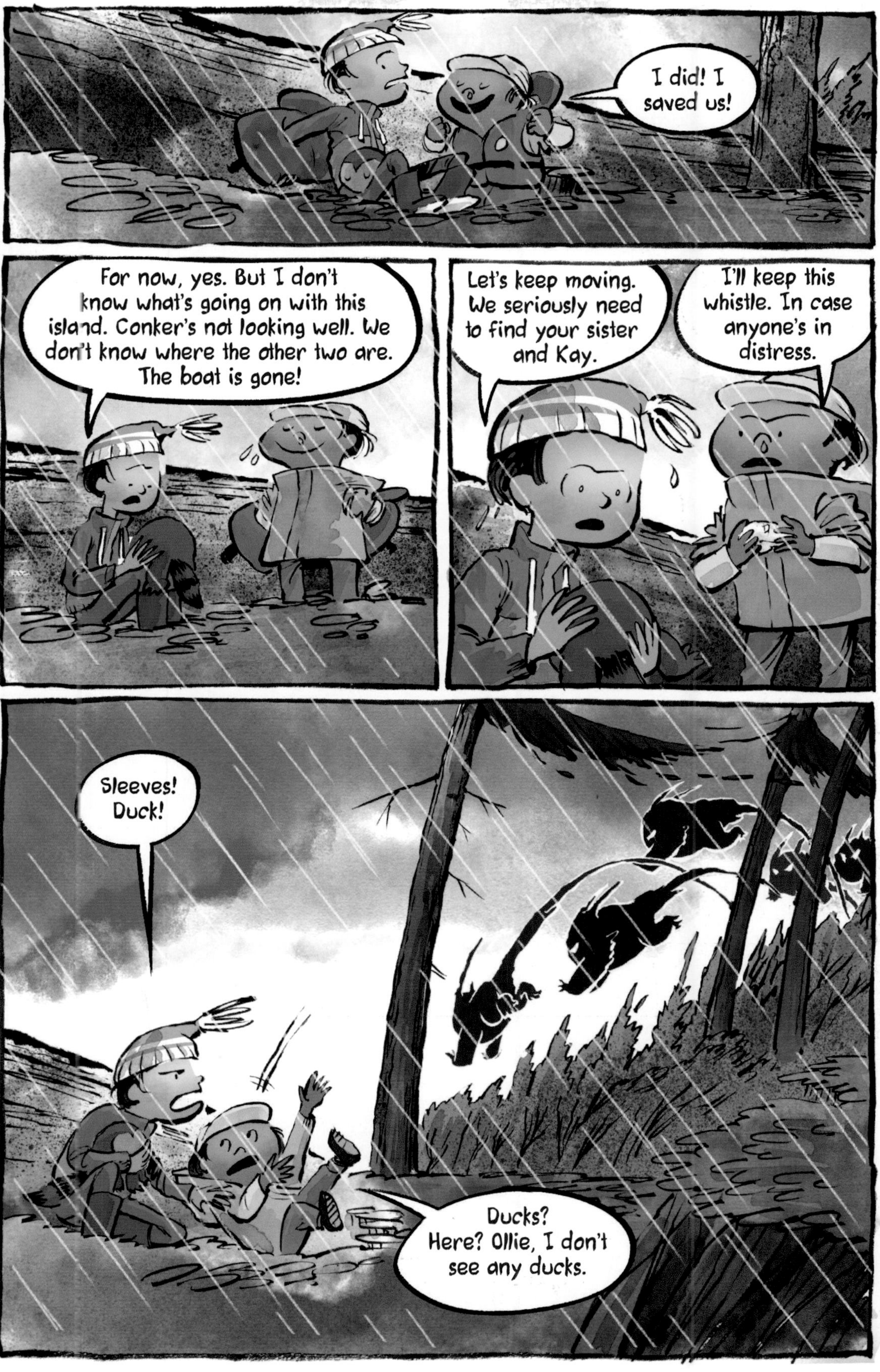
I did! I saved us!
For now, yes. But I don't know what's going on with this island. Conker's not looking well. We don't know where the other two are. The boat is gone!
Let's keep moving. We seriously need to find your sister and Kay.
I'll keep this whistle. In case anyone's in distress.
Sleeves! Duck!
Ducks? Here? Ollie, I don't see any ducks.

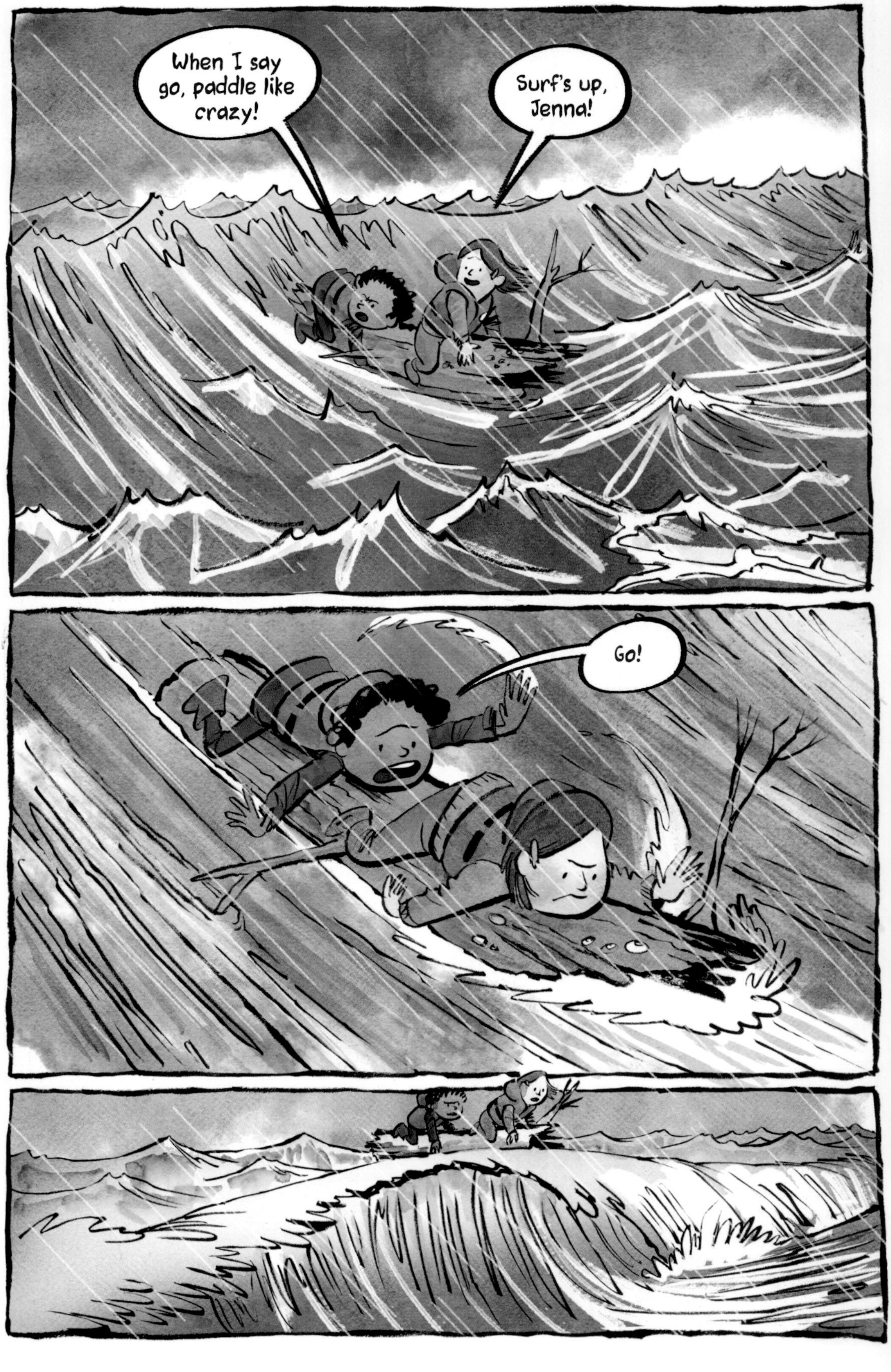
When I say go, paddle like crazy!
Surf's up, Jenna!
Go!

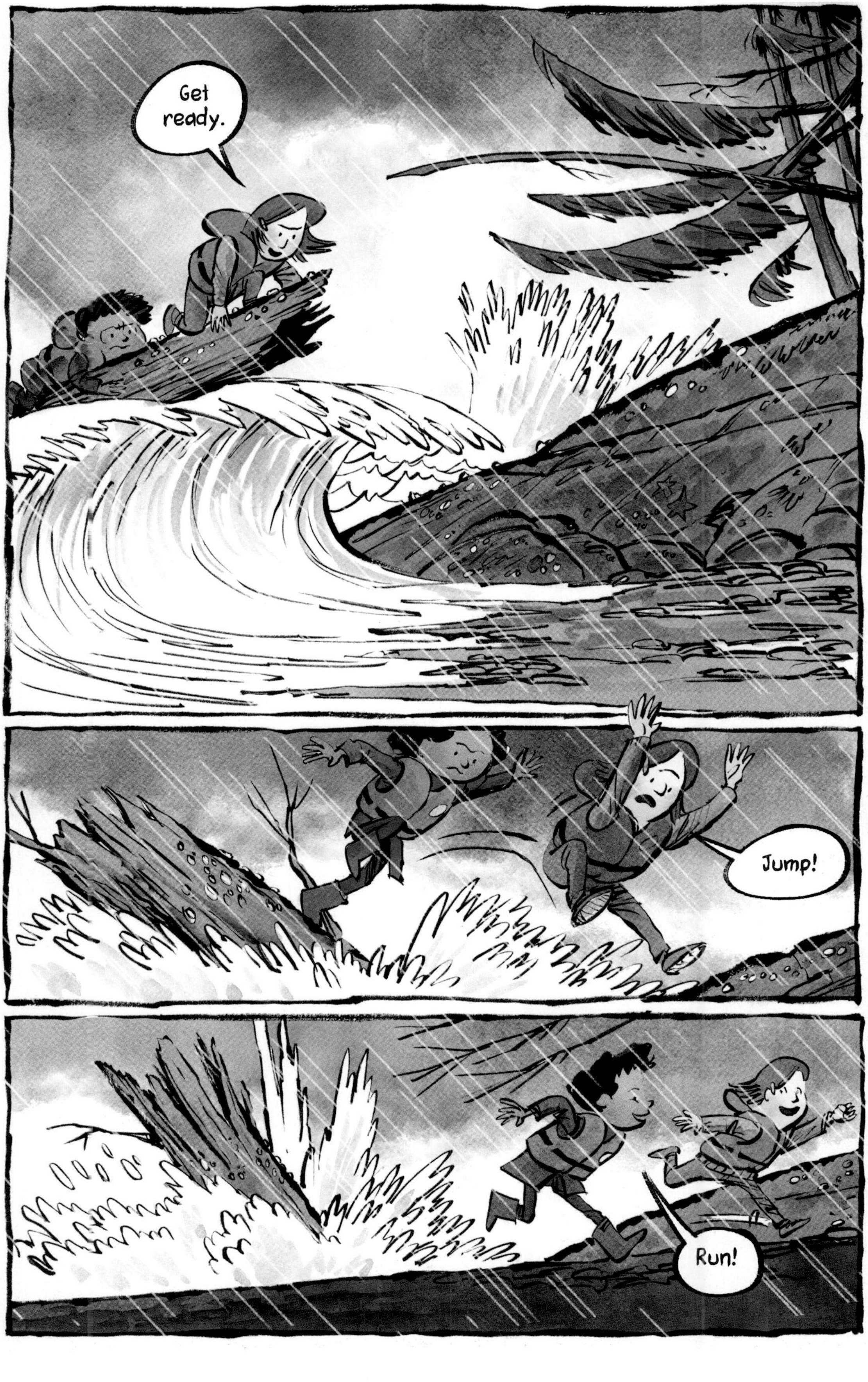
Get ready.
Jump!
Run!

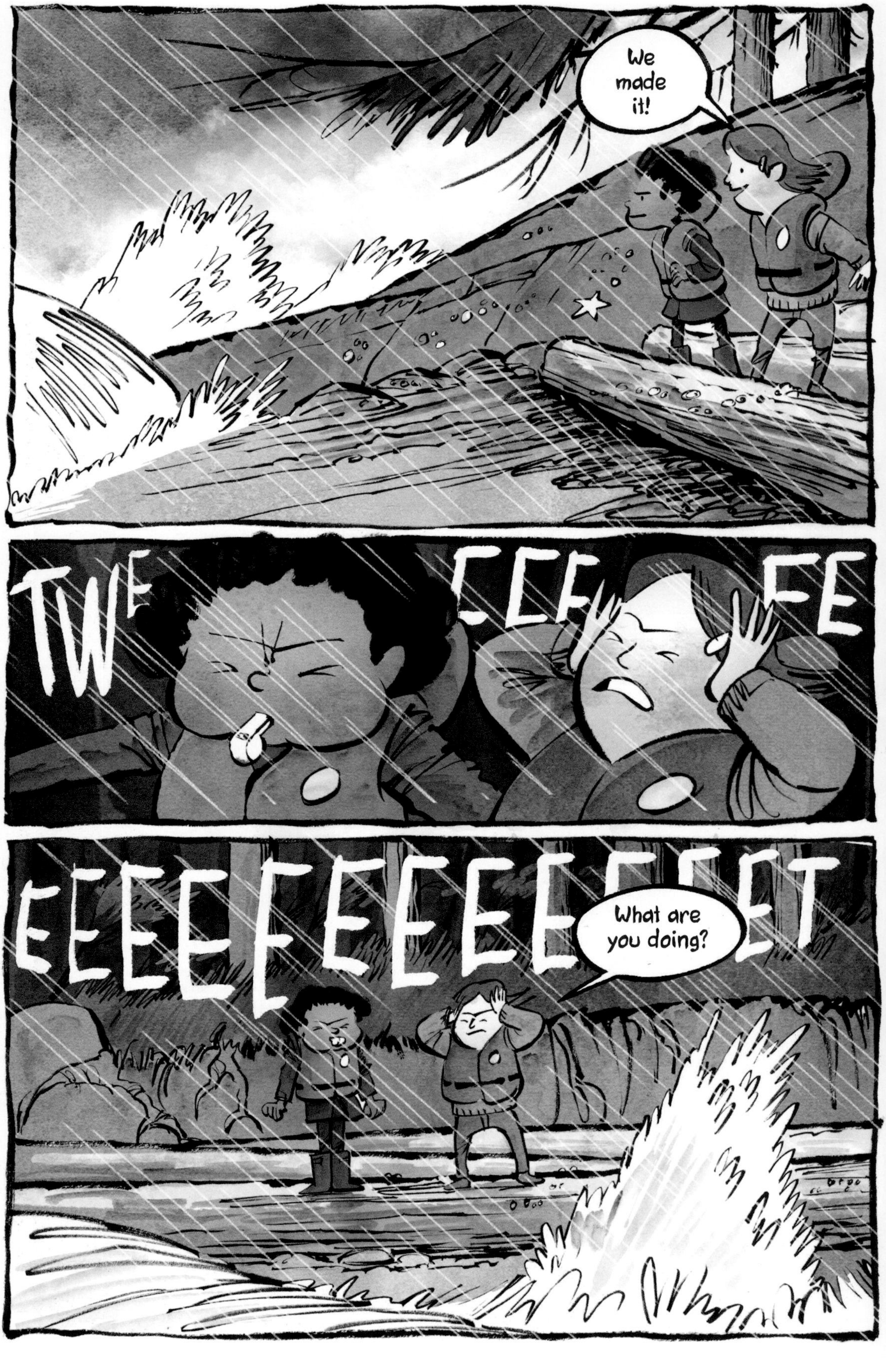
We made it!
TWEEEEEEEEEEEEEEEEEEET
What are you doing?

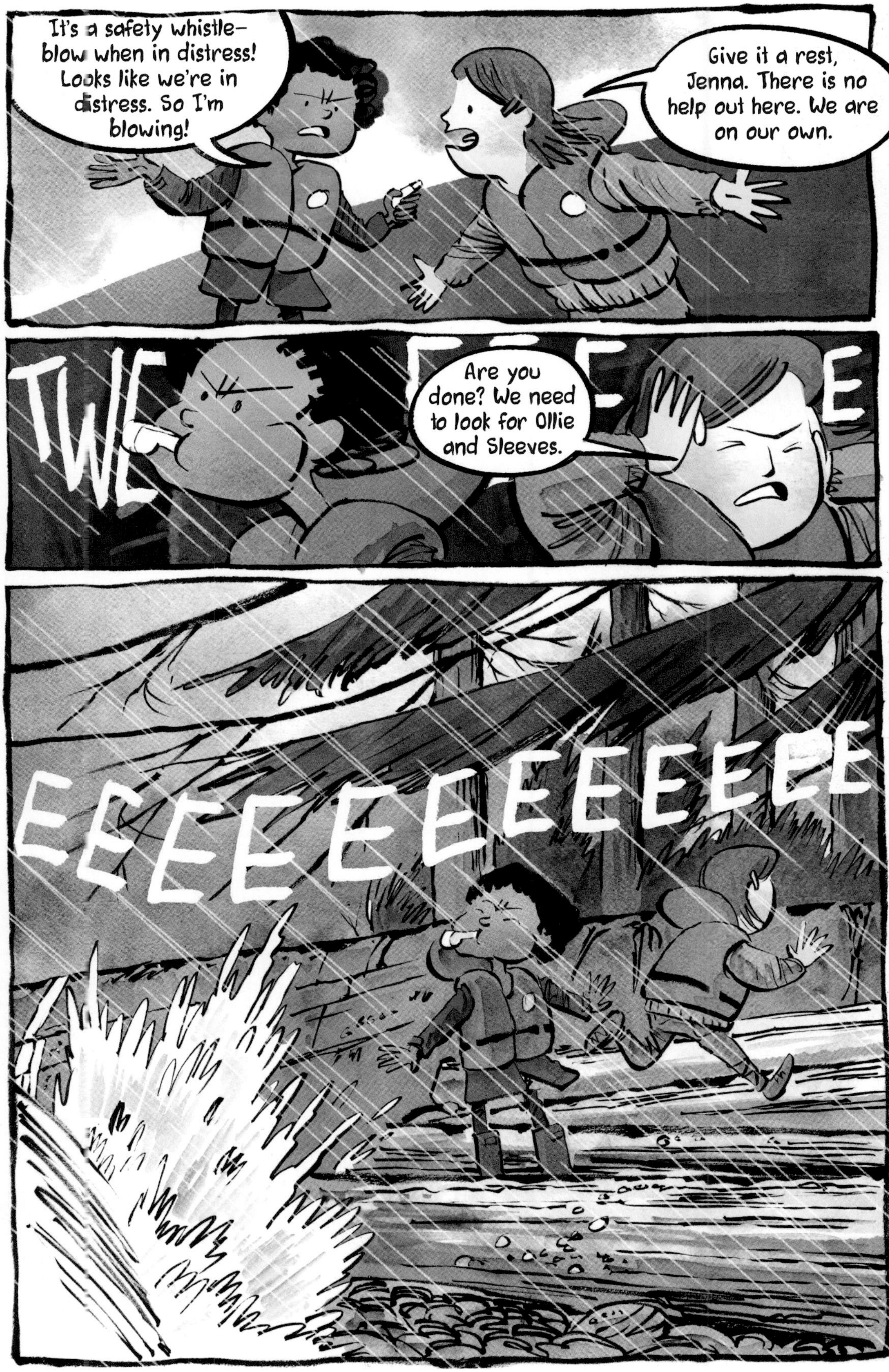
It's a safety whistle-blow when in distress! Looks like we're in distress. So I'm blowing!
Give it a rest, Jenna. There is no help out here. We are on our own.
TWE
Are you done? We need to look for Ollie and Sleeves.
E
EEEEEEEEEEEE

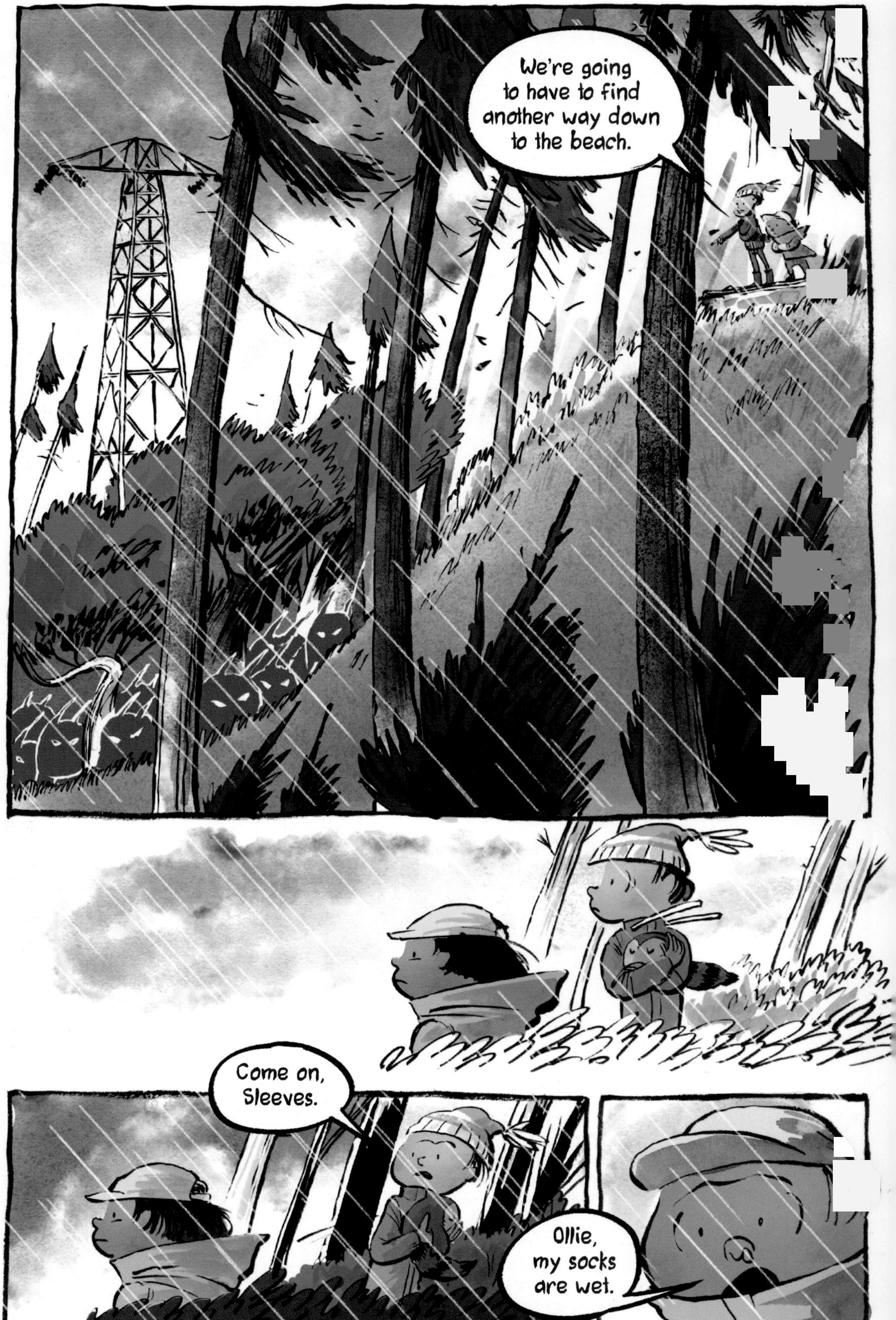
We're going to have to find another way down to the beach.
Come on, Sleeves.
Ollie, my socks are wet.

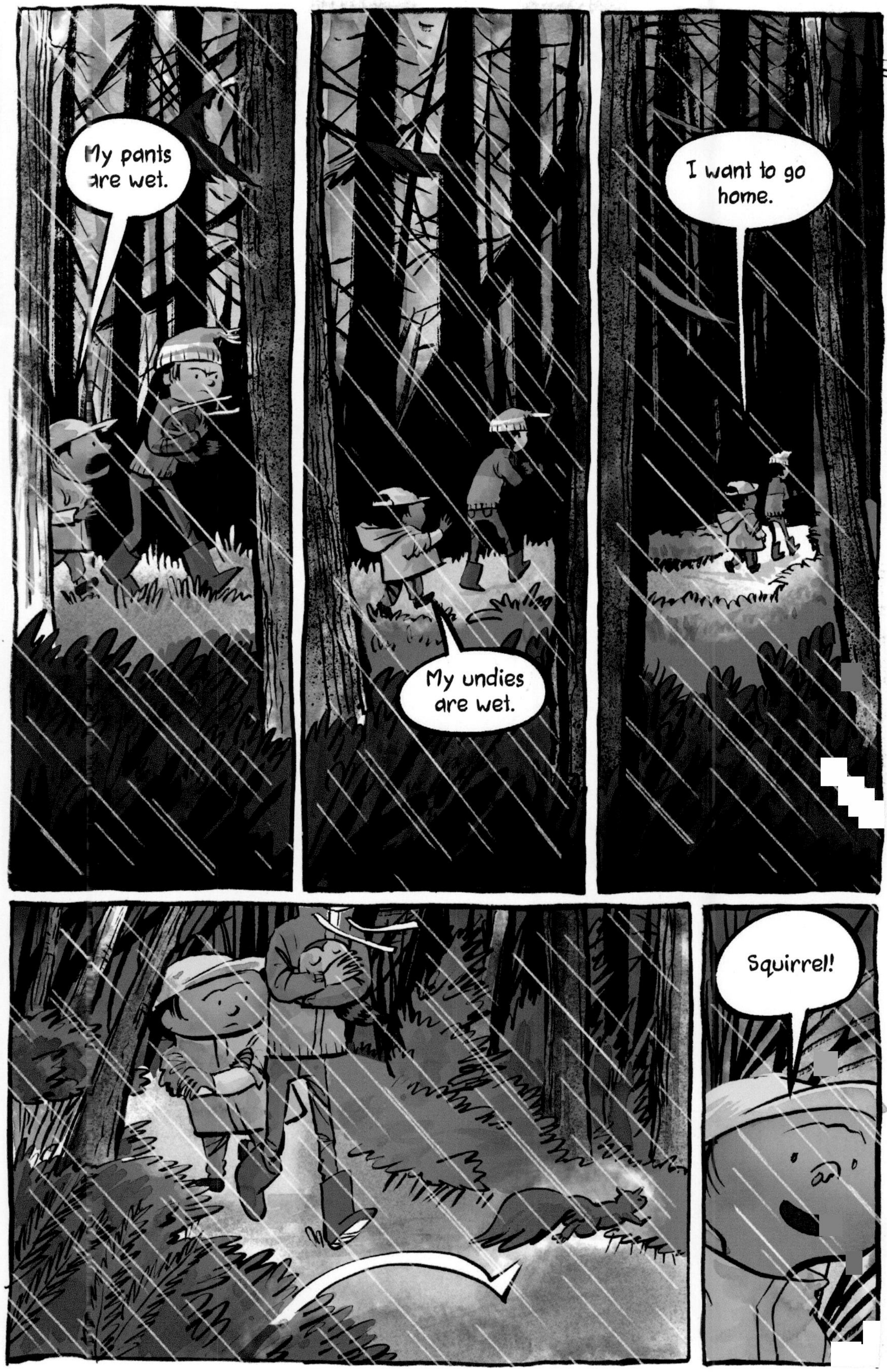
My pants are wet.
My undies are wet.
I want to go home.
Squirrel!

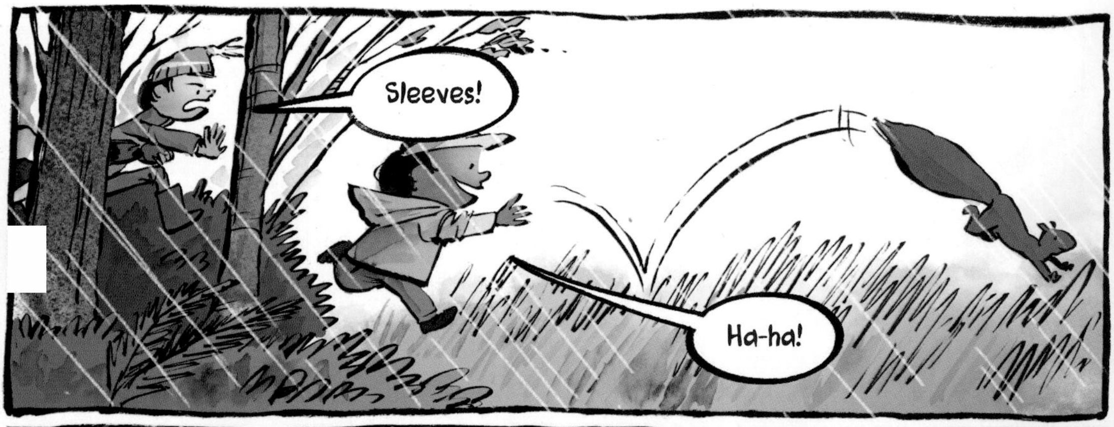
Sleeves!
Ha-ha!

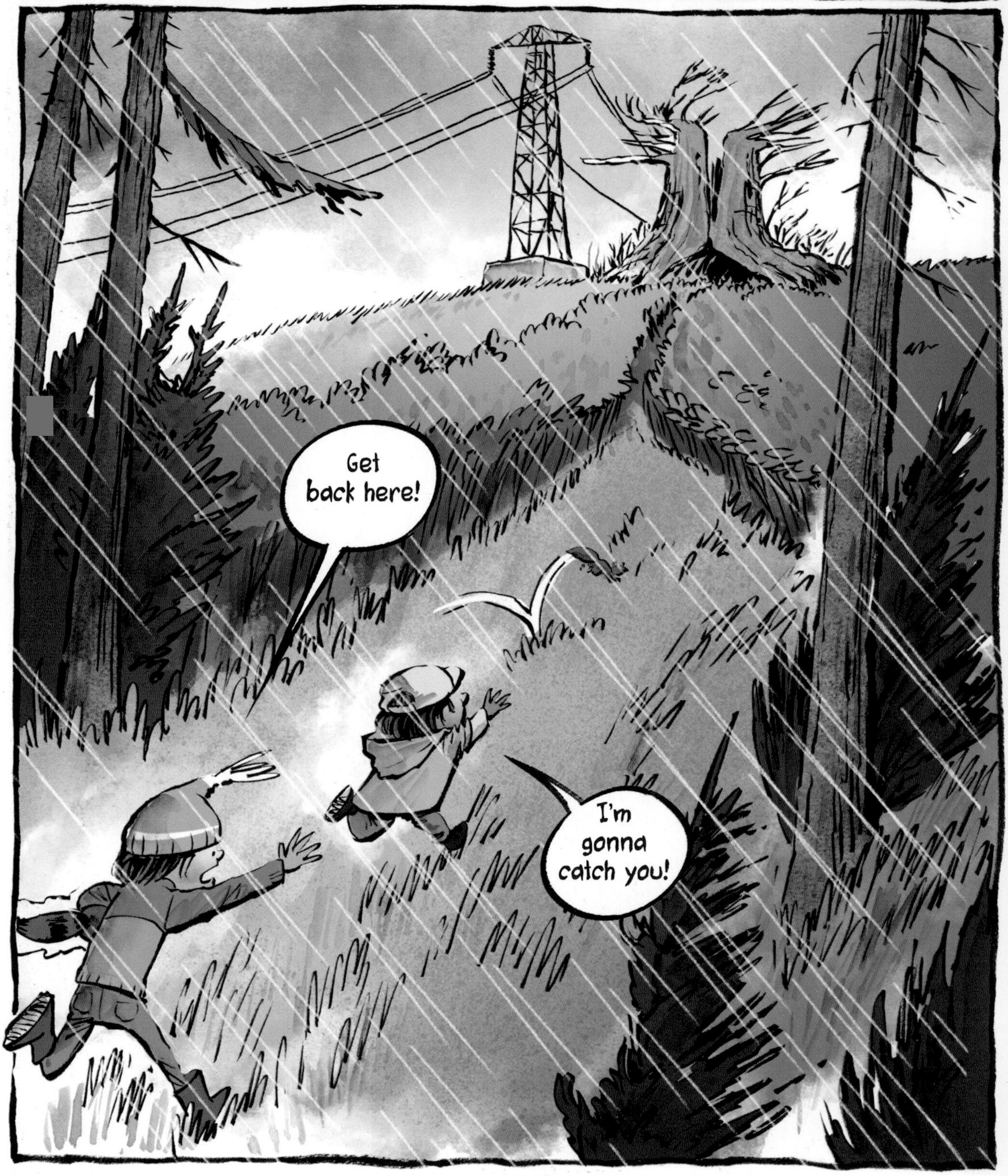
Get back here!
I'm gonna catch you!

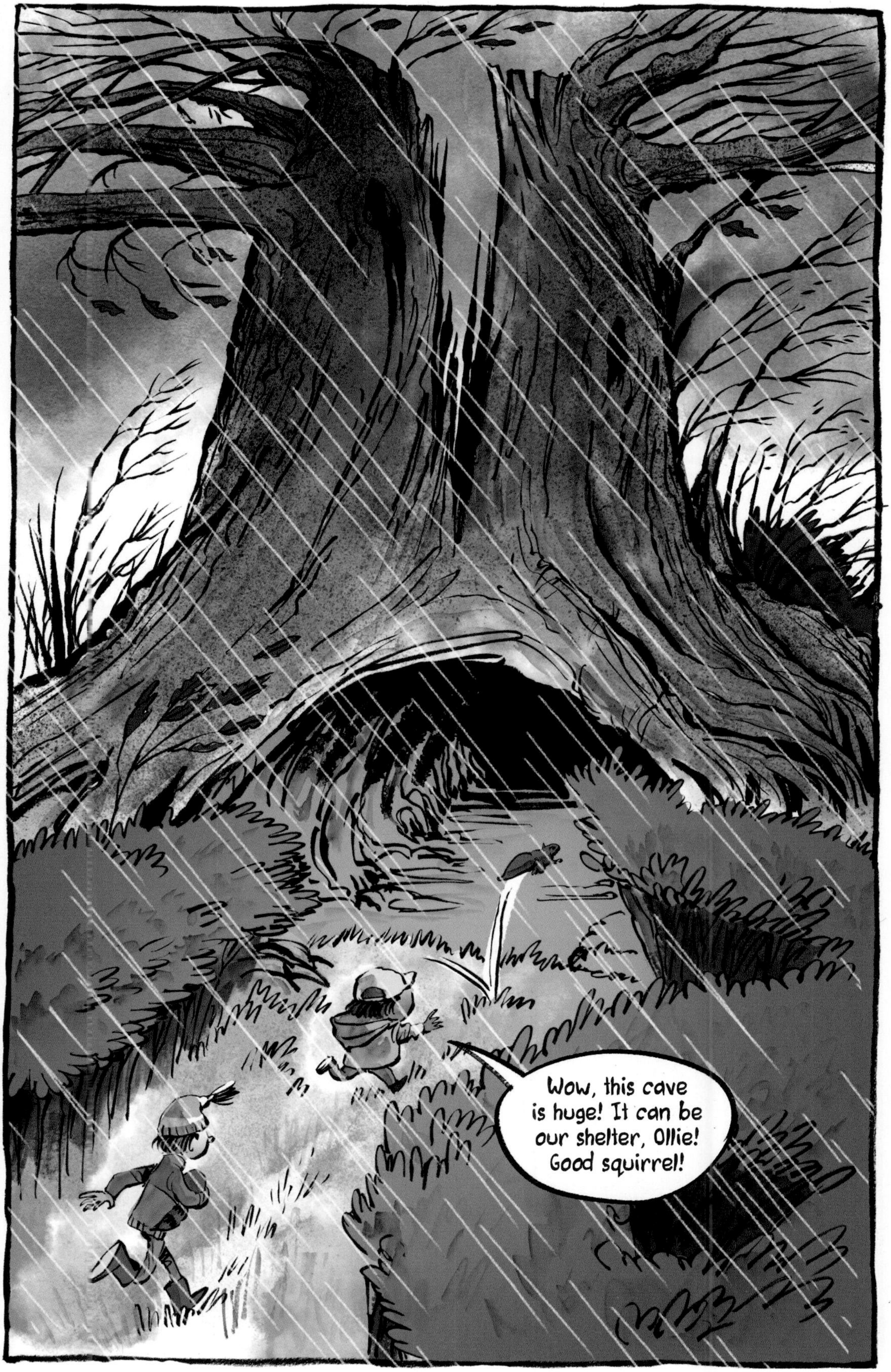
Wow, this cave is huge! It can be our shelter, Ollie! Good squirrel!

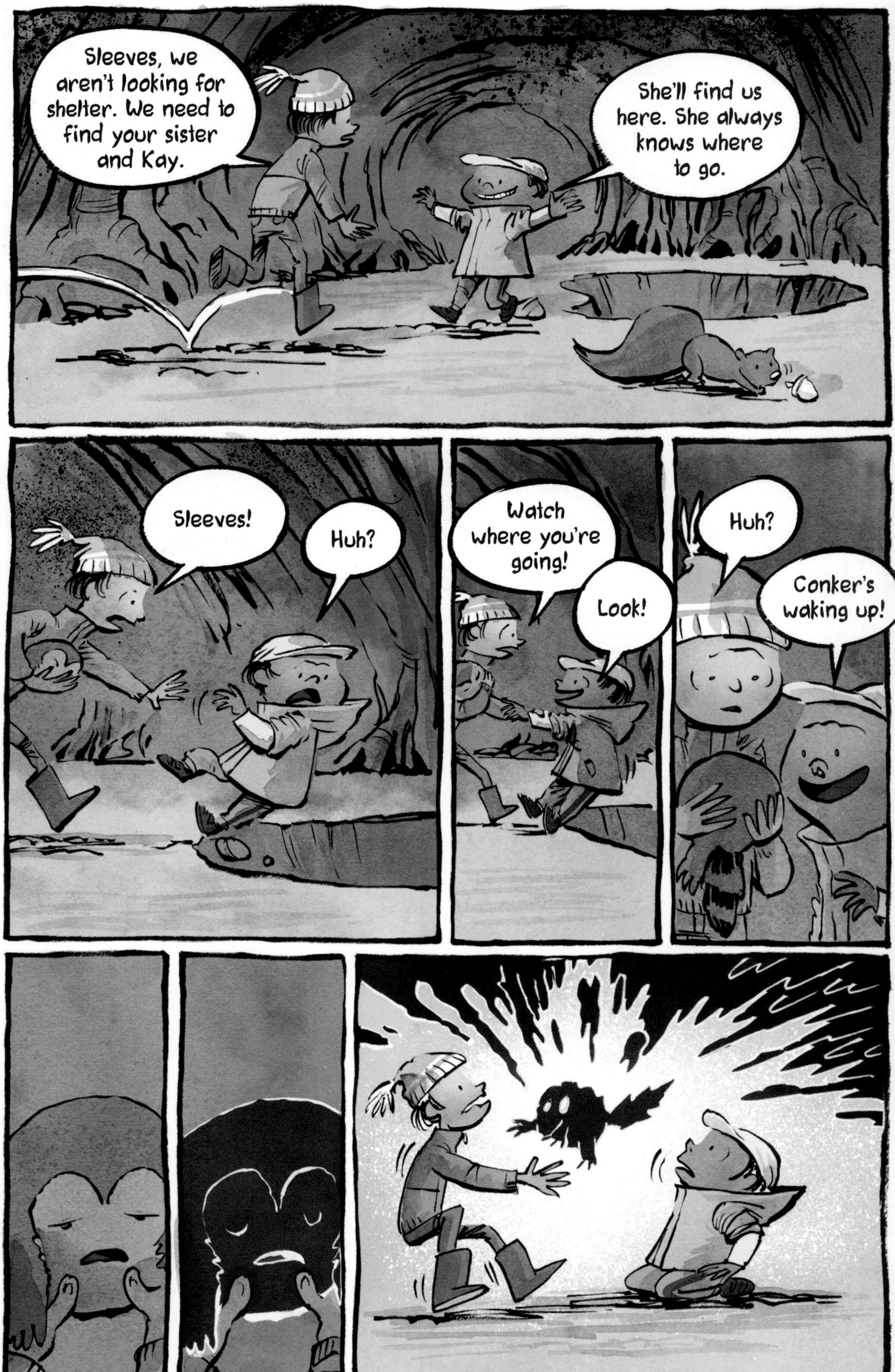
Sleeves, we aren't looking for shelter. We need to find your sister and Kay.
She'll find us here. She always knows where to go.
Sleeves!
Huh?
Watch where you're going!
Look!
Huh?
Conker's waking up!

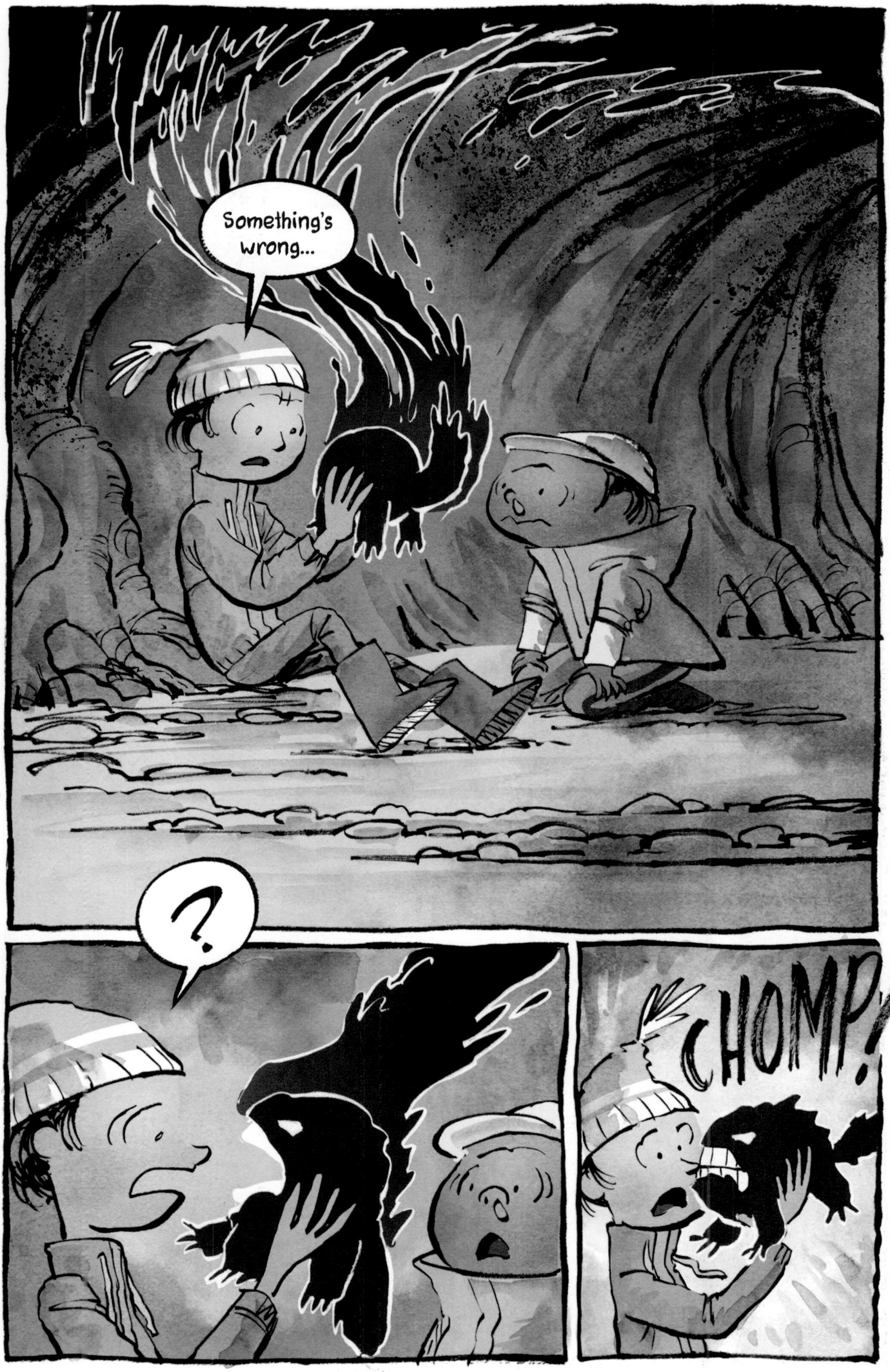
Something's wrong...
?
CHOMP!

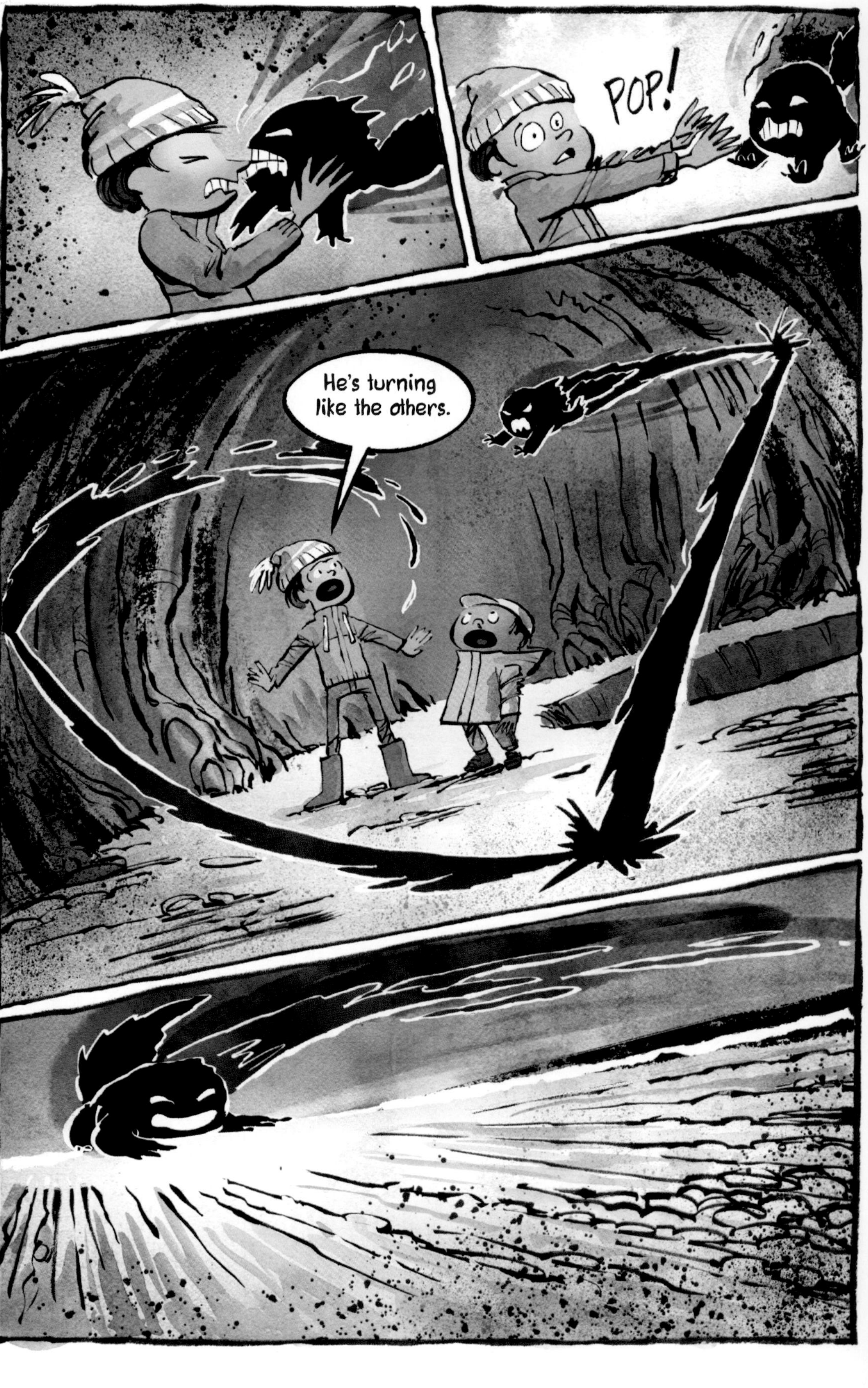
POP!
He's turning like the others.

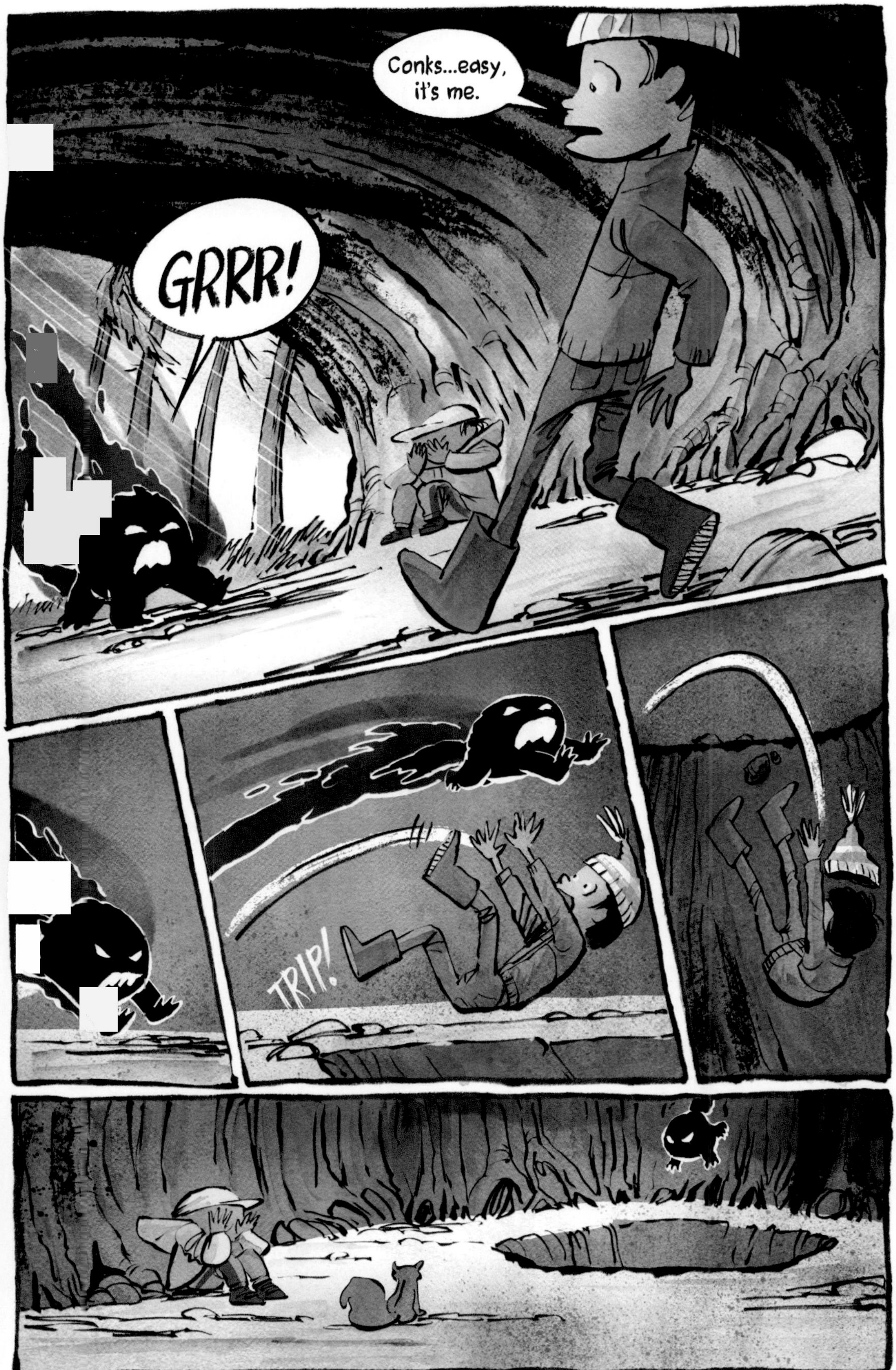
Conks...easy, it's me.
GRRR!
TRIP!

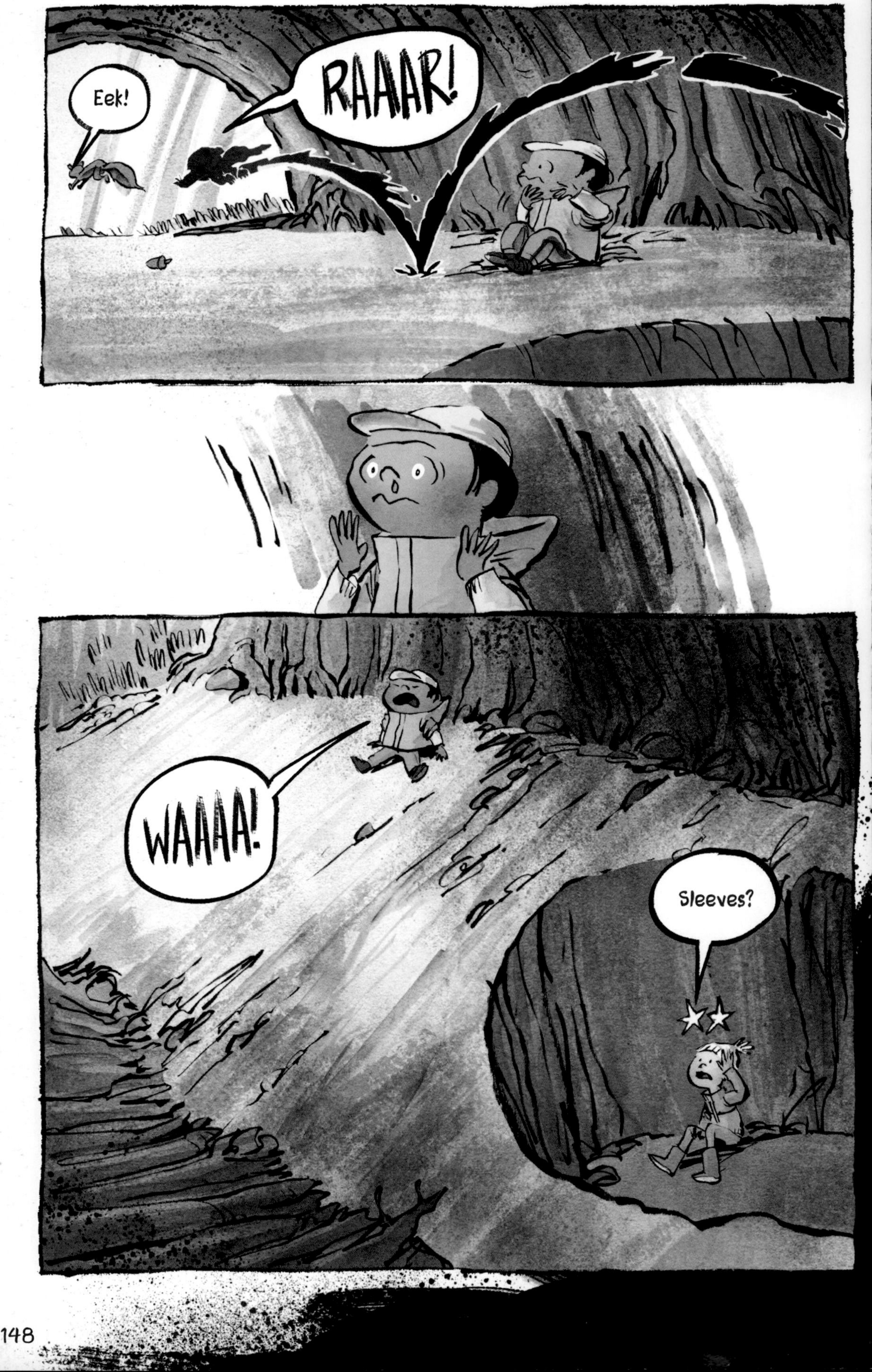
Eek!
RAAAR!
WAAAA!
Sleeves?

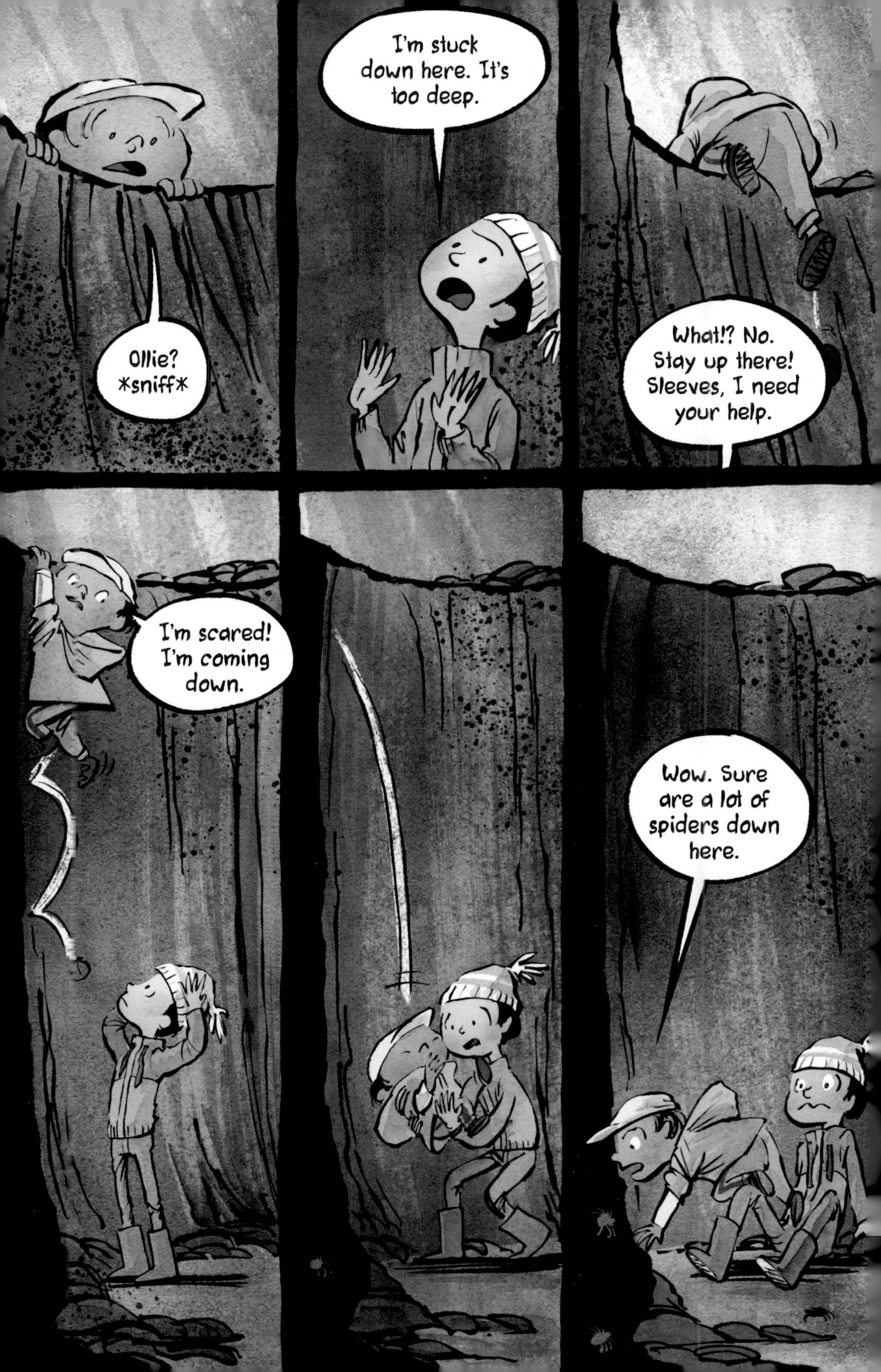
Ollie? *sniff*
I'm stuck down here. It's too deep.
What!? No. Stay up there! Sleeves, I need your help.
I'm scared! I'm coming down.
Wow. Sure are a lot of spiders down here.

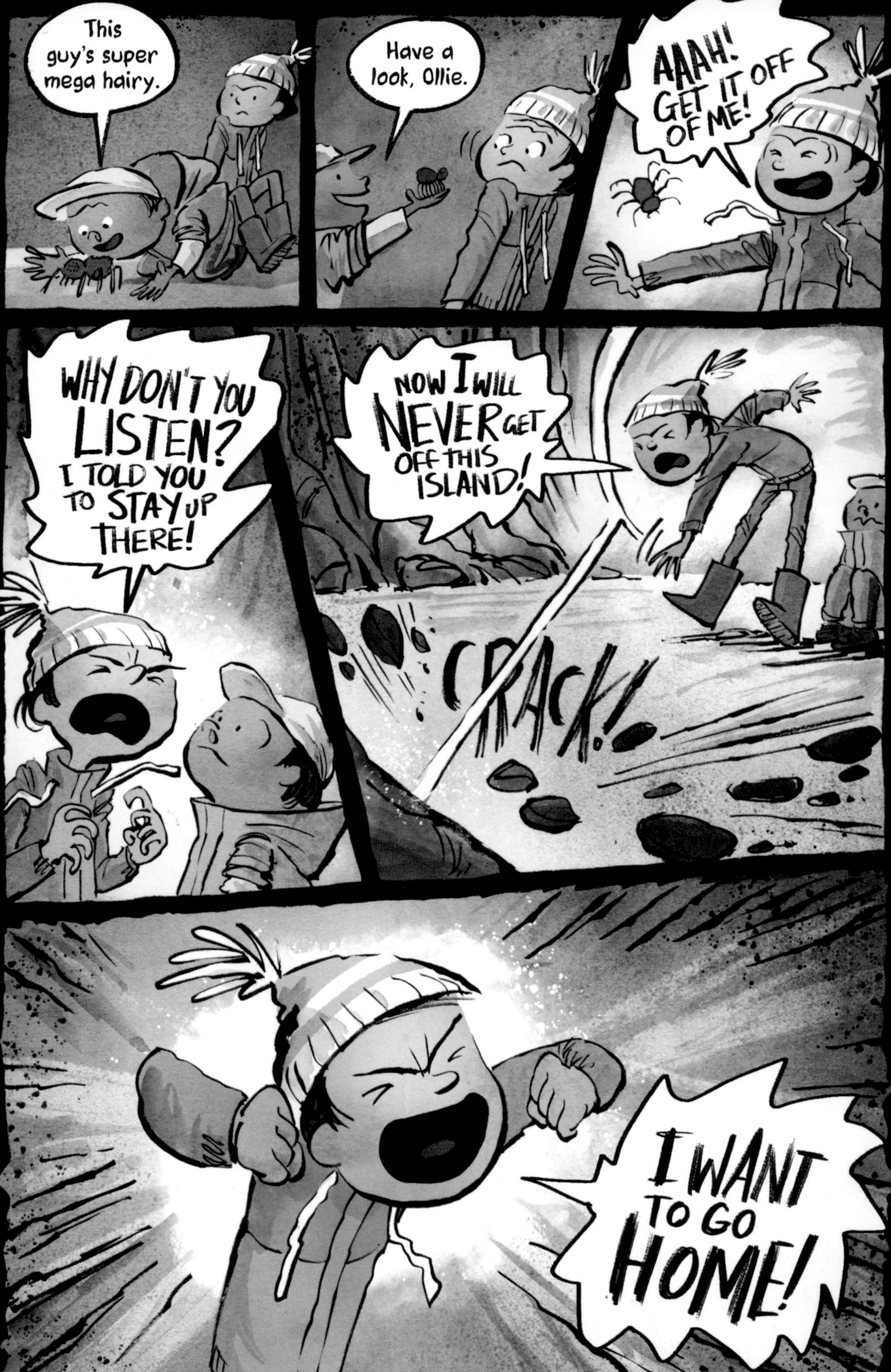
This guy's super mega hairy.
Have a look, Ollie.
AAAH! GET IT OFF OF ME!
WHY DON'T YOU LISTEN? I TOLD YOU TO STAY UP THERE!
NOW I WILL NEVER GET OFF THIS ISLAND!
CRACK!
I WANT TO GO HOME!

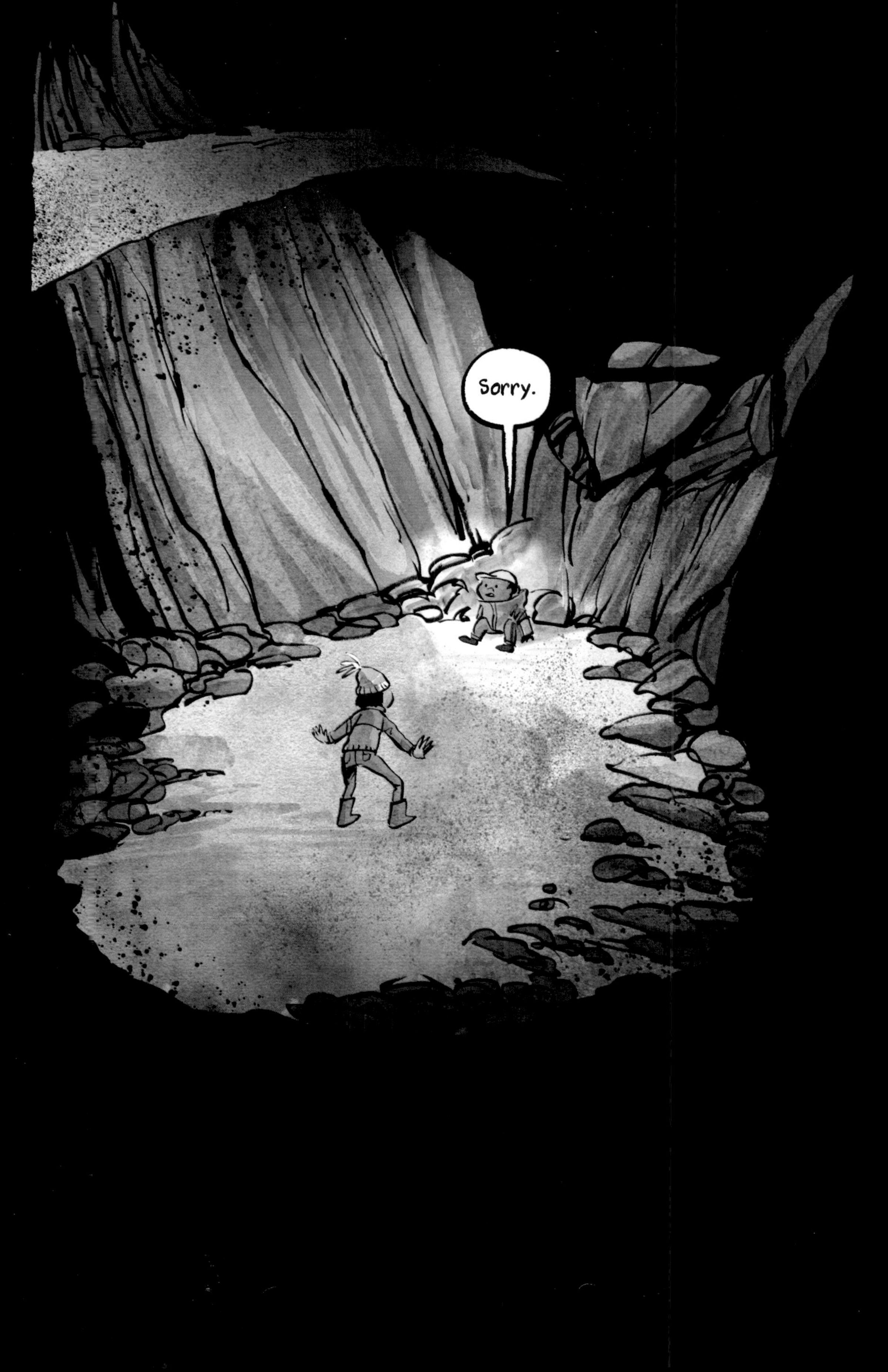
Sorry.

CHAPTER FIVE

Stuck

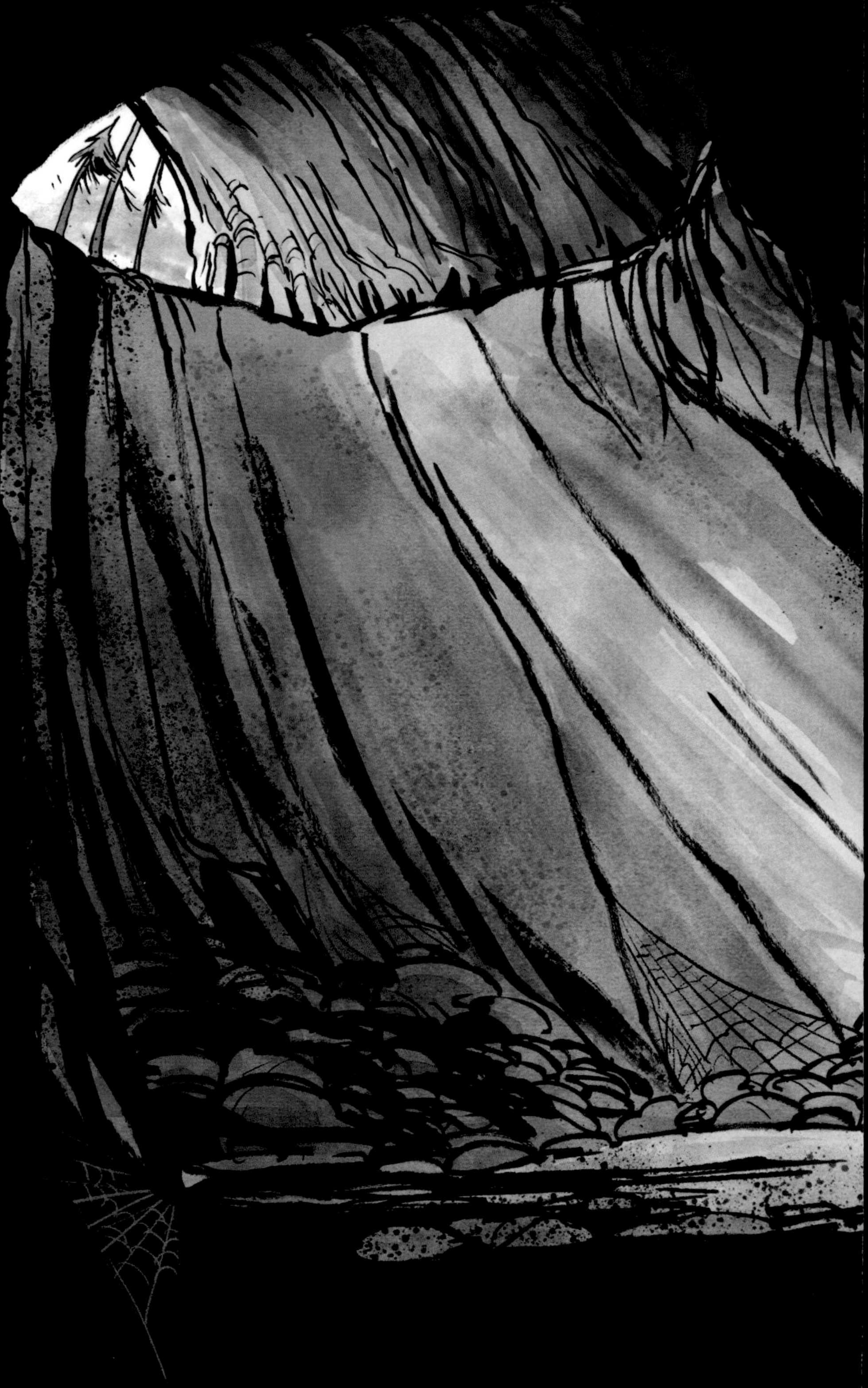

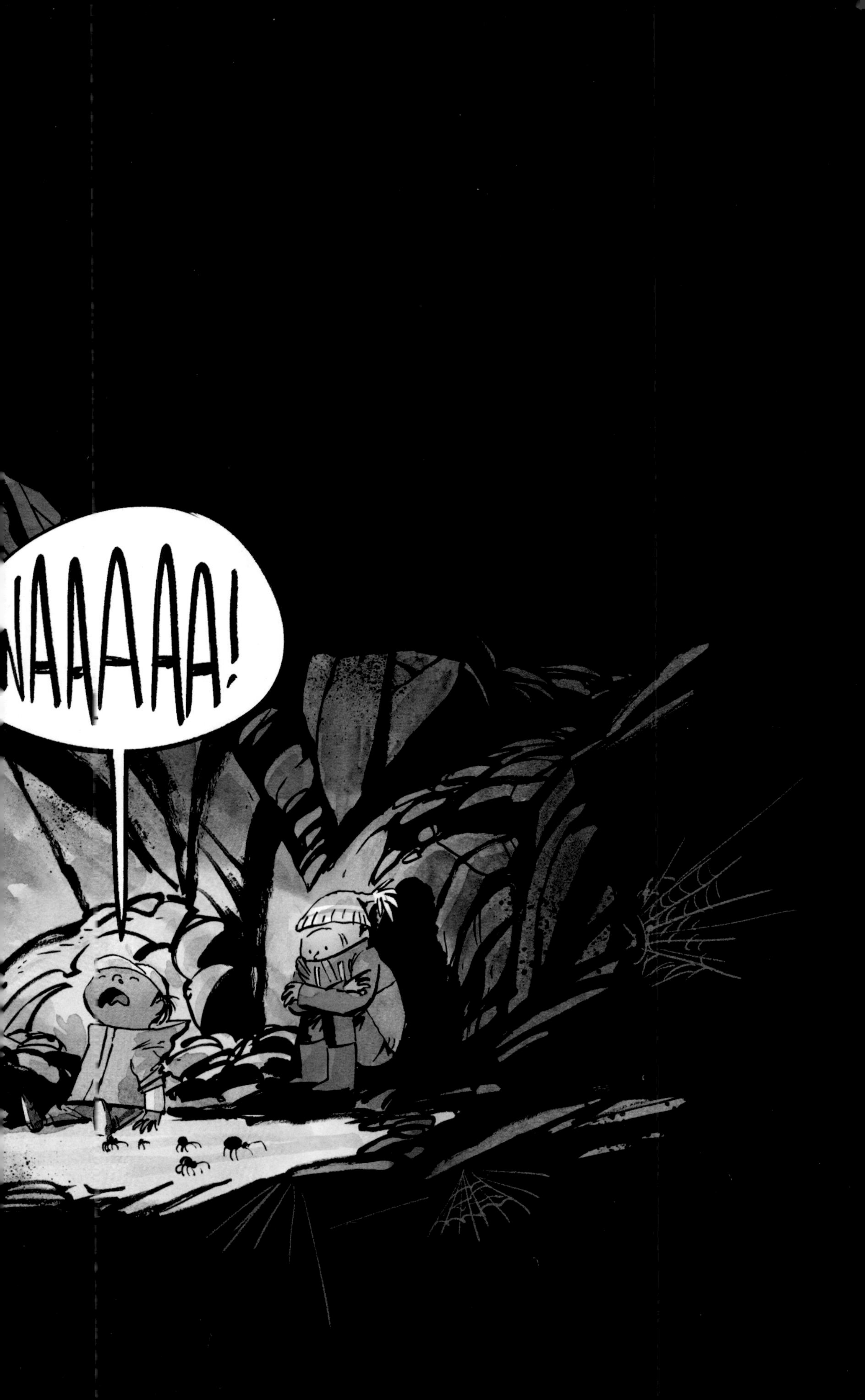
AAAAA!

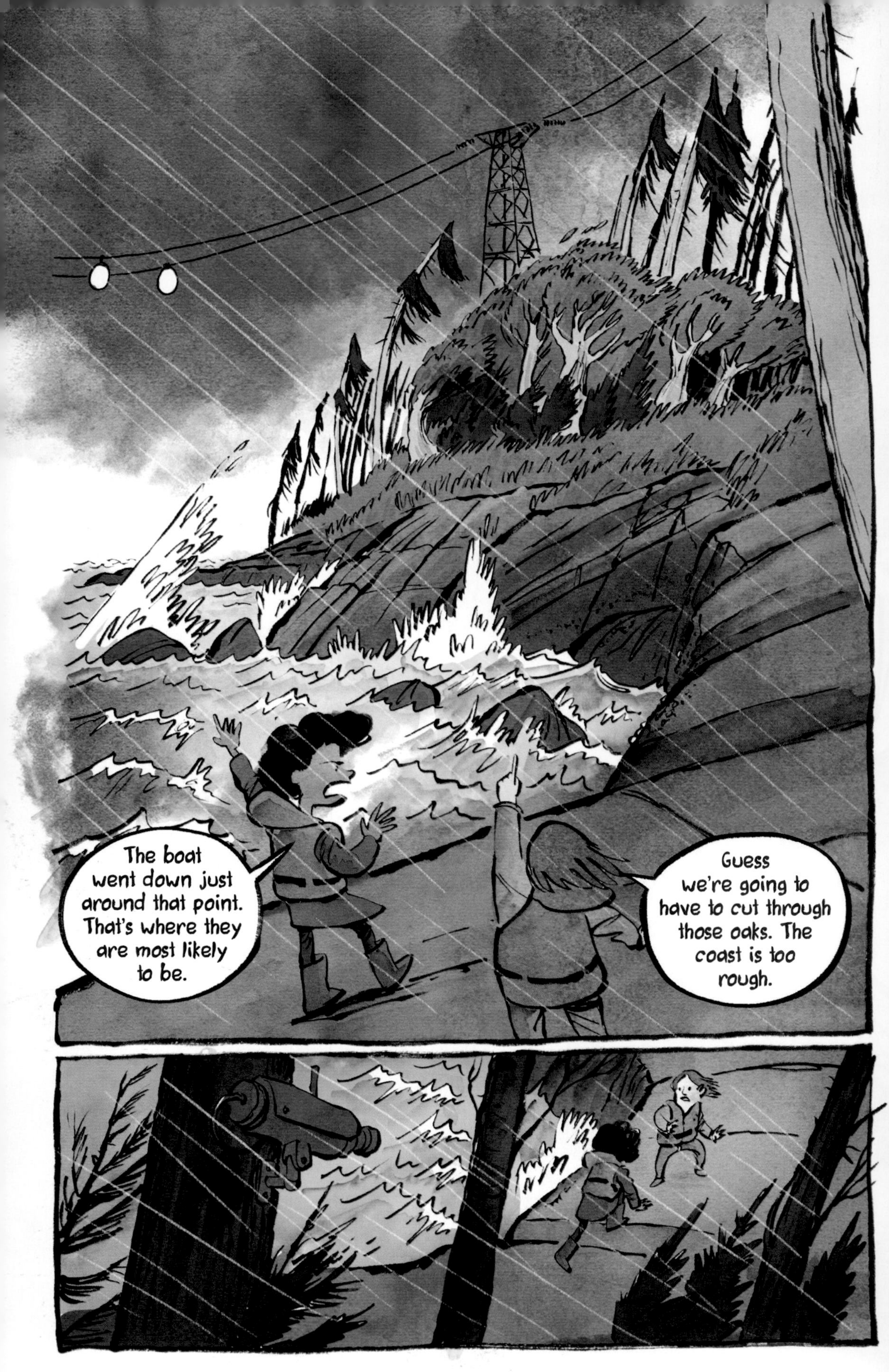
The boat went down just around that point. That's where they are most likely to be.
Guess we're going to have to cut through those oaks. The coast is too rough.

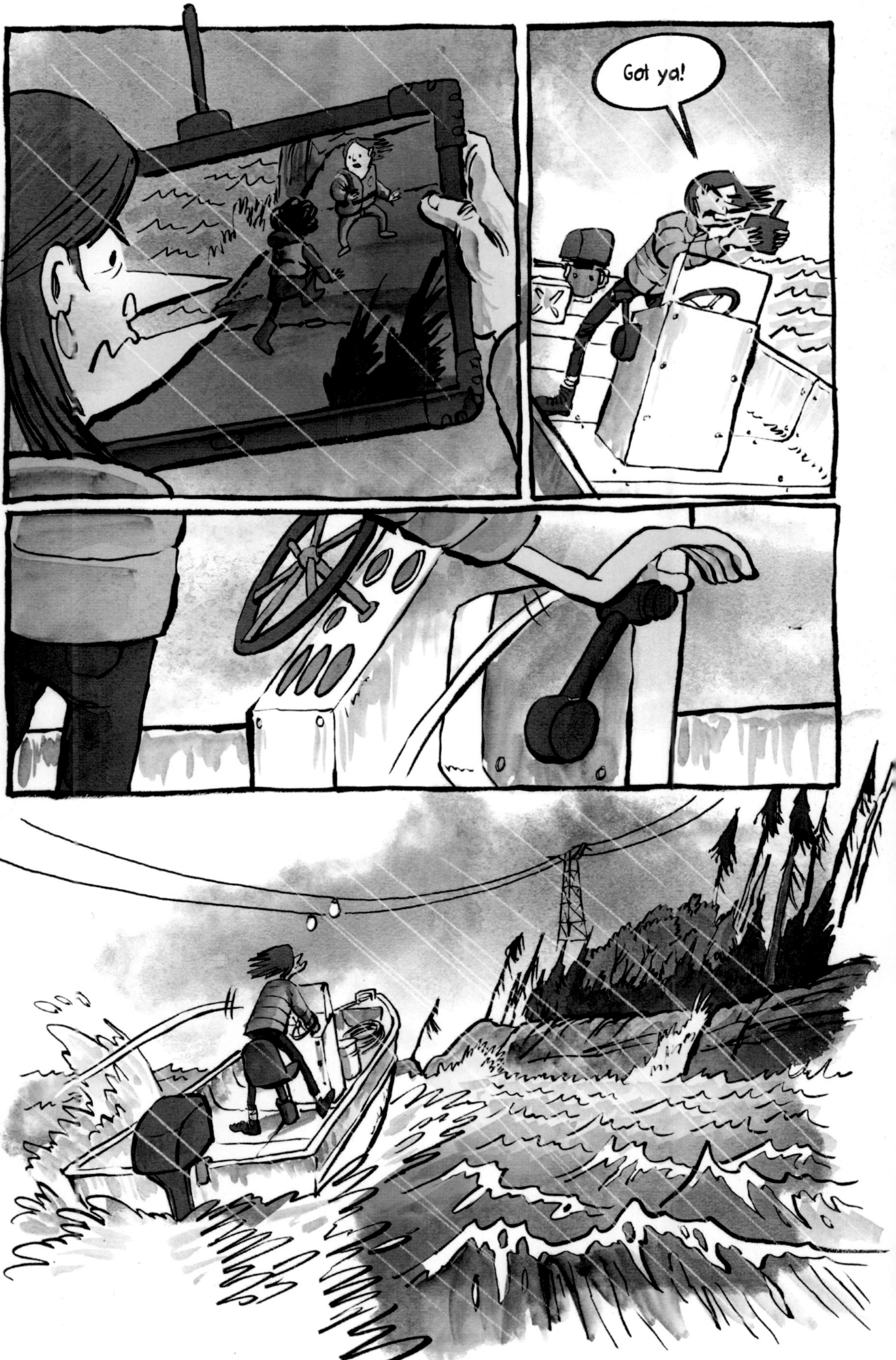
Got ya!

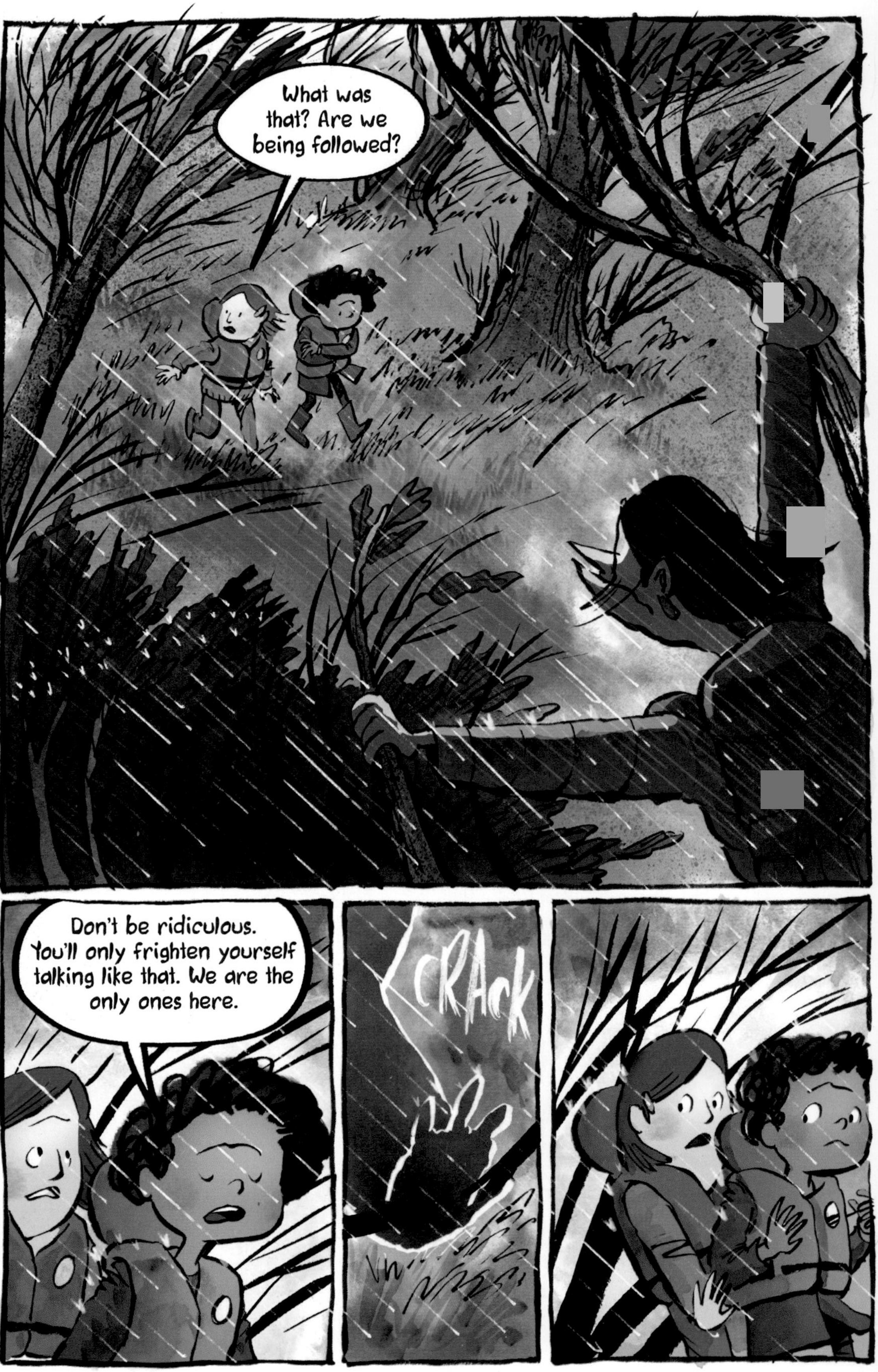
What was that? Are we being followed?
Don't be ridiculous. You'll only frighten yourself talking like that. We are the only ones here.
CRACK

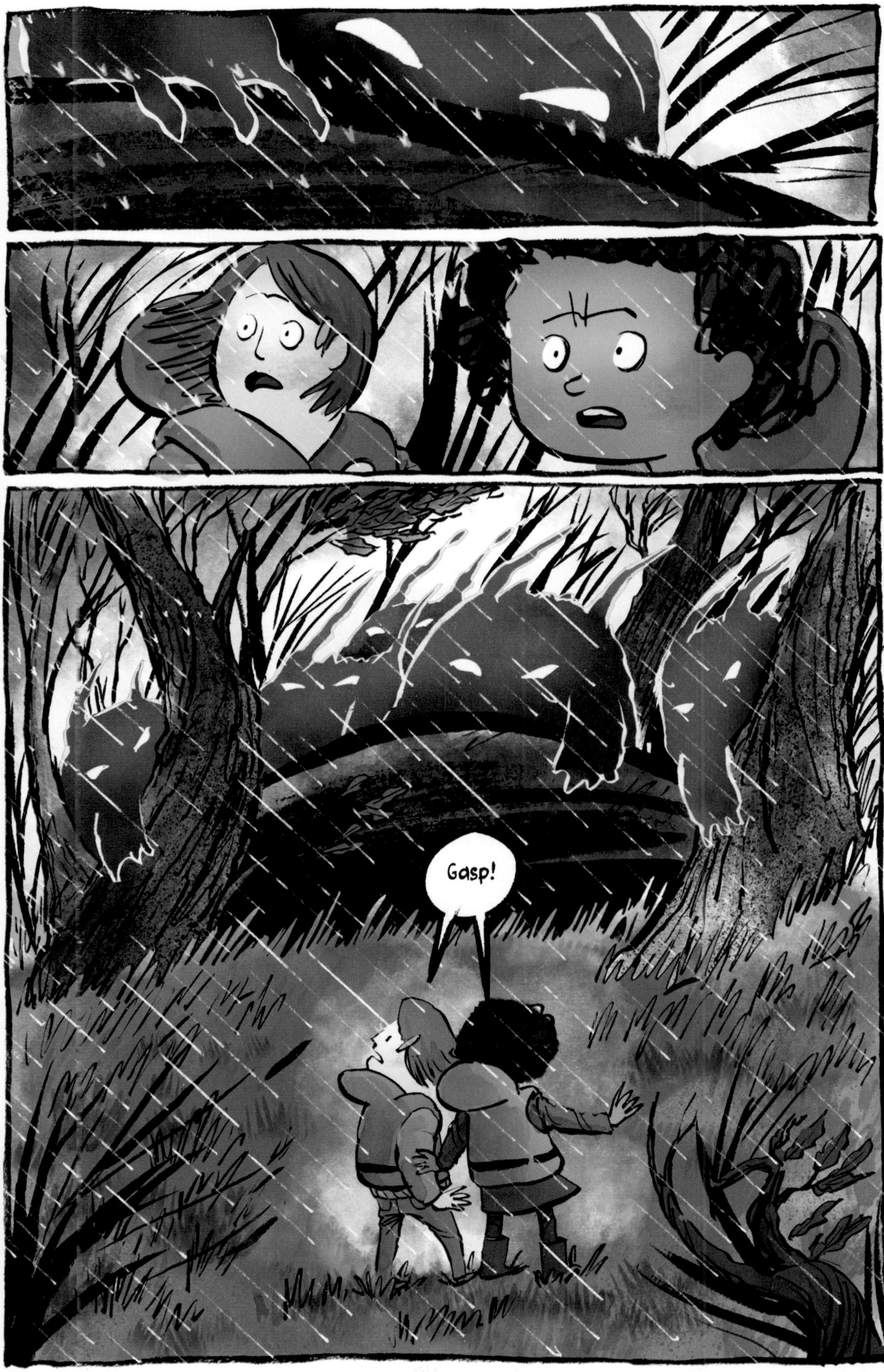
Gasp!

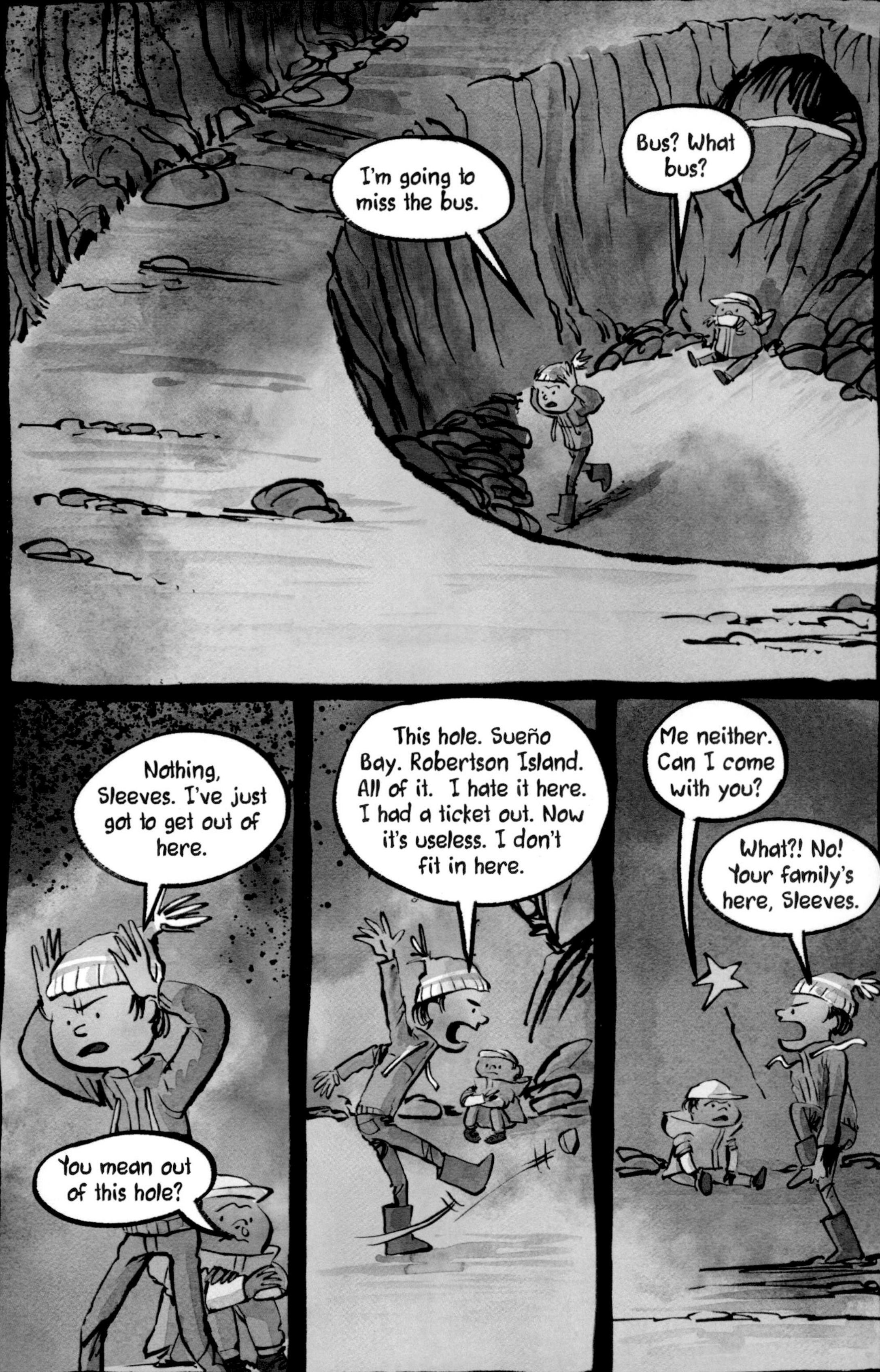
I'm going to miss the bus.
Bus? What bus?
Nothing, Sleeves. I've just got to get out of here.
You mean out of this hole?
This hole. Sueño Bay. Robertson Island. All of it. I hate it here. I had a ticket out. Now it's useless. I don't fit in here.
Me neither. Can I come with you?
What?! No! Your family's here, Sleeves.

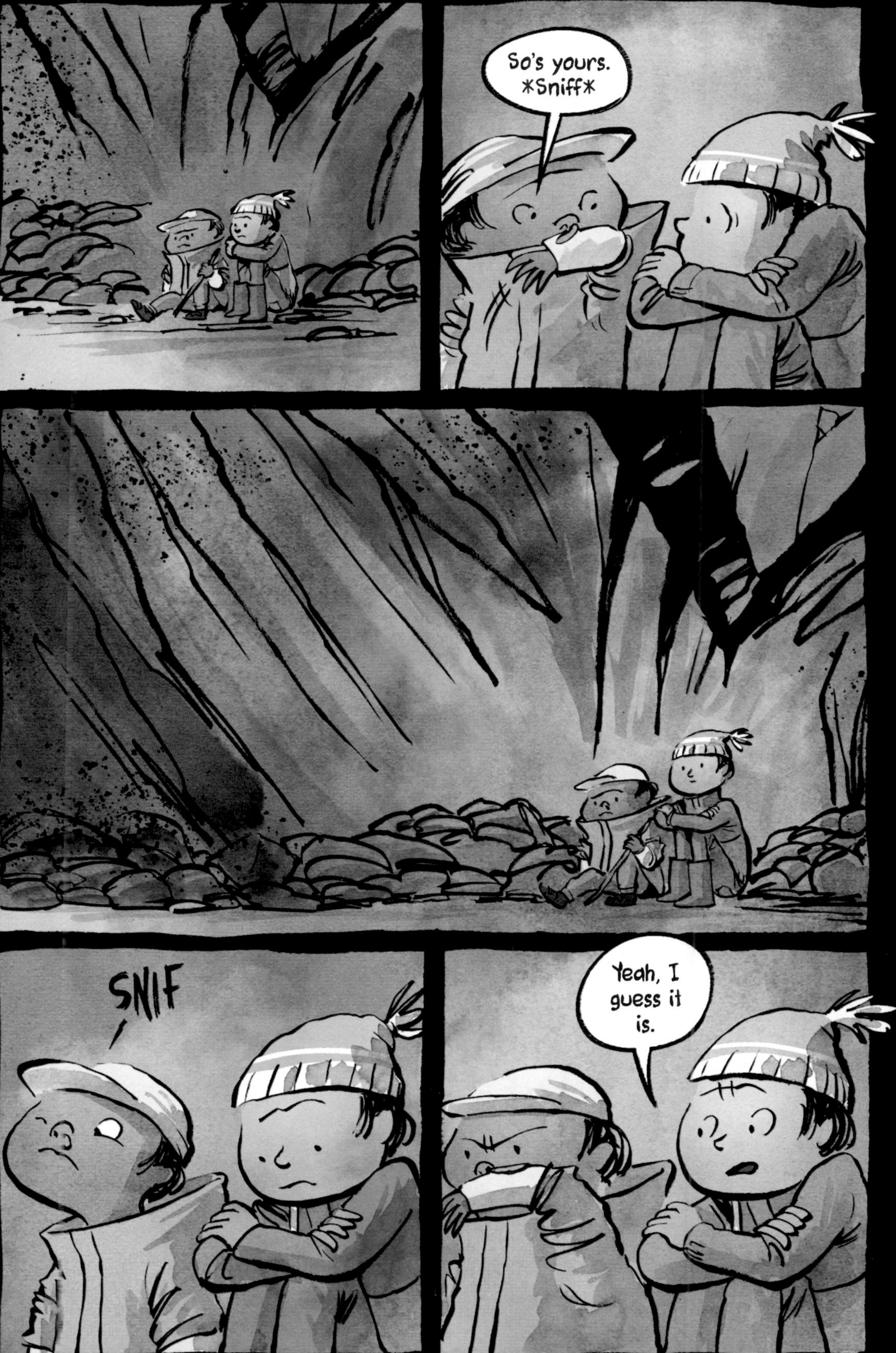
So's yours. *Sniff*
SNIF
Yeah, I guess it is.

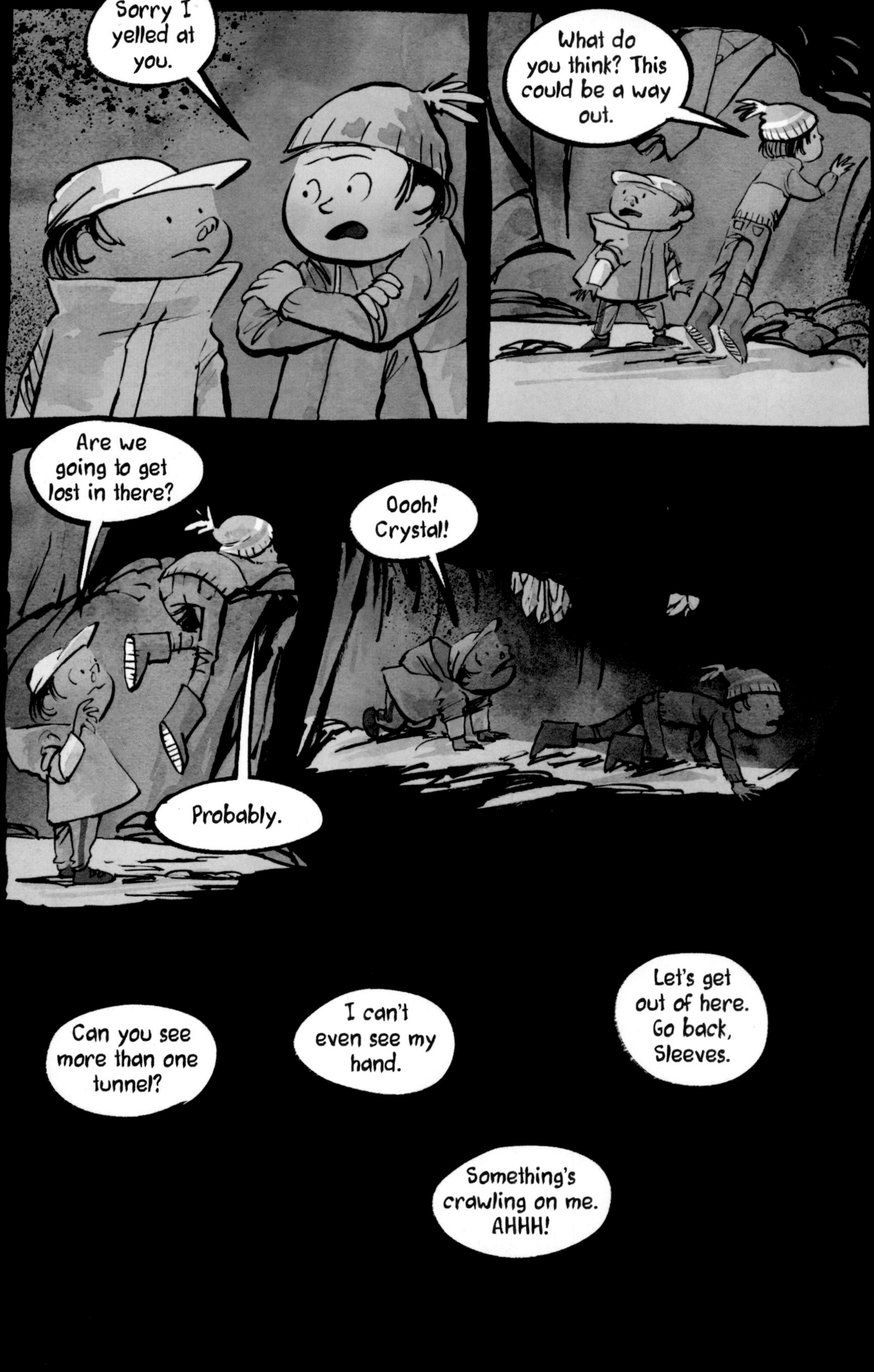
Sorry I yelled at you.
What do you think? This could be a way out.
Are we going to get lost in there?
Probably.
Oooh! Crystal!
Can you see more than one tunnel?
I can't even see my hand.
Let's get out of here. Go back, Sleeves.
Something's crawling on me. AHHH!

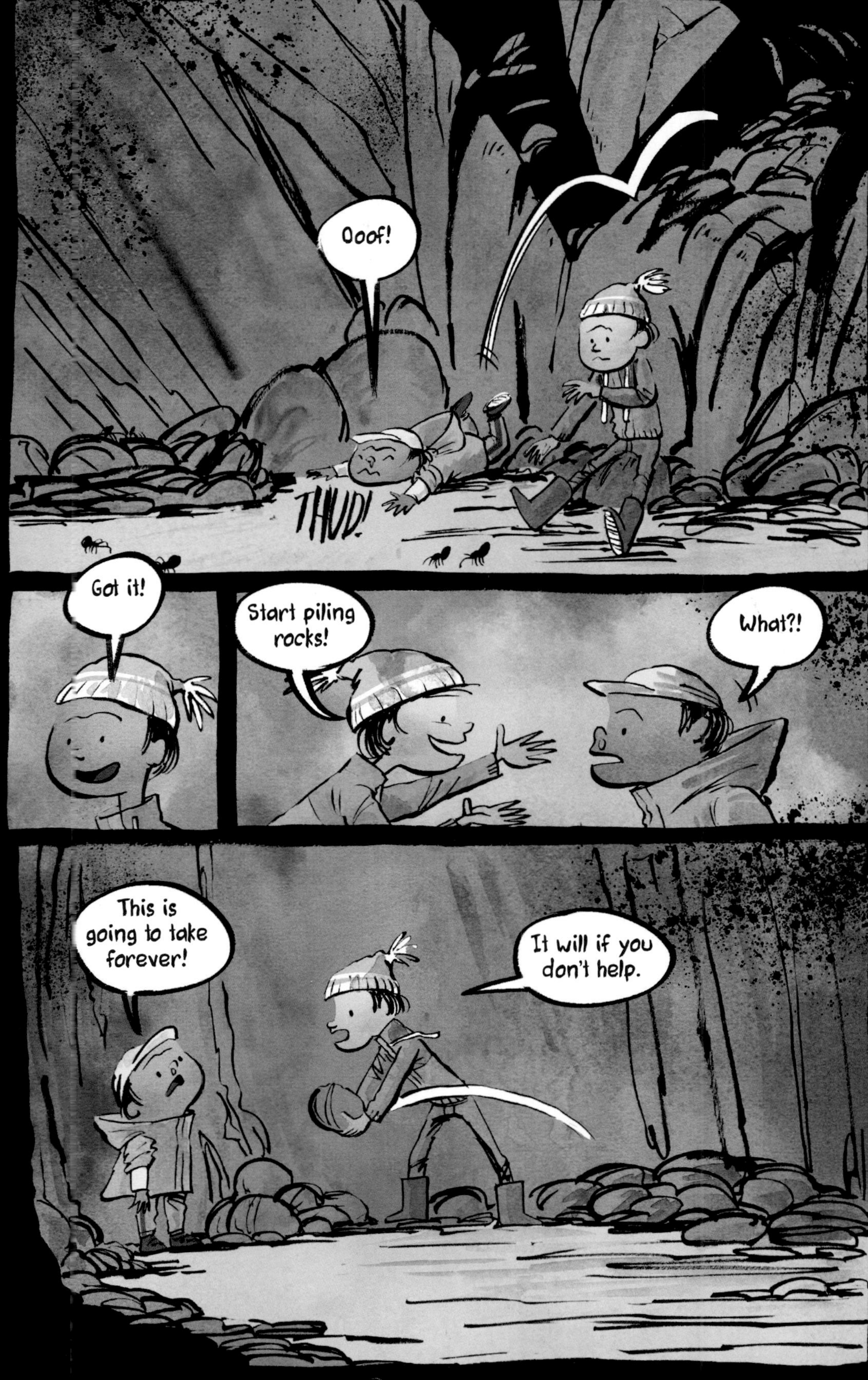
Ooof!
THUD!
Got it!
Start piling rocks!
What?!
This is going to take forever!
It will if you don't help.

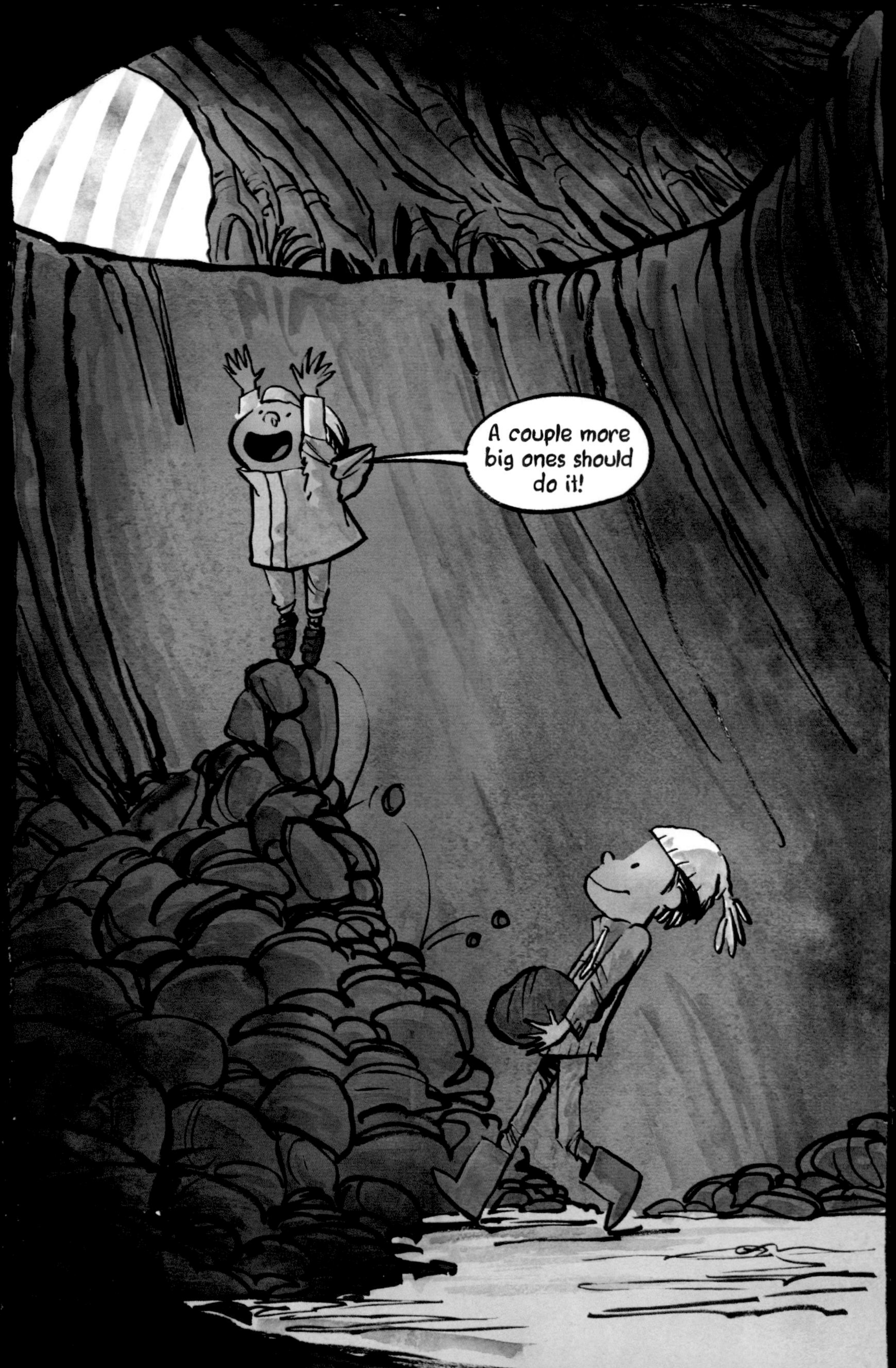
A couple more big ones should do it!

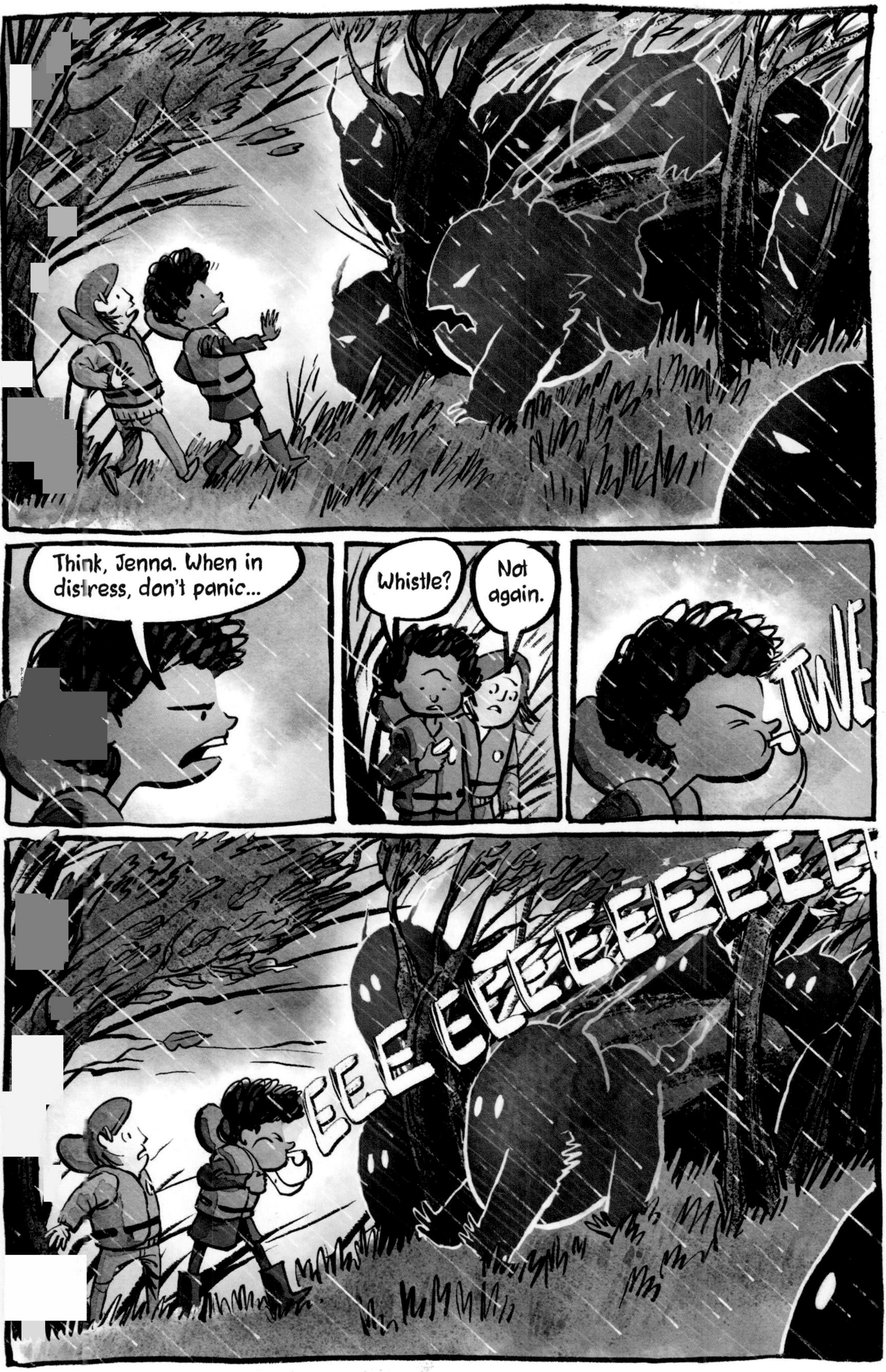
Think, Jenna. When in distress, don't panic...
Whistle?
Not again.
TWE
EEEEEEEEEEEEEEEE

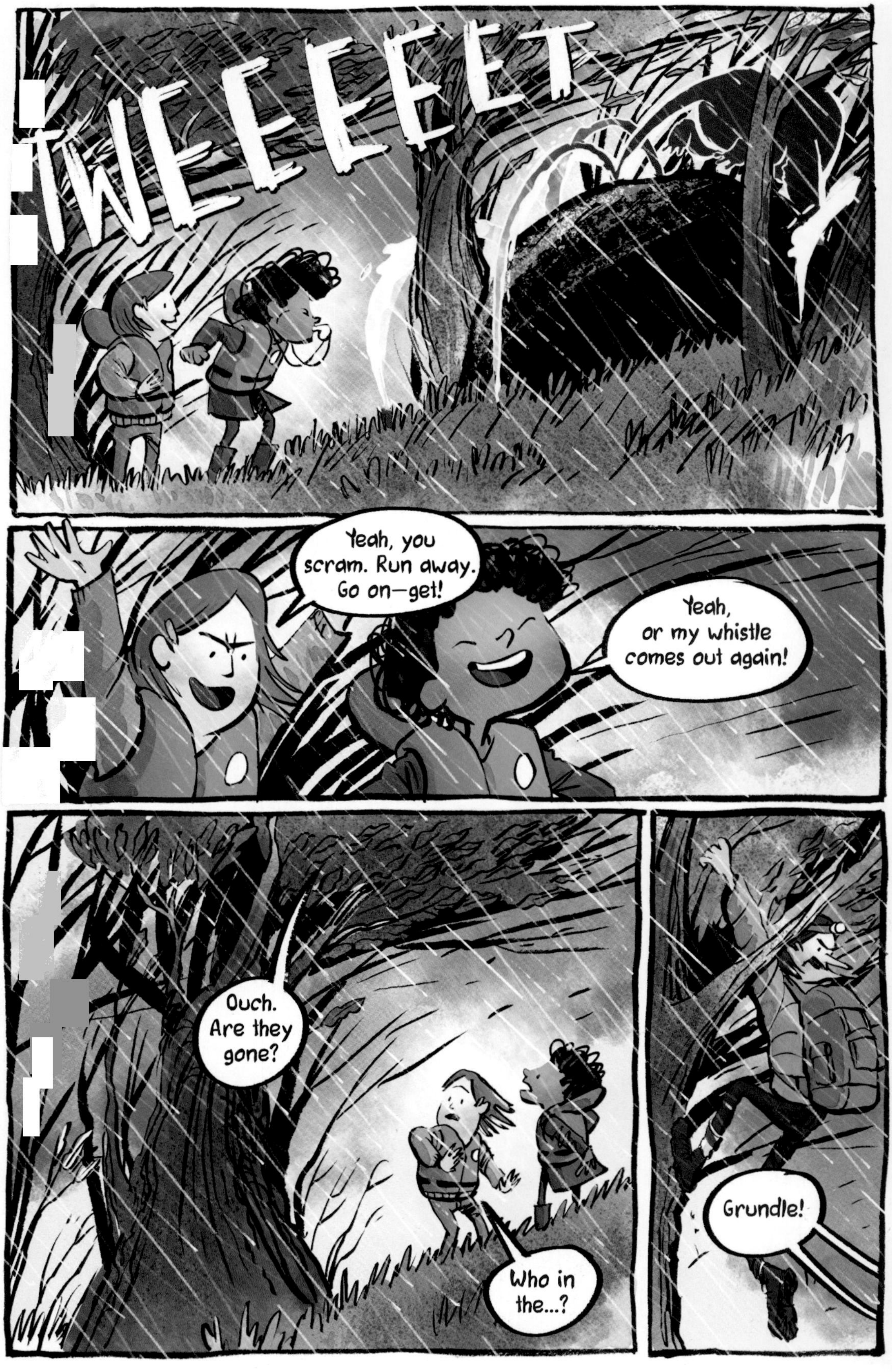
TWEEEEET
Yeah, you scram. Run away. Go on—get!
Yeah, or my whistle comes out again!
Ouch. Are they gone?
Who in the...?
Grundle!

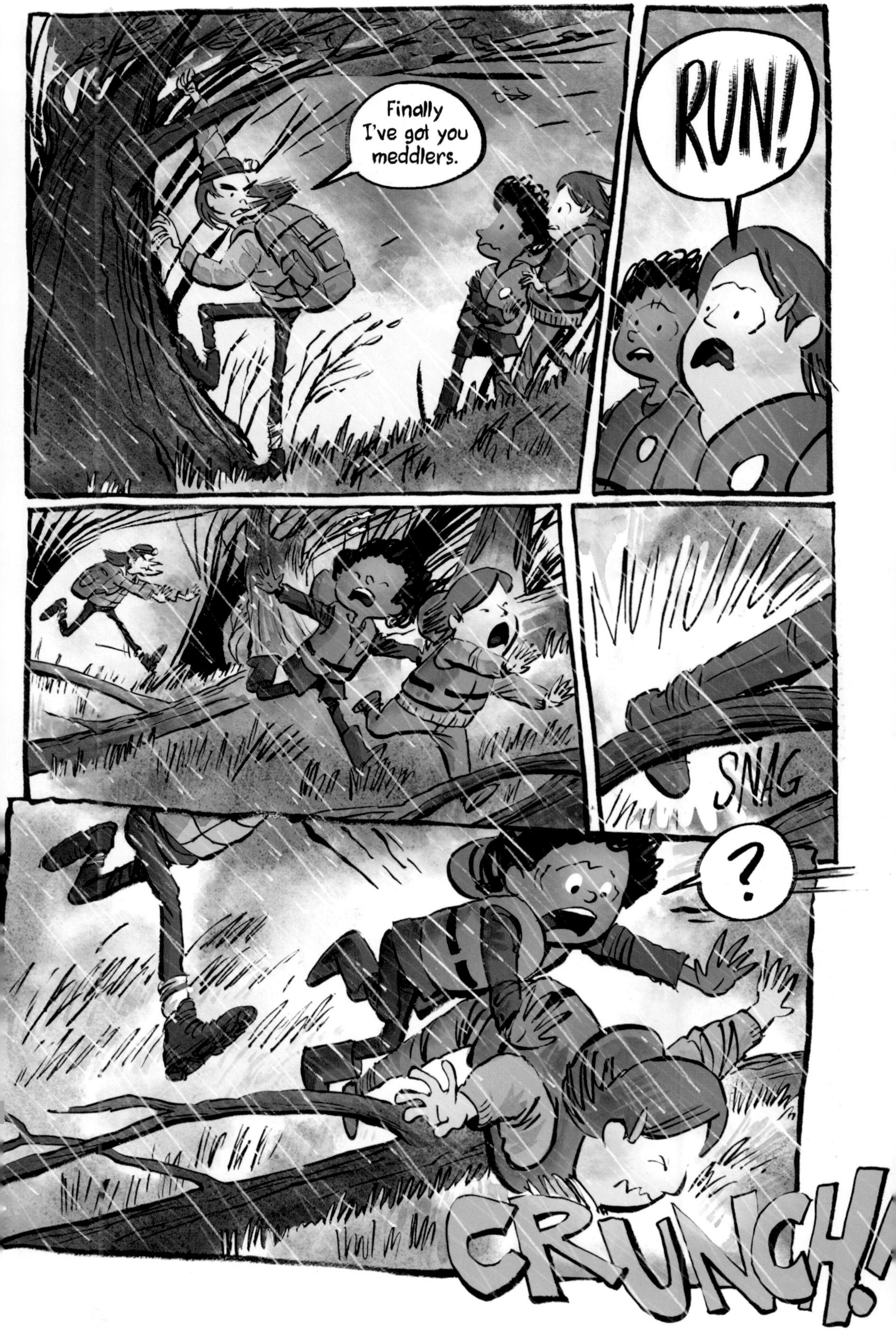
Finally I've got you meddlers.
RUN!
SNAG
?
CRUNCH!

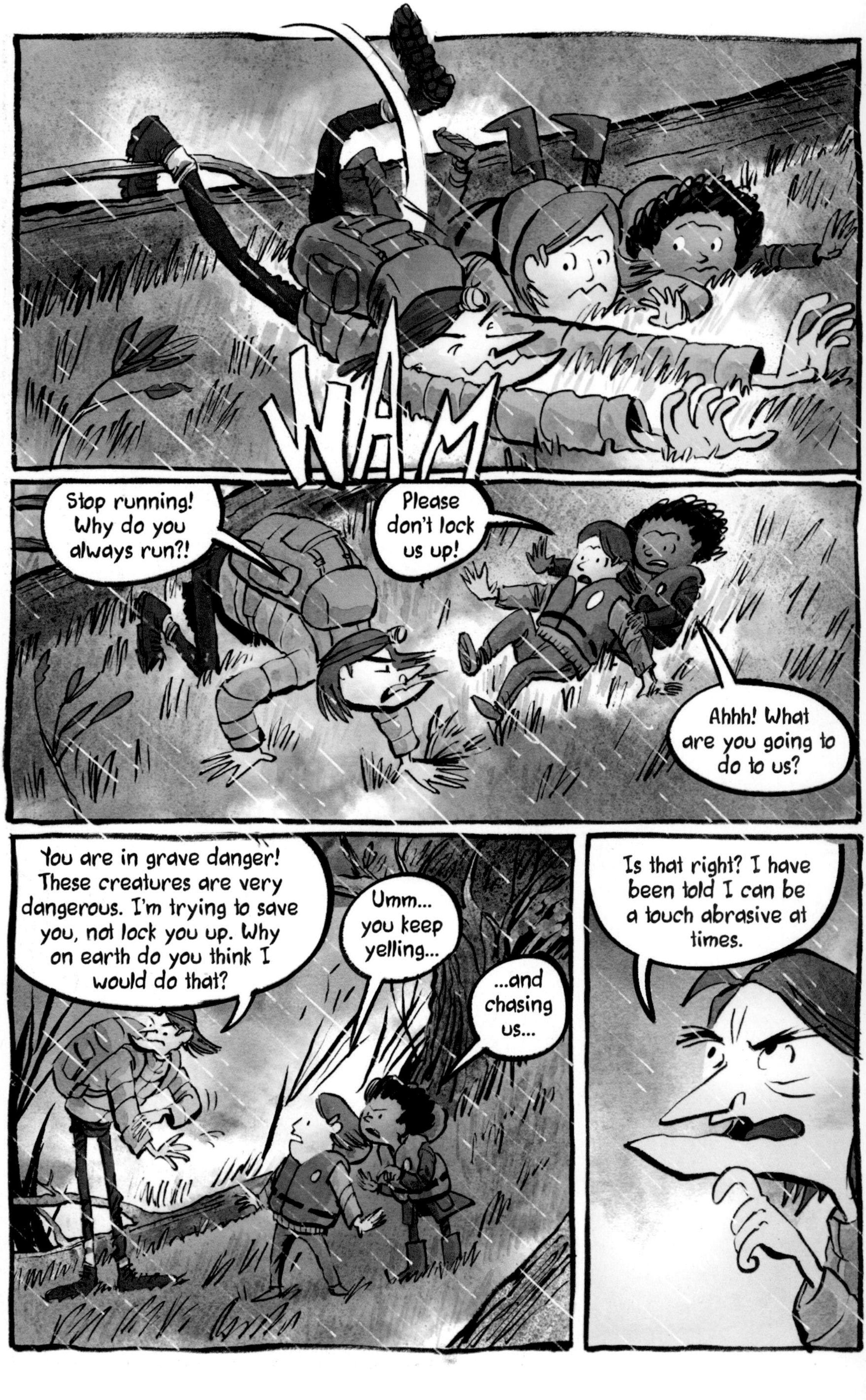
WAM
Stop running! Why do you always run?!
Please don't lock us up!
Ahhh! What are you going to do to us?
You are in grave danger! These creatures are very dangerous. I'm trying to save you, not lock you up. Why on earth do you think I would do that?
Umm... you keep yelling...
...and chasing us...
Is that right? I have been told I can be a touch abrasive at times.

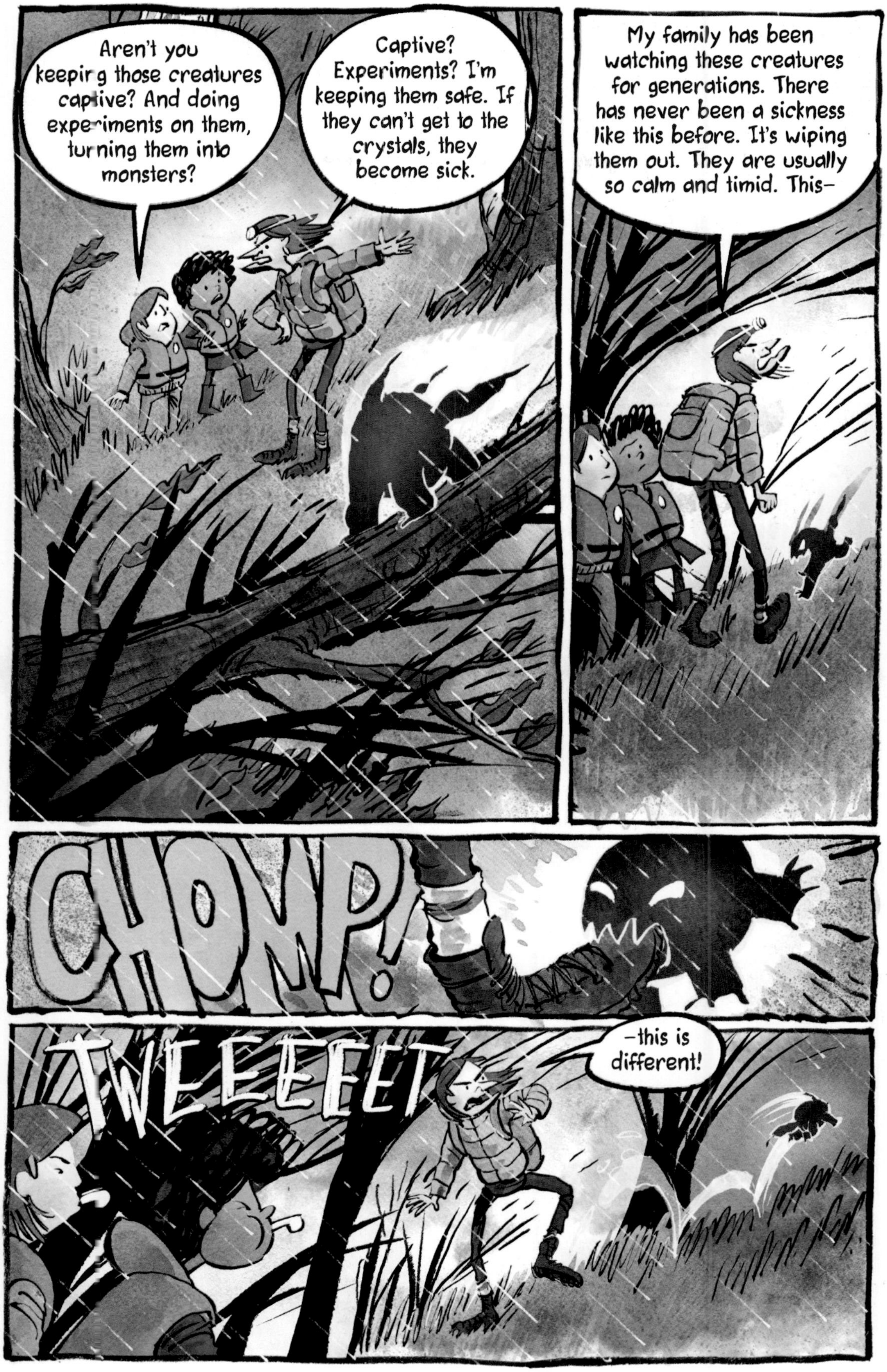
Aren't you keeping those creatures captive? And doing experiments on them, turning them into monsters?
Captive? Experiments? I'm keeping them safe. If they can't get to the crystals, they become sick.
My family has been watching these creatures for generations. There has never been a sickness like this before. It's wiping them out. They are usually so calm and timid. This–
CHOMP!
TWEEEEET
–this is different!

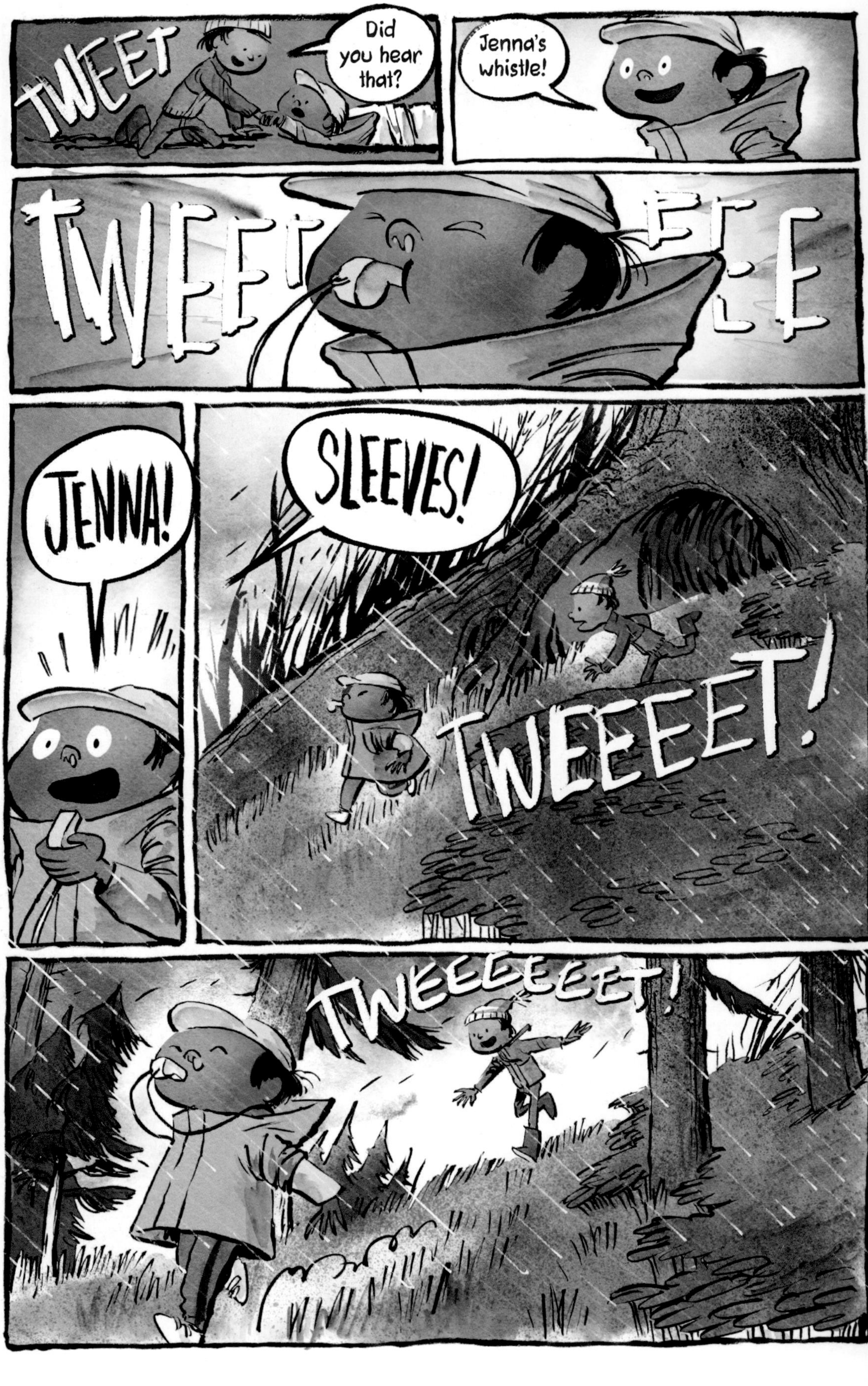
TWEET
Did you hear that?
Jenna's whistle!
TWEEEEEE
JENNA!
SLEEVES!
TWEEEET!
TWEEEEEET!

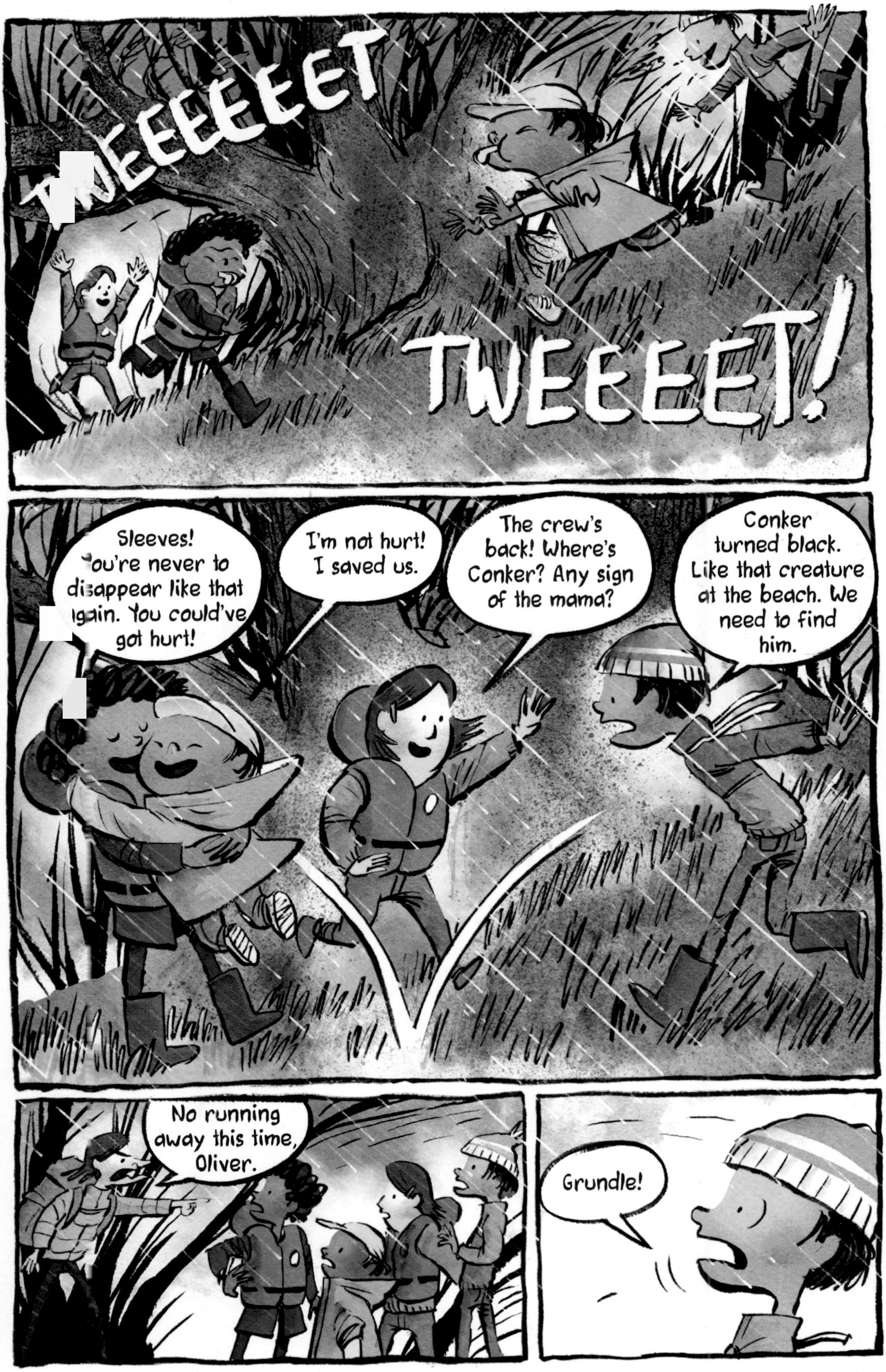
TWEEEEEEET
TWEEEEET!
Sleeves! You're never to disappear like that again. You could've got hurt!
I'm not hurt! I saved us.
The crew's back! Where's Conker? Any sign of the mama?
Conker turned black. Like that creature at the beach. We need to find him.
No running away this time, Oliver.
Grundle!

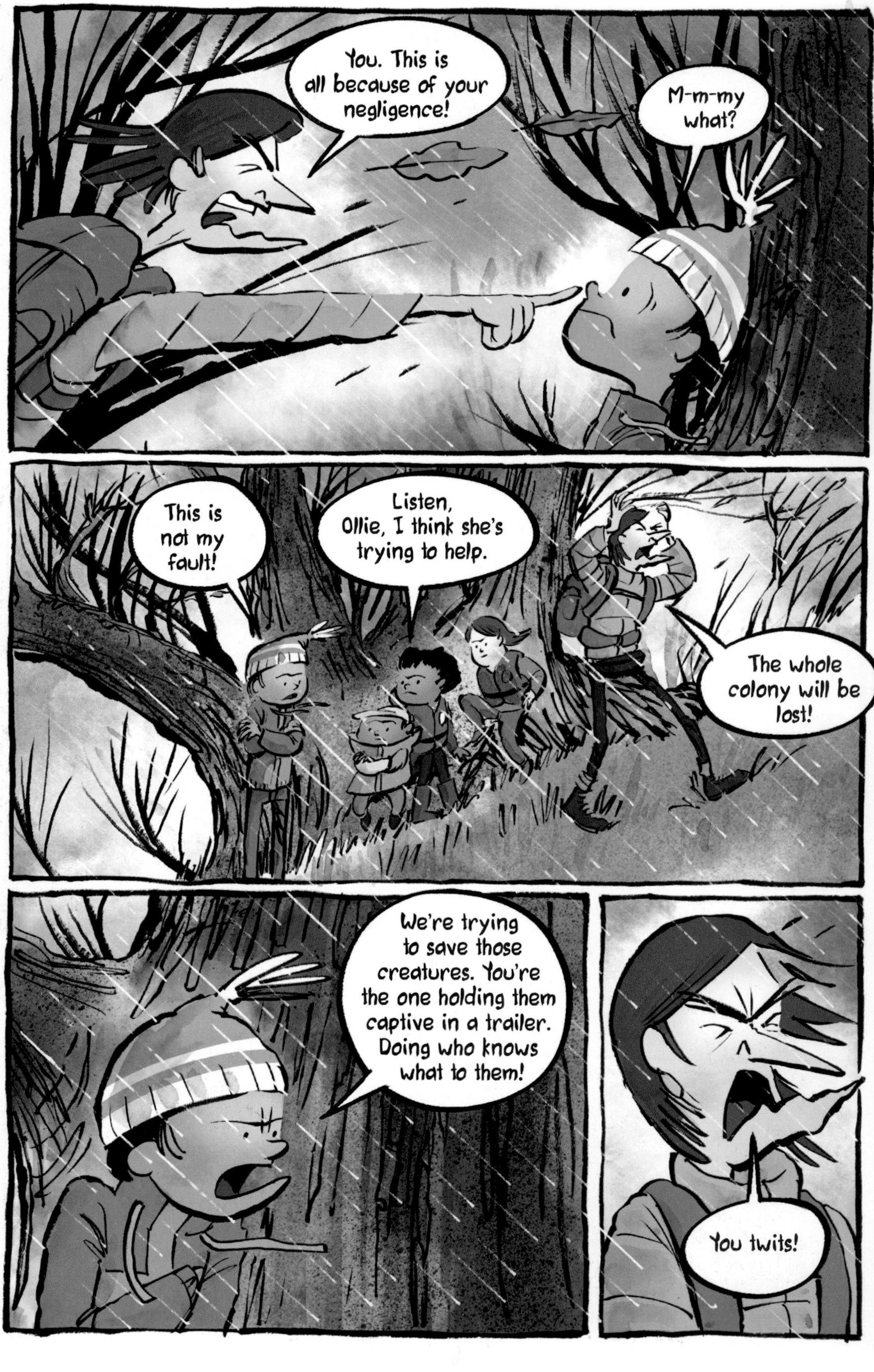

You. This is all because of your negligence!
M-m-my what?
This is not my fault!
Listen, Ollie, I think she's trying to help.
The whole colony will be lost!
We're trying to save those creatures. You're the one holding them captive in a trailer. Doing who knows what to them!
You twits!

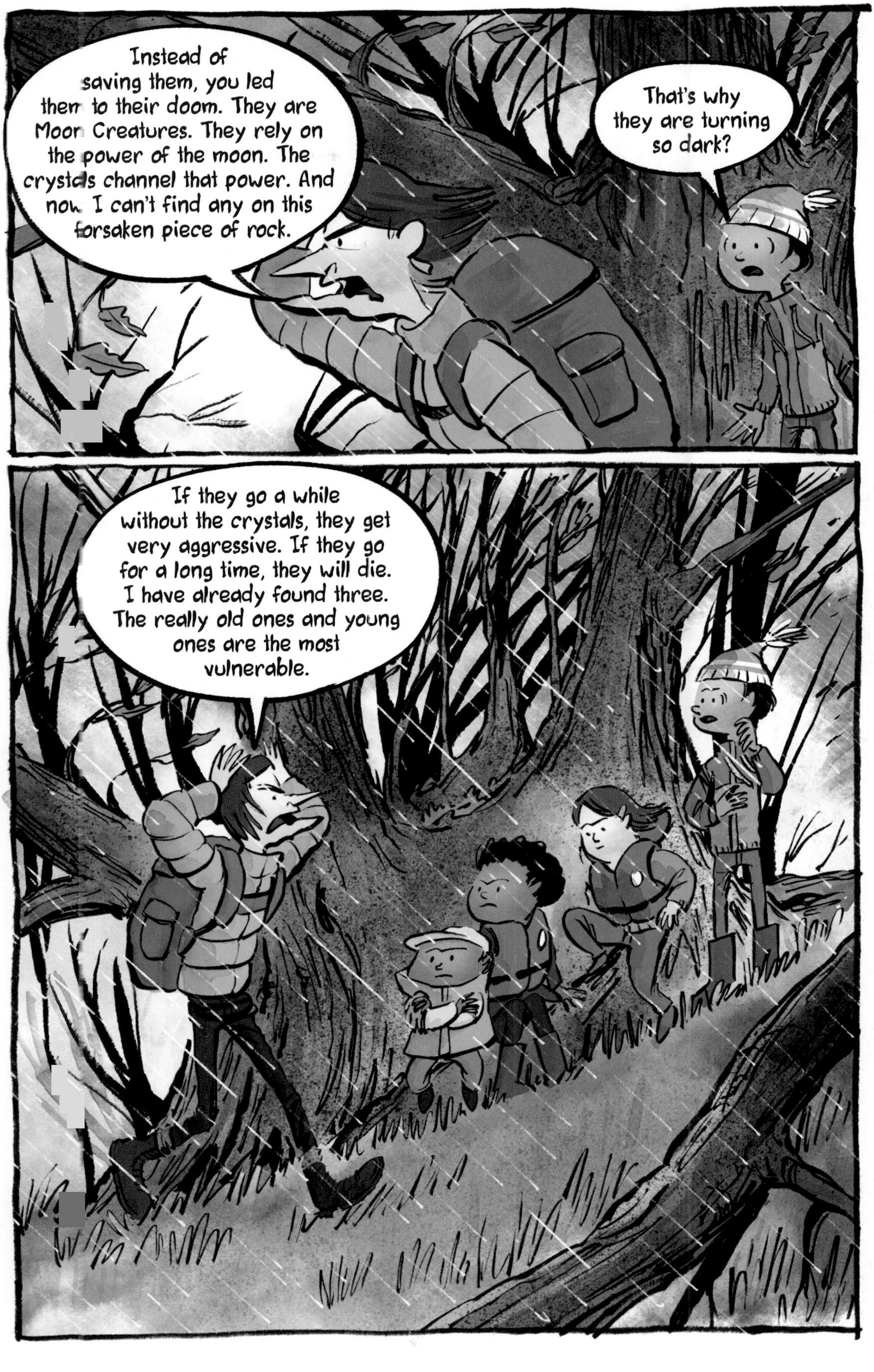
Instead of saving them, you led them to their doom. They are Moon Creatures. They rely on the power of the moon. The crystals channel that power. And now I can't find any on this forsaken piece of rock.
That's why they are turning so dark?
If they go a while without the crystals, they get very aggressive. If they go for a long time, they will die. I have already found three. The really old ones and young ones are the most vulnerable.

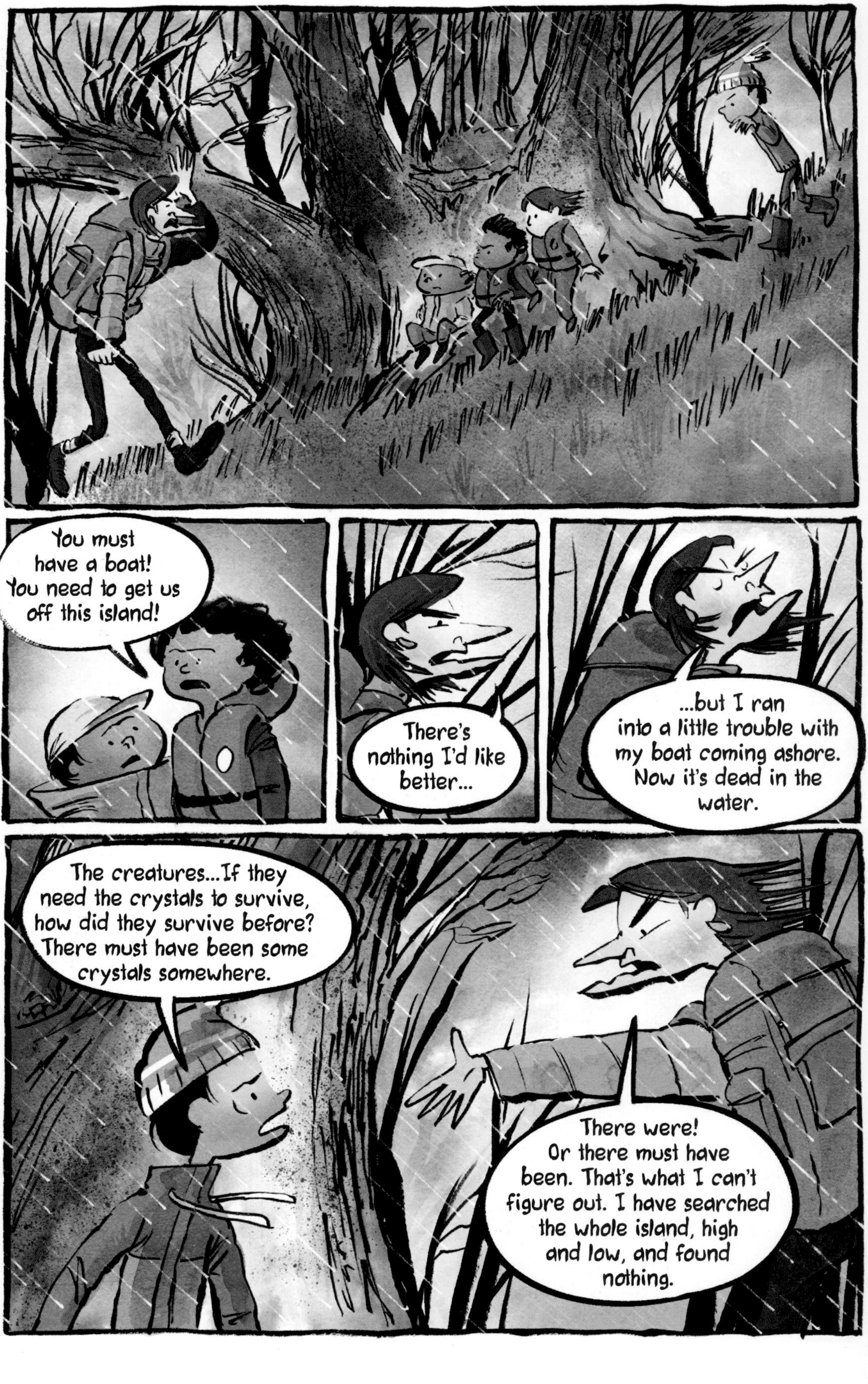
You must have a boat! You need to get us off this island!
There's nothing I'd like better...
...but I ran into a little trouble with my boat coming ashore. Now it's dead in the water.
The creatures...If they need the crystals to survive, how did they survive before? There must have been some crystals somewhere.
There were! Or there must have been. That's what I can't figure out. I have searched the whole island, high and low, and found nothing.

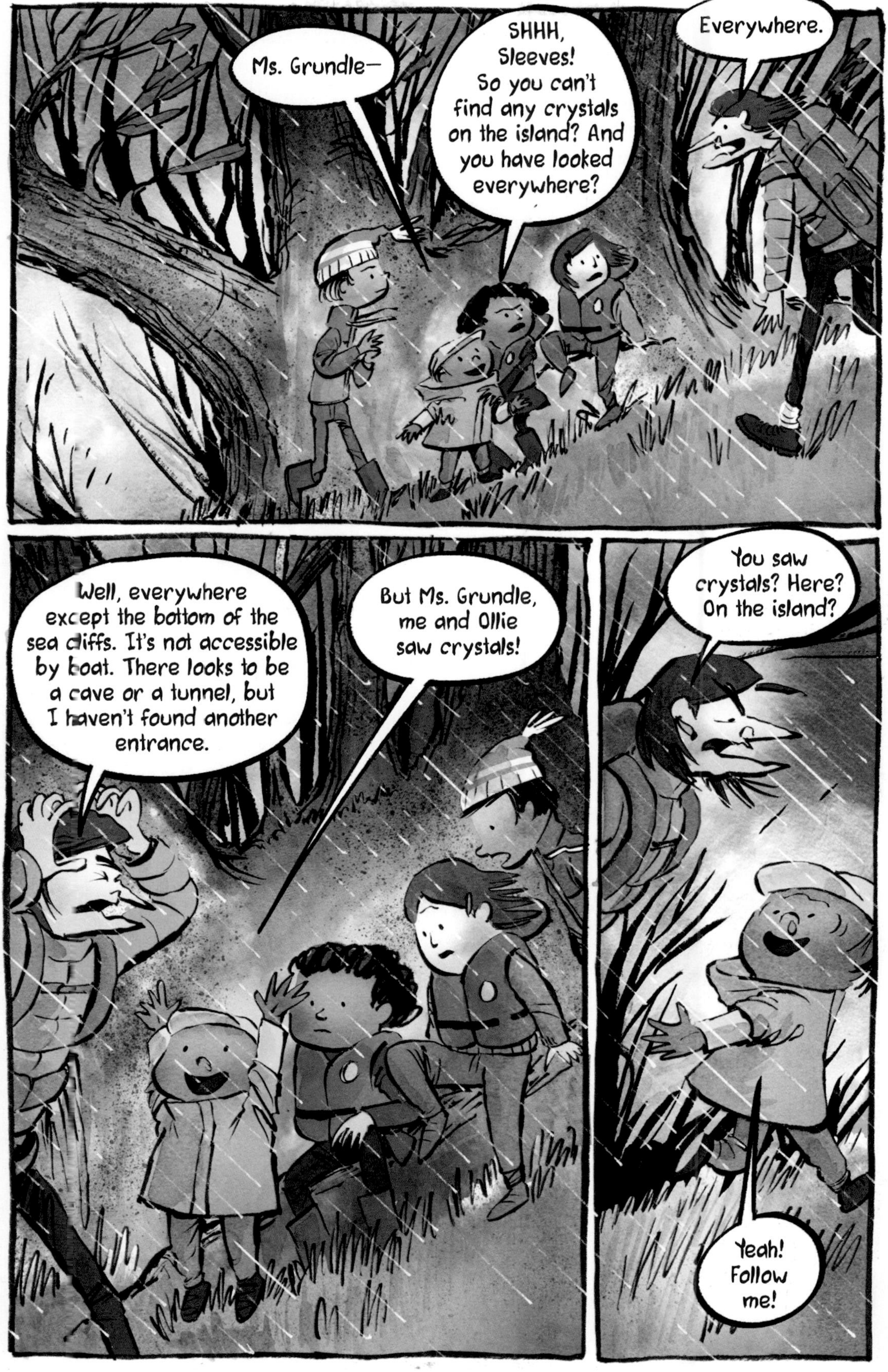
Ms. Grundle—
SHHH, Sleeves! So you can't find any crystals on the island? And you have looked everywhere?
Everywhere.
Well, everywhere except the bottom of the sea cliffs. It's not accessible by boat. There looks to be a cave or a tunnel, but I haven't found another entrance.
But Ms. Grundle, me and Ollie saw crystals!
You saw crystals? Here? On the island?
Yeah! Follow me!

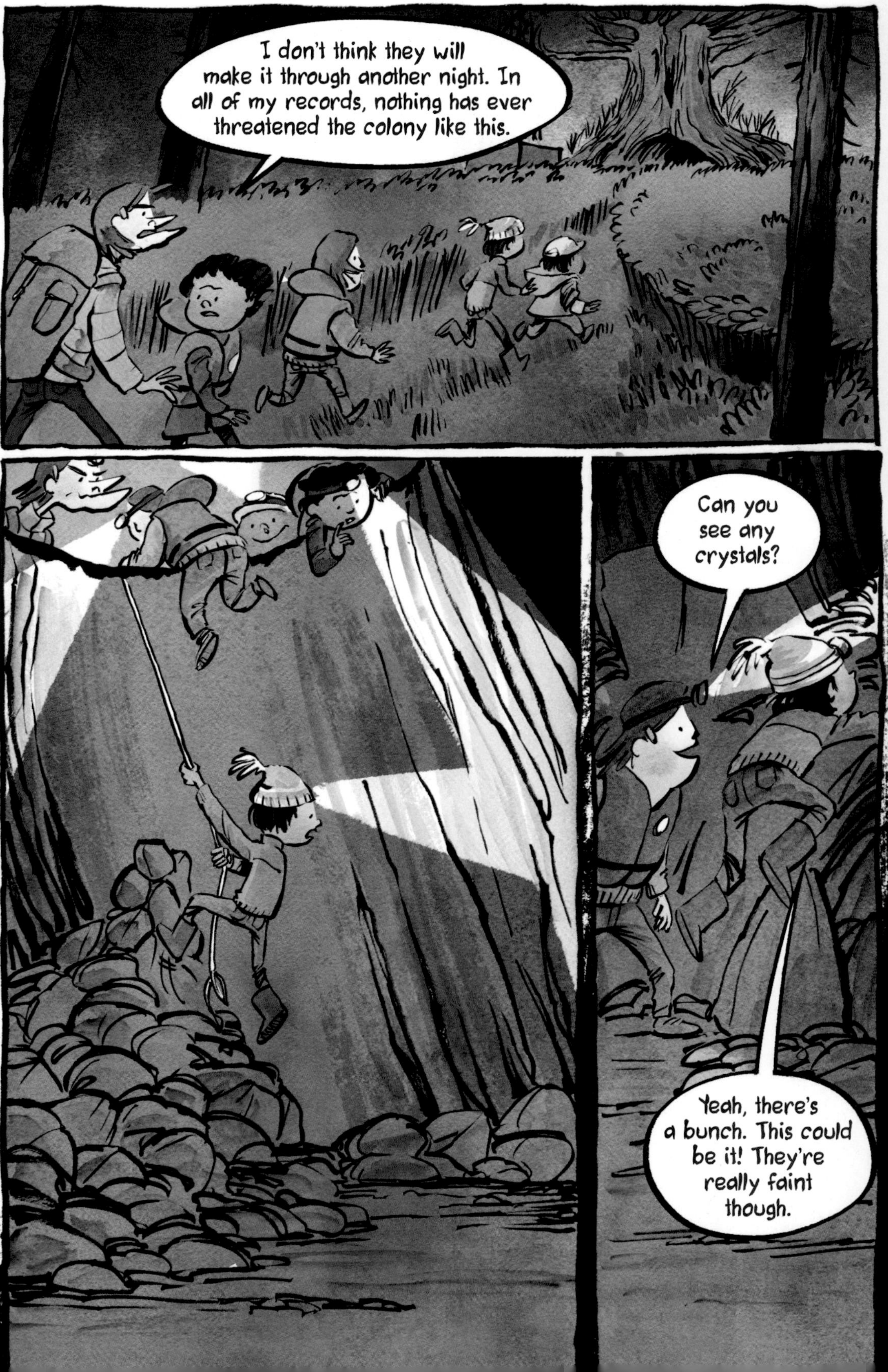
I don't think they will make it through another night. In all of my records, nothing has ever threatened the colony like this.
Can you see any crystals?
Yeah, there's a bunch. This could be it! They're really faint though.

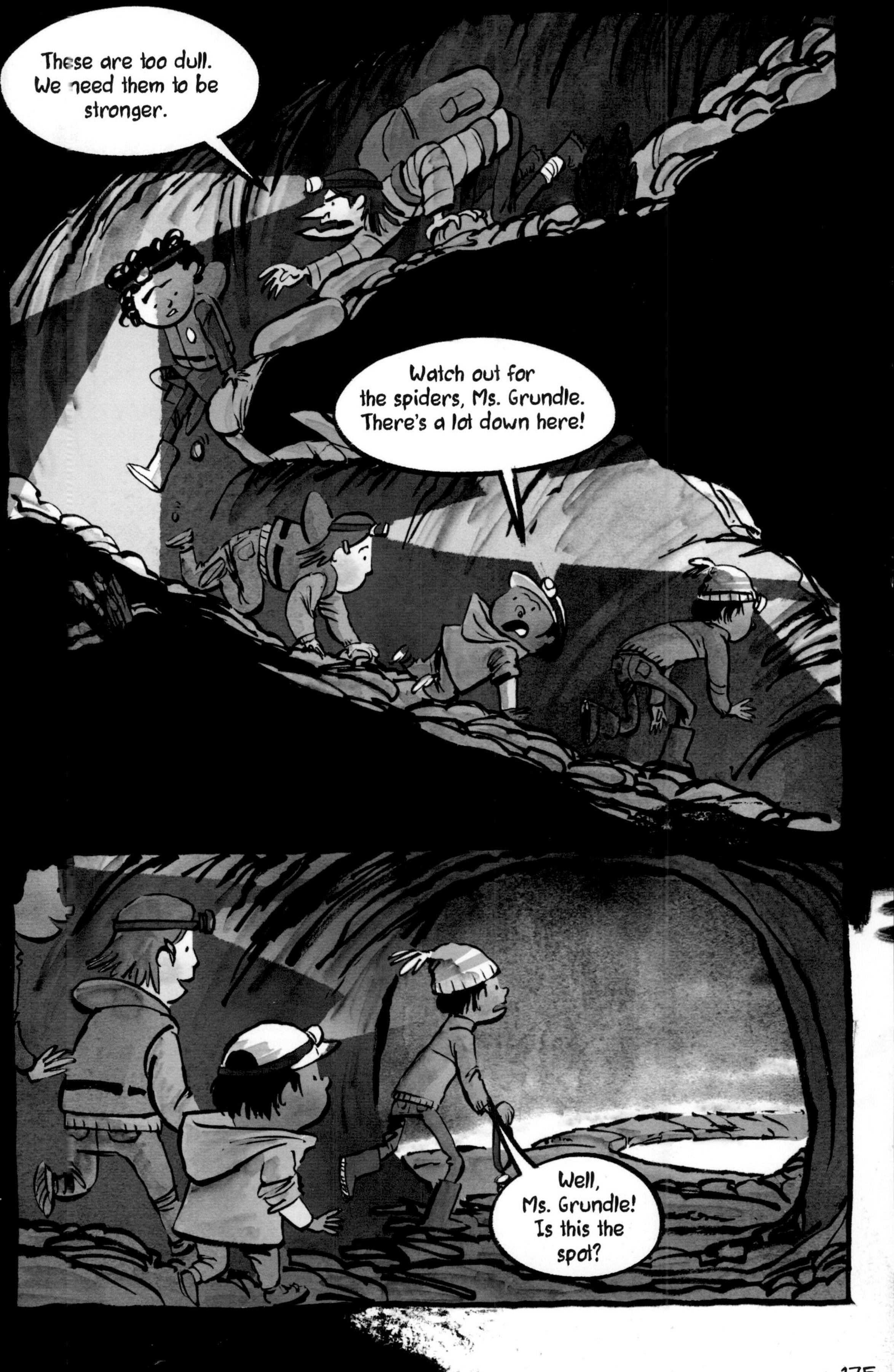
These are too dull. We need them to be stronger.
Watch out for the spiders, Ms. Grundle. There's a lot down here!
Well, Ms. Grundle! Is this the spot?

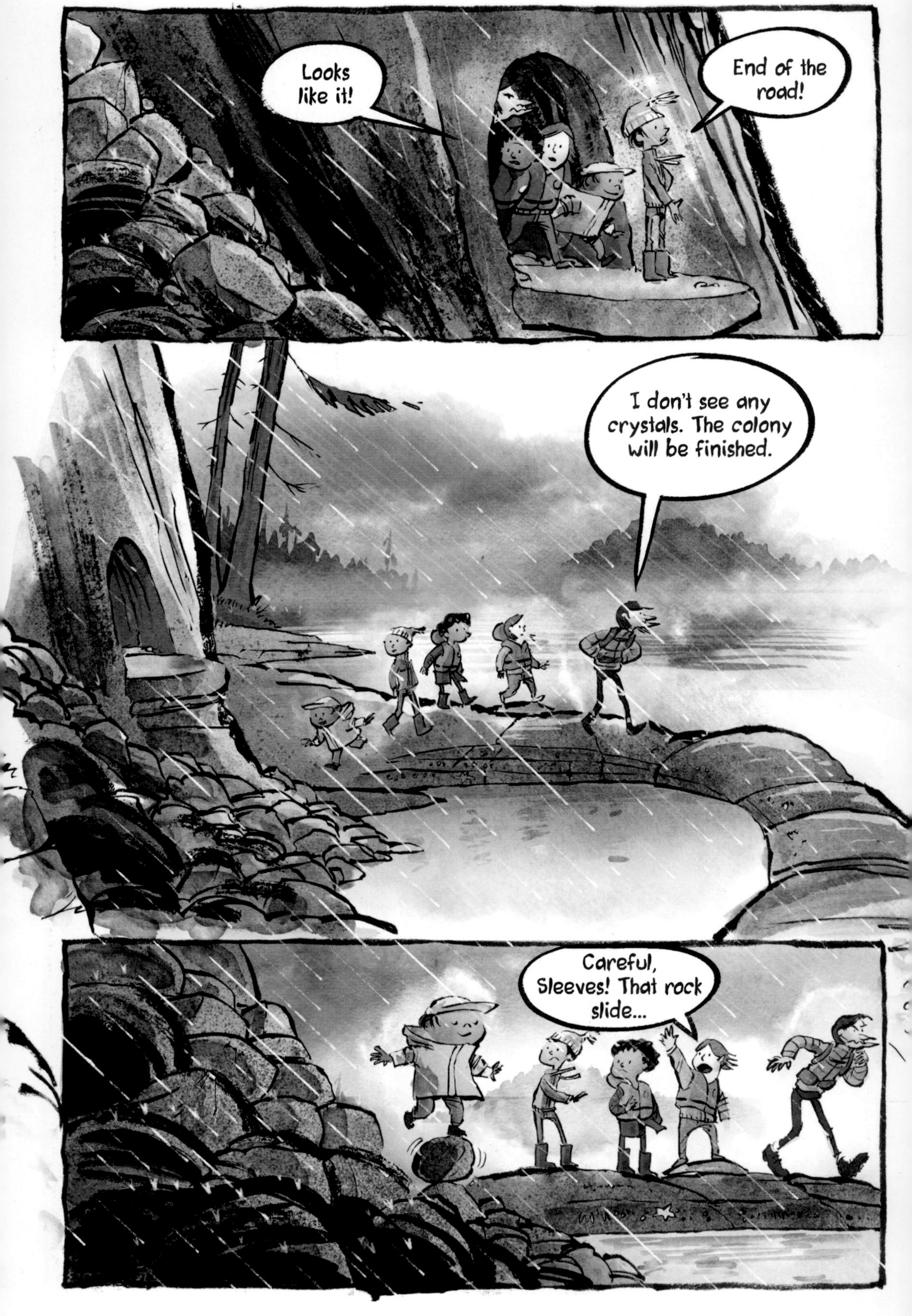
Looks like it!
End of the road!
I don't see any crystals. The colony will be finished.
Careful, Sleeves! That rock slide...

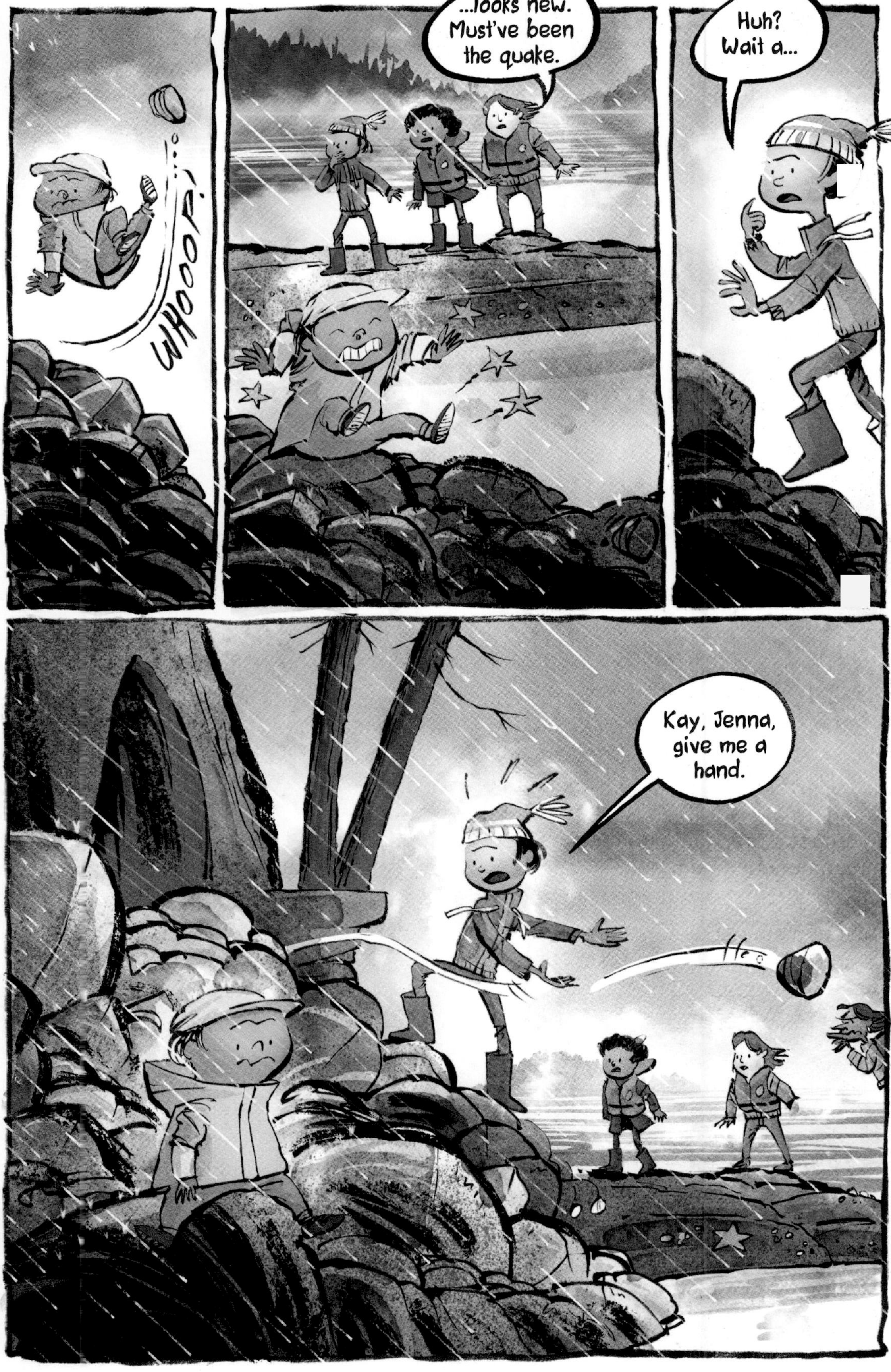
WHOOOP!
...looks new. Must've been the quake.
Huh? Wait a...
Kay, Jenna, give me a hand.

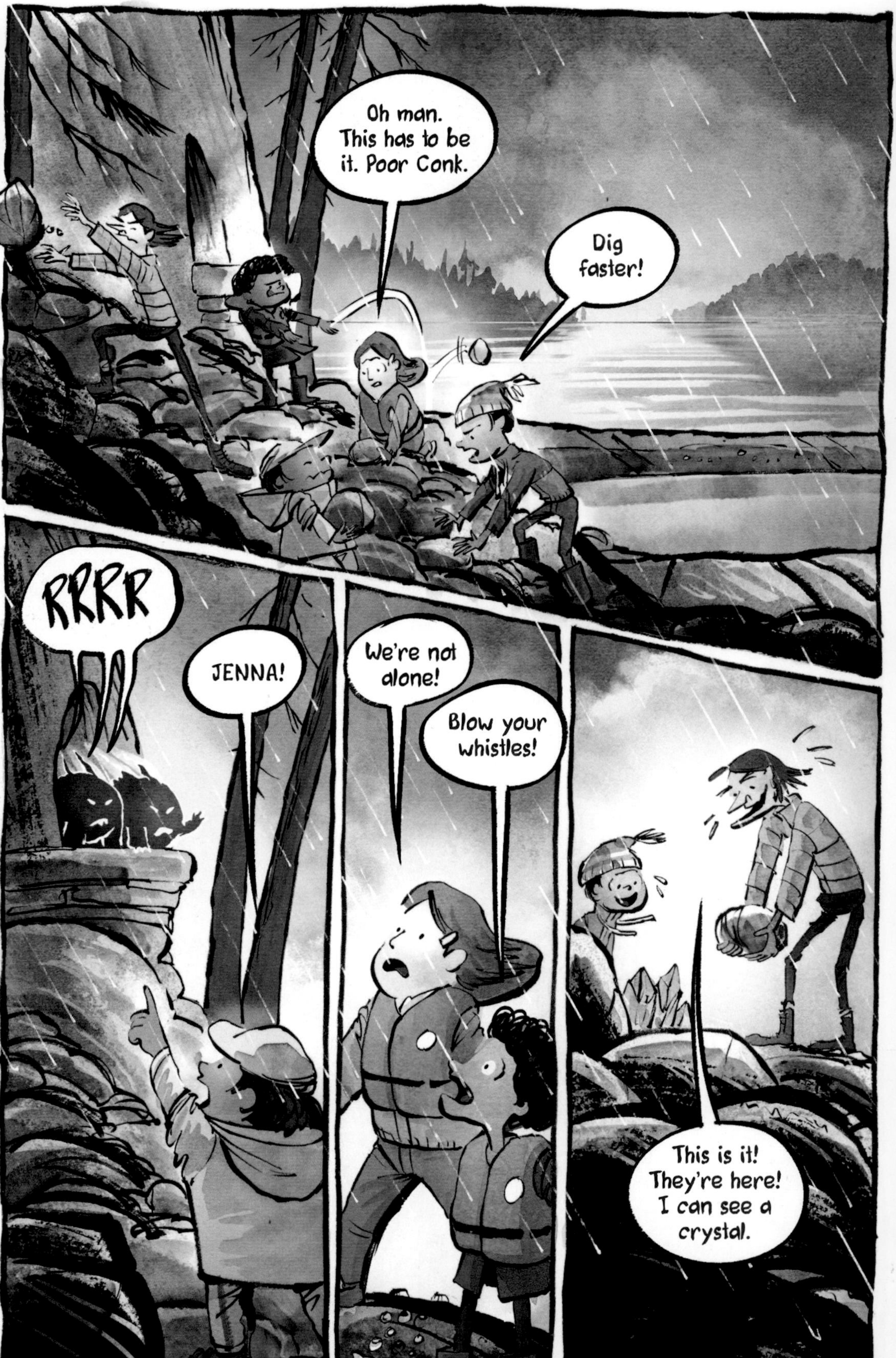
Oh man. This has to be it. Poor Conk.
Dig faster!
RRRR
JENNA!
We're not alone!
Blow your whistles!
This is it! They're here! I can see a crystal.

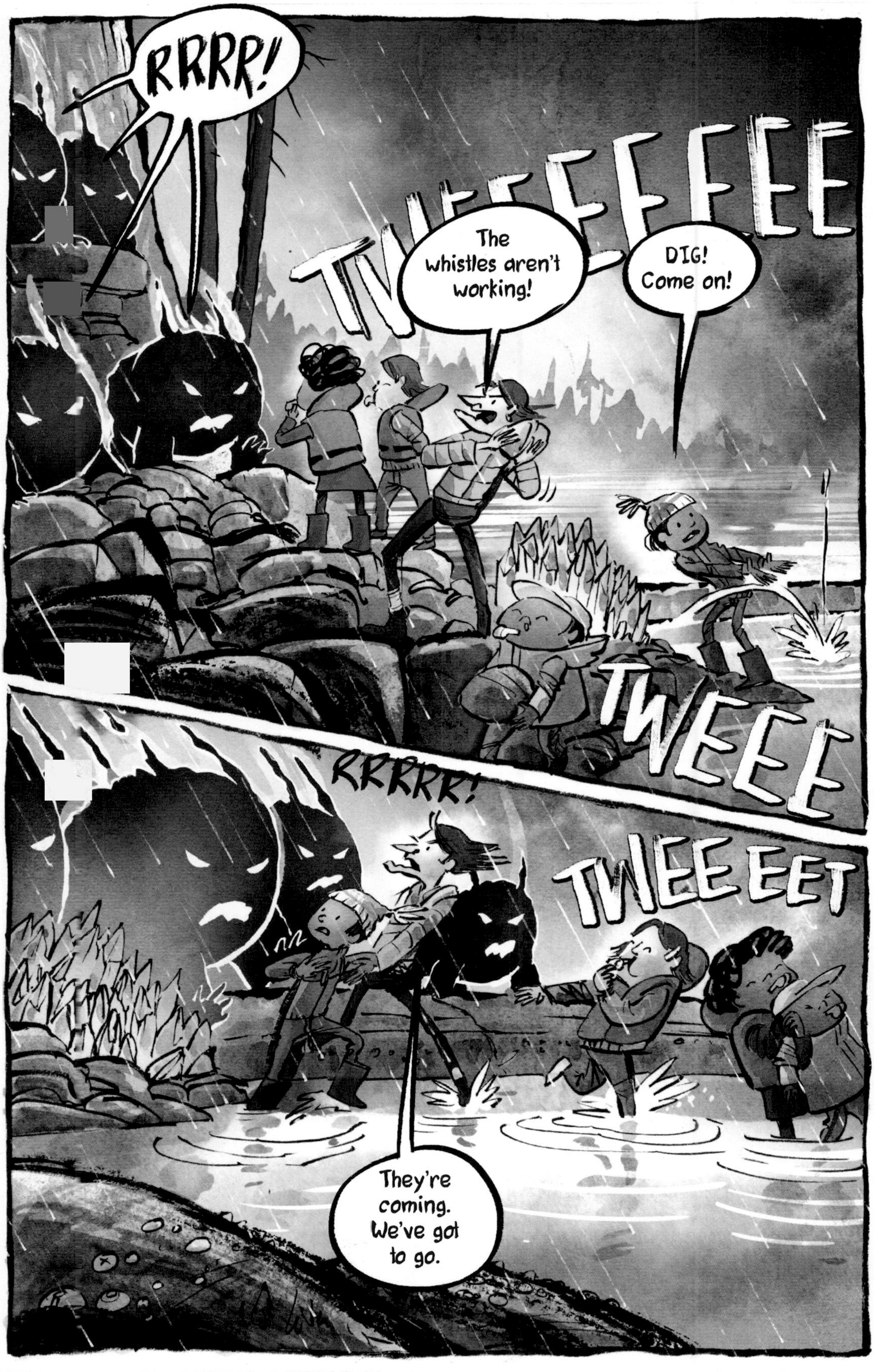
RRRR!
The whistles aren't working!
DIG! Come on!
TWEEE
RRRRR!
TWEE EET
They're coming. We've got to go.

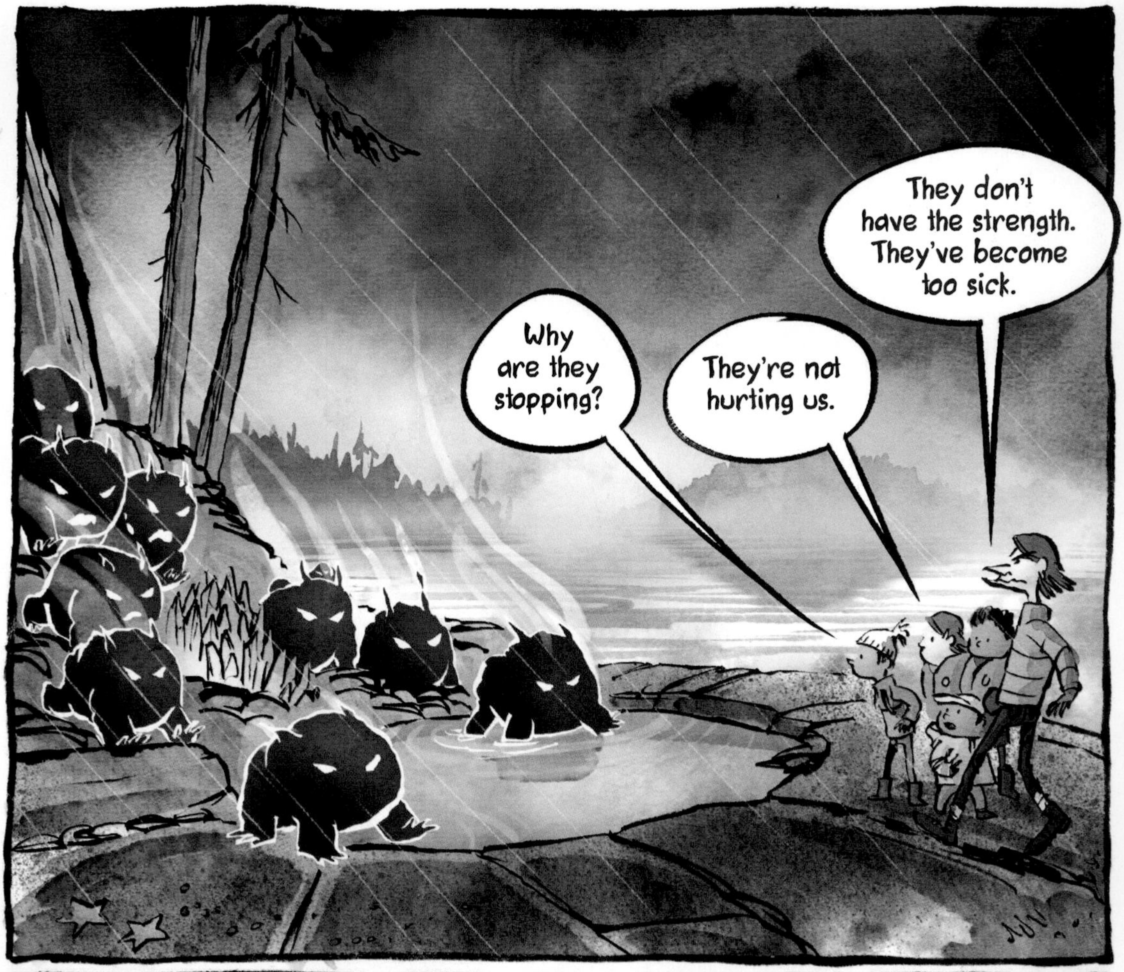
Why are they stopping?
They're not hurting us.
They don't have the strength. They've become too sick.

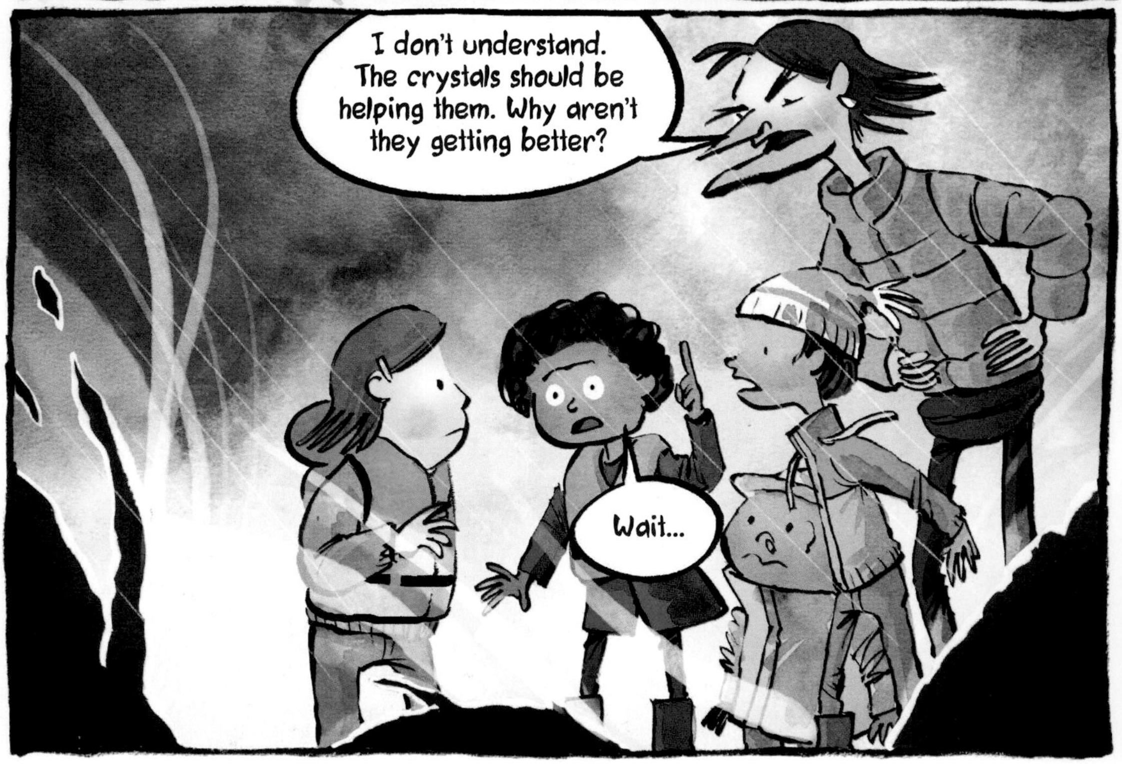
I don't understand. The crystals should be helping them. Why aren't they getting better?
Wait...

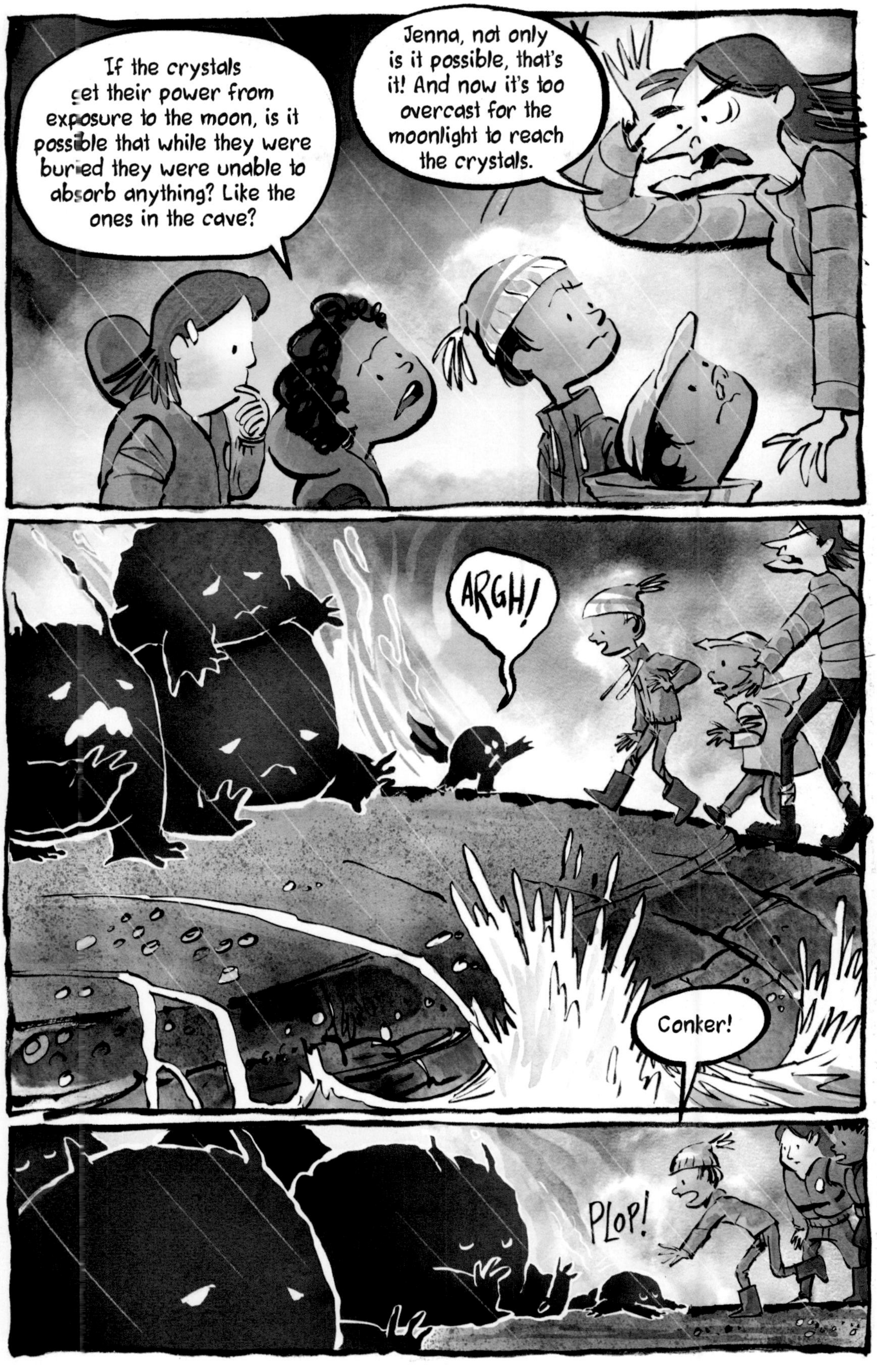
If the crystals get their power from exposure to the moon, is it possible that while they were buried they were unable to absorb anything? Like the ones in the cave?
Jenna, not only is it possible, that's it! And now it's too overcast for the moonlight to reach the crystals.
ARGH!
Conker!
PLOP!

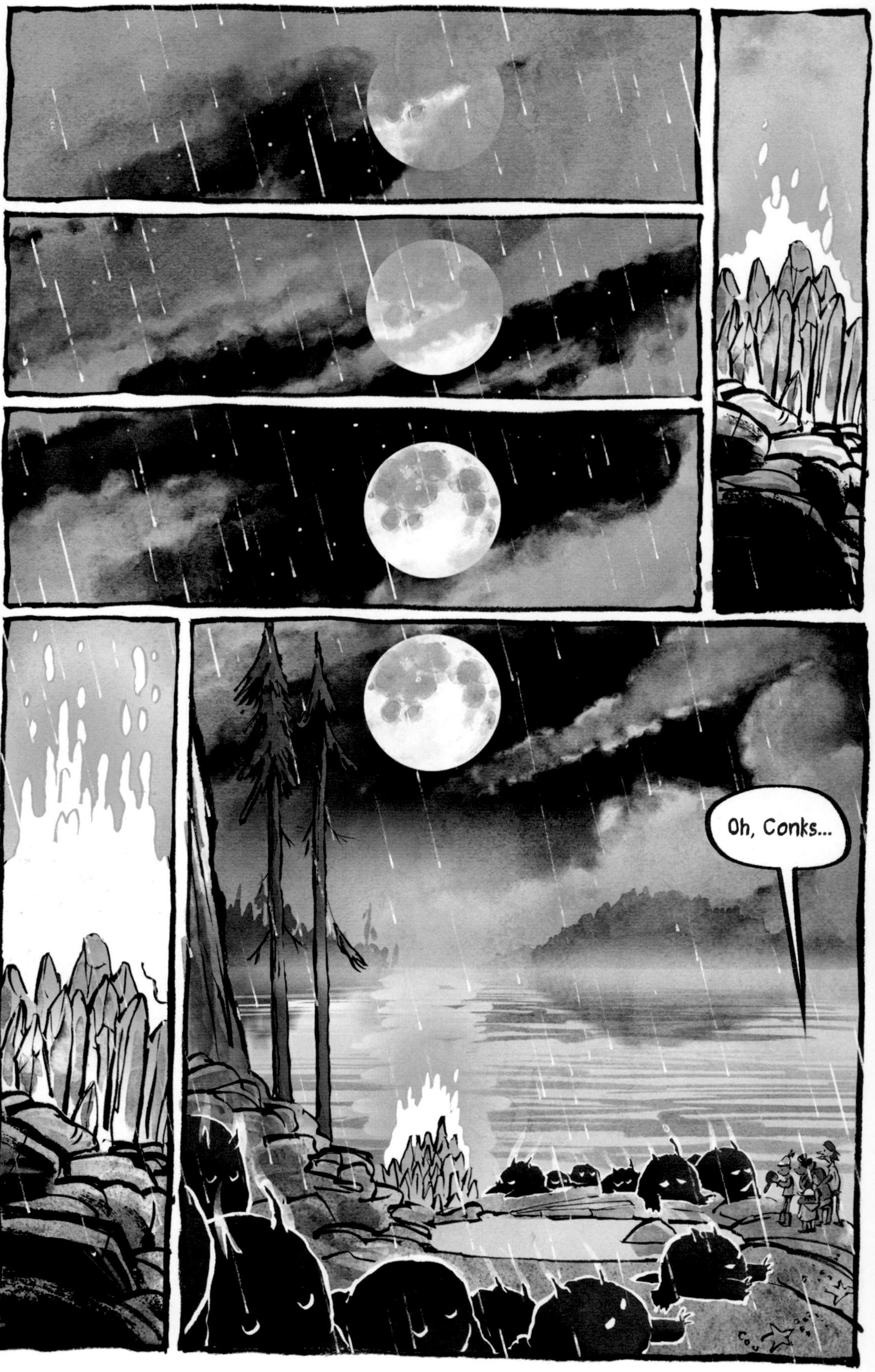
Oh, Conks...

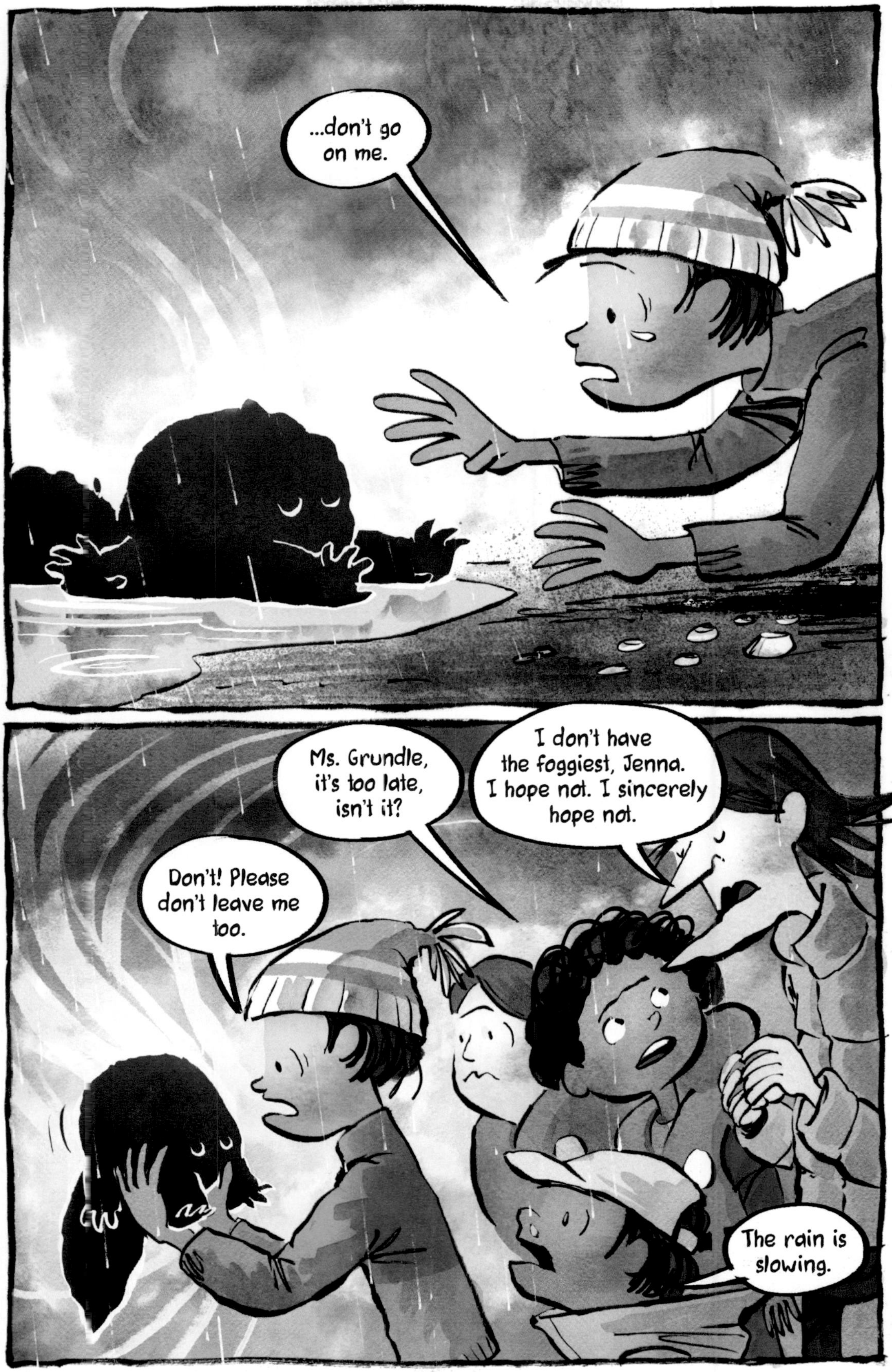
...don't go on me.
Ms. Grundle, it's too late, isn't it?
I don't have the foggiest, Jenna. I hope not. I sincerely hope not.
Don't! Please don't leave me too.
The rain is slowing.

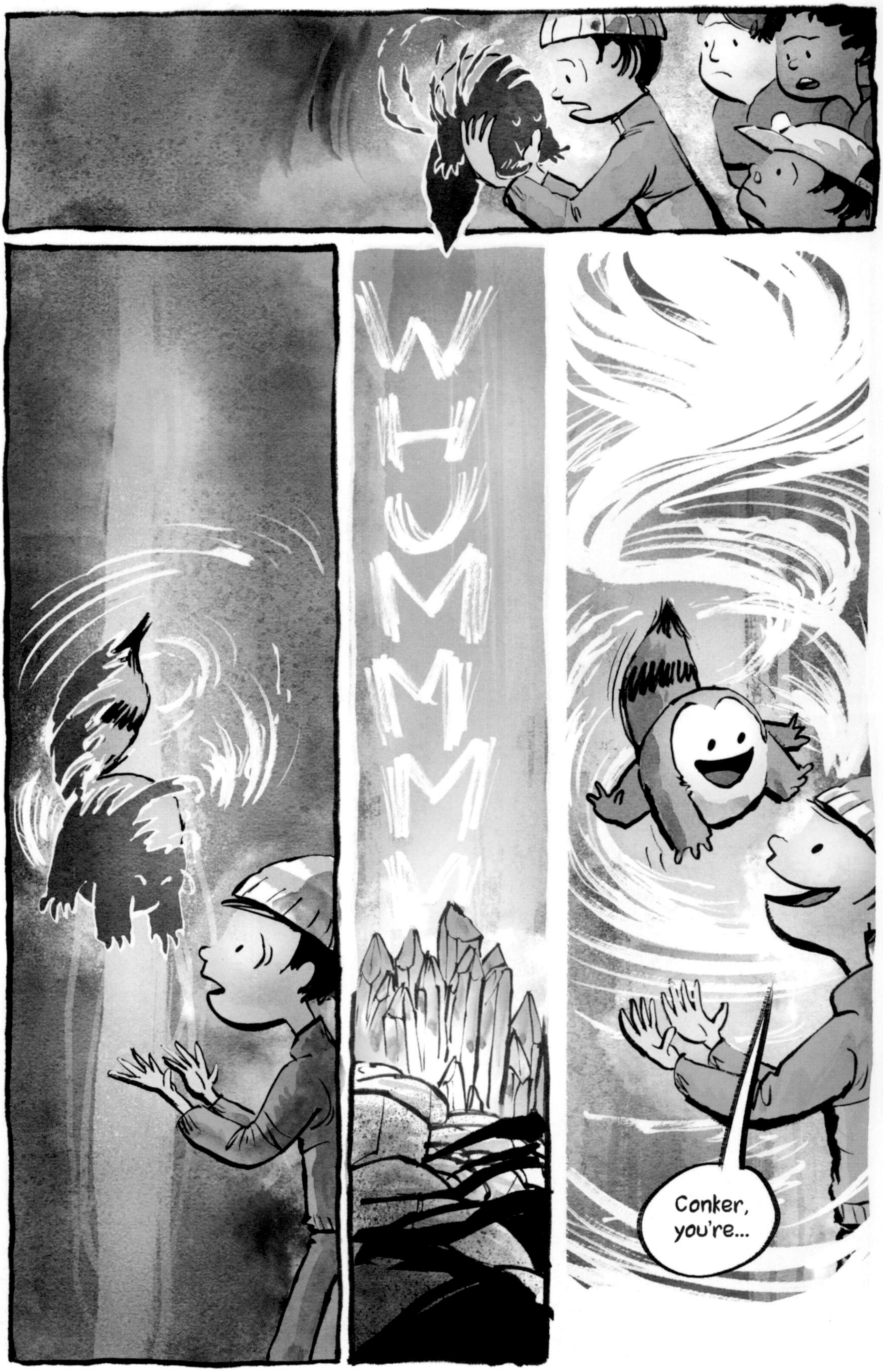
WHUMMM
Conker, you're...

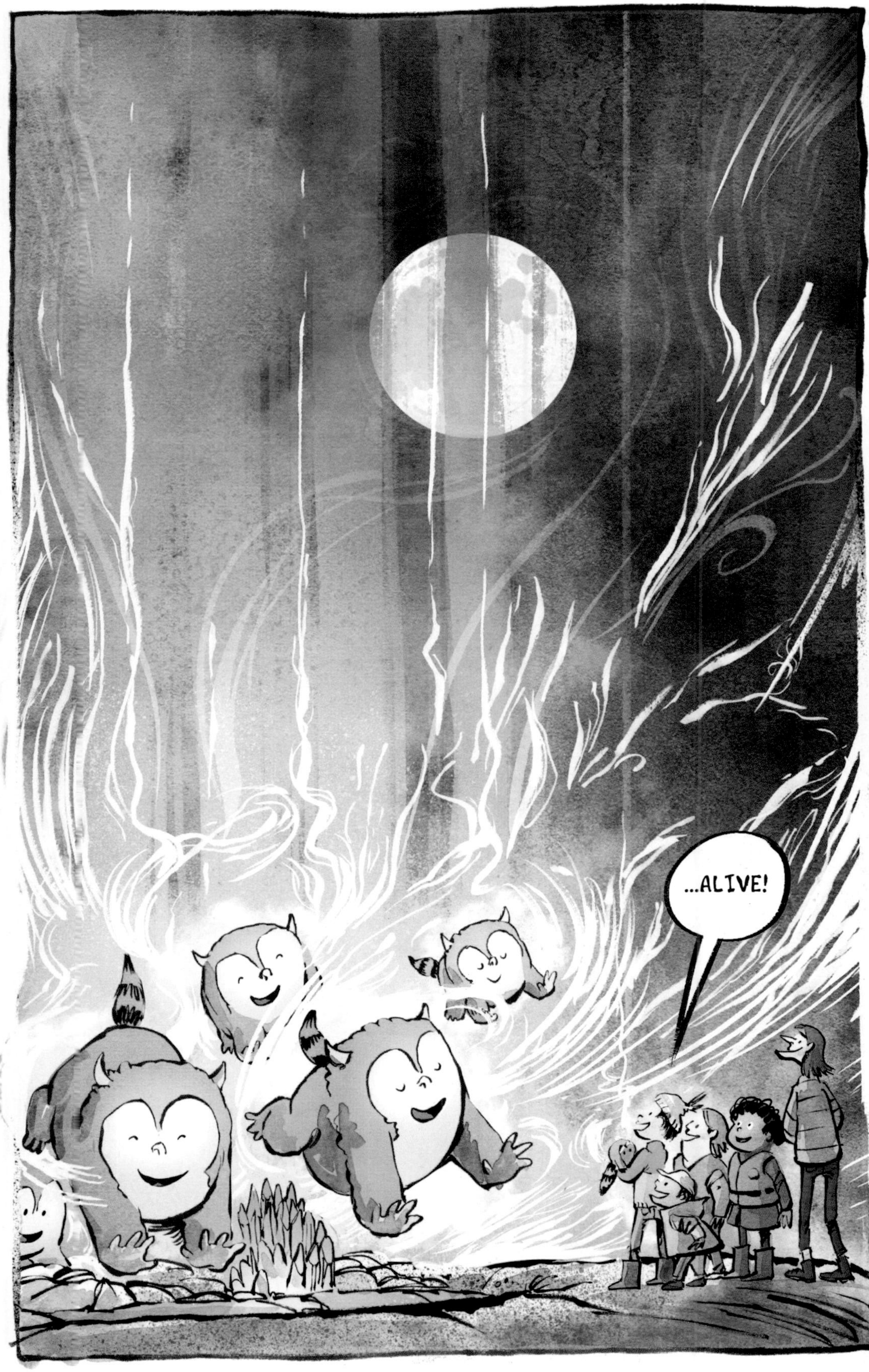
...ALIVE!

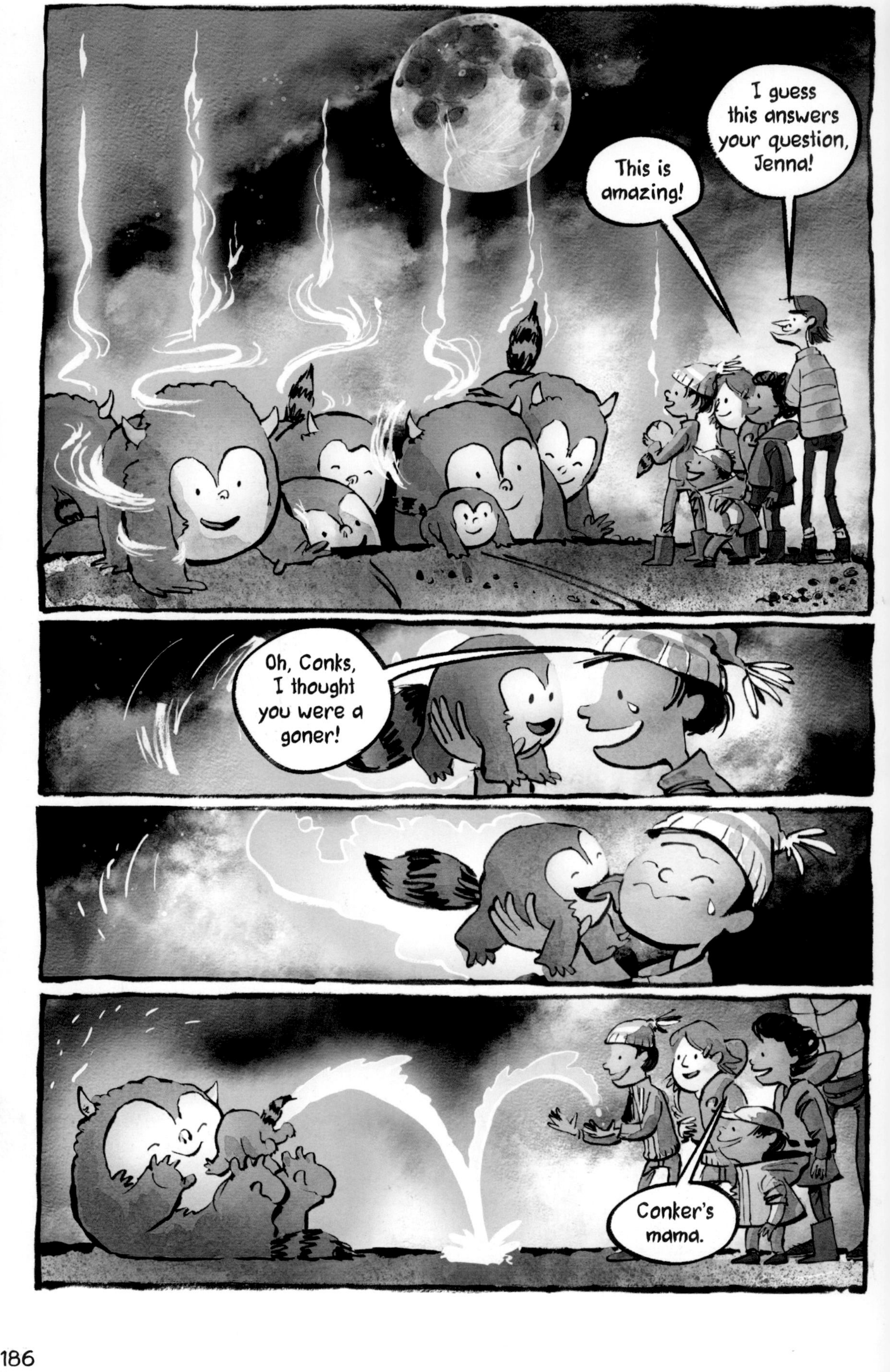
This is amazing!
I guess this answers your question, Jenna!
Oh, Conks, I thought you were a goner!
Conker's mama.

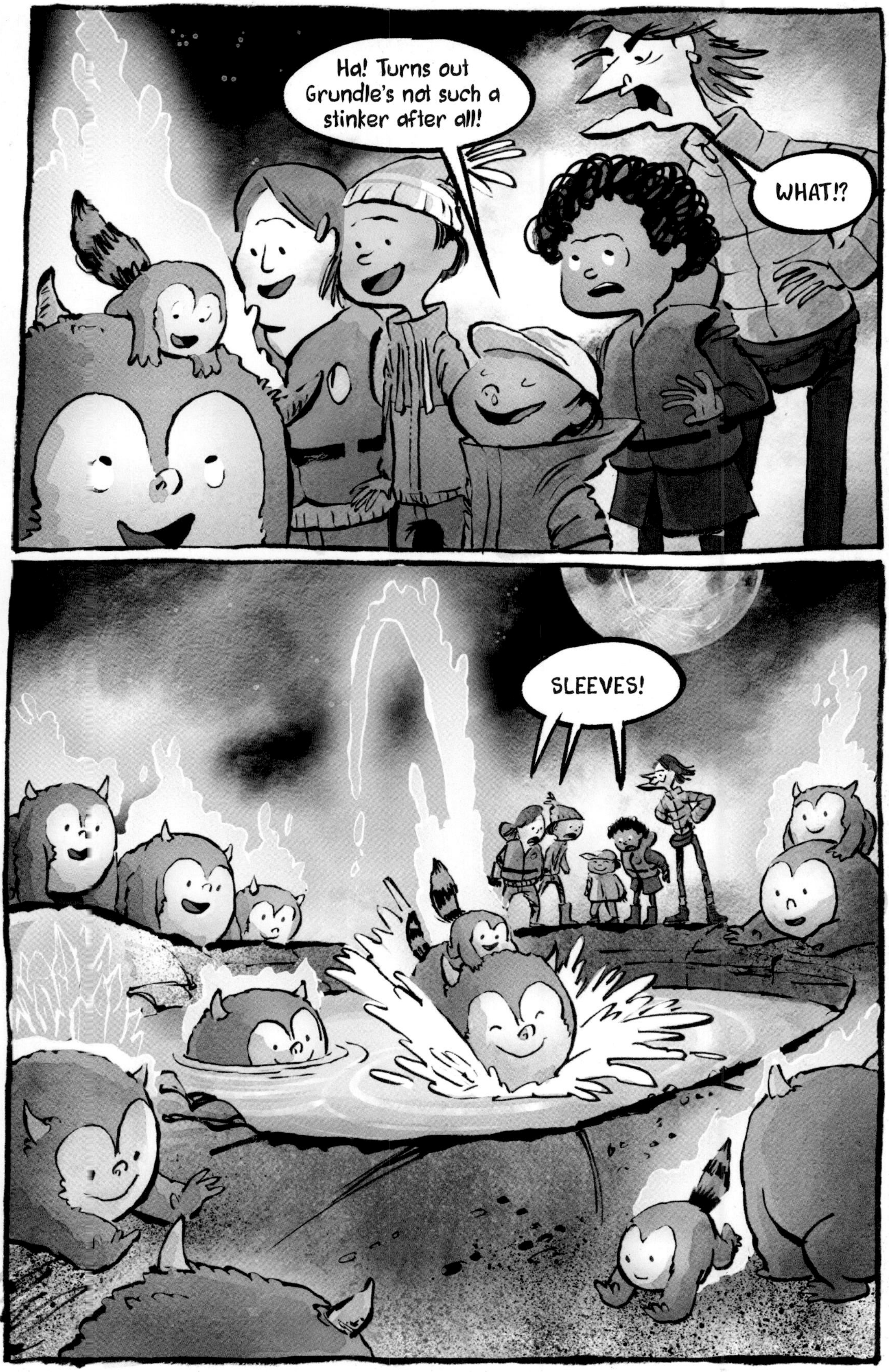
Ha! Turns out Grundle's not such a stinker after all!
WHAT!?
SLEEVES!

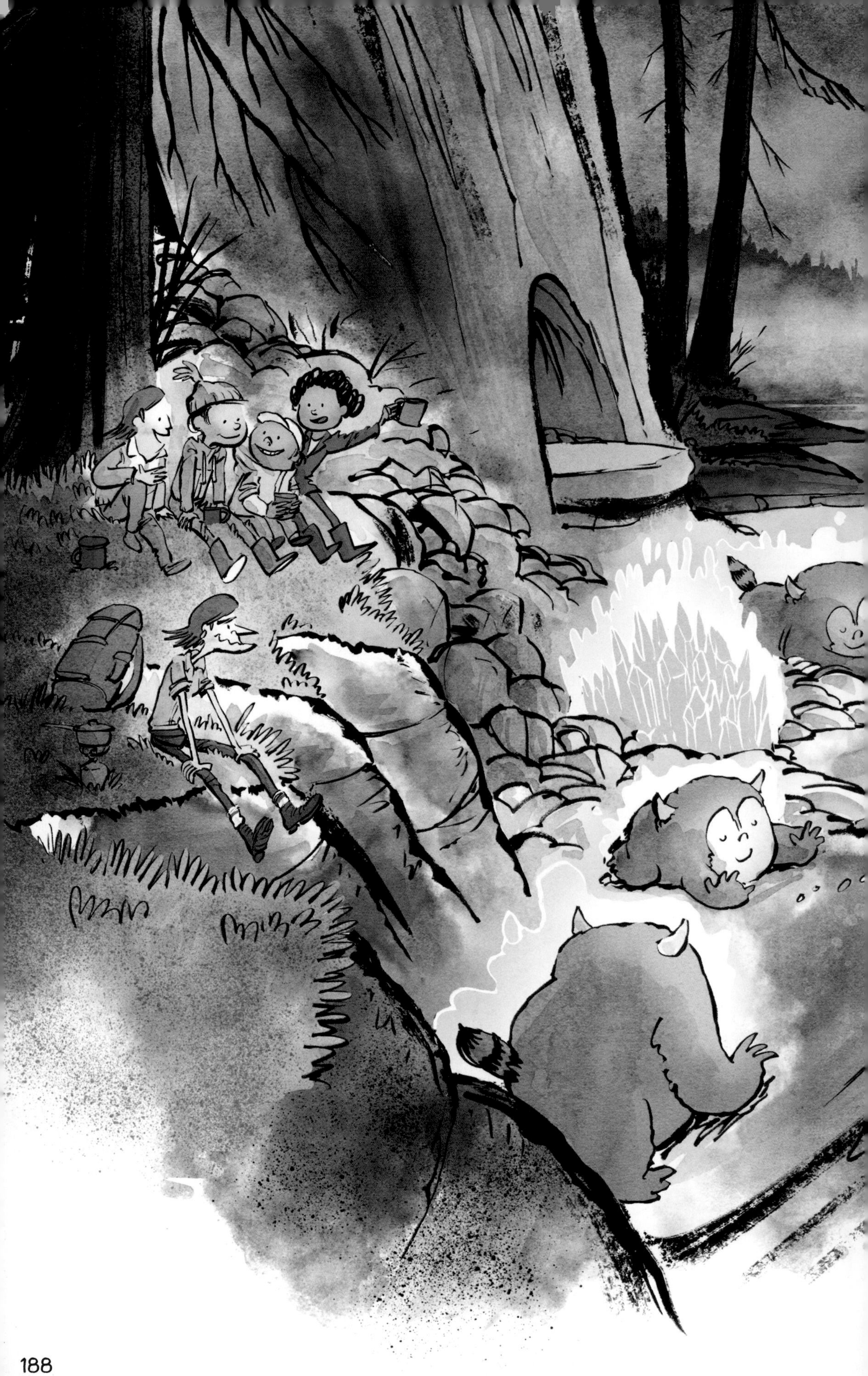

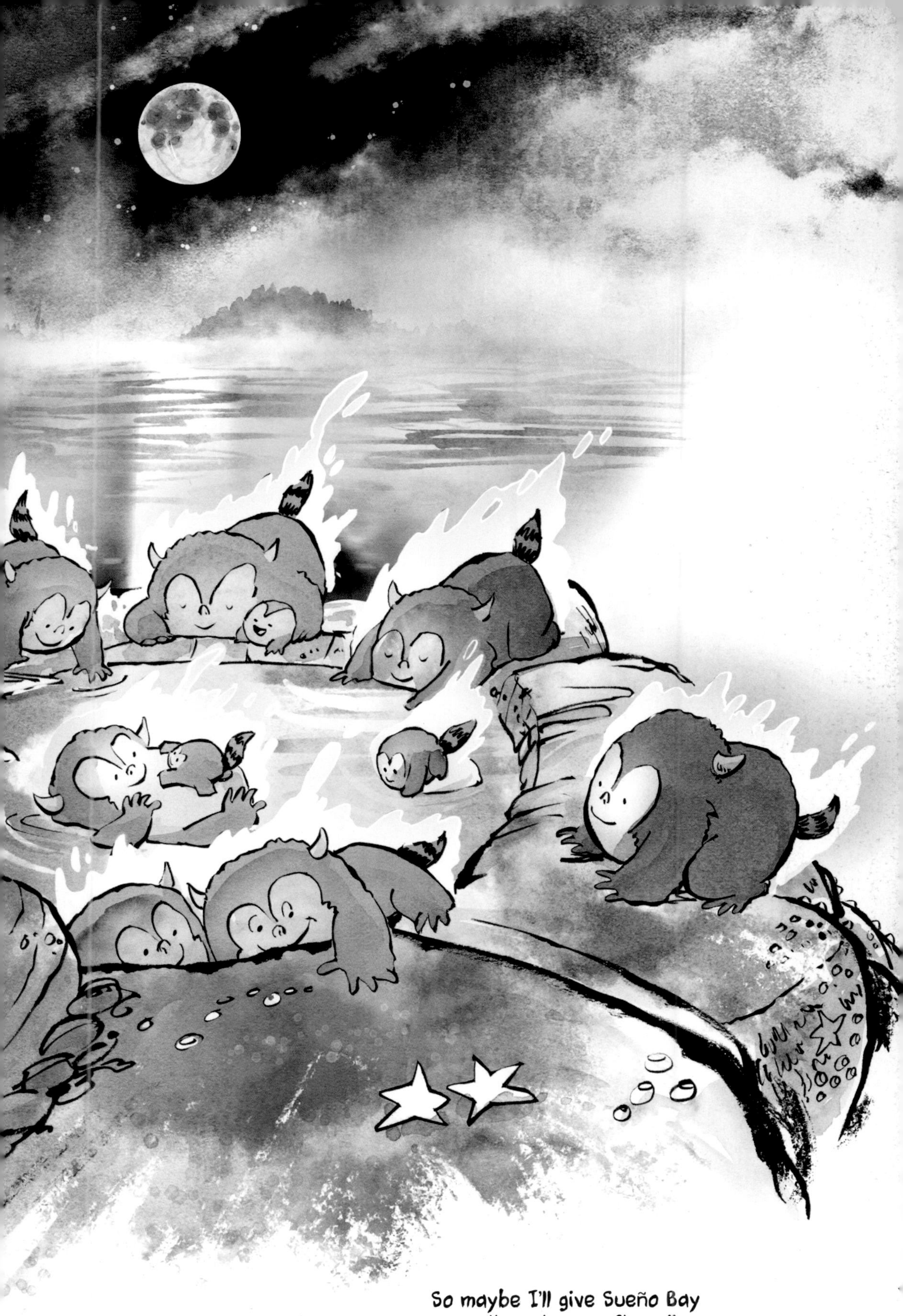

So maybe I'll give Sueño Bay
another chance after all.

husband-and-wife team **NANCY** and **MIKE DEAS** enjoyed collaborating on this project. Nancy grew up on a farm on Mayne Island, British Columbia, where she wandered the forests and beaches. She has a great love of travel and adventure. Nancy holds a Bachelor of Arts from the University of Victoria. Mike is an author/illustrator of graphic novels, including *Dalen and Gole* and the Graphic Guide Adventure series. While he grew up with a love of illustrative storytelling, Capilano College's Commercial Animation Program helped Mike fine-tune his drawing skills and imagination. Mike, Nancy and their family live on Salt Spring Island, British Columbia, a magical and mysterious island that inspired Sueño Bay.

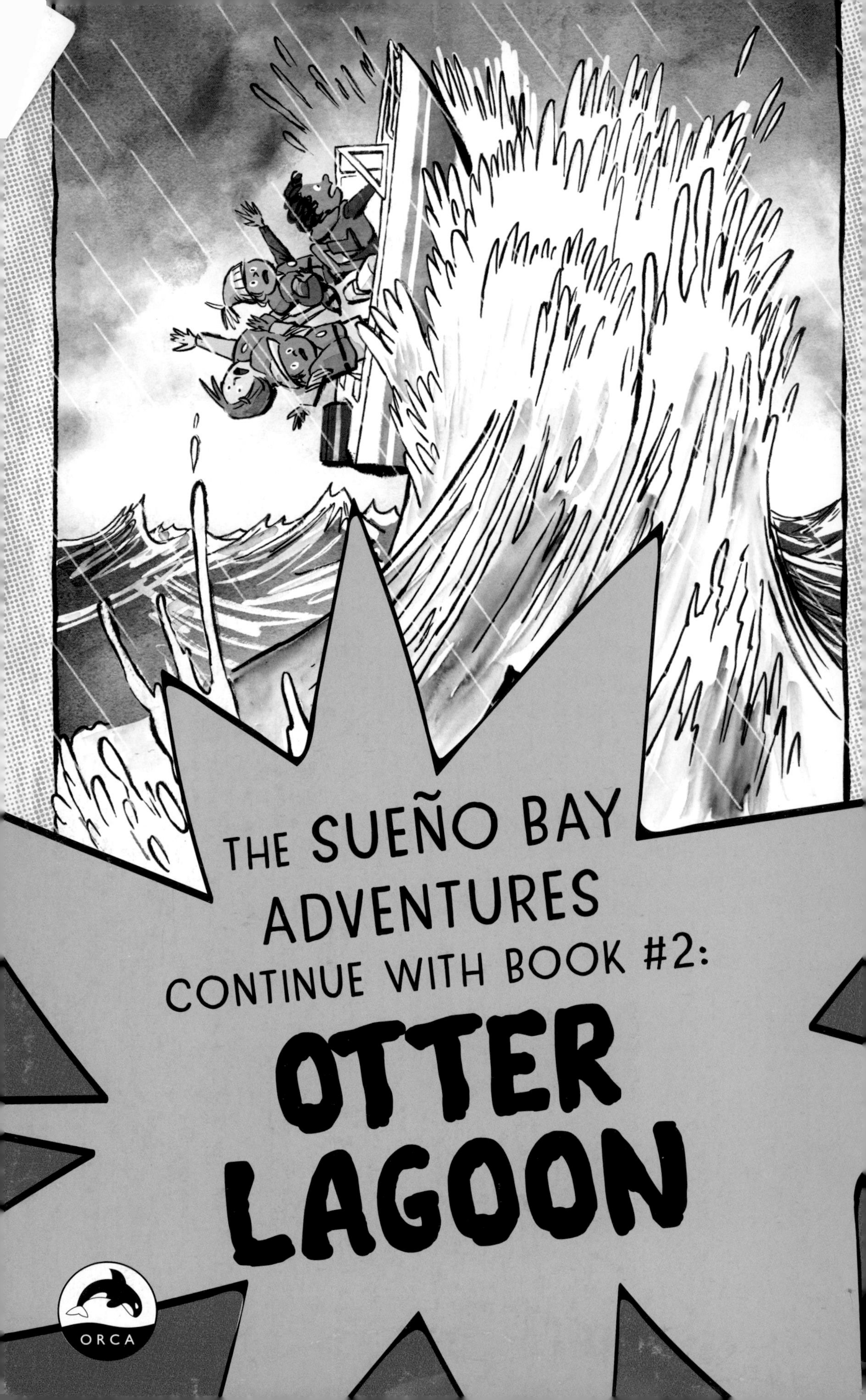

THE SUEÑO BAY ADVENTURES CONTINUE WITH BOOK #2:

OTTER LAGOON

ORCA